CÉLESTIAÁ:

PRODIGALSUN

BY MICK CARTY

COPYRIGHT

DEDICATION

IN MEMORY OF MARTIN GUNN, JIMMY MARTIN

& ALL GOOD MEN TAKEN TOO SOON

ACKNOWLEDGMENTS

With many thanks to Rita Gunn, Brecken Haverstock & everyone
who has encouraged and pestered me to get this finished.

EXPLICIT CONTENT WARNING

This title contains explicit sexual content, violence, foul language
and character opinions and theories that may cause unintended offence.

CONTENTS

PROLOGUE

Thin wisps of silver cloud drifted, wraith-like, across the gleaming disc of Lunaá; sitting high in the blackness, silently watching over the intertwined realms of Elŷsium and Kiípos. The crispness of the clear dark skies, augmented by the softest of cool breezes, created a glasslike shimmer on the rippling water of Elysia Harbour; Lunaá's bright reflection casting its light back onto the vessels and structures surrounding it. Idle boats swayed and creaked, bobbing gently on the water as it softly lapped against the many jetties.

The harbour taverns and restaurants were heaving; the hubbub of patrons and musicians all competing for supremacy, their carousing deafening. Fiddles, pipes, and accordions accompanied hearty, sometimes breathless songsmiths, as they worked their way through well-practiced party pieces. A hurdy-gurdy player cranked out ancient, traditional folk tunes, recalling times long gone. Men and women danced, as they had on many campfire evenings, or encircled by Romani wagons, in the Carpathian Mountains of Kiípos.

The revellers were, thankfully, all too much in their cups, too invested in their songs, to notice the hunched demeanour, and furtive, but purposeful movement of the visitor. Although illuminated by the moon's reflection, the hooded figure slunk along the boardwalk, carefully avoiding attracting attention; weaving their way through the delirious throng like a silent river meandering through gaps in the rocks and stones; onward, never stopping for breath.

Reaching the outer jetty, the visitor turned, taking a long last look, ensuring that none were aware of, or interested in, their presence; that no one was taking notice of the figure carefully climbing down in the darkness onto the ancient boat. They scurried across the deck, chasing their own moonlit shadow, and entered the lowered cabin, snapping the door shut behind them.

The tiny, poorly ventilated deckhouse was stuffy and cramped; a stale warmth, a musty scent, and a thickness in the air all suggested a lack of recent use. The ancient wood groaned and strained as it undulated, gently rising and falling on the evening tide. On a thin shelf, a candle-lit lantern provided a dull, strangely orange light and, in the corner, sitting on a small stool, was another dark, heavily cloaked figure.

"You summoned me, Lord Eris?" the visitor asked, a fearful quiver in their voice. "Do you think it wise to meet here... on Charon's boat?" The sitting figure raised their hands and pulled the heavy hood back, revealing a beautiful black-haired woman.

"*Lady* Eris, for your information," came the reply; her diction soft, her enunciation perfect. Curious eyes inspected the new arrival; a curl of her lip confirming her disdain, her contempt, as she immediately assumed a position of superiority. Creating chaos and destruction came easy to Eris, but she could never stomach being in the presence of those beneath her; their stench polluting her beautiful nose; their bleating, worm's words an assault on her ears. No. She would keep this meeting short and remove the pungency forthwith. Whether the stranger survived the encounter, would be determined by the next few minutes; and whether Eris liked what they had to say.

"My apologies, my lady," the visitor spluttered, "but we, *everyone*, have always presumed you were a man. We didn't realise..."

"Of course you didn't realise. When one is the goddess of strife and discord," the woman sneered, "it does no harm to keep confusion to the fore. I have, in previous times, it's true, been thought a woman by many, but I prefer to keep the insects guessing. I am the mistress of verisimilitude; an expert of the appearance or semblance of truth or reality. It is very easy, very enjoyable... very believable... to blame men for everything. Their egos, their pride... their lust for sex, ownership, and control drives everything they believe in. Circe did us a great service, making humans such poor imitations of our image." She glanced about the dim cabin. "And where better to meet than right under the noses of the enemy?"

The visitor pulled their own hood back. "I'm sorry, my lady, but I don't understand why you have summoned me. I assumed my service to Lord Haáde was complete. That I had fulfilled his commands."

Eris stood, removing her cloak to reveal a magnificent teal silk stola. As she tossed her outer garment onto Charon's dishevelled bed, she ran her finger along the dusty shelf, rubbing her fingertips in disapproval. She was not, in any way, intimidating to look at; but, diminutive, with a slim, shapely figure, her youthful complexion belied the vindictiveness and malice that coursed through her every fibre. Beneath her beautifully manicured pencil-thin eyebrows, her dark green eyes, so cat-like in their intensity, flayed the visitor; drilled right through them; unnervingly narrowing as she frowned.

"*Complete?*" A disbelieving tone marked her incredulity at the naivety of her visitor. "Your service to the Shadow-lands is eternal! It is never *complete!*" she spat. "You may have fulfilled the tasks set by Pasiphae, but, as you well know, she is no longer the mistress of Hades. Although my creator, her usefulness had long since expired, so now there is a new queen for you to serve."

"I'm sorry, I still don't understand, my lady."

Eris let out an exasperated sigh. "Do you really think Lord Haáde would so thoughtlessly murder his own wife? On a whim? On the pleadings of a mewling, simpering, cross-breeding harlot?" She nonchalantly fingered, and scrutinised, Charon's belongings, giving an occasional nose scrunch in disgust. The visitor took a breath, about to speak, but remained silent as Eris held her finger to her lips in a shushing gesture.

"Is it your belief that our master is so easily influenced?" She again glanced sideways at the visitor. "Pasiphae had become a liability. Her reckless attack on Kiípos was not what Lord Haáde had planned; not what he wanted. How could it be? The endangering of the supply of the life essence? His desire for the throne of Sólaás, for revenge over his bastard brother, is as strong now as it has ever been, but Pasiphae was jeopardising his *actual* plan. A plan trusted only to his closest advisor, his confidante... his *bedmate*. There is a new queen now; one with the wit, the wisdom... the cunning... the sexual stamina... deserving of the Dark Lord."

Eris seemed lost in her words, having an almost orgasmic experience. She slowly brushed her hands down her breasts, her midriff, pulling her stola tight against her; emphasising every curve of her figure. Her eyes closed, and head bowed, she gave a long gasp of unadulterated pleasure, before glancing up at the visitor with a contemptuous smirk. "It is not important that you understand; only that you *obey*."

"What is it you require of me, my lady?"

"While Pasiphae was expendable, her removal essential, the demise of Lady Circe was, however, an unexpected bonus. A glorious victory was won, and Elŷsium now believes Hades poses no threat. Access to both Kiípos and Elŷsium has become much easier, hence my presence on this stinking vessel. The new potentates may wield executive power in Elŷsium, but they are not Circe. They are blind to my presence, and my... *tinkering*. They are also ripe for the picking... any time our lord chooses."

An icy sweat coursed down the visitor's back and forehead, the little beads giving an uneasy, almost itching sensation. But the visitor knew better than to fidget. It was common knowledge that Eris had a 'short fuse', an explosive temper. It seemed even more frightening now, knowing she had concealed her true self, her true gender, for so long; actually convincing people she was someone else entirely. And yet, here she was, revealing herself openly. A terrible shudder sped the cold sweat in its descent as the visitor considered the implications of this.

"We shall allow the new custodians of Kiípos a grace period; a honeymoon, to pat themselves on the back, and to restore Kiípos' long term worth to our lord. With that in mind, what news have you?"

"I know not the reasons behind it, my lady, but Lady Cassandra is to petition that they build an army. With the increase in life essence making its way from Kiípos, they intend paring off a huge number in preparation for war; training them to be battle ready. It may be as many as half the combatants in the Battles of Purification. Perhaps more."

"Ha!" laughed Eris. "And of what use do they think their army will be? Against us? Against *him*?" She looked at the visitor as if they had insulted her. "They can amass as many soldiers as they like. It is of no concern," she added dismissively. "And what other futilities has the Trojan planned?"

"Cassandra is forming a group... a cadre. She calls them 'Élementaá', and they are to go to Kiípos; their mission is to free women from the bondage and tyranny of men, apparently."

Eris laughed heartily, disbelieving of what she was hearing. "She thinks that misogyny is the fault of men on Kiípos? That the prissy little lambs there can be free of their yoke? What precocious nonsense. But what else can we expect of a deluded human, schooled in the romantic haverings of a dreamer? Male dominance starts with Helios and Haáde; from there stems the natural law that we, womankind of Célestiaá and humanity, should be grateful for the benevolence they graciously bestow upon us. Men think they complete us with their phallus; honour us with their seed. They believe we are nothing without the men who make us. Whether this is just or not does not matter; Circe could no more change this misguided belief than I could." Her laugh halted, as abruptly as it had started.

"But it is they who should be grateful. For the pleasure we give them; for the heirs we birth them. We let them have their thrones, and their illusion of power, but all men come to women for what they desire most. Well, at least, the heterosexual ones do. However, many men detest women for simply being women." Eris gave a throaty, dirty laugh, then considered the visitor's claim. "Men have physical dominance, certainly, and they use this to torment women, particularly on Kiípos. I see no harm in allowing the Trojan her little avocation; it will keep her busy, distracted, while we plant the seeds of their submission. It will be interesting to see how this Élementaá fare; men will not simply hand over their hegemony because a pretty face asks them to. The Trojan is a fool if she thinks otherwise. Oh, but I do love a little bloodshed." She nodded as she considered the outcome.

"This Cassandra and I do have one common goal, however; to see womankind in its rightful place, and not just as an adornment to male conceit. We may have differing methods, or expectations, but in this we agree. It shall be my life's culmination, my greatest achievement, when I deliver Lord Haáde with the daughter, the heir, that Pasiphae could not provide. The *woman* who shall ultimately rule the universe."

She scoffed, petulantly screwing her face as she became aware once more of the visitor's presence. "You shall continue to do what you've been doing, but will report directly to me from now on."

"Yes, my lady. But..."

"But, *what*?" snapped Eris.

The visitor shirked at the latest verbal attack. "I fear they now suspect me. Or, at least, they suspect someone. Ever since their return from Hades, they have restricted access and information to a select few. They know that someone alerted Hades to their incursion; and that Hades knows of Elŷsium. I fear..."

"*You fear?*" mocked Eris. "You fear? Believe me when I say, fool, that you do not yet know what fear is. You will bring everything you learn to me, or else you shall face my justice. Then... *then*... you shall truly know what it is to fear."

"Yes, my lady," whispered the visitor with a fearful bow. "And my family? They are safe? May I see them... have some proof of their health?" The visitor's throat immediately tightened. Their breathing became laboured; a clawing, grasping struggle for oxygen.

"You dare ask me for proof?" Eris asked insouciantly, replacing the latest piece of Charon's clutter to pique her curiosity. She smiled at the visitor, enjoying the fear and panic in the face of the suffocating minion, before relaxing her invisible grip. The visitor fell to the floor, gasping and coughing and wheezing, their hand grabbing the stool and pulling it, too, to the floor.

"You wish to understand? Well, understand this, you pusillanimous wretch! Whatever arrangement you had with Pasiphae is *done*. Your privileged existence... *here*... is now at my pleasure. Your family's privileged existence in Hades, is at my pleasure. You no longer have a *deal*... no longer have *bargaining* rights. You ask me for *proof*? You shall have no proof. What you will have, is my assurance that should you fail us, or betray us, your family will suffer the most unspeakable tortures ever experienced. Even Hades can learn new tricks, new ways to exact and prolong pain. Do you now understand?"

The visitor, still on their knees, gasping for breath, nodded. "Yes, my lady. My apologies, my lady."

Eris returned to her tinkering, turning a small figurine in her hand; screwing her face in bemusement. "Why do men need childish things?" she muttered to herself, before turning once again to her visitor. "What I will give you, is the knowledge that *He* is coming... soon. The plan is now in motion; measures are being taken to ready the universe for the new order, and we must all play our part. Elŷsium, and whatever pitiful assemblage passes for an army, will soon receive a long overdue reminder of the fragility of its existence. I intend spending some time here; learning whether this paradise is as perfect as they say; testing the weaknesses of the population; preparing for Caátastroph."

A wicked smile formed on her lips. "Having some... *fun!*"

She glanced down at the kneeling lackey, her eyes thinning to cat-like slits, her tone more menacing than ever. "Make the most of your idyllic life, helot, for darkness and disaster are about to visit."

1. THE LUMINARY'S DISMAY

We are all the product of *Chaos!*

We are all part of the whole.

All of us. Every plant. Every creature. Every microbe. Part of the universe. Our atoms, our life energy, our souls and consciousness; all contributing to the *'Eternal Return'*; the reality that the universe and all existence and energy are recurring, and will continue to recur, forever and always. Thus, it is true to say, no-one, or no living thing, ever truly dies. We all continue to exist—in one form or another—and that should make us extremely happy.

But happiness never lasts, does it? I'm sorry, but that's how it is. That's how it *always* is.

If I told you that the end of times... Armageddon... Ragnarok... The *Apocalypse*... was inevitable, what would you do? What *could* you do?

If I told you to *run... would* you? *Could* you? And, if you could, where would you run *to*?

All good things, all good times, must end at some point, and, I suppose, Kiípos has seen its share of good times. Hasn't it? It already has, it's true, come very close to the end of times, but not even Pasiphae's reckless tampering, or man's self-interested flirtations with disaster, compare to what is coming. I have seen worlds die before, and it is never pretty. It is never *painless*. There is always great......

I'm sorry. I'm getting ahead of myself, and that is not the way to tell a story... or to give a warning. Yes, yes, I know I've given warnings before. I know, on previous occasions, I prognosticated on the imminent demise of this joyous little rock. At least, back then, there was a chance—even if just a little chance—of avoiding complete and utter destruction. Now?

I had hoped our next meeting would be a pleasant encounter. That I could regale you with tales of the immense progress and developments that were helping restore Kiípos to her former glory. That I could bring you exciting news concerning our friends and comrades in Elŷsium, and their tireless efforts on both Kiípos and Lunaá.

But, no. No.

I'm afraid recent disastrous developments have taken away any enthusiasm for idle chitchat. Doomsday is almost upon us; the universe shall reclaim all physical life, and, in its place, will be nought but dead space. We are *all* dead men walking, as the parlance goes.

Kiípos has circumnavigated Sólaás but once, since last we met, and much has transpired. Joy and sadness. Gain and loss. Life and death. But it all counts for nothing. It is all meaningless. How did it all fall apart, I hear you ask?

So quickly. So completely. So hopelessly. Surely, you may think, there is something to be done? Someone who can rescue the situation? Well, I have pondered, and I have calculated, and I have gone over everything. Every. Single. Detail. I have recollected and remembered everything I've ever seen; every plan or gambit or ruse that ever was. But, no matter what we do, *he* will still come; and he will, in his wrath, his superstition, and his ignorance, bring with him the end. He will usher the way for the Mother of Darkness; The Queen of The Dead. And her all-consuming hatred shall facilitate the death of light... returning us all to whence we came; the Nothingness.

Of course, if you insist, I shall re-evaluate the situation once more, just for your benefit; just so you can understand the futility of having some hope of reprieve. If I have missed some fact, or overlooked some escape route... *please*... enlighten me. I will not take offence; in fact, my joy would be limitless. I am not a strategist, or a planner. I... well... I just *observe* things. And, for the first time in my existence, I find I do not know the *right* path; the path that will help lead us away from this unavoidable doom.

But, and it pains me to say this, my ego and hubris have blinded me to my own failings... *my* personal weaknesses. Why haven't I intervened before, you ask? It is true I am privy to sights and sounds, events and phenomena, unseen by the mortal eye. But it is also true, despite previous denials, there are things that even *I* do not see.

The contrivances and machinations hatched in the darkness of Hades. The lofty proclamations, and the indifferent ignorance of Sólaás. Even the actions and discussions of my master, Lord Aether, are beyond my ken. I see only what Célestiaá allows me to see, and, to my shame, I realise that is not, perhaps, as much as I may have led you to believe. And, even if I were to know such things, to have seen such things, what could I possibly do about it? I am impotent; unable to affect. I am a fraud, yes. But only in the sense that I, too, have been, if not deceived, then *misinformed*.

But, let's recap. See if we can come up with something helpful.

It seems such a long time ago, but is it really only one human year? All seemed so hopeful, so optimistic, and so safe back then. Our reluctant heroes had defeated Pasiphae and her selfish ambition; returning home bruised and broken but, ultimately, victorious. The impending assault on Kiípos, and the usurping of the throne of Sólaás, quelled only by a noble act of sacrifice and selflessness. Prisoners and homeless souls were granted freedom and rest; albeit at significant cost. There is still the yawning chasm of grief left by Circe's departure; an empty echo replaces the sound of her sweet voice, and the hearts of two particular men, and one distraught woman, can never truly heal.

It has not been, however, a simple case of Kiípos returning to its former healthy state; the damage inflicted by man has cut deep, leaving scars that will take an eternity to diminish. The chaotic helter-skelter of Kiípos' weather systems continue to wreak havoc, with floods, heatwaves, drought, and famine exacerbating an ever-increasing humanitarian disaster. The demise, too, of Man's nuclear obsession has left a terrible legacy of poison and destruction, with whole swathes of previously fertile land rendered uninhabitable.

Whole genus', species, families and categories of animals, birds, insects, fish—rather than thriving in man's demise—continue to disappear as Kiípos lurches further toward self-destruction. While, in contradiction to the disappearance of many, other strands of insect and reptile species thrive in the increasing temperatures; migrating to previously unreachable, colder continents; spreading their venom, their poisons and diseases into previously immune lands.

Disease is now working hand-in-hand with starvation and dehydration in reducing the diminishing human population. Medicines, drugs, and medical care from hospitals, doctors, and clinicians are almost impossible to find. And, as humans are prone to do, war rages everywhere as fresh water becomes the new 'oil'.

The nation state paradigm—the idea of country and citizenship—has long since evaporated in most places. Lawlessness is rife, as those whom laws once held in check, now enjoy the fruits of society's collapse. Anarchy prevails, and new micro-communities have formed, with many disparate groups laying claim to newly established territories. New borders—regularly disputed—etch themselves into the landscape as governments implode; their armed forces fragmenting into localised militias, led by opportunistic, ambitious warlords, intent on protecting their own particular fiefdoms.

It is an amazing facet of humanity, how willing they are to concede their freedoms to the unsavoury, the unsuitable, the undeserving, in exchange for protection from other equally desperate clans. Man will, happily, surrender his choices, his responsibilities, his liberties, in an agreement for the provision of nothing more basic than food and water. The explosion of man's numbers—his ravenous exploitation of Kiípos' resources—has, unfortunately, led to a species unable to fend for itself. The mass production, the industrial spoon-feeding of meats, vegetables... in fact, everything the simplest human requires in order to see the sun rise each morning, has rendered most individuals utterly dependant on others. The individual knows not how to grow food; knows not how to rear the animals on which they have so readily feasted. In truth, most have no idea in how their *daily bread* came to find its way onto their plate. Some, dare I say it, do not even make the connection between that lovely fillet, that most juicy cut of meat, and the chickens, the pigs, or the cattle, that are slaughtered on a bewildering scale. Most have lived in blissful ignorance of most everything around them... so long as they have food in their belly.

The individual will become supplicant, or acquiescent, to the demands of those who profess to *'provide'*. It is not a new characteristic, of course; so-called 'democracies' have often elected the most unsuitable, self-serving narcissistic individuals simply because of how they look, or how they talk. People hear what they want to hear; believe what they want to believe. Say the right things—even the most transparent of lies—and the sheep will follow. Strange, then, that animals would never allow the stupid, the weak, or the selfish, to lead their packs; yet humans readily facilitate the rise of the most obnoxious... abhorrent... *dangerous* of their kind. And then inexplicably find themselves protecting their *'protectors'*. It has never ceased to fascinate me.

The fortunes of the female—the women and girls of Kiípos—have never fallen lower than they are now. It is almost as if, after *'The Ripple'*—the wave that rendered electricity extinct—man's baser, more primitive urges have resurfaced. Rape, murder, slavery - all, now, the only future many females, young or old, can see before them. Women are, in every sense, the property of the dominant male. The time for a saviour has never been more urgent.

Humanity and Kiípos are at a precipice; a point where the very survival of the once-predominant species is now looking unlikely. A point where Célestiaá, Naátúr, and Mother Ella, must redouble their efforts in restoring the natural equilibrium of the Universe's garden, just to ensure its survival. But, even if successful in this venture, it will all be in vain, anyway. For, when *he* comes, all that was once good will be gone; snuffed out like a dying candle and, in the darkness that follows, forgotten, as the Nothingness returns once more. When *he* arrives, there will be no Eternal Return, no Sólaás or Hades. No Kiípos. No us. A world gone mad, in a universe of diminishing light.

It will be much simpler if I were to show you events since the trip to Hades. Perhaps then you may see something I've missed. Something that can give us at least some hope for the future. I should warn you, there are things I am aware of, and shall report on, *now*, that were hidden to me back then; intrusions, and coercions, trespasses and betrayals that I should have seen, but was blind to. To my eternal shame.

And, now, as we are so comfortable in each other's company, may I remind you, as I am an Asexual Intersex, of indistinguishable gender, and do not wish to be associated with the unrestrained barbarity exhibited by the dregs of the human male, you respect I no longer wish to be *referred* to as 'male'. You understand? Thank you.

Let us rejoin Cassandra, Ella and Katherine. I shall not recall the sickening actions of her spouse that led to this intervention, but we can listen in, and view, as Katherine comes to a very important decision.

Close your eyes and, once again, allow me to show the ripples.

11. GIRLS' NIGHT

"Are you sure, Katherine? This is what you want?"

"I'm sure. Ye've said I'm to protect women. I'm sure that means *all* women. And I'll need help... I can't do this alone, can I?" Her hand rose to her mouth once more, biting deep into the apple for a second time. The sweet juice washed her senses; cleansing her as it rushed through her body like a river of enlightenment. Slowly awakening her awareness of the situation she now found herself in; boosting her strength, her enthusiasm... reassuring her in her decision.

She giggled, an almost childlike chuckle, as a tsunami of strange new feelings surged through her. She felt, if not drunk, then *tipsy... giddy*; as if just returned home from a girls' night out. Her vision was a little blurry, her balance a little unsteady. She held her hand up before her, chuckling again as her fingers seemed to fatten and shrink, then stretch extremely thin, her eyes finding difficulty in focussing. "I feel... *woooh!*" she said, gently waving the apple in the air. "But, boy, do I see things now."

The apple crunched once more between her teeth, releasing more flavour... more energy... and more knowledge of her new self, her new duties... and her new allies. "If I am to do this," Katherine continued, making sense of the tasks set before her, "then I have to *find* these women. I don't know them, or where they are... but I'll find them. And I'll need *her* wi' me."

Cassandra looked down to the little girl, a frown betraying her thoughts. "And what do you think, Mother?"

"Will I have to give her an apple?"

"They are *your* apples, Mother... it is for *you* to choose to whom you give them."

Ella looked to Katherine, who smiled in understanding; the fuzziness in her head now melting away. "What do you think I should do, Mummy?" Katherine crouched beside her daughter and took the little girl's hand, nodding to the half-eaten apple in her own hand.

"Well, Sweetie. I've learned so much already... just from three wee bites o' yer apple. My fear, and confusion at... this," she said, looking around her at the tragic scene; looking to the beautiful woman who had brought them back from the dead, "this *mess*... has gone. I already understand... well, *kind* o'... what Cassandra is askin' o' me... askin' o' *you*." She smiled and gently shook her head at the irony of what her first action was to be. "I feel I know so much about her I didna know before. I think I can understand who she is, and why she did what she did; why she was so horrid to everyone. She's no' had a happy life, Sweetie... no-one who ever really cared for her, or loved her... like I love you. She was a victim, every bit as much as you or me. And, I think, she would benefit from our forgiveness and understandin'... and one o' your apples. I'm sure she, too, will learn, just as quickly as I already have. But it's your decision, Ella."

The girl thought for a moment, then looked around to the three inanimate shells lying by the dining and coffee tables; the lifeless, defunct corpses of what had once been the Gallagher family. Around the room, several candles still burned; now just little, misshapen stumps of wax, sitting in hot liquid pools; the flickering wicks, smelling of burnt braided cotton and over-burnt wax, struggling now in providing a gloomy, depressing half-light.

Katherine's unfinished meal still sat on the puke, blood and bile covered table; pushed to the corner in her futile, frantic last grasps for life. A large smudge of blood, with several rivulets running toward the floor, stained the wall by the living room door. Many other random driblets spattered the surrounding wall, floor and furniture; testament to the force with which her husband had slammed Katherine against the wall.

Allan's body lay where it fell; his pants around his ankles, his bare buttocks reflecting a strange illuminance in the faltering candlelight. The bulk of his toned, muscled frame—the massive, overwhelming brute that had proven too powerful for Katherine—was now nothing more than a contorted lump. Cassandra's silver sword had ended the violence... the rape.. and the life of the rapist bully.

By the coffee table... *against* the coffee table, was Ella's former self; sitting almost upright—so childlike in her pink 'Peppa Pig' pyjamas—as if watching the television; the table's sharp corner penetrating the cracked skull atop her limp, broken, blood-stained neck. A tragic, real-life rag doll... an innocent who stumbled into the wrong place, at the wrong time, becoming yet more wreckage in the maelstrom of her father's frenzied, alcohol-fuelled meltdown.

Ella smiled at her mother, who now, like herself, looked resplendent in her new lilac stola; the bloating facial disfigurements of her assault left behind on the half-naked contortion slumped around the table leg. "Should we no' forgive Daddy, as well?" she asked. Katherine looked up to Cassandra, unsure of what to say. The Mistress of Elŷsium stepped over, then crouched alongside Katherine.

"What you see here," she said, perusing the tragic scene around them, "is beyond the gift of our forgiveness. Your daddy crossed a line, Mother, and committed the absolute worst atrocities that any man can commit against women. There can be no absolution for Allan Gallagher; no place in Sólaás for a rapist and murderer. I know he was your father, but there is no saving the soul of this man. Do you understand?" The little girl nodded sadly. Cassandra stood once more, pausing only to ensure Ella's acceptance of her explanation.

"Are you absolutely sure you wish this girl to come with us, Katherine? She will become your companion... your responsibility... for all time. Are you sure this is what you want?" Katherine gave Ella a hug, then stood to face Cassandra, determination written across her face.

"This wee one here," she smiled again at Ella, "will be very busy learnin' lots o' new stuff... meetin' lots o' new, interestin' people." She playfully squeezed Ella's nose, and they both laughed. "I'll miss her terribly. But, while Ella's preparin' for her new life, I know I, too, will have a lot o' hard work ahead o' me as well. And I think *she* should be the first woman I save, don't you?"

Cassandra embraced Katherine. "I knew you were the woman to lead Élementaá," she said. "So, if you want her with you, then we shall go get her... before the Valkyrie take her." She held her hand out to Ella, who hesitated, uncertainly raising her own. "Is there something wrong, Mother?"

"There's just one thing."

"Whatever you need, you just have to ask."

"What'll happen to Crumbles... and Bentley?"

Katherine gestured toward the rear of the house. "We have two horses outside; two much-loved members o' our family." Ella looked up at Cassandra, nodding in agreement.

"Is it possible to take Bentley and Crumbles wi' us?" asked Katherine. "We'll be doin' a lot o' travellin', I take it... and we'll need *some* sort o' transport."

Cassandra gave a little laugh. "Don't worry, Katherine," she said, "I have it all taken care of."

"No, no' just now," replied Katherine, shaking her head. "When we return for our tasks. We'll need transport if we're to reach the places we'll have to visit. We can't expect to walk everywhere, an' there are no *buses* any more," she laughed. "The horses've been sufferin' lately, an' they'll die without us here, anyway. At least this way we can take care o' them."

"Mmm," thought Cassandra. "You make a good point."

Katherine smoothed her daughter's hair with her hand, gently cupping her cheek. "Dinna worry, darlin'... I'll make sure she takes care o' him."

Ella smiled, reassured slightly. "She can borrow him, but make sure she crumbles his biscuits properly, Mummy. He'll no' behave for her, otherwise."

Cassandra paused, considering the unexpected proposal. "You realise we can't take... living... breathing... creatures with us?"

Ella eyed Cassandra, a sudden worried look spreading across her face. "Ye won't hurt them, will ye, Cassandra?"

"They won't feel a thing, Mother. I promise," she smiled, reassuringly, as she thought for another moment. "It makes perfect sense your mounts should have the same celestial protections as you both," she confirmed, nodding.

Katherine looked puzzled. "Celestial protections?"

"Didn't I tell you, Katherine? You are the Divine Creator, the Mother Superior of Élementaá. You are not immortal, but nothing in *this* earthly sphere can kill you now." She shrugged her shoulders. "You will still feel pain, can still be hurt, but, as you have already *died*, there is no more for you to fear. I shall provide you with suitable tools and weapons... as well as a means of inter-dimensional travel. Having these horses will make localised travel much easier, too. Yes, a superb idea."

Cassandra closed her eyes, as she concentrated, raising her left hand slightly forward. Her diamond ring glowed brightly for a second. She smiled as her eyes opened once more. "It's done," she assured her companions. "Now, we should leave this sadness behind," she said, "and let's go get our girl."

A solitary candle lit the large hotel room.

The dimness, made more depressing by the musty smell of stale sweat and beer, provided a perfect deathly shroud for the cold, naked figure lying on the dishevelled bed. The putrid, sickly sweet smell of death was now making its presence known; emanating from the pale white body splayed across the centre of the bed. The mess of red hair and her traumatised, terrified visage, were completely at odds with the beautifully oiled limbs and her once youthful allure.

Underwear and clothes lay scattered about the room, as did many empty beer cans and overflowing ashtrays; the scene suggesting a sorry end to a lively evening of drink and sex. The room was always generally untidy, anyway; with several drawers left partly open, loose pieces of clothing hanging out; the wardrobe door, too, lying open. Scattered across the dressing table were assorted makeup items, with more clothing flung over the backs of chairs. The silence seemed almost respectful in the face of the girl's passing on.

A bedazzling light swelled from the centre of the room, briefly filling the space, allowing the unseen entrance of the celestial trio. As the light faded, the stale smells caused each to place their hands over their noses. "It smells like Hades in here," noted Cassandra, the sudden pungency almost overwhelming.

Katherine surveyed the scene and, taking her by the shoulders, turned Ella to face her, with her back to the bed. "Don't look, Ella. It's no' very nice," she said. Cassandra placed her hand on Katherine's shoulder.

"It's best if Mother *does* look, Katherine. Life and death will become very regular responsibilities in her future now, and it's something she will have to deal with."

"It's ok, Mummy," the little girl said, turning back to face the bed. "I've already seen you, me and daddy. I'm ok."

Cassandra and Katherine exchanged eye contact, smiles, and both felt immense pride in the little lady who now had the unenviable task of restoring the world to full health. Cassandra readied herself, raising her hand once more and, again, the ring emitted a brief bright light.

"Melanie! Wake up, Melanie!" She lowered her arm, now holding a bright red stola. The ethereal essence, the very soul and personification of the murdered woman, slowly woke and raised herself from the now-empty shell she'd occupied in life. She turned, lowering her legs over the side of the bed, and sat for a moment, curious as to the delegation before her. As she took solid form, there came the realisation of earlier events; the attack by Allan, her desperation in trying to fight him off, to breathe, to stay alive. Just as panic was about to overwhelm her, Cassandra spoke again, softly and reassuring.

"Please relax, Melanie. You are at peace now; with an exciting future before you... if you accept it. I believe you know Katherine, and Mother Ella. My name is Cassandra, and I have a task for you." She held out her arm, offering the girl the red stola. "Please put this on. We must go on a journey, and have delayed long enough."

Cassandra's words, calming and lovingly delivered in her beautiful gravelly Aegean voice—which seemed tinged with a hint of Scottish brogue—had the desired effect. Melanie took the garment and slipped it over her head. "Am I dreamin'?" she asked with a sigh.

"No, you're not dreaming," Cassandra confirmed, gently squeezing the girl's hand. "But you have left your earthly life behind, and *this* may take some getting used to. So, relax, and..." She turned to Ella and smiled. "... please accept Mother Ella's gift."

Ella stepped forward, her arm outstretched, offering a glistening red apple. As the older girl smiled, Ella cocked her head to the side. "That's the first time I've ever seen ye smile properly, Melanie," she said. "Ye should smile more often. It makes yer eyes shine." Melanie was overwhelmed by the unexpected friendliness, and tears welled up in her eyes as she accepted the apple.

"Thank you, Ella," she sobbed. "That's the nicest thing anyone's said to me in a long, long time. And thank you for this..." She held up the apple, before taking a bite. Her eyes flickered sideways to her right, and fear took hold as she acknowledged her former employer; the wife of the man she'd stolen; one of the many women she had betrayed. "Kathy? I'm sorry, Kathy. I'm so... so sorry." Her upset intensified, her tears flowing heavier. "Please dinna hate me." Katherine approached the sobbing wretch and held the girl's head to her, stroking her hair.

"Sshh," she whispered. "I know ye now. I'll look after ye from here on."

"Wow," Melanie squealed, as Ella giggled excitedly. Stepping out from the light, the girls looked at each other in wonder, and the group made their way up the short path to the paddock area where the horses had been resting. "You should get used to this," Cassandra said. "Travelling through the Diávasi will become a regular occurrence for you all." Darkness surrounded them but, in the faint moonlight, they could make out the static forms by the makeshift stable. The horses looked as if asleep, lying partially on their sides, legs folded underneath with their chins resting on the ground. Ella ran forward, desperately looking about the field. "Crumbles!" she called. There was silence... until, just to their right, emerging from the shadows, appeared the familiar nodding heads, languid strides, and snorts, of the two horses.

Crumbles was a light-brown chestnut, with white markings on his head and lower legs; a small horse, but a horse all the same. *'He's a horse, not a pony,'* Ella would make sure to tell everyone. She smiled broadly as the white stripe down his muzzle nuzzled into her, and she wrapped her arms around his neck in a loving hug.

Bentley was a large bay. Towering over his counterpart, a chocolate-brown body with a black mane and ear tips. Both his front legs had an unusual black and white 'swirl' around the ankles. He moseyed over to Katherine and gave his customary snort and nod, dropping his head and ears, looking for the enjoyable scratching that she would give his ears and neck.

Ella turned and beckoned Melanie over. "Come meet him, Melanie," she offered. The older girl approached, warily at first, but her confidence growing as she gently patted his neck. She had seen Crumbles many times at the stables, but had never had actual contact with him. "Hello, handsome," she said, smiling as he rubbed his head into her.

"He likes ye," Ella confirmed.

"Does he?"

"Aye! Ye'd know if he didn't," the little girl said seriously. "He'd pin his ears back and show ye his teeth. I dinna think he'd bite ye... but I wouldn't take that chance." From nowhere, Ella produced an oat biscuit. "Ye need to seal his friendship wi' a biscuit, Melanie," she advised. Then, in a whisper, "crumble it up first, then let him eat it off yer hand."

Melanie smiled and did as instructed. Crumbles eagerly snaffled up the oats, then gave some grateful head nods. "That's how ye keep him on yer side," said Ella, with a little wink. As she petted Bentley, Katherine watched the two girls interacting with interest. She wrapped her arms around the girls and gave them both a squeeze. Melanie leant her head against Katherine's shoulder. "Ye ok?" Katherine asked. The red-haired girl looked up, nodding with a smile.

"Thanks, Kathy," she said.

"Thanks? What for?"

"My head's startin' to clear now. I can remember everythin'. Well, most o' it. I'm surprised ye're no' tryin' to strangle me... like... he..."

Katherine pulled her tight, once more. "I have no actual idea what any o' this is," she said. "But, wi' every passin' second, I'm becomin' more aware o' *why* we're here... all three o' us. Cassandra's givin' us a new life, a new purpose in that life. I'm seein' ye properly for the first time, Melanie." She laughed. "No' as a husband stealer, or a cheeky shit o' a lassie… but as someone who needs me, needs Ella, needs Cassandra. I can see that ye didna have a childhood; no love, no guidance or support. I can't change what's happened to ye before, but I can make sure, from now on, ye have somebody on yer side." She kissed the top of the girl's head. "We're yer family now."

"Please dinna be nice to me Kathy, I dinna deserve it," Melanie said, as she wiped a tear from her eye.

"Ye've been scrappin', and fightin', since ye were a bairn, Melanie. Ye never got the *chance* to deserve it. I chose ye 'cause I want ye to have that chance. You an' me? We've got fuckin' loads to do together. An' we're gonna give loads more lassies that fuckin' chance. We're gonna kick some arse."

"It's time we were going, ladies," interrupted Cassandra. She looked at Ella, then at the horses, with a slightly concerned expression. "Keep the horses close, Mother. They may find this a little unsettling." Ella nodded, placing her hands on Crumbles and Bentley. Once more, a brilliant light surrounded them for several seconds, before fading back to the darkness.

They were now standing at Geata Dhè. "This is how you shall make your way across the dimensions," said Cassandra. "But, first, you must make the trip to Elŷsium, and you will all sleep for a time. On the other side, you shall be reborn, and we can then prepare you for your new lives." Cassandra turned and placed her hands on Katherine's shoulders. "On the other side, Katherine, you'll be reacquainted with Jacob," she smiled. "He's looking forward to seeing you again."

Katherine looked over her shoulder, taking one last glance back toward Strath-sealgair. She looked around the darkness of the clearing, the moon's illumination giving a strange prominence to Jacob's abandoned car. There was a stillness, however; a calm, peaceful air; broken only by the gentlest of breezes rustling the leaves of the thousands of trees bearing witness. She had lost count of how many times she'd visited these stones over the years—with Jacob, or with Ella—but there was a difference in this trip; a realisation of a wondrous journey ahead. A new life beckoned, and Katherine was determined to make it on *her* terms.

"Can I ask one more thing?" said Katherine. "When I step through this... this gate? Can I do this as *me*? No' as someone who people want me to be?" Cassandra looked puzzled.

"I'm no' Kathy, or Katherine... I'm *Katie*!"

Cassandra gave her companion a tight hug. "Well then, Katie. We had best get going."

III. A NEW HOME

Geata Dhè, Strath-sealgair July 1987

"Ye make a very decent sandwich, ye know."

"One o' the benefits o' bein' an independent man," he laughed.

"Aye," retorted Cissy, "only 'cause your mum has ye well trained, eh?" She leaned into him, chomping away on the perfectly balanced mix of sliced ham, cheese and tomato.

"There's a very fine art to gettin' it right," advised Ray, as he twisted the cap off the thermos flask. "If ye put too much o' one thing, it takes over, an' yer as well no' havin' any o' the other stuff. And the bread's really important. Ye've got to have fresh bread." He poured a cup of piping hot tea into the small plastic cup, then held it up, ready for Cissy to add some milk. Ray nodded his head. "Aye, it's about the balance."

Cissy smiled. She looked Ray in the eyes, quickly glanced down at the cup, then returned her gaze. "No chance o' ye starvin' then, Smiler?" she laughed.

He poured a second cup as he considered the question. "Only if we have to survive on your cookin'," he laughed.

"Ye cheeky shit!" Cissy squealed. "Yer mum says I'm gettin' better," she chuckled.

"Aye, an' she tells my dad he'll get the hang o' that piano some day."

Cissy thought for a moment, then looked out down Glen Affric, her legs dangling down over the steep edge of the slope. "Aye, well, ye don't love me for my cookin', do ye?"

Ray watched her staring into the distance. "I love ye for every reason there is," he whispered. "An' a million more besides."

Cissy turned to face him, her heart fluttering, as it did every time he made her feel like a goddess. She *was* a goddess, of course, but Ray didn't know that. He just had this amazing ability of reminding her how privileged she was; how lucky she had been to find *this* man, among the billions she could have met. She leaned forward and kissed him, gently, slowly. Making every microsecond of contact between them mean something.

The sun was high, and the lack of any breeze helped make it one of the hottest days of the year. A day off work, a picnic at Geata Dhè, and the solitude, of just themselves and the singing of the birds, brought a feeling of glorious delirium to the two young lovers. Life could not get any better than this, surely?

"Ray?"

"Aye?"

"What would ye say… if I asked ye to get a house with me?"

He took another bite of his sandwich. "Could we afford it?"

His answer reassured Cissy; he hadn't rejected the idea out-of-hand. "Well," she said, "ye've got yer wage from the mill, and I'm workin' full-time at the cafe, so there's that. An' we're no' exactly big-spendin' party-goers, are we?"

Ray continued chomping away. Cissy hated keeping anything from him, but she couldn't tell him she'd never allow them to be poor, or to struggle needlessly. Money was not an issue; she had, within the beautiful jewels on her finger, the means to create all the riches anyone could possibly desire. But how could she possibly explain suddenly coming into a vast fortune? Or how, occasionally, when she was supposed to be working at the cafe, she'd actually be in Elŷsium? No, she'd top up her wage carefully; just enough to help, but not enough to raise suspicion.

"I'm sure my mum and dad would help, if we needed it, but I wouldn't like to ask too much o' them. They've been brilliant to me.. to us.. so far. An' everythin' they've done for Eric…"

"So, ye're no' against the idea?'

"Against it? No!" he affirmed. "I'd love it, just the three o' us." He took another bite of his sandwich, squeezing the last inch inside his mouth. "But where are we gonna find somethin' that would suit us, that we could afford? I don't want some tiny wee flat. It'd have to be somethin' nice, for you and Eric; somethin' wi' a wee garden, eh?" He slurped from his cup. "I don't finish my apprenticeship for another year; that'd give us a wee bit more, though."

"Well...," Cissy said, enthusiastically. "It just so happens that I've seen an empty house. Up School Road. It's a small three-bed semi, wi' a garden at the back. It's near the stables, and there're loads o' paths and walkways..."

"Whoah," laughed Ray, holding his hand up. "Ye've done yer homework, eh?'

"Aye," blushed Cissy, "I've been thinkin' about it for some time. The rent's quite cheap, and the landlord's desperate to get somebody in. It'll need a bit o' work, but... What do ye think?"

Ray looked deep into her eyes. "I'd live in a ditch if it guaranteed bein' wi' you," he said, leaning his forehead on hers. "No' sure Eric would be too happy, though. Aye, let's check it out," he nodded.

They both stared down the Glen, munching on their snacks, drinking their tea; marvelling at the scale of the beauty before them. Cissy looked up, shielding her eyes, as the flicker of a Golden Eagle broke the stillness, hovering high above its intended prey. Cissy pointed up, and Ray's eyes followed.

"God's country," he muttered.

"Aye," agreed Cissy, linking tightly into her man. "God's country."

A large jolt, as the wheels dipped into a slight hollow in the ground, broke Ray's introspection. The carriage rumbled up the track, circling around a dense group of firs, before the first signs of the village broke through the gaps in the trees. "Welcome to Rimel, Dad," said Jacob. "Ye know ye can both stay at the villa if ye want to, don't ye?"

Ray peered out the window, trying to catch a glimpse of the new home that had been arranged for himself and Eric. The dappled sunlight flashed through the gently swaying leaves; the interchanging light and shadow making it impossible to determine the detail of the approaching structures.

"Aye. Thanks, son. But…" He glanced across at Eric, sitting silently, as always, in the opposite corner of the cab. "… I think it'd be better for us to have a wee bit o' privacy. Just 'til we get used to all o' this. Ye understand?"

Jacob nodded. His own arrival at Elŷsium had been confusing… terrifying, even; the speed of events hampering any sense of comprehension and acceptance. But, with the support of his mother—Circe—and Cassandra, he could eventually come to terms with the huge upheaval. Death, afterlife… even the realisation that he was the son of a celestial goddess.

Ray and Eric, however, had no such support. Their path to Elŷsium was far different; the car accident was only the beginning. Pasiphae's Reavers had intended taking all three of them from the car, but succeeded only in removing Ray and the eldest of his sons; hauling them down through the darkness into Hades. Their earthly death had been tough enough to cope with for Jacob—he was just a boy, after all; had he known of the nightmare they had then endured..?

"He's still no' spoken?" Jacob asked, quietly.

"No' a word," replied Ray. "He hasn't uttered a word since the day o' the accident. I don't know if he *can* still talk, but he mumbles and screams in whatever passes for sleep."

The years in Hades had left their mark; not, it seemed, physically, as the men's appearance and outward health continued to improve the longer they were in Elŷsium. No, there was a far deeper wound; a hidden, ugly black scar, with the memories eating away at both Ray and Eric; the constant vision of Pasiphae's sadistic smile, and the echoes of her shrieking screams and laughter. "Do ye want to talk about it? What ye went through? Do ye want to talk about mum?"

What was there to talk about, thought Ray? He'd mourned the loss of Cissy when she'd died; and for every day after that. Seeing her again, for however brief a time down in Hades, still didn't seem real to him. Did it actually happen? How could he believe what he'd seen, when he wasn't entirely sure about anything that had happened since the car crash?

He held his gaze inwards toward Eric, then looked at Jacob with as much of a smile as he could muster. "One day... maybe," he said, before returning to look at the upcoming village. "When it doesna make me scream inside, I'll sit down an' tell ye all about it." Jacob clasped his dad's hand, gently squeezing. Eric sat silently, staring out the other window.

"Well, the countryside around here's beautiful, an' quiet. Ye'll both have peace," Jacob said. "Ye can arrange a carriage anytime ye want to come down to Strath-sealgair Villa, or to visit Elysia." He laughed. "I'm no' gonna be much o' a tour guide, though, Dad. I'm still tryin' to get to know the place m'self. There are other towns and cities, like Gellane, but I've no' had a chance to visit any o' them yet."

"We've fixed up a lodge for you and Eric; nothin' fancy, just as ye'd asked for. Ye'll have yer own workshop as well. Naebody to bother ye. Unless ye want them to, o' course."

Ray smiled. "Thanks, son. We'll need a bit o' time to ourselves. Just to let us adjust to everythin'. These clothes, for instance," he said, tugging at his tunic. "How does it work here? Food? Wages, all that sort o' stuff?"

"It's easy enough, Dad. Ye make what ye want, as good as ye want it. Ye give it to whoever wants it, or needs it. Ye carry out work, or repairs, for whoever needs work done. Ye get food, clothes, whatever ye need, from whoever makes it, or grows it... as much as ye need, as much as ye want. There're regular markets in Rimel, Gellane, and Elysia that ye can use. There's no greed here, or hoardin', or any need for material wealth. Ye see what people need and ye provide it; and they do the same for you. It's like barterin', but without exchange rates. There's no money involved. Just everybody doin' their bit."

"Like communism?"

"No. Like a commonwealth. A community." The carriage pulled up with a jolt. "Nobody goes hungry.

Nobody lacks the work that they want to do. Everybody's important. Everybody contributes, and there's always someone to help ye out."

"Mmmm," mumbled Ray. "Sounds too good to be true. I thought I had a job for life before. I thought I had a life before."

"The clothes?" Jacob added, "well, the formal togas an' tunics are only really worn in places like Strath-sealgair Villa, Elysia an' Gellane. Everywhere else, well, ye'll see when ye're in Rimel." Jacob glanced at his still-silent brother in the corner. "Take all the time ye both need, Dad. I'll see ye regularly; I'm back an' forth to Elysia every few days. So, too, will Charon... *Joe*! He an' Brunhiíld pass here all the time. There're loads o' things happenin' right now, lots o' changes bein' made."

"Mmmm. *Joe*!" muttered Ray. "That's somethin' else I'll have to get used to."

Jacob opened the carriage door and stepped down, looking expectantly for a welcoming face. The carriage had pulled up in the village's Main Street, and several passers-by looked on curiously. To their right was the saloon, but, across to his left, by the baker's shop, a loud laugh drew his attention.

He grinned as he found who he was looking for. "Biro, here, will look after ye both. Help ye settle. Won't ye, Biro?"

Ray jumped down, then looked up to see the man-mountain approaching. Biro was charging his way up the slight incline toward them. His heavy stomping feet and the sound of his hands clapping against his white apron to get rid of the flour, were an amazing sight.

"Ahh, Master Jacob," exclaimed the baker, his enormous smile concealed by his even more enormous beard. "So good to see you again." He held out his hand to Ray. "Welcome, Master Raymond. My name is Biro, but, around here, I'm known as 'Grind'. We have all been looking forward to your arrival at Rimel; we have lacked a skilled carpenter for far too long in these parts." As Biro squeezed his hand, Ray gave a slight wince as he felt his bones crunch.

"Careful, big guy," laughed Jacob. "Don't want to incapacitate anybody wi' yer enthusiasm, eh?" Biro nodded, an embarrassed look on what they could see of his face.

Ray smiled as he shook his hand, loosening his tightened fingers. "Nice to meet ye, Biro. Don't know about bein' a skilled carpenter, though. It's been a long time since I held any tools."

Biro slapped his hand firmly on Ray's shoulder, a serious look now in his eyes. He took a little, sideways glance at Eric, who had now stepped warily from the carriage. "You are among friends now, Raymond. You have a new life ahead of you. Both of you. And you will have all the time, all the privacy you want, in order to settle in to that new life. We will be here whenever you need us. We shall be invisible when you don't."

Biro strolled over to Eric, holding his hand out in welcome. "Hello, young Eric. Welcome to Rimel." He laughed out loud—a bellowing, thunderous roar—but immediately contained himself, realising how nervous Eric actually was. "Don't worry, young sir. It's not just old grizzlies like myself here. We have many young men and women, all of whom cannot wait to meet you." Biro turned, looking for someone in particular. "Ah, here she is," he said. "My daughter, Jael, with some water and towels. I'm sure she and her friends will be much more to your liking."

A young girl, a teenager of about seventeen or eighteen, approached from the saloon, carrying a heavily laden tray of glasses, a jug of water, and several damp towels. She was as tall as Eric, with a bob of shoulder-length black hair circling her pretty face. Strong black eyebrows arced across the lively brown eyes that shone beneath and looked directly at him; looked into him, it felt like. She had a thin, straight nose that rounded cutely at the end, and her thin lips grinned cheekily at him. He couldn't help himself as he eyed her figure; the loose, thin white linen blouse, highlighted by the sunshine, trying, but failing, to hide her cleavage as she bore the weight of the tray. The brown cotton trousers hung loosely, too, but still defined the curving lines of her hips. "Would you like some water?" she asked cheerily.

Eric nodded, embarrassed that she may have caught him admiring her; embarrassed that he was thinking lustful thoughts about the girl. Unaccustomed to the clothes he was wearing, he felt embarrassed about that, too; that his long, thin white legs looked ridiculous as they stretched from below the short white tunic.

There was no other visible reaction; no smile, or obvious interest; just a passive acceptance as he reached his hand out for a towel. "Will you be working at the sawmill?" Jael asked. "Or, maybe, you might even prefer to work here, at the bakers?" She smiled again. Eric's lips curved up, slightly, just for a second; just the merest hint of a smile, a reaction. "Hmm," said Jael. "I can see I've got my work cut out." She looked straight into Eric's eyes, holding her gaze for a few seconds, before turning toward Jacob and Ray.

Biro had made his way back over to the two men. "We have fully stocked the cabin with food and firewood; the workshop with tools and equipment. And we have diverted branches of the stream directly past the workshop and cabin, so you'll always have a ready supply of fresh water. There is a horse and waggon at your disposal, too, Raymond. When you're ready, I'll take you up there."

The cabin was far more impressive than Ray could have imagined. It wasn't huge, by any measure, but it was spacious, warm, and comfortable. It spanned two floors; the living area on the ground level, and the sleeping quarters in the upper space.

The front door opened to a large, square living room. The exposed beams, wooden floors, and panelled walls provided an authentic rustic atmosphere; whoever had prepared it for them had also been meticulous in ensuring the home was immaculately clean.

To the left was a striking rock fireplace, stretching from floor to ceiling; crafted from large blocks of cut stones, as well as river stones and fieldstones in their natural shapes. A black iron surround housed a pile of unlit logs and wood cuttings, stacked neatly in the clean, unused hearth. The artisan rock work continued to the nearest left-hand corner of the room, with a stunning stone staircase winding up around the back of the chimney breast to the bedroom area above.

Directly ahead, at the rear of the cabin, were two sets of wooden French doors; the wall of glass gleaming bright as the sunshine streamed through, filling the entire space. A large square glass coffee table, surrounded by comfortable-looking armchairs and sofas, sat proudly in the centre of the room; various oil lamps, statuettes, and other paraphernalia punctuated certain focal points; all totally out of step with the mainly Greco-Roman world they'd found themselves in at Strath-sealgair Villa. It reminded Ray of the sort of cabin you'd book for a luxury getaway in the mountains; if you had the money, of course. It now just needed someone to make it 'lived in'.

In the far-left corner, to the left of the French doors, was a doorway to the kitchen area. He poked his head around it, impressed with the comprehensive range of equipment and cupboards surrounding the large island, but wryly noted there was no sign of a fridge-freezer. Sitting neatly on the island was a massive basket of fruit and vegetables; the scene looking every inch like the ideal, staged photo you'd see in country and farmhouse magazines. Very beautiful, very rustic... very surreal.

Ray carefully opened the French doors and stepped outside onto a long porch. As with the front porch, there was a generous, but not excessive, space, as the rooms upstairs extruded out, forming a perfectly proportioned cover. Two wind chimes tinkled in the gentlest of breezes; a rocking chair sat idly waiting to rock someone to sleep, and there was something magical, too, about the view. To his left was a fenced off garden area; already populated with beautiful, healthy shrubs, flowers, and trees. Four wooden steps led to a path, heading off down a gentle grassy slope to a second group of small cabin buildings. This was his workshop; his own sawmill and carpentry studio; sitting at the beginning of a track that led into the clump of trees at the bottom of the hill, before winding its way up the hill toward Rimel. A small corral area was home to a large-looking black horse, who was running and jumping and frolicking his time away and, to the side of the mill, sat a long covered four-wheeled waggon.

Ray gazed out at the vista before him. Trees surrounded the cabin in all directions. The path to the sawmill descended a narrow valley and stretched out toward the quickly flowing stream that ran from behind the cabin and down through the settlement. The feeling of the warm sunshine falling on Ray's skin, and the pleasant birdsong piercing the otherwise silent scene, immediately left him feeling far calmer, and more relaxed, than anytime he could remember. This was the perfect privacy both he and Eric needed.

He envisaged sitting drinking in the hum of frogs, crickets, and wind chimes on a summer's night. Feeling the cool night breeze, watching the fireflies and stars, forgetting about everything else in the world. It didn't feel like it yet, but this could be home.

A creaking groan from behind him, brought him back to the here and now. He turned to find Eric had laid claim to the rocking chair. The young man didn't say a word but, for the first time since the day of their accident, Ray saw his son smile.

He sat up, gripping the sheet so tightly he could feel his fingernails stabbing into the palms of his hand. The blackness of the room surrounded him, the blackness of his despair filled him. Sweat poured from every part of his body, running down his torso, his arms, his forehead. Tears streamed from his sore, bloodshot eyes; his gulping sobs making his breathing erratic, hurried and forced. He stared into the black void. Looking for her face. Listening for her voice. Waiting for her attacks.

There was no sign of her. There was nought but silence and darkness. Yet, still he watched. Still, he waited. The curtains fluttered as a breeze came through the open window, making him jump, his head snapping to the right, seeking the hidden interloper. There was no sign of her... but she was there. He knew she was there; waiting for him to relax, to let his guard down. She'd stayed hidden since they'd arrived here, but he knew she was just biding her time; taunting him, tormenting him. She did this regularly, taking great pleasure in his anxiety, his torment, his fear.

He watched for her, all the time. Even now. Sitting in the darkness. Sitting in the silence. Sitting in a pool of his own urine, the sheets soaked in his own warm, wet, fearful discharge. He daren't move lest she hear him, lest she reveal herself. He couldn't take it again. Not again.

He tried to tell himself that she was dead, that he had seen her die. Murdered at the hands... by the sword... of her own husband. He had seen her sliced apart by the giant black sword, wielded by the giant black shadow-man. He had heard her scream as the blade fell; heard her evil curses fade as she turned to dust. He knew all of this, and yet... in his mind, Pasiphae lived on.

His dreams were all too realistic, all too accurate. How she would whip him with her leather straps; drag her blades slowly down his skin, shedding thin lines of his blood. How her warm tongue would work its way up the bloody trails, drinking up the bright red liquid. If she wasn't torturing him, then she'd be tormenting him, teasing him, using him. She took great pleasure in arousing him; stroking and gently squeezing his genitals; taking his reluctant hardness in her mouth whilst working her hand on his length. Then she would mount him, thrusting herself, satisfying herself; soaking him in her juices till he could hold out no more. Afterwards, when he had ejaculated, she would rub her sex, and his discharge, into his mouth; making him drink in a sick show of power... and control... and humiliation.

Tonight he dreamt of the beatings, of her screaming insults in his face, of her taunts. Of how she would make fun of his emaciated body, grabbing and pulling at his testicles; stretching and smacking his penis, laughing hilariously like a child each time. He dreamt of being left chained and hanging in his manacles for days at a time; being force fed the mouldy, putrid gruel the Hadeans called food, washed down with stale, warm water. The many times his distressed intestines flushed stinking, watery faeces down the back of his welted legs. The constant cold and darkness of his dungeon cell, and the shrieks and screams of the many other unfortunate souls suffering the same unbearable fate. Tonight he dreamt that he just wanted it all to stop.

A faint light to his left startled him, and he scurried back in his bed, back against the headboard. "It's ok, son," the man said. "It's only me. Ye're safe, Eric. Ye're safe, son." Ray walked to his son's bedside and placed the lantern on the side table. The large unsightly wet patch stood out on the brilliant white sheet and, not for the first time, Ray carefully sidled onto the bed, shuffling alongside his distraught son. Eric jumped as Ray placed his arm around his shoulders, staring at his father through glazed, red-rimmed eyes.

Ray understood the fears, the dreams and the hurt... he had exactly the same experiences... exactly the same nightmares. He pulled Eric to him, cuddled him, reassured him... talked softly to him until his eyes could finally close; hopefully finding an almost peaceful unconsciousness. Almost... but never fully. Another tear-filled night, watching his son slip further away.

IV. THE BOULÉ

"Are you sure you won't need me?" Marro asked.

Jessica watched his face for any sign of humour. It seemed a strange question; there was nothing he could do that both she and Cassandra weren't more than capable of. The meetings with the Boulé were not something that Marro had any need, or business, attending; particularly today's gathering, which was an opportunity for Cassandra to receive official permission to proceed with her plans of forming a defence force for Elŷsium. Putting it down, simply, to his desire to be with her as much as possible, she replied, "no, we'll be fine." She placed a soft kiss on her lover's lips, then smiled. "Cassandra has already decided on how she'll approach the Boulé. They cannot possibly refuse her request." She threw the cover off, swinging her legs out of the bed, and sat on the edge, running her fingers back through her hair.

Marro raised himself, his hands on her shoulders, kissing the back of her neck. "I wouldn't be too sure," he said. "There are many things the Boulé will deliver, but consistency of logic is not one of them." Jessica shivered, as he slowly traced his fingers down her back, sliding his hands under her arms, softly squeezing her breasts; kissing the side of her neck. She moaned as his right hand brushed down her front, between her legs; her thighs parting automatically, accepting his soft caresses. She leaned her head back, kissing him fully and deeply before pulling away with a smile.

"I love you," she said, her eyes shining as brightly as her smile was wide. "But," she added, leaning her forehead against his, "I.. *we...* have work to do." Her right hand cupped his cheek, as she kissed him passionately once more, before breaking away with a giggling laugh.

Marro lay back on the bed, leaning on his elbow, watching Jessica as she skipped off toward the bathroom. He smiled, glorying in his contentment, in his joy, in everything. It seemed surreal, thinking of how he had reached this point, but life really couldn't be any better. His resolve to travel to Hades with Jacob's party had been at the risk of losing Jessica; at the risk of losing himself. He did not consider himself a brave man, but accompanying the others was something he felt he could not avoid, if he was to look himself in the mirror again. The rewards of his courageous decision, despite his own feelings on the matter, far outweighed the relative dangers he thought he would face; dangers eased on instructions given him by Brunhiíld.

He'd spent the entire period at the Dark Lands readying the boats for their hoped-for escape. The waiting was tortuous; pacing back and forth, ignorant as to the progress of his friends; indeed, they were now more than friends; they were family. As time had passed, his hope had all but faded, until, out of the darkness, in a tiny boat, came Circe; an unexpected interloper, an unexpected source of hope. Little did Marro know at that point, this would be the last time he would see the beloved matriarch of Elŷsium.

When his 'family' came stumbling back through the tunnel door, bleeding, barely alive in some cases, stunned through their traumas, the obvious absence of the daughter of Helios had broken their hearts; wounded them, more than any Hadean sword could ever manage. The tears of the inconsolable fell for the entire journey home. Marro, of course, had busied himself tending to the wounded; reassuring, and feeding, the starving liberated prisoners - the family Jacob so long thought dead.

They had spoken little as they made their return to Elŷsium; the boy, not at all. Charon had steered them through the darkness, back onto the River of Transcension, before he, too, fell victim to his wounds. At that point, it had been Marro who had taken control of the boats, guiding them home through the silence. Haste was crucial; Brunhiíld, in particular, had serious wounds that could only be alleviated by returning to the healing aura Elŷsium's borders gave. The channel leading into Elysia Harbour brought much relief to the Frenchman; he'd survived the trip and returned home to his lover; a blessing they'd hoped for, but thought impossible.

Jessica strolled back toward him, towelling her wet hair. Marro smiled, raising an eyebrow in appreciation at her nakedness, drinking in the beauty of her form. "I think you should climb back in here," he suggested.

Jessica laughed and flicked her towel at him. "I would then need to take another bath and, while I'd love to... *satisfy* you, that would only make me late. And there is no way we can be late for this meeting." She sat on the bed and leaned over to kiss him. "What do you have planned for today?" she asked.

Marro leaned back against the headboard, his hands behind his head. "I have the not-so-simple matter of welcoming the delegation from Lunaá," he laughed. "They always treat their visits here as some form of... school trip. I believe it would be simpler looking after a hundred toddlers, rather than a dozen, or so, Demi-gods."

Jessica leaned over and kissed him. "In that case," she advised, "you'd best get yourself cleaned up for your crèche duties." Marro grunted before jumping up, chasing the shrieking woman back toward the bathroom.

The Ephor sipped his water as he listened; nodding in agreement now and again, taking notes occasionally; but all the time, making mental calculations of the resources required. As leader of the Boulé—the council and caretakers of the constitution of Elŷsium—his was the deciding vote; over-ruling all others, if that was what was required. Master Jossa, and the four Archons, sat in an arc around one half of the enormous circular table. Theirs was the responsibility of government, of administration, of allocating employment and resources.

To his left, sat Archon Lusanne of Gellane Province, scribbling away furiously; documenting every word; her hand a blur as her quill flew repeatedly from parchment to inkwell and back. Occasionally she would pause, looking up as if to ask a question, then return to her writings, having thought better of it. A serious woman of great diligence, her attention to detail was legendary, with some joking she could recount her every bowel movement since the day of her earthly birth. Lusanne would counter that, sometimes, people needed reminding of what they *actually* said, as opposed to what they liked to think they said.

To his right, Archon Tima of Elysia; a seasoned politician of some standing, but a man who had no hesitation in showing his disinterest. He lounged, fanning himself in the stuffiness filling the room, staring out to the veranda. This gathering, to his mind, was a waste of time, having already determined what his answer to Cassandra's request was to be. He would much rather be out enjoying the sunshine; meeting the people of Elysia and hearing more of what they required; not sitting here, struggling for breath, listening to a rambling, incoherent plea for the impossible.

The other two Archons were each capable orators and campaigners in their own right, when it came to securing resources for their own provinces. But, equally, when it came down to it, each was more likely to accept the decision of the Ephor.

Jossa placed his glass on the table, staring at it as he sat quietly, stroking his chin while considering the representations. After a short time, he looked around the table, making eye contact with each of the attendees; his hands forming a steeple, his fingertips touching.

"And you base this... this... hypothesis... on what?" he asked.

Cassandra forcibly sat back in her seat, exhaling sharply as her impatience finally broke. "Were you not listening, Master Jossa?" she snapped. "Lady Circe, prior to her death, gave this vision to me. We *must* act." Jessica placed her hand on Cassandra's; an effort to calm her.

"A *vision*?"

"Yes! A vision. A reactivation of my foresight, I suppose, showing an imminent battle at the Elysian Fields."

"And have you had any further visions, my lady? Any additional information you can give us? When we can expect this battle? With whom we shall engage in battle?" He looked at Cassandra with head tilted low, his brow furrowing, his fingertips tapping each other; like a headmaster interrogating a misbehaving pupil.

"*Argh!*" screamed Cassandra, pushing her chair back violently as she stood, toppling it behind her. "A war is coming, Master Jossa," she asserted. "We don't know when. We don't know with whom. But it will come all the same. We must begin building an army—a defence force—immediately. We shall need barracks, weapons, rations... everything, in fact, that we do not yet possess."

Jossa picked the glass up once more, holding it to his mouth with both hands; not drinking or sipping, just thinking... and tapping. The group around the table waited patiently; even Cassandra had hushed, allowing the Ephor time to consider the requests. She had not expected the past would come back to haunt her; that those who needed to hear them, would ignore her warnings, once again. Not everyone, certainly—Jacob, and Jessica and Marro, they all took her word; or, at least, that's what they told her. Were they just humouring her? Lying to her? Jossa continued tapping his glass as he mused. "It's all very irregular, my lady," he said, at last, looking aside to each of his fellow councillors. "Perhaps we should take more time to consider the proposals."

"Do you not believe me?" Cassandra asked, holding her hands out in despair.

Jossa gave a short, condescending chuckle. "It's not that we don't believe you, my lady," he ingratiated. "Its just that, well, it would take a massive realignment of our food supplies, our carpenters, our farriers, our builders. My, we have no one experienced in the manufacture of weapons; how are we to arm these new... soldiers?"

"Weapons?" exclaimed Cassandra. "You fixate on weapons? Where do we find our weapons for the Battles of Purification? Who makes *these* weapons, I ask?"

"*These* weapons," he countered, "as you well know, are symbolic tools. They are not weapons of *war*, not the weapons of *proper* soldiers. They would be of limited value... *if* we had to use them in genuine conflict." He chuckled again. "And how do we decide on which life essences are to be spared the trips to Solaás or Hades?" His face suddenly straightened, taking a more serious appearance. "What are we to say to Lord Helios when he asks why his tribute has disappeared?"

Cassandra banged both her hands on the table as she leaned forward. "Tell me, Master Jossa," she asked, angrily staring at the table in front of her, avoiding looking directly at the Ephor. "Would you be asking Lord Jacob these same questions if he were here?"

The Ephor laid his glass down, then settled back in his seat, brushing his toga down as if expelling some invisible crumbs, or some non-existent dust. He looked dryly at Cassandra, steepling his fingers once more, fingertips tapping furiously as his patience waned. "If Lord Jacob were here, my lady," he said coldly. "I'm sure he would have something more tangible than a... a... *vision*... to back up his requests."

"*Arrgh!*" Cassandra repeated, turning toward the door; making as hasty an exit as her anger would allow. Jessica's jaw fell, shocked at the sudden departure of her friend. She stood, her head twisting back toward the door, then back to the Ephor. "May I...?" she blurted. "May I...?"

Master Jossa waved his hand in dismissal. "Yes, yes! See to Lady Cassandra, Jessica," he ordered. "Tell her we shall consider the requests put to us and will get back to her in due course." Jessica bowed, before grabbing her notes and scurrying out of the conference room.

Cassandra was already some considerable distance down the corridor, taking her anger out on several vases; sending them crashing to the floor in a display of uncharacteristic, immature fury; like a child throwing a tantrum. Jessica broke into a jog, pulling her stola up as she ran. "Cassandra!" she called. "Calm down, Cassandra! He's just being important. He's just trying to remind everyone of who he is, that's all."

Jessica caught up with her friend, who was now banging her fist against the wall. "He's just being..."

"He's just being a fucking man," bellowed Cassandra. "A fucking panjandrum! I thought Elŷsium immune to the rampant chauvinism that soaked through the very atmosphere of Kiípos. But, here we are; finally seeing the arrogance, the entitled superiority of man assert itself in our Elŷsium." She screamed as she pushed another vase onto the floor. "What is the point in being Mistress of Elŷsium if an officious oaf can overrule me at every turn? If a self-important clerk can ignore Mother's warnings?"

Jessica cocked her head to the side, pursing her lips and crossing her arms in disapproval; watching quietly as Cassandra paced back and forth, raging, screaming obscenities and cursing all men. As she turned, Cassandra's eyes caught Jessica's, instantly feeling the reprimanding glare and, just as instantly, feeling the embarrassment wash over her. "Feel better?" asked Jessica.

A maid came rushing around the corner, in response to the sound of smashing vases. She stopped to assess the mess, before heading off to fetch a broom and dustpan.

Cassandra stood rigid, her deep breaths leaving no doubt as to the depth of her anger. "No!" she replied. "I do not feel better." Jessica placed her hand on Cassandra's shoulder and sighed.

"Don't let him get to you, Cassandra. Since Circe's... since we lost Circe, many of the administration, particularly the males, have felt a little lost. They've felt that, by unconditionally accepting you and Jacob as their new leaders, they are betraying her memory in some way. It's nonsense, of course, but there you have it."

The maid returned with the cleaning equipment and made to sweep the shattered vases. "Its alright," Jessica advised. "Cassandra will do that." The young girl looked puzzled; uncertain what to do next. Jessica held her hand out for the broom, smiling at the bewildered domestic. "It's ok," she reassured. "You can continue your other duties. We'll deal with this."

"So, because these men have some sort of orphan complex, I am to bite my tongue? I will not be silenced, Jessica. I had enough of that in my earthly life; I refuse to be ignored, or ridiculed again."

Jessica smiled and embraced her friend. "There, there," she said, holding out the broom. "Now, sweep." Cassandra humphed and heyed, grudgingly grabbing the broom and setting to work. "Keep your powder dry 'til Jacob gets back—then you can get things moving. How long will he be away?"

Cassandra slowed her sweeping as she considered the question. "Well, he's taking Ray and Eric to their new home at Rimel—well done for arranging that so quickly—so, probably a day or more."

"My pleasure," replied Jessica with a curtsey. "Those guys must really need some normality—if you can call Elŷsium normal. Must have been, well, *hell* for them."

"Mmm," agreed Cassandra. "They were in a terrible state. I think they're on the mend—physically, anyway. It will probably take some time for them to get Pasiphae and Hades from their minds; if they ever can."

Jessica watched as Cassandra waved the broom from side to side; a sweeping motion, certainly, but ineffective and pointless. Her concerns over Cassandra were growing, and were hardly eased by the intransigence of the council, the Ephor in particular. The trip to Hades, and the death of Circe, had taken much out of Cassandra; far more than she was prepared to admit. Her recovery of Katie from

Kiípos had been a welcome distraction, but now the reality of her loss was hitting home, as she had time to brood.

With Jacob away, it fell to Jessica to console and support the new Mistress of Elŷsium. But that was easier said than done. Circe had been an ever-present in Cassandra's life in Elŷsium for thousands of years; now she was gone, and the doubt, insecurity and paranoia of Cassandra's earthly life was in danger of resurfacing. Everything was happening quickly, with the intended recruiting of an army, and the formation of Élementaá, very much in everyone's thoughts. The Ephor was not alone in resisting Cassandra's pronouncements and premonitions; Jessica, too, was not entirely convinced, given the lack of detail, but did not have the heart to tell her friend as such.

It pained her to doubt her friend, and to see her unsuccessfully burying her grief as she strove to assert herself as the new matriarch. There was a quiet resistance, a reluctance to accept Cassandra as the new sovereign; many saw Jacob, a half-Célestiaá, as the heir apparent. Cassandra had only been Circe's ward, her assistant, her accessory; she was surely not capable, or deserving, of such regal responsibilities. Surely?

"But I shouldn't have to rely on Jacob for the Boulé to listen to me. Circe placed the responsibility of leadership and recovery in my hands; in the hands of women," Cassandra said, abruptly halting her sweeping. She raised her hand and stared at the Célestiaá Ring. "If men cannot see this, or accept this, then, as Élementaá will have to do on Kiípos, you and I shall have to assert our authority here in Elŷsium. By peaceful means, if possible; by other means, if necessary." Her smile, and the threatening tone of her voice, chilled the bones of Jessica. "Now, enough of this," Cassandra added, leaning the broom against the wall. "Time for some wine."

⁂

"You were a little... disrespectful, Master Jossa," Archon Lusanne berated. "Lady Cassandra is, whether you like it or no, the custodian preferred by Lady Circe. She is the chosen partner of Lord Jacob. You really should..."

"Yes, yes, yes, Lusanne," interrupted Archon Tima. "We are all well aware of the positions held by various..." He swirled his hand around. "... people," he concluded. Lusanne glared at her colleague. "But that does not mean we can allow just anyone carte blanche with our resources." Tima returned her glare.

Master Jossa sat deep in thought. Lusanne was right. He *had* been offhand with her, and yet, he could not help but think Cassandra's requests were a little... unhinged. Certainly he thought them a little self-indulgent. Elŷsium, to his mind, was a sanctuary; untainted or unconcerned by such negative phenomena as war. To even consider the building of an army, with the resources and logistics required to service it, at a time when Elŷsium was being stretched enough, was nothing short of folly.

The never-ending trail of souls, incoming from Kiípos at an already overwhelming rate, was creating no end of problems for the clockwork precision of Jossa's logistical machine. The Battles of Purification were an exercise of meticulous detail and timing but, now, even they were

64

evidencing signs of the compromise required in dealing with the perpetual influx. "Perhaps you're right, Lusanne," he conceded. "But I cannot see any way in which we can possibly approve this rather... bizarre... request. We are struggling to accommodate the current crop of combatants as it is. If we were to build this army, we should require all our artisans working full time creating a completely new infrastructure."

"And," sighed Tima, "I should not have to remind you of the promises made to begin construction of a new housing sector to the north of Elysia. We have been waiting... well, it seems like forever. And now we have had to relocate the Boulé... *here*... to Strath-sealgair Villa. Further reducing our standing in the eyes of Circe's descendants."

"If I may," a mousey voice interjected. The three senior councillors stared over the table to where Archon Sitlis, of Leriathe, sat, previously unnoticed. A diminutive woman, short in height, if not spirit, Sitlis was the youngest member of the Boulé. Elected overwhelmingly by her peers in the large town, situated to the northwest—following the transcension of Rachael, her predecessor—she was a clever, practical woman. She struggled, however, to assert herself in the company of her fellow Boulé members. She stood—an attempt to make herself more noticeable; make the council take her more seriously.

"Yesss?" drawled Jossa. "You have something you wish to say, Archon Sillis?"

"It's *Sit*-lis," she corrected. "It's Sit-lis, not Sillis."

"Oh, for pity's sake," groaned Tima. "Get on with it, girl!"

The small, fair-haired woman screwed her nose at the rudeness of her peer. "Weee...," she drawled back, gesturing to the other Archon, who, too, had been excluded, thus far, from the discussion. "Weee... were wondering why Lady Cassandra, or Lord Jacob, for that matter, do not simply use the Célestiaá Rings in assistance. I'm sure Lady Circe would have."

Tima shifted impatiently in his seat, continuing to fan himself. He looked to Jossa, waiting for the Ephor to state the obvious. Unable to contain himself, Tima gave a condescending laugh. "Oh, my dear," he said pithily, "if it were so simple, do you not think we would have suggested such a course of action?" He peered over his fan, his eyes wide, mocking in their intensity.

"Archon Tima, in his own way," sighed Jossa, "is correct, my dear. The rings, or at least, one of them, were useful when in the possession of Lady Circe. Now, I fear, they are but mere decorations. Certainly, until such time as Lady Cassandra or Lord Jacob, learn to wield them effectively. They are not the masters of the rings just yet, and we cannot, therefore, rely on their usage."

"But...," persisted Sitlis, "shouldn't we be encouraging both to practice their skills, so that we may have some benefit from the rings? We do, after all, have two rings now at our disposal."

Tima got up and walked toward the open balcony. He was a flamboyant man; expressive and demonstrative in everything he did. His togas were always bright; the jewellery adorning them, spectacular. To him, life was a stage on which he was born to perform, and every utterance a performance; a trait many of his current contemporaries found rather irksome at times. "Lady

Cassandra *has* had some practice, though, hasn't she?" He turned and took a quick glance at Jossa, before continuing outside. Jossa's patience was wearing thin. Nevertheless, he kept his calm demeanour.

"She has, it's true, developed her skills in inter-dimensional travel, having visited Kiípos a short time ago. But that, and some minor creative conjurations, is the extent of her abilities thus far."

"So how, pray tell, does she intend creating her Élementaá, this hobbyhorse that fixates her, if all she can manage are a few parlour tricks?" The room fell silent as everyone turned to look at Archon Mylos, of Halfland Moors. He was not a man who said much but, when he spoke, he did so quietly; his gruff voice was barely audible, so as to encourage his audience to pay complete attention.

"I thought you asleep, Archon Mylos," said Lusanne, with some amusement. Mylos returned her gaze, impassive and unimpressed.

"Do not mistake my silence for disinterest, Archon. My input here is every bit as important as your own. I speak only when I have something worthwhile to say, not merely for the effect of it." Lusanne, feeling a little chastised, sat back in her chair. "Archon Sitlis, though a little presumptuous of my support, makes a relevant point," Mylos continued. "We are facing overwhelming demands on our resources, and yet the very people we consider our 'leaders' offer us little more than fanciful nonsense. A *vision*. Are we to waste any more of our time on the dreams of someone who, let's face it, has ascended to prominence through adoptive good fortune?"

Lusanne gasped. "I'm afraid I'm finding it difficult to accept the levels of vitriol being displayed here. I cannot ever recall such bitterness."

Tima retook his seat. "Archon Mylos is right. Consign this foolhardy request to the bin, Master Jossa. Allow Circe's waif her divertissement, her Élementaá; but let us get on with the business we are tasked with, and let's hear no more about building an army."

"I agree," chimed Sitlis.

"And you, Archon Mylos?" asked Jossa. "You agree with Tima and Sillis?" The brooding Archon nodded his head slowly, before resting his chin on his fist. Sitlis threw her hands up in despair. "It's Sitlis," she murmured to herself.

"Well, that seems to carry the motion," said Jossa, banging his gavel down. "Lady Cassandra can proceed with her Élementaá project. But we refuse the request for a defence force."

Archon Lusanne sat in shock. "That's it?" she asked. "End of discussion? You have all demonstrated nothing but rudeness, disrespect and, dare I say it, as I never thought I'd see it here, of all places, outright misogyny. I am ashamed to be part of what has transpired here today." She got slowly to her feet, and, looking at each of her fellow-councillors, shook her head. "I shall return immediately to Gellane. I do not feel the welcome here that I once did." And, with that, she was gone.

V. NAÁTÚR

Katie lay on the bed, enjoying the warmth, the birdsong and the sunlight streaming through the open window. A light breeze brought a cooling air to the room, keeping the temperature at a comfortable level. Although a little stiff, she felt refreshed, having had a long, deep sleep on the boat that brought them here.

The room decor was bright, with a light blue ceiling matching the floral murals that framed the white stone walls. Several couches, busily populated with cushions, sat neatly against the walls, suggesting a space that not only served as a bedroom but also for social gatherings. The furniture, and the various ornaments, vases, jugs and glasses that sat on the tables were all designed with a very feminine aesthetic, but were a curious mix of Roman, Greek, Norse, African and Japanese. The smell of the abundant fruit, piled high in a beautiful China bowl, filled her nostrils and, in the pleasant warmth, made her think of summer.

Her head rested back against the wall, her eyes closed, thinking through all that had happened since... since...

She blanked the incident with Allan out of her mind, focussing instead on her meeting Cassandra; the change in Ella... the change in herself. Eating the apple had somehow filled her head with names and faces, places she must go, tasks she must perform. It was just snippets of information, no details or explanations—a confused to-do list that made sense one second, then, almost immediately, felt completely absurd—but she knew this was what *fate* meant her to do. Fate! Is that what it was? Was there such a thing? How else could she explain where she was? How she got here? It still surprised her, too, that she had brought Melanie with her, after all that had happened; but, yet again, she knew it was the right thing to do, and felt an enormous sense of pride that, already, she had saved someone's soul.

She ran her hand over her bald head. A look under her light top cover confirmed that the baldness was everywhere; her head, her face, her arms and, thinking of how she had always hated grooming '*down there*', her legs and pubic area. There was a strange feeling of acceptance; a contentment with her perfectly smooth body; a satisfaction at the unblemished femininity of her naked form. She felt perfect, immaculate... *divine*; as if cleansed of impurity, not just in her physical form, but in all things.

A giggle at the doorway to her right broke her reverie, and a smiling little face peered through the gap. "Are ye awake yet, Mummy?" Katie sat up, holding her arms out in welcome. Ella ran to the bed and leapt onto the bottom end; kneeling, giggling with excitement. "I can make bluebells, Mummy! Ye should see the bluebells I've made."

Katie laughed and squeezed her daughter tightly to her. Ella wore a yellow peplos, her hair tied back with a matching band. She looked the picture of health and happiness, her face radiant and joyful.

"Bluebells, sweetie?"

"Aye! There's a huge garden, and I can make bluebells. Ye've been sleepin' so long, Cassandra let me make bluebells." The little girl was bubbling with enthusiasm. She giggled once more, then, looking in awe at her mother, said, "ye're really beautiful, Mummy. Even wi' no hair, ye're really beautiful."

"Thank you, Ella," Katie replied with an enormous smile, stroking Ella's hair. "You're really beautiful, too, but how did your hair grow back so quickly?"

"Cassandra said that children don't lose their hair 'cause they don't need to be reborn like adults do. And I'm only beautiful 'cause you made me, Mummy." The little girl's face turned serious. "Cassandra says *I'm* goin' to make loads o' beautiful things, but first I've got to meet my new teachers." She raised herself up on her knees as high as she could and, with great excitement, added, "they live on the moon, Mummy!"

"On the moon?" Katie repeated, excitedly. The little girl squealed with laughter and threw herself into her mother, hugging her tightly. "Well, then," Katie added, turning to lower her legs to the floor, "I think it's time I got up, don't you?" A light dizziness caused her to pause as her feet pushed against the cool floor. She took a breath and stood, unsteady at first, before stretching herself as fully as she could manage, her long arms reaching toward the ceiling. A cursory look around the room located the doorway to the bathroom. A shower would be most welcome, and she had an urgent need to pee.

"Can ye see any clothes anywhere, sweetie?"

Ella looked very businesslike and knowledgeable. "There's a huge bath in there, Mummy. And lots and lots o' dressin' gowns. And over there," she said, pointing to a doorway in the opposite wall, "is a huge wardrobe. I've got my own room too, Mummy, just like this one, and I'm keepin' it tidy, honestly." Katie smiled and took a more considered look around her. A long, hot soak *would* be even better than a quick shower.

"Right then. Mummy'll have a hot bath, then ye can show me around the place. Deal?" Ella nodded enthusiastically. She jumped down from the bed and, taking her mother's hand, led her toward the bathroom.

"Cassandra asked me to look after ye, Mummy. She said to make ye comfortable and..." Ella paused while she tried to recall Cassandra's instructions. "Comfortable and... somethin' else, Mummy." Katie laughed and walked slowly, and rather stiffly, toward what she hoped would be a toilet. "Do ye want me to find ye somethin' to wear, Mummy?"

"That'd be brilliant. Thank you, sweetie." The girl ran off toward the walk-in closet, leaving Katie to discover the splendour of her rest room. Steam rose from the huge sunken pool, with little islands of suds and bubbles drifting aimlessly in little, circular paths.

Bright brownish orange terracotta walls surrounded the large space, with full size mirrors built into several cavities. The floor was tiled with brown and orange hexagonal tiles that spilled down the walls of the bath, covering the base, which had an intricate orchid design tiled into it. There were several tables with vases containing orchids, chrysanthemum, and roses dotted neatly around the walls. Shelving on either side provided either perfumes or gels, or towels and robes. At the end of the shelving to her right was a small, partially covered cubicle where she hoped she would find a toilet.

On having relieved herself, Katie indiscriminately lifted an orange-coloured bottle and gingerly stepped down into the hot water. She let out a large exhalation as the sudden heat caught her breath, and she lowered herself below the surface. Ella came through the doorway, her excitement as high as ever. "I've found a yellow dress, just like mine, Mummy," she said.

Ella took her sandals off and sat on the edge of the bath, dangling her feet in the hot water. "Cassandra's told me where to take ye when ye're ready, Mummy. We're gonna meet our new teachers, then have lunch, then get shown about the villa and gardens. I've already explored a'place, Mummy. So, if ye need to know anythin', ye can just ask me." She paddled her feet as her mother washed. "Then, tomorrow, we both begin our trainin'. I havena seen Jacob yet, but Cassandra says he's dyin' to see us again. I hope he likes my bluebells. I'll show ye when ye've finished, Mummy."

"Well, in the meantime," said Katie, laughing and splashing soapy water at her daughter, "get in here an' give yer mummy a big cuddle."

Ella squealed with delight as she removed her peplos, before jumping down into the bath with a massive splash.

"This way, Mummy!"

The Gallagher ladies walked, hand in hand, down the long corridor, gazing awestruck at the statues, tapestries, paintings, and various urns, vases and carvings that brought colour and vivacity to the otherwise surgical cleanliness of the white walls. They stopped to inspect one particular canvas. It was a beautifully detailed watercolour, depicting the view through Geata Dhè and down Glen Affric; a summer's day brought to life through the eyes of someone who'd obviously held great love and affinity for the place.

"Nae place like hame, eh?" The man's voice caught them both by surprise, and they turned in unison, searching for the source.

"*Jacob!*" squealed Ella as she ran toward the new arrival. She jumped up toward him and, as he caught her in his arms, they twirled around several times, locked together in a tight hug. His sudden appearance struck Katie dumb, unable to move, as all of her previous sorrow at losing him for a second time evaporated; her joy and relief at seeing him was overwhelming. She remained motionless, fingers on her lips, trembling now, as a gargantuan wave of intense emotion raced through her, and tears spilled freely down her cheeks.

Jacob lowered Ella to the floor and looked up to Katie. "Suits ye," he smiled, pointing to her hairless head. He held his arms out as he strolled toward her. He looked different; not just because of the toga, although Katie was impressed by how well it suited him. No, he looked healthier - happier, even, than she'd ever known him. He stood taller, more sure of himself; a man finally at ease with himself, by the look of it.

She fell into him, squeezing her arms tightly around him, resting her head on his left shoulder.

"I thought I'd lost ye," she sobbed. Jacob pulled her tightly to him, his head leant onto hers, his hand on the back of her head. He sighed.

"Ye did," he confirmed, "and it wasn't a pleasant experience." They embraced for what seemed a lifetime, then Jacob leaned back and looked at her, before stretching up, placing a kiss on her forehead. Katie leaned forward, an attempt to kiss him, but Jacob pulled back, a subtle shake of the head saying 'no'. He then smiled at Ella. "I promise we'll catch up properly later, and we can compare horror stories. But, now that ye've found me again, ye might wish I'd stayed lost." He turned toward the room at the end of the corridor. "There are some... *people*... here to meet you both. They'll be yer... well... yer tutors, yer advisors. Has Cassandra explained everythin' to ye? What yer new responsibilities are?" Katie linked arms, pulling Jacob tightly to her as they walked down the rest of the corridor. The hubbub of what sounded like a large crowd grew as they approached the doorway.

"I've got a rough idea o' what I'm supposed to be doin', but no idea how I'll do it," she laughed. "Cassandra said I'll be 'Protector of Women'... and I know there're some girls... women... that I've to seek out. To recruit. But I've no' got a clue what I'm recruitin' them for. Bein' honest, Jacob, I've no' really got a clue about any o' this. One minute I'm thinkin', '*aye, I've got this*', then, the next, my brain goes to mush." Jacob smiled as he recalled his own confusion on arriving in Elŷsium, and squeezed Katie's hand as it rested on his arm.

"Once ye get yer head around this, an' realise it's all real, ye'll find it all a little easier. It took me ages. They must've thought I was as thick as two short planks." He stopped walking and looked at Katie. "And a lot has happened in a short time, but we can talk about that, too, later." Ella ran ahead, pausing as she reached the doorway, peering into the room at the assembled group. She turned, eyes wide, and smiled in delight at her mother. Jacob gestured with his head for her to enter. "In ye go, Ella. They're all eager to meet ye."

The little girl waited, a little uncertainly, until her mother had caught up and, taking her hand, strolled into the room, with Jacob following. An immense space opened before them, with long, high white walls stretching for some considerable length to a columned veranda, the bright sunshine outside creating a blinding glow in the doorways. A long, beautifully polished oval table, surrounded by high-backed chairs, all neatly tucked under at regular intervals, filled the centre space. Several fruit bowls, water jugs and glasses sat untouched in the ornately decorated centre area.

The group stood beyond the table, in the sunshine's glow, and they fell silent as the mother and daughter entered. As one, they bowed, then knelt on one knee in deference. "Welcome, Mother!" they chorused, heads lowered, awaiting the blessing of their new matriarch. Jacob stepped forward and, lowering himself to Ella's height, whispered, "they'd like yer permission to stand, Ella."

"Please, stand," she said, looking back to Jacob for reassurance. 'Well done,' he mouthed. The cohort rose, once more in unison, before breaking, spontaneously, into a round of warm, welcoming applause. To the right, a small, elderly woman stepped forward; her short, deliberate steps a contrast to the tumult of clapping hands. She stood no taller than Ella. Her beautiful white silk stola shone with an almost halo-like glow as the sunlight bursting through the veranda doors seemed to shine directly on her. Her long white hair, wrinkles and frail demeanour suggested a woman of great age, but the smile she gave to Ella felt like a brand new day.

Ella turned to her mother, eyes wide; an awestruck, amazed look of bewilderment. A massive smile forming as realisation took hold. "Mummy! She's the Moon!" Ella whispered. The woman approached, holding out both hands to Ella, who instinctively responded in kind. The hands met and clasped, an instant bond forming, an immediate transfer of thought, emotion and understanding. The ladies embraced as if long-parted old friends; the beginning of time, meeting Kiípos' last hope.

"Welcome home, Mother," said the old lady. "Our broken hearts can heal once more."

"Are ye the Moon?" asked Ella. The woman smiled and kissed the girl's forehead as the applause faded.

"Ah, the Moon! Yes... yes... I suppose I am the Moon. Not physically, of course, but figuratively... metaphorically. My name is Selêne. I am the curator... the caretaker... of Lunaá, the moon, and I am delighted to meet you, Mother." She looked around at her eager companions. "We are all delighted to meet you." Selêne, still holding Ella's hands, looked up at Katie; her pride in her daughter written across her enormous smile.

"Congratulations, Katherine. You have raised our mother beautifully; we couldn't have asked for any more from you. She is a delight, and I'm now sure, with Mother Ella, we can restore Kiípos to the magnificent fertile garden she was before man's neglect." The old woman, once again, stretched her short, thin arms out. Katie bent down and hugged her. "I shall, personally, take care of your daughter." Selêne smiled as she looked again at Ella, before her eyes looked into Katie's. "But she is, at last, where she was always meant to be. *You* are, at last, where you were always meant to be." Her hands clasped Katie's tightly. "Ignore my inane rambling, my dear. All shall become clear soon."

The ancient woman focussed her attention once more on Ella, who had waited patiently, albeit excitedly, to meet her new friends. Selêne gestured for Ella to take the centre seat at the nearest side of the table, and the eager child pulled, with great effort, the heavy chair out from under the vast slab of wood. "Shall I help?" offered Jacob.

Ella smiled, shaking her head. "It's alright, Jacob," she grunted, her tongue then sticking out to the side of her mouth as she heaved, "I can manage." Jacob eyed Katie with immense pride, and he made his way to his seat at the end of the table with a satisfied smile. Katie sat to Ella's right, and Selêne took the seat at the opposite end from Jacob.

The assemblage made their way quietly to the other seats, sitting only after Mother Ella had taken her rest. The girl sat, almost stretching to lean onto the table, gazing around at the impressive gathering before her. Selêne tapped a glass with a knife, drawing everyone's attention. "Welcome, welcome, welcome to you all," she said, with a joyous flourish of her hands. "It has been far too long since we had cause to celebrate, but here we are," she looked across at Ella, "rejoicing at our new beloved Mother, and at the dawn of a new era for Kiípos. We also give great thanks for our new earthly ambassadors, Ladies Katherine and Melanie. It is our greatest hope they find swift success in restoring the fortunes and stature of not only the human female, but also the well-being and growth of all humanity. Welcome, too, everyone, to the first day, the birth... of Élementaá." Once again, the group burst into applause.

Selêne raised her hand, and the applause ended. "But we must also give thanks, thoughts and beloved remembrance for those we have lost; Lady Circe and Mother Gaea. Without them, there would be no us. And without us, there would be no hope." A respectful hush descended and the heads of all assembled lowered in deep thought, as if in prayer. After a short time, Selêne addressed Ella. "With your blessing, Mother, may we begin?"

Ella looked toward Katie, but, rather than seeking reassurance, she smiled as she stood. "Let's begin," said Mother Ella with certainty, confidence, and authority. Katie took a deep breath as her love, pride and admiration at the blossoming of her little girl stunned her. Ella, without looking, took her mother's hand, giving her a gentle reassuring squeeze as she retook her seat. "We have work to do."

Selêne nodded to Jacob, and the Consort of Elŷsium stood. "I suppose we should begin by introducin' our esteemed visitors." He looked to the man to his immediate left and smiled. "Please keep it brief, eh?" The large man stood with a grunt.

"If you insist." He was tall, broad-chested and muscular, and his dark red toga gave him a fearsome, impatient look. A thick black beard, with equally thick, curly black hair and eyebrows, framed a rather serious looking face, and, with an air of dismissal, he spoke... curtly and concisely. "I am Kronos, Master of Time... of which I regularly seem to be denied," he said, before giving a rather forced, insincere bow. He then sat, almost as quickly as he had got to his feet, with an annoyed sideways squint at Jacob. Jacob smiled, knowingly, then nodded to the woman next to Kronos.

She was thin, athletic, with cropped black hair and, unlike most of the other women in the room who wore stola, she wore a white knee-length tunic. She was pretty, her actions carried out with an androgynous smoothness, her boyish figure somehow exuding great femininity but, also, great masculinity. Her gaze fell on Katie, and she smiled wickedly, looking her up and down. "My name is Nike, and I proffer the gifts of speed, strength and victory to those who are deserving. And...," she gave another wicked, seductive smile, "I can be very friendly... with the right partner." Selêne tapped her glass impatiently.

"That will be enough, Nike!" she muttered, with an air of disapproval. Nike bowed toward the old woman. "Yes, Selêne. My apologies." As she sat, she gave another suggestive smile, and a wink, to a blushing Katie. A ripple of quiet laughter worked its way around one side of the table.

"Forgive my sister," a mellifluous, pleasant, voice broke in. "She is lacking in neither confidence or impudence, but she does also have some humility and respect, even if she rarely shows it." The woman, who could easily be mistaken for a man, looked remarkably like Nike, but didn't dress like her. Wearing a loose blouse and trousers, she bowed… then sat down again. After a few seconds, she stood once more. "I am Dionysus, cultivator of plants and vegetation. And I welcome you to Elŷsium." She bowed again, then sat down again. She stood once more. "I love your bluebells, Mother." Then sat again.

Selêne looked down to her feet, shaking her head in disappointment, tapping her knife frantically against the glass. "Can we please have someone present themselves in a manner that will shed a positive light on us all?" she complained. "Mother will think us all fools and flusters if this carries on." Jacob stood, taking control of proceedings, introducing each of the seated guests.

"In clockwise order, Ella, we have… Kronos, Nike… Poseidon, master o' water and sea creatures… Boreal, keeper o' winds and air… Hephaestus, fire… Erebus, darkness, rest and sleep." He smiled at the next woman. "Demeter, *Goddess* of Agriculture, Fertility, and the Harvest." Demeter laughed out loud.

"Oh, Jacob. I shall have words with Cassandra. She has told you before about teasing us Naátúr. Unless, of course, you *truly* see me as a goddess." She winked at Jacob. "In which case, Cassandra had best keep an eye on her man." The words hit Katie like a sledgehammer. Jacob and Cassandra? Of course. That's why he pulled away when she tried to kiss him. Her mind was in a whirl, but Jacob pulled her attention back when he resumed the introductions.

"Artemis, mistress o' the hunt, and twin sister o' Apollo, who isn't in attendance here for… well… *reasons*." Katie noticed a little contempt in Jacob's voice when he mentioned Apollo's name.

"Hestia, Curator o' Domestic Life. Dionysus..." Jacob paused when he looked at the last woman in the group. "And, with the exception o' Mother Ella, the most important person in the room... Athena. A veritable goddess... o' wisdom and courage, law and justice, and strategic warfare. A magnificent, talented woman. The woman tasked wi' the raisin' o' Elŷsium's armies, and the trainin' o' Élementaá." Athena stayed silent, but bowed her head in gratitude.

Jacob walked around the table to where Katie sat. "Don't worry about all o' these unfamiliar names an' faces, Katie. Most are just here out o' curiosity. Ye'll be workin' closely wi' Athena; she'll be yer immediate link from Kiípos. You and Melanie are about to be given some amazin' abilities, and some mind-blowin' tools and weapons that ye'll need when ye go back down there. Athena'll make sure ye know how to handle yerselves." It rather surprised Katie at how assertive, and in control, Jacob was with the gathering. There was an authority about him she'd never known before; a confidence, an air of assumed superiority, without acting superior. He was the boss, and everyone around the table knew it. He then gave Katie a cheeky, knowing, smile.

"It's no' all good, though," he warned. He looked to the tall figure sitting in the corner. Katie hadn't noticed them until now. Had they been there all the time? They stood and approached Jacob.

"Why, Jacob," chastised Séntinell, in a mocking tone. "First you tease Demeter, and now you tease me. What are we to do with you?" They smiled, then, bending down to hug Jacob, rubbed his hair. "Cheeky boy!" Séntinell turned to Katie and, hands held out, took hers in a warm, friendly greeting. "My dearest Katherine," they said. "It is such a pleasure to meet you both. Our hearts can never overcome the loss of our beloved Mother Gaea, but we can rejoice in knowing we now have Mother Ella to herald a new epoch for Kiípos. We can have hope, too, now that we have Katherine, The Divine Creator, to bring liberation and prosperity to the many disparate genders of mankind; *all* now struggling to survive in the aftermath of Pasiphae's annihilation of man's societal structure."

The tall figure stepped over to Ella's chair and kneeled. Their great height towered over the little girl, but, taking Ella's hands in theirs, they bowed their head. "Mother Ella, I am Séntinell. The Lumináry. I am the physical representative of My Lord Aether; the Primordial god of the upper air, the atmosphere, space, and heavens. With his blessing, I am here to pledge my service, in whatever way is required." They looked into Ella's eyes and smiled.

"I love your beard," said Ella, smiling in return. Séntinell gave a little gulp, disarmed by the unexpected compliment, then kissed her hand.

They took Katie's hand and, looking to both ladies, said, "I can only stay a short while, this time. I have a task at the outer edges of the Galaxy that I cannot put off but, while I am here, I shall teach all you need to know about *Chaos!*, and what our roles, all of us, will be in the next chapter of the Universe."

"We can leave the lessons for later," Jacob smiled. "We don't want to overwhelm our new guests, do we?" Séntinell looked, with puzzlement, at Jacob, then at the Gallaghers, before realising that there were other formalities to be observed. Jacob made his way back to his seat. "Cassandra is, at present, welcomin' Melanie and…" He smiled warmly at Ella. "... Crumbles and Bentley, to their new home." He looked around the table.

"Now, down to business!"

Cassandra and Melanie had already taken their seats at the large round dining table, but there was still no sign of the rest of the group. A massive buffet lay on a table along the wall by the veranda, sitting untouched, waiting, too, for the expected diners.

"Can I ask somethin', Cassandra?"

"Of course you can... anything."

Melanie thought carefully before speaking again. "I was... vile... awful, a complete pain in the arse. I stole her husband, sold out people I worked wi', did some... disgustin', shameful things." She raised her hand and quickly wiped away a tear. "Why do ye think Katie brought me here?"

Cassandra looked into the girl's eyes, thought for a second, then smiled. "Why do *you* think she brought you? Was it a punishment? Spite? Or... was she offering you a second chance? A chance of redemption, perhaps?" Melanie fiddled with a napkin as she gave the question some thought.

"When I first... woke... I was terrified. I saw Katie standin' over me and expected her to thump me. But, almost immediately, I felt calm. I saw her and Ella, and they... well, they looked beautiful. Angelic. And when Ella gave me the apple, I couldna help but feel... couldna help but feel their love. It was the strangest sensation, Cassandra. I've never felt anythin' like it before."

Cassandra stood behind the young girl and placed her hands on Melanie's shoulders. "I agree," she smiled, "love *is* a strange sensation. And I cannot tell you how much it pleases me you have, at last, experienced this feeling. It must be extremely difficult to give love, when you have never received love." She bent down and kissed Melanie on the top of her bald head, then took her seat once more.

"When I revived Katie... resurrected her... I offered the chance to improve the life experience of every girl, every woman on Kiípos. I asked that she save the souls of certain women; to muster a corps, a group of worthy mothers, daughters, sisters... acting together under common direction; to overturn man's violent dominance over womankind." She poured a glass of wine for them both.

"Katie argued that, despite the imbalance of the genders, it was unfair to blame all men for the injustices inflicted by a few; that *all* good souls were worth saving. She named you as the first good soul that should be saved; that you should be the first name on her list."

Cassandra sipped her wine, and Melanie dried her tears. "Whether she acted out of forgiveness, or malice, is not important. Katie wanted you as the first of her sisters in the great fight that's coming."

"The great fight?"

"You do not expect men to simply hand over their control, their self-appointed entitlement, without a fight, do you, Melanie? If anything, since the ripple, men have intensified their grip on those weaker than themselves; unrestrained by the rule of law, or even moral decency. No. While your mission is one of emancipation, I have no doubt it shall involve much bloodshed. Élementaá is the long overdue scalpel that shall, literally, cut out the cancer of misogyny and oppression, and you shall be Katie's chief proponent in her crusade. If you do not wish to be part of this great liberation, you merely have to say so. *You* are in control of your destiny now."

Melanie sat quietly for a second. "Ye know, I always thought I *was* in control... that it was my choice to be like I was." She looked at Cassandra, a dawning realisation, an anger growing inside her. "I wasn't though, was I?"

"You became what men wanted you to be; what you *thought* men wanted you to be. You did what you had to do, in the life that was given. *That* is why Katie chose you, Melanie. You were not her enemy; you were simply someone trying their best to survive; another soul that required saving. And, in Katie's mind, if she could save you, then she knew she had what it takes to save anyone." Cassandra sipped her wine again, then smiled.

"I too, required saving, many, many years ago. For different reasons, it's true, but I found my true self here, in Elŷsium. I found love, and family. When I revived you, I revived the true you; not the wretch that had scraped and salvaged the wreck of a life, but the real you; Eve Melanie Gilmour Ross."

"Eve!" Melanie sighed. "They named me after my mum, but she was a cunt. That's why I dropped it when I got to Strath-sealgair."

"Well, here, in Elŷsium, I know that you too can find love... and family."

The sound of whistling came from the corridor. "And here is the first of that family," Cassandra smiled. "Best prepare yourself." Melanie felt a shudder run down her spine. In through the door came a tall, blonde whirlwind, her cape already removed and flying toward the chair in the corner. Her long purposeful stride carrying her past the two slightly stunned guests, toward the waiting banquet.

"I am fucking famished," she declared, to anyone who may be interested. Without fuss, or even any selective interest, she plucked up a huge chicken leg and ripped a chunk, rather unladylike, into her chomping mouth. Cassandra laughed quietly, shaking her head at her friend's unapologetic entrance.

"Good day, Brunhiíld," she said.

"Guid day tae ye, sweet lady. How the fuck are ye?"

Melanie broke into a massive smile. Did she detect a mocking Scottish accent from the blonde giantess? The strong, muscular woman turned to inspect the sitting girl, pulling a chair and thumping herself down as she ripped another chunk of chicken from the bone. "Hello," she bellowed. "Which one are you? The red or the brown?" She stared at a confused Melanie as she continued chewing, patting her head, indicating that she meant hair colour.

"Er... red?"

"Ah, the husband-stealer!" Melanie sank into her seat. "Let me tell you something, little thief. You try to steal my man and I shall cut your tits off and shove them down your throat. Yes?" Melanie felt sick as she nodded sheepishly.

"Oh, Brunhiíld, stop teasing the girl. There is enough strangeness already to terrify the poor child, without you flexing your muscles. Don't worry, Melanie, Brunhiíld is just toying with you. I think."

Brunhiíld stopped chewing. "Am I?" she asked. She winked at Melanie then ripped another chunk. "Charon sends his apologies, Cassandra. He is running a little late: several boats came loose in the storm last night, and he is assisting the locals in returning them to the quayside. Apparently there were, too, one or two brawls in the harbour bars last night. Strange we've never had this happen before." She stared, once again, at Melanie. "Welcome, Melanie. I am Brunhiíld." Melanie swallowed, and squeaked, "Hi!" Suddenly, there seemed a more serious air to events, and the people she was meeting.

The room was suddenly throbbing with voices as the group entered en masse. Katie approached, bending down and hugging the girl from behind. "You ok?" she asked. Melanie nodded, then gave a rather relieved smile.

"Aye," she replied. "Just gettin' used to the new faces, eh?" She nodded toward Brunhiíld, whispering, "that yin scares the shit out o' me." A waving hand caught her attention and she could see Ella smiling warmly at her from the end of the table, gesturing for her to come over.

"Melanie," the girl said, "there are some people ye need to meet." Ella sounded very formal, very grown up, nothing like a five-year-old. She took Melanie's hand and led her over to where a group of three people were stood talking. "Jacob," she called, as she pulled at the man's toga, "this is Melanie." The man turned with a smile. He looked down at the small girl before turning to the taller. "She's my beautiful new sister," Ella added. Melanie felt her heart surge, and she looked down to the little girl, who was gripping her hand tightly, with a massive smile lighting her face. "This is Jacob," she added. "He's my best friend."

Jacob bent down and hugged Ella, then turned to Melanie. "Welcome to Elŷsium, Melanie. Nice to meet ye," he said. "Lookin' forward to yer new 'job'?" he laughed. She could see the warmth in his eyes. And she couldn't help but reciprocate as the corners of his mouth pushed up into the most pleasant smile; it was no wonder Katie was stuck on him.

"I've no idea what I'm gonna be doin'," she admitted, "but Cassandra and Katie both seem to think I'll manage." Jacob turned to his companions and drew their attention to Melanie. "Hi," she said, awkwardly.

"This is Selêne, *Taskmaster* of Naátúr," he laughed, as the little old woman kicked his shin. She looked at Melanie, studying her. "There is a lot of pain behind those beautiful eyes, child," Selêne said softly. "I can see we will have to convince you of your worth." She reached out for a hug and Melanie bent down to oblige. "It will be a joy to see you blossom into the woman you are, the woman you don't yet know."

"Right then," said Jacob, rubbing his hands, "let's eat."

VI. THE RED KITE

Geata Dhè, Strath-sealgair July 1988

"I love comin' up here," cooed Cissy. "There's nothin' better than the fresh air, the views, and the complete privacy. And, we have it all to ourselves." She spread the blanket out, then turned in the direction of the laughter. Despite being weighed down by the large picnic backpack, Ray was chasing little Eric around the stones. She found the mix of the man's laughter, and the child's hearty chuckles, infectious to where she couldn't help herself but laugh along with them.

"Ray! Ray!" she called. "Bring the backpack over here… then ye can play to yer heart's content, ye daft arse." The man looked over to where she was kneeling on the blanket. He gestured with his head, and young Eric looked over, holding up a wild flower he had picked. Ray bent down, whispering something to the boy, who then nodded furiously before running toward her, the flower held aloft.

His little legs awkwardly pounded their way through the longish grass as he approached. "Mummy, Mummy," he breathlessly gasped, "I've got ye a bonnie flower." As he reached the edge of the blanket, he fell to his knees, into the outstretched arms of the waiting woman. They hugged tightly and, as he leaned back, Eric said, "ye can put it behind yer ear, Mummy."

Cissy smiled, taking the now-half-squashed flower carefully from his little hand. She brushed her hair back, sliding the stem behind her ear, making sure it was secure, before letting her long hair fall back into place. "How do I look?"

Eric's face lit up. "Bootiful," he exclaimed. "Dinna take it aff, Mummy!" Cissy cupped his face in her hands, her eyes taking in his childish enthusiasm and innocence. She felt immense pride that she was, at the very beginning of things, responsible for such beautiful little beings. That, between herself and her father, Helios, they had created such wonderment in the coldness, the darkness, of the universe.

Her eyes moved up to see Ray approaching; panting, out of breath, and looking just a little sweaty. The walk up to Geata Dhè had taken most of the morning—little Eric's wee legs could only go so fast, after all—but they were here now, and could spend the entire afternoon relaxing. Ray pulled the pack from his shoulders and lay it on the blanket.

There was a secondary bag, tied through the loop at the top of the backpack, which he undid and opened. Inside was a small football, and a bright red kite, both of which he removed and placed to the side.

"Why don't you two have a wee kick about while I sort the food out?" Cissy suggested.

"I would, but I think my auld legs wouldna make it," laughed Ray. Eric kicked the ball—in that awkward way toddlers have about them—and chased after it, laughing and giggling. Ray smiled at Cissy. "Ye ok?" he asked. "Ye've been affy quiet this morning."

She looked up, a huge smile, and wide eyes, putting his mind at ease, and his heart into overdrive. "I'm just perfect," Cissy replied. "How could I no' be, wi' my two favourite men, and a picnic on a sunny day, at the most beautiful place on earth? How could I be anythin' other than happy?" She reached up with both arms, pulling his face down to hers as he leaned over, kissing him with everything she had.

A sudden gust caught the kite and snapped it against Ray's leg. "Aaahhhh," he chirped, picking the toy up. "Looks like we'll get to fly this thing, after all." He turned, looking for his son, who was using two of the great stones as goalposts. "Eric!" Ray called. "Do ye want to fly the kite?" The wee boy looked back and immediately ran toward his dad. As he approached, Ray undid the neatly secured ribbon and string.

"Now," said Ray, with a very serious tone. "My Granda' always told me that, when ye let yer kite fly, ye're sendin' a message to God. And, if he…"

"Or She!" interrupted Cissy, as she carefully removed the thermos flasks from the backpack.

"Or *She*!" corrected Ray, "reads yer message, then he…"

"Or She!"

"Or *She*!" he corrected again, flicking out a play slap toward Cissy. "Or She, will grant ye a wish. Would ye like a wee wish, Eric, eh? Would ye like that?"

The boy nodded eagerly.

"Now, we don't have to write it. All ye have to do is close yer eyes… *Properly*! Then make a wee wish for what ye want. Don't tell us now. Keep it to yersel'." There was a momentary pause, then Eric opened his eyes, and his smile stretched from ear to ear. "Did ye do it?" asked Ray. "Did ye make yer wish?" Eric nodded frantically. "Right, then," said Ray, getting to his feet. "Let's go deliver yer message."

He handed the string to Eric, looping it around his tiny hand for security. "Now, when I say 'go', we have to run as fast as we can, over toward the stones. Do ye think ye can do that?"

"Aye, Dad! I can!"

"Can ye run really… *really*… fast? Fast enough to take the kite all the way up to the top o' the sky?" Eric nodded enthusiastically, his small face appreciating the seriousness of the task at hand. Cissy watched in silence, her heart overflowing with love.

"Go!" laughed Ray.

They ran through the grass, the string stretching out, until eventually becoming taut; the breeze gripping the red quadrilateral, and Eric's wish soared high into the sky. The boy looked up, with wonderment in his eyes, his arms raised, pushing his wish ever higher. The red message darted and weaved, flashing across the brilliance of the blue sky, pulling tighter on the wee boy's hand. The string slowly unwound from Eric's hand, and the kite flew off, high on the rushing air; flying over the Glen, soaring upwards, shrinking into the ether; delivering its message to the heavens. Eric closed his eyes, repeating his wish, then let go of the string.

"Aw, that's a shame," said Ray, crouching beside his son, as they watched the kite disappear into the blue. He was intrigued, though, to see a broad smile on the boy's face. "Are ye no' upset at losin' yer kite, Eric?"

"Oh no, Daddy," he squealed. "My wish has gone wi' it!" The boy looked Ray square in the face, giggled, then ran off to retrieve the football.

Ray laughed, scratching his head. "Well, that's a turn-up," he said to Cissy. "Wonder what he wished for?"

Cissy patted the blanket, urging Ray to sit. She leaned over and whispered into his ear. "I hope it was for a wee brother or sister, eh?"

It took a few seconds for the news to sink in. Ray clasped Cissy's shoulders, their eyes locked together. "A wee…?" Cissy nodded excitedly, her eyes filling with the happiest of tears.

"Aye, Raymond Corrie. Yer gonna be a dad again." They fell into each other, embracing tightly; realising their already-idyllic world was going to be even more perfect.

"God, I love ye so much," gushed Ray.

"For every reason there is," she whispered.

"An' a million more besides," he whispered in reply.

Ray ran the plane along the line of the flat oak spindle, lowering himself so his eye could assess the surface; ensuring there were no indents or bumps. He smiled as he ran his finger along the smoothness, the hard wood feeling almost soft to his touch. For the first time since working in the mill at Strath-sealgair, he allowed himself a sense of satisfaction; a pride in the quality, and application, of his work. At long last, he believed he could make himself useful; that he could make a worthwhile contribution. At long last, he felt that he and Eric could feel at home.

He laid the spindle down and stepped back to admire his latest handiwork; a rocking chair—or, at least, the parts of a rocking chair waiting to be assembled. Eric had taken such pleasure from the chair provided with the cabin—a small but important sign that he may, at some point, recover from the ordeal in Hades. Ray was loath to remove anything that may bring some normality to his son's recuperation, but felt *he'd* like a chair too. The pieces lay on his workbench, as if arranged for an exploded view diagram; the headrest at the top, the seven flat spindles lying neatly spaced below, and the scooped seat— painstakingly shaped to suit *his* backside cheeks—at the bottom. To either side were the long side-pieces, comprising armrests, front and rear legs, and the ornately curved rockers; each part carefully designed and cut to slot into the next, negating the need for glue or pins.

He was about to assemble the chair when the squeaking and creaking of a passing waggon outside caused him to pause. "Hey there, Handsome!" The faint sound of a young girl's voice brought a smile to his face— Jael. There was no hint of a response, but Ray knew Eric would try his best to raise a smile; Jael seemed to have that effect on him.

Ray clapped his hands together, brushing the sawdust from them, and made for the workshop door. The door gave a tremendous groan as he pushed it open. It wasn't dark in the workshop, but there was enough shade to make him squint as the bright sunshine outside flashed in his eyes. As his vision adjusted, he looked up the short hill to the cabin and saw Jael jumping down from the back of the cart. "Hi, Mister Corrie," she shouted, her arm outstretched in an enthusiastic wave. "Brought your supplies up for you. Save you a trip down to the village." Ray smiled. Sure, it would save a trip down, but it also meant that Jael could have an afternoon with Eric; and that made Ray's smile widen.

Since they'd arrived at Rimel, Jael had made it her mission to bring Eric out of his introversion; to have him actually speak to her. She was now a regular visitor; this time bringing the supplies, chatting endlessly as she unloaded the sacks of vegetables, trays of poultry, churns of milk, eggs, and the wonderful bread and pastries her father made. Ray still found it hard to believe how, just by offering his undoubted talents as a carpenter—doing repairs, or making furniture—the surrounding community provided everything he and Eric could want, or need.

It surprised him, too, just how willing and available the people of Elŷsium made themselves in trying to help. Jael was typical of that philosophy. Ray made his way up to where the girl was offloading a sack of potatoes. She dragged the sack to the edge of the waggon, then paused, turned, and smiled warmly at Eric. "You gonna watch me struggle here, Eric?" she asked. She placed her hands on her hips. "I can manage myself, but I'd prefer some help." Ray held back, watching his son. Again, the faintest hint of a smile cracked his lips—just for a second—then Eric rose from his rocker and made his way down the steps.

Ray sat on a log, leaving the youngsters to get on with things; not because he didn't want to help, but simply to allow Eric to come back from the edge—to assimilate himself into the new world in which they found themselves. Jael continued to chat away, neither expecting, nor waiting for, an answer from Eric. Ray listened as she spoke of her family, her friends; what she did in her spare time, or what she wanted to do in the future. It was an unchallenging monologue that brought warmth, and comfort, and Ray could see how relaxed and at ease Eric was. He still didn't talk, but neither was he cowering in a corner.

Jael continued to direct the unloading and, once the task was complete, she led Eric back to the steps at the porch. As she sat down on the top step, she patted the space next to her, intimating Eric should sit. He did as instructed. Ray watched curiously as they just sat there, leaning against each other, looking out down the valley; looking like any other pair of teenagers, anywhere. Jael turned her face to look at Eric; letting out a little chuckle when he returned her smile. Eric's face was transformed; relaxed, peaceful, content. The fear that he'd carried since Hades was gone, and in its place, was a look of hopeful optimism.

Wiping away a tear from his eye, Ray looked at Jael, considering how wonderful the change she was effecting on his son. 'What a remarkable young woman you are'. He raised himself and made his way toward the cabin. "Would ye like to stay and eat wi' us, Jael?" he asked. "We're plannin' on havin' a rabbit stew tonight. If I can get the thing skinned, that is."

"Oh, I can do that for you, Mr Corrie." The girl looked at Eric and smiled. "Would you mind if I stayed, Eric? I can help you with the vegetables, too, if you'd like." Eric smiled and gave the slightest nod of his head. "Looks like you're stuck with me," she chirped. "Shall we get started on those vegetables?" Eric nodded again and pushed himself up from the step, smiling at his father as he turned to enter the cabin. Jael, too, stood and turned toward the door, giving Ray a confident, satisfied smile.

'Thank you,' he mouthed. 'Thank you.'

The two teenagers sat on the steps to the lodge; the large metal bowl of water in front, and between them, on a lower step; the small sack of potatoes behind. Slowly and deliberately, they peeled each potato, their small knives slicing through, separating the skin and discarding it at their feet. They then carefully placed the little white tubers into the cleansing water, ready for boiling later. Every now and again, Jael would look at Eric, assessing him, considering him. It seemed to her that keeping him busy was the best form of therapy, the best way to draw his mind from his nightmares, and the ever-tormenting memories.

He returned her gaze, and smiled, enjoying the simple task before him; enjoying the relaxed company, and the absence of any demand, any expectation. Jael took a deep breath. "Do you know we have a Harvest Festival each year, Eric?" The boy shook his head. "Oh, yes," Jael continued. "We celebrate on the Sunday nearest the harvest moon. That's the full Moon closest to the autumn equinox. All the farms and homesteads surrounding Rimel come together at the saloon, the ale house tavern, by the bakery. There's food and drink, stalls and games, and music and dancing. There are even sports, of a sort, and competitions, and it's a chance to meet up with friends again." She chuckled. "Of course, we can only have the fun after all the hard work's done. Everybody mucks in, collecting and bailing the crops; the hay, the corn, wheat... everything, really. There's always something to do at the harvesting."

She watched him, deep in concentration, as he tackled a particularly awkward-shaped potato. *'Be gentle with him,'* her mother had advised. *'The boy has suffered terrible horrors that none of us will ever fully understand.'* There were no physical signs of the tortures he'd endured—they'd all, bar his silence, disappeared as he'd settled in Elŷsium—but Jael sensed the inner turmoils of her friend. She noticed the little jumps whenever he heard a loud noise; the panicky twists and turns if he thought someone was approaching from behind. He would constantly check his surroundings, making sure he was never left alone. *'Remember, that sense of humour of yours is not to everyone's tastes. The boy may easily feel insulted, taunted. Watch what you say, Jael.'* Her mother was always overly dramatic with everything, but, Jael knew she was right.

"We usually work in pairs, you know, for the harvesting... and, of course, the festival. It's nice to have a partner to go with, and to dance with." Eric continued his peeling, with no apparent response to her little hints. He looked at her again, smiling as he firstly placed the peeled potato in the water, then plucked another from the sack. His eyes dropped back to his work. *'Mmm,'* thought Jael, *'this might take some time.'*

Her hand reached into the sack for another potato. "No-one would expect you to help with the harvesting but, if you'd like to go to the festival, I could take you." She glanced sidelong, but still no response. "All my friends are eager to meet you, you know." She laughed. "They're probably all bored seeing the same old faces, but yours..." She looked at him again, studying his hair, his eyes, the smooth curves of his jawline... the way his nose shone at its tip. "Yours... is... well," she whispered, "yours is beautiful." She gasped, surprised at how she'd let it slip out. There had been no intention of being quite so familiar; she wasn't even sure if she liked him... in that way... until this very second.

Jael jumped up, taking a couple of steps down, the peelings around her feet flying everywhere, and turned to look at Eric. "I'm sorry," she blurted. "I'm sorry, I never meant... I didn't..." The young boy stopped peeling and looked up, his eyes meeting hers. The cares and worries, the fear, even the skittish nervousness that seemed to hang over him like low, dark clouds were gone. In their place, shining like the sun breaking through those clouds, was a smile big enough to warm Jael through the coldest of winters. She smiled back, disarmed, at ease, and more sure of herself. She lowered her chin, plucking up the courage to actually, properly, ask the question. "Would you like to go with me, Eric?"

Eric placed the potato and peeler carefully on the step. He pushed himself up, stepped down to where Jael stood, and wrapped his arms around her. As he pulled her tightly to him, Jael let out a little squeak of delight and responded in kind. They didn't speak. They just stood, slowly swaying, entwined in each other's arms, enjoying the closeness, the warmth... the affection that had been building, but had never been demonstrated until now. Pulling back a little, their eyes met, and their smiles widened, their connection strengthened. Eric remained silent, but he hugged Jael once more.

"Right," she said, "let's get these spuds on to cook." She looked down at the peelings scattered across the steps. "Best collect these for the compost, eh?"

Then, for the first time, Jael heard Eric laugh.

VII. HEART TO HEART

"I'll leave you two to talk," said Cassandra. She smiled at Jacob, giving a long, loving look. Her eyes fell to the floor. An unsure expression crossed her face as she remembered a very similar situation she'd found herself in, not so long ago, just for a second, before she smiled again. Then, with a bow of her head, she turned to leave the room; content, despite the risks and uncertainty of her decision, that Jacob and Katie have this time to themselves.

Katie watched as the woman departed, her graceful walk and elegant composure bringing an ironic smile to Katie's face. "So... you and Cassandra, eh?" Jacob looked thoughtfully at her.

"It's..."

Katie stopped him. "Please dinna say '*it's complicated*', Jacob. That's what men always say when they want everythin'. When someone wants to have their cake and eat it too." Jacob sighed. "Don't worry," Katie continued. "I understand. She's fuckin' gorgeous. Fuck's sake, I think I'd be tempted if she flashed that smile at me. She's amazin'. And... after everythin' that's happened lately, I don't think it'd be a good idea to piss off the woman that's brought me..." She gazed about the deserted room, the sunlight streaming through the veranda doors like heavenly sunbeams. "... here! Wherever, or whatever, here is."

"It is complicated, though, Katie. I love you... I do... but I also love Cassandra... and... well, there's a bit more to it all than just you and me. Cassandra is amazin', and she knows how I feel about ye. That's why she's left us alone to talk; she knows I've a decision, a choice to make, and she's allowin' me time to figure it all oot."

Katie poured herself another glass of wine. "That night," she said, suddenly changing the topic, "after the restaurant, I'd decided to leave Allan." Jacob looked at her attentively, but said nothing; he just listened. "Ye were home again. I felt alive again; I had somethin' to cling to, to look forward to, and all I had to do was leave my shitebag husband. Then..." Katie paused, recalling the first time her husband had raped her; the terror as she lay in bed that night; the confusion as to what that meant for her hastily arranged plans for liberation from the prison of her loveless marriage.

"After we got home, Allan just lost it. He was jealous. I think he knew we were done before I did, and he wanted to get his control back." She looked deeply into Jacob's eyes. "He always saw ye as a threat, even when we were kids. I think he was the only person who took any joy from yer accident; delighted that ye were taken away to Glasgow. But I always felt he was worried that, one day, ye'd come back."

"He always was a cowardly bully," said Jacob. "He was never good enough for ye. Neither was I, Katie. No' really. Ye deserved the very best. I'm sorry."

"Well, sorry or no', then came... what was it Cassandra called it? The 'Ripple'?"

"Aye," confirmed Jacob. "They're callin' it the Ripple back on Kíípos... Earth."

"The world went to shit," Katie continued, "and, once again, ye'd disappeared off the face o' the Earth. Disappeared from my life. I went lookin' for ye, but ye were nowhere to be found." She took a sip of wine. "Ye don't fuckin' hang aboot long, do ye?" she laughed, choking as she held back her tears. Jacob took her hand, squeezing gently. "And I was left trapped wi' a man I hated, wi' nowhere to go; cryin' constantly over all the lost years without ye." Her hand slowly wiped away a tear. "Ye never did say why ye didn't get in touch, all those years," she said, her eyes looking directly into his.

Jacob looked down at his glass, turning it in his fingers while he considered her words. "I still can't answer that properly," he offered. "I've never felt good enough. For anythin' really. Losin' Dad and Eric, my black leg, bein' taken to Glasgow—all o' it reinforced how little control I had in my life." He glanced up at her. "Any time I thought o' ye, I'd tell myself to get on the phone. Look ye up. Just... make contact... just do it." He swallowed the dregs from his glass. "And then I'd bottle it. I'd bury my head in my work, and focus on somethin' else."

Katie poured some more wine. "Ye could have called anytime... and I'd have come runnin'," she said.

"I know," he sighed. "But after a time, well, it got easier and easier to distract myself. It got easier to convince myself that ye wouldn't be interested. That ye'd forgotten all about me."

Her hand clasped his tightly. "I'd never forget about ye. Never stop lovin' ye. But... here we are," she said, looking about her once more. "Elŷsium! Heaven! Paradise!" She laughed. "I can remember us arguin' wi' the RE teacher at school, convinced that there wasn't a God, that when yer dead, yer dead. Now we are actually in heaven, and we still can't be together. But this time there's a bloody gorgeous Trojan-Goddess shaped reason for it. What the fuck did we know, eh?"

"It's a long story, goin' right back to the beginnin' o' everythin'," he said. "At least you werena tied to a bed listenin' to Séntinell lecturin' ye." Jacob explained *Chaos!*; how the Earth came into being, and his celestial family. About Cassandra, and her short, tragic life. About the woman in black, the falls, and why the Ripple had been wrought. He explained about arriving in Elŷsium; how his leg had healed; and about the fateful trip to Hades.

"I found, and lost, my mum. Circe! I lost and found my dad and my brother. It's been a fuckin' whirlwind o' events, emotions, and experiences. I've, quite literally, felt like a leaf bein' blown aboot in a hurricane; always one step behind, always expectin' to wake up from the most fuckin' weird dream—or maybe it's a nightmare—I've ever had." He stood, then walked to the veranda, taking a deep breath of the fresh air, enjoying the warmth of the sun on his skin. Katie joined him.

"But there's no wakin' up. This is it, Katie. Elŷsium. It seems like heaven but, as my mum was quick to point out to me, it's no'. It's another steppin' stone on our way to our true destination; Sólaás. There are people, like Cassandra, who've been here since the very beginnin'. Some, like yersel', have only just got here. It's an idyllic life in Elŷsium; a simple but beautiful life. But there's death here, too. People *can* die. There's no sickness, or murder or any sort o' crime; none o' that shite. But accidents happen; or people decide the time's right for them to join Sólaás. Suicide in this place isn't desperate people feelin' they've no option, no way out. It's a conscious decision to transcend."

"But, surely there's still grief for the families and relatives?" Katie asked.

"Aye, there's still a sense o' loss. But loss here, though, isn't the same as we had back there, Katie. There's no grief, no' really. Grief is the love ye didn't get a chance to give in life; here, there's no denyin' yer love. No, it's a celebration — a fulfilment o' everybody's true destiny. Sure, we miss people when they're gone. But we're all just universal energy, makin' our way through the... the... *system*; constantly re-energisin', constantly recyclin', and findin' Sólaás is the culmination o' our experiences and contributions in our earthly existence. It's taken me a wee while to realise this about my mum, too. She's no' gone completely, she's just returned to the universe."

Katie smiled, taken aback at how certain Jacob was now; how authoritative he had become since their last meeting. It seemed strange to her, too, how accepting she had become of her new circumstances; how easily she could come to this decision. "I would've left Allan in a heartbeat, Jacob, just to be wi' ye. He was a bastard. He raped and murdered me, fer fuck's sake. But now? Seein' ye wi' Cassandra? Seein' how her eyes light up when ye're wi' her? I couldn't, *wouldn't*, ruin this for her, even though she's given me the chance. There's somethin'... *special*... about her. I don't just mean that she's pretty, or funny or kind. She's... she's... *woman*! Not *a* woman, but the very essence of womanhood; wi' the strength, and fragility o' every woman. I know Selêne said the same about me, but it's Cassandra that should be the aspiration of women. And, while I love ye more than ye can ever know, I already feel an unbreakable loyalty to that woman; perhaps even more than to you." She playfully punched his arm, then embraced him; not as a lover, but as a friend would. "She's given me a job to do, back on Earth, and I'm no' gonna let her down. Do ye understand, Jacob?"

Jacob kissed her cheek. "This is our reality now, Katie. And reality isn't done wi' us." He turned, looking directly at her, now with a very serious tone in his voice. "Cassandra has chosen you as leader of Élementaá, and ye'll be returnin' to Earth wi' Melanie. Ye'll be taught all ye need to know, be given all the tools ye'll need to succeed, and to survive. Once ye've found all the people ye'll need, wi' Cassandra's help, you and Ella, and the rest o' Élementaá and Naátúr will perform the most amazin'... well... first aid, I suppose. Ye'll help get Kiípos back to where she needs to be. And that's why I have a request for ye, too."

He turned and gestured for them to retake their seats, pouring another glass of wine for each of them. He held up the Célestiaá Ring for Katie to inspect, displaying the twin diamonds, and the surrounding gems. "My mum explained to me the significance o' this ring to the Eternal Return, and the ongoin' glitch that's... well..." He took a sip of wine, wincing as the acidic tang hit his throat. His eyes met Katie's, but, just for a second, there was no warmth, no happiness. "Cassandra's become consumed by the idea o' endin' the patriarchal dominance on Kiípos and, to a certain extent, I agree wi' her. But much o' the problem isn't caused by men alone, it's the result o' the Eternal Return's drainin' effect on decency and morals. There's no easy fix to that, but... look... all I'm askin' is that you and Melanie don't just go on a killin' frenzy against men."

Katie laughed at the ridiculousness of the suggestion. "A killin' frenzy? For fuck's sake, Jacob, it takes me all my time to kill a spider. What do ye think we'll be gettin' up to?" She sipped her wine as she chuckled.

"When ye go back down there, Katie, you and Melanie'll be seen as fair game for any o' the men that take a fancy to ye. Ye're gonna have to defend yerselves, and I don't want ye developin'... well... developin' a taste for it. There's still a lot o' good men, decent people. Ye'll be careful, won't ye?"

She smiled, comforted, but a little confused, by his concern. "Aye," she nodded, "I'll be careful."

Jacob looked for a second, then smiled. "Good. Good. But, anyway, there's a far bigger... issue. There's a war comin'."

"A war? Wi' who? When?"

"Ah, that's the tricky bit. We don't know who wi'... or when... but Cassandra's seen it, in a vision my mum showed her."

"And ye believe it?"

"If ye'd asked me that back in Strath-sealgair, I'd have laughed it aff as nonsense. But I've seen so much that ye wouldn't believe, Katie. I've been to Hades; seen Haáde and Pasiphae, and their rank, stinkin' soldiers. I've managed to control, and create things, wi' this Célestiaá Ring. Nothin' too impressive so far, I'll grant ye, but I think I'm slowly gettin' the hang o' it."

He sipped his wine. "When Athena has sent ye aff on yer first tasks, she'll set about buildin' oor armies properly. Providin' the Council can get their heads out their collective arses, that is. We'll be keepin' our eyes on two fronts; you and Élementaá on Kiípos, and whoever... whatever... is comin' for us."

VIII. THE SWORDS & THE STONES

Melanie couldn't help herself. Her hand repeatedly made its way to her head, brushing the sharp red stubble that was now poking its way through. She looked at herself in the mirror. In place of the beautiful silk stola she'd worn previously, was a white cotton vest, and black cargo pants, tucked under elastic at the top of black leather laced calf boots. 'I look like a fuckin' skinhead,' she mumbled to herself.

"Are ye ready?"

Melanie turned to find Katie standing in the doorway, similarly attired. "Fuck's sake, Katie," she moaned. "Are they takin' the piss?"

Katie laughed as she entered. "Don't think the bonnie dresses'll be very practical for what we'll be gettin' up to," she said. She brushed her hand over Melanie's head. "Ye look grand, and it'll grow back quickly," she advised, as she then rubbed her own head. "At least mine seems to be."

"Will there be a hairdresser to style it when it does, do ye think?" Melanie mused. "Another thing, there's no' a stick o' makeup anywhere in this place. How the fuck do the women look so fuckin' good?"

"You have more to worry 'bout than hair and face paint!" The sharp, angry voice caught both women by surprise. In the doorway stood a small Japanese woman; a stern, impatient look on her face. "Lady Athena request you come... now!" She turned sharply to leave, before calling over her shoulder. "When I say request... I mean order!"

"Holy shit," said Melanie, "what the fuck've ye got me into, Katie?"

The older woman laughed, a little nervously. "Fuck knows," she replied, "but I seem to have got m'self into it as well." She nodded toward the door. "You first."

"Aye, that'll be fuckin' right! You're the boss here. So, lead on, Boss."

They hurried out of Melanie's suite, trying to catch up with the speedy feet of the small woman. She wore a dark blue keikogi, with silver sandals and, strapped across her back, was a long pole, with a padded cover at the top, shielding what could only be a blade of some sort. An ornate bun held her scraped-back black hair in place, and her pale skin looked almost white against the darkness of her clothing. She disappeared out a door at the end of the hallway and, as the door slammed shut, the girls felt the need to run after her.

They pushed the door open, almost falling through it, and exited into a small courtyard. On a bench in the far corner, sat Athena, with the Japanese woman down on one knee, head bowed, before her. There was a table with a water jug and goblets and, behind those, a burgundy coloured cloth covered several long, thin items. Katie and Melanie made their way over, and both Athena and the Japanese woman stood to face them. The little woman kicked her sandals off.

"This is Chiyoko," said Athena. "Child of a thousand generations! Onna-musha, and member of the bushi class. You," she said, staring at Melanie, "will test your skills against her." Without a word, Chiyoko threw a long, thin pole in Melanie's direction. Caught by surprise, Melanie stared at the pole as it hit her face before falling to the ground.

"Ow," she squealed, "that's no' fair, ye wee fucker." The Japanese woman was already making her way purposefully toward the stunned girl, spinning her own pole and catching Melanie behind her ankles. With a broad sweep, she was flying, and thumping onto her backside. "Ow, for fuck's sake," yelled Melanie. Chiyoko's pole then whacked the side of her face, and Melanie could feel the blood ooze from the little cut nipping at the corner of her mouth. Chiyoko smiled at her.

Katie made to move forward in assistance, but Athena put her hand on her chest, stopping her. "No," she said, firmly. Katie held back as ordered. Athena sat back down and watched.

Melanie wiped the blood from her mouth. She looked at the other woman, who was now walking in a circle around her; prowling like a tiger about to pounce, her pole spinning threateningly in her hands. She was shorter than Melanie, but probably around the same age, if not slightly older, judging by her smooth features. The mocking smile confirmed her confidence, her complete dominance and control of the situation. Melanie looked down and grabbed the other pole and, with a grunt, got back to her feet. Chiyoko immediately halted her progress as she swung her staff, again catching the side of Melanie's head. She was stunned now, and stumbled to the side.

"Right, that's fuckin' it," she said. "Ye want a fight, ye little shit? Well, I'll give ye a fuckin' fight." She gripped her pole with both hands and swung it toward Chiyoko. The little woman simply ducked under the swoosh, then swung her own weapon, once again catching Melanie's ankles and tumbling her to the ground. "Fer fuck's sake," screamed Melanie, spitting out dust and red, blood-filled saliva. She looked over to Athena, who was watching with interest. 'Ye want a fuckin' show, is that it?' thought Melanie. 'Right, enough o' this shite!'

She got back to her feet and, once again, wiped the blood away from her mouth. Her eyes locked onto Chiyoko's, and she mirrored the other woman's turning circle. As she pushed on her standing leg, she lunged forward, swinging her pole down. Chiyoko stood on the balls of her feet, raising her staff and blocking the assault, easily pushing Melanie aside. Her right leg swung, catching the unbalanced girl behind the knee, buckling her leg. The staff, yet again, smacked into the already bruised cheek, sending the helpless girl face down into the dust.

Melanie quickly looked up. There was no self pity this time, no hesitation. She was up in a flash, hurtling toward her adversary, thumping into her. Both women fell to the ground and Melanie pinned Chiyoko's shoulders down. "Enough, ok?" she screamed, her tearful face just inches in front of Chiyoko's. The Japanese woman smiled, then, catching Melanie completely by surprise, leaned forward and kissed her fully on the mouth. Melanie recoiled back away from her downed opponent. "What the fuck?"

Chiyoko wasted no time, spinning over and thus pinning Melanie to the ground. She smiled, then bowed her head, before standing quickly. She extended her hand to Melanie, pulling her to her feet. "Next time we use blades," she said.

"Aye, that'll be fuckin' chocolate," mumbled Melanie. She rubbed the small of her back, as the pain throbbed through her. Katie ran over to assist her comrade.

"You okay, Mel?"

"Ow! No. My arse is absolutely killin' me, an' my cheek feels like it's broken. Fuck's sake," she complained. "Thought I was back in Murphy's Bar for a second." The two women turned back to Athena. Chiyoko once more knelt in front of her mistress, standing only when Athena gestured her permission. Athena looked at Melanie.

"Tell me, Melanie. You had this woman at your mercy. This woman who had repeatedly hurt you, showing you little consideration as she wounded you. Why did you not hurt her in return?" Melanie was brushing the dust from her vest and pants.

"Listen, I already hurt good people before... back there. I was a selfish little cunt. I've no' fuckin' idea what all this shite is, but I'll be fucked if I'm goin' to ruin a second chance at... at... at whatever this fuckin' shite is. If ye don't like it, ye can fuck off, ok? Ow!" Her mouth was still bleeding, and the pain in her cheek was getting worse by the second. She was fighting to hold back her tears as she looked at Katie. "Can I get a drink o' water please, Katie?" Katie hugged her injured friend. "I really felt like throttlin' the little bastard," Melanie whispered.

Chiyoko poured some water into a goblet and, as she passed it to the wounded girl, smiled and whispered, "well done!" Athena finally stood, studying Melanie's tear soaked face. "No one has ever spoken to me in this way, Melanie," she observed. Katie stepped forward, positioning herself between Melanie and the Naátúr.

"My apologies for my friend," she began, "but..." Athena raised her hand, stopping Katie in her tracks.

"Please do not apologise, Katie. We had no doubts about your own credentials for the tasks that lie ahead of you. However, and please do not take offence, Melanie, we were not entirely convinced of your choice in companion. We doubted her courage, and we doubted her temperament and self-control." She placed her hand on Melanie's shoulder. "But, for an untrained novice to get close to, let alone upend Chiyoko, well now, that takes something rather... special."

"She was lucky," smiled Chiyoko.

Athena nodded. "Perhaps, Chiyoko. But our ladies will need as much luck, as they will courage and determination. Can you train these girls? Are they worthy of the blades?" Chiyoko walked around the two bewildered Scotswomen, seriously scrutinising them.

"Yes, mistress. I think so... but..." Melanie and Katie watched the short woman as she circled them. "But what?" asked Melanie impatiently.

"But..." Chiyoko continued. "I think we have underestimated what these women are capable of. I think this one..." she said, looking at Melanie, "may also be capable of using a bow."

"A *bow*?" Melanie was totally confused now.

"The blades will be an excellent start but, if Élementaá is to grow and prosper, we should give these women as many tools as possible." Athena nodded, thoughtfully, then pulled the burgundy cloth from the table. Below it lay two long swords; their slender, single-edged blades were two and a half feet in length and glistened brightly in the sunlight. Their ornate inscriptions seemed to speak to the women, as the light ran down them, highlighting every little twist and turn. A twelve inch grip, easily long enough to accommodate two hands, was wrapped with black and red leather in a criss-crossed manner. Blood red silk cords hung from the circular guard. Behind the swords lay two black lacquered wood sheaths; the ornate red markings making the scabbards seem every bit as important and symbolic as the swords themselves.

"Take them, please," said Athena. "They should become part of you, for they shall be an extension of you. Chiyoko will teach you the martial arts, the meditation, and fighting skills you shall require, but the blades will be far more than just a sharp weapon. They will be a conduit for the abilities you are about to receive."

Katie and Melanie stepped forward. "You first," said Katie, with a smile.

Melanie selected a sword and sheath, and gasped as the metal gleamed in the sunlight running up and down its length. She swung it from side to side, amazed at how easy it was to control. "It's very light," she said to Athena.

"Harmoniaá, herself, forged these swords. High carbon steel, threaded with titanium, mined from the craters of Lunaá. The blade shall cut with the heat of Harmoniaá's furnace. It will stay sharp and true; never dulling, never breaking, never failing." Katie, too, was now getting a feel for her sword, swooshing it from left to right, twisting and turning, testing her mobility.

"They are the only blades of their kind," continued Athena, "forged specifically for you, and they shall compliment the Harmony necklaces you shall receive later. We shall furnace further blades as Élementaá grows."

Athena gestured to Chiyoko, who made toward the door, bowing as she held it open for her mistress. "I shall see you again soon, ladies," she said. "But, for now, you shall receive the other gifts, and complete the first parts of your training." She departed, leaving the two women still enthralled by the ease with which they were wielding the swords.

Chiyoko remained bowed until Athena had disappeared, then turned to face Melanie and Katie. "We begin at dawn. Sleep well, and do not be late."

The two women half-bowed, unsure as to whether it was expected of them. "What time's dawn?" whispered Melanie.

"No' got a fuckin' clue," whispered Katie in reply.

As they made their way back indoors, a man of short height with a lightly tanned complexion, clothed in a white tunic, greeted them. He smiled as he approached. "Ladies," he said warmly. "My name is Marro. Jacob has asked that I bring you both when you are ready."

"Where are we headin'?" asked Katie, walking alongside the new acquaintance. Melanie followed, her aches and pains making every step seem like a punishment.

"To the Tholos of Circe," he replied with a smile.

"The what o' what?" asked Melanie.

"The Tholos is a commemorative monument erected in thanks to Lady Circe. It is the nexus by which we still give thanks for her energy and presence; the eternal flame through which Jacob and Cassandra draw their influence and guidance. All you think you know about the universe, about yourselves, is about to change," he added cryptically. Marro glanced at Katie, who smiled in return as her eyes caught his. "Jacob did not exaggerate," he said warmly, glancing next to Melanie. "Scottish women are exactly what we need for this task."

Melanie snorted. "No' sure if yer flirtin', or takin' the piss," she said.

Marro laughed. "Oh, Melanie," he chuckled. "I am not ashamed to say that both you ladies would be far too much of a handful for one such as I." He saw the affronted look on Melanie's face. "I mean that as a compliment," he smiled. "At any rate, I am happily taken."

"Pity," replied Melanie, as she linked into Marro's left arm. The Frenchman smiled at the unexpected gesture.

"Jessica and Cassandra are trouble enough," he laughed. "It is perhaps fortunate that you shall spend much of your time on Kiípos. I doubt Elŷsium could survive all four of you making mischief at the same time."

"Cheeky bastard!"

Marro turned, laughing. "I'm not wrong, though, am I?"

Katie, too, linked arms with him. "Bet ye've got some juicy stories, eh, Marro?"

"Many. But I cannot betray the trust I am privileged to enjoy."

"Well, that's a buggar. Nothin'? Ye won't tell us anythin'?"

Marro smiled and held out his hand, gesturing to a door. "This way, ladies," he laughed, as he led them out into the gardens.

A vast sea of bluebells overwhelmed their senses; a deep violet-blue carpet, stretching for over a hundred yards, with a narrow path through the centre coming to a sharp, perfect end as it reached the vast lawn. The sweet aroma of millions of drooping flowers, many of which were bobbing under the weight of hundreds of bees, swelled their nostrils.

"Oh my," smiled Katie, "she really has made bluebells."

Marro laughed. "I think Mother Ella has ensured we shall not be found lacking in bluebells ever again. Did you know, Katie, the bluebell symbolises constancy, humility, and gratitude? Characteristics, I sense, your little girl has in abundance. She is an absolute joy. You must be so proud?"

The trio made their way slowly down the path, scanning side to side. "Aye," confirmed Katie. "She's my wee girl, right enough."

Across the lawn sat the Tholos of Circe; a large, white circular construction with a vaulted roof. A Doric colonnade ringed the outside, and a Corinthian within; exquisite carvings and inscriptions adorned the surrounding columns. Three marble steps led to the centre, in which sat a white marble plinth, holding a polished marble hearthstone. In the centre of the hearthstone, a beautiful blue and orange flame, about two feet in height, danced and swayed. A small bowl of delicately cut and drilled stones, a variety of colourful rocks cut from the craters of the moon, sat in front of the flame, with two delicate steel chains laid alongside a small dagger.

A small group had already taken their places at the top of the steps. Selêne held her hands out in welcome, embracing first Katie, then Melanie, before guiding the women toward the inner circle of the tholos. Jacob waited with Cassandra and Ella to the left side, Cassandra holding Ella's hand. On the right stood Poseidon, Boreal, Hephaestus and Séntinell. The serious faces, and the solemnity of their demeanour, reinforced the importance of the gathering. Katie took Melanie's hand as they walked nervously, uncertainly, to the centre of the memorial.

"Your swords, please ladies," said Cassandra, gesturing to the plinth. "You first, Katie," she instructed. Katie unsheathed her blade and laid it gently on the plinth. Cassandra took the dagger and pricked her own finger. She then placed a drop of her blood on the sword's blade. Katie stepped forward with her finger outstretched in readiness. "No jokes about 'little pricks'," she whispered to Melanie, who immediately let out a muffled giggle. The dagger painlessly pricked Katie's finger, and she squeezed her blood onto the blade next to Cassandra's. Melanie followed the same ritual with her own sword.

Each of the waiting Naátúr stepped forward and took two stones. They then pricked their own fingers, placing a blood drop on both stones and the swords. They laid a stone beside each of the blades, then stepped back, heads bowed. Séntinell took their turn, followed by Ella, who was taking everything in her stride.

Selêne laced each group of stones onto its own chain, beckoning the women forward. They both knelt instinctively and, as she hung the chains snugly around each woman's neck, Hephaestus pinched the ends, creating searing heat, sealing an unbreakable joint.

"Please place the blades through the flame," Cassandra urged. "This will bind us all to you through the sword, and the stones." Katie and Melanie did as instructed, the hissing of the blood drops, and the dark blue puff of smoke sending a ripple down the arms of each. A warmth flowed through both women; like that comforting feeling when eating hot soup when you're cold.

"Katherine Margaret Sully Gallagher. Eve Melanie Gilmour Ross. These are the Harmony Stones," said Selêne. "They imbue the gifts of the gods, allowing you privileged control of the elements; earth, water, fire, air and space. Nature is now your ally, to call upon as you require." The women sheathed the swords and were then embraced by each of the party. "The stones are part of you now," continued Selêne. "The chains are of the same alloy as your sword, and sword and stones together give immense power. They cannot be removed... by anyone. You are now Élementaá; Champions of Naátúr; Soldiers of Elŷsium."

The group applauded loudly, then gathered around the two women. Séntinell gestured to Jacob, then slowly walked away from the chattering crowd. "Ye want to talk to me, Séntinell?" Jacob asked.

The tall figure looked down, smiling awkwardly. "Yes, Master Jacob. I'm afraid I shall have to take my leave a little earlier than planned. Lord Aether has ordered I attend an audience with Lord Helios on his behalf. It appears news of his daughters' demise has now reached his ears. And, it seems, he has not taken that news well... not well at all."

"Mmm," muttered Jacob. "And what does that mean for us?"

Séntinell once again looked down at Jacob. "I'm sure it is just a simple matter of... clarification. I shall update him on the circumstances of this tragedy, and reassure him that, in the hands of his grandson, Kiípos is on the mend." The smile was false, and, despite the reassurances, their concerns clear.

"Mmmm," Jacob repeated, not entirely convinced. "Should I come wi' ye?" he asked.

"Oh, no!" Séntinell immediately held their hands up in protest, fear filling their eyes and straining their smile. "No one approaches Sólaás without prior permission from Lord Helios," they said. "Indeed, I am not sure that your human half could withstand the solar breach required to enter the Sun-world. Or, for that matter, how Helios may react to your presence. No, no. I shall visit alone. Ease his broken heart." The look on Séntinell's face betrayed their fears. This was not the simple briefing that was being made out.

Cassandra broke the awkward silence as she joined them. "And what are you two plotting?" she asked.

"Oh, nothing of concern, my lady," lied Séntinell. "Just a simple task that shall take me from you a while. But I shall return as soon as I can." They looked at the two woman admiring their new necklaces. "Your champions shall have need of whatever knowledge I can give."

IX. LUNAÁ

"May I help ye?" Ella offered.

"You may, Mother," replied Selêne, smiling as she raised her arm for Ella to link into it. "Not because I need your help, but because I already treasure your company, and feel much the happier with you beside me." Ella returned the smile and clasped her arm with Selêne's. "When we step through the Diávasi, Mother, you may be a little surprised at what you find."

"Do ye think so? Is it all white? Will I be able to make more bluebells?"

Selêne patted her hand. "Oh, you'll be able to craft so many new things, but, all in good time, my dear. We'll have to get you settled in first. And we have a special friend for you to meet."

"A special friend? Someone to play wi'?"

"While I shall be with you most of the time, it may be difficult for you not having your mother, or your old friends with you. So, we have selected... well, you'll see."

The little old woman chuckled mischievously. "Now, are you ready?"

Ella nodded, hardly able to contain her excitement. "Am I really goin' to the moon?" she cooed.

"You are," confirmed Selêne, taking a short step forward into the light. Ella matched the small steps of her mentor, her eyes widening as they ambled through. After just a few seconds, the light thinned as they exited the other side, and Ella gasped at the magnificent garden they found themselves in. The lush, soft grass beneath her feet felt like the deepest of carpets.

In front of them, a large pond, stretching the length of the garden, rippled under the merest hint of a breeze. Around the banks of the pond, groups of Maples, Acers, and a variety of smaller shrubs broke up the extensive greenery of the lawn. On the left bank, sat a white, single-story wooden building, with a high sloping roof, beautifully and clearly reflected in the water below. From the door of the building, a thin bridge arced over and across the water to a path leading through the trees. Although obscured by the trees, Ella could tell that the path led up a long, steep staircase. Poking above the height of the small copse, was another, larger white building; much like Strath-sealgair Villa.

"Welcome to *'Tranquility'*, Mother," smiled Selêne.

Ella skipped forward, to the edge of the pond. Hundreds of black and golden carp and goldfish weaved their way through the clear water, ignoring the millions of tadpoles that busied themselves along the length of the bank. Thousands of underwater shrubs and plants swayed in the motions of the purposeful fish. Birdsong filled the air, and the sunshine warmed the skin. Ella turned to

Selêne, her smile as bright as the sun. "It's beautiful, Selêne," she cried. "It's beautiful."

Selêne nodded her agreement. "But, Mother," she said, holding her chin as if in deep thought, "don't you think there is something missing?"

Ella's face beamed in delight as she realised instantly what Selêne was referring to. "Bluebells?" She danced and spun in excited delight. "Can I make some bluebells, please, Selêne?"

Selêne approached, holding her hand out in readiness for Ella's. "This is your garden, Mother. It is for you to decide how it looks. The little building will be your school, and," she paused, looking up the hill to the villa, "that is your new home. If you'd like bluebells, then you can have as many as you wish." The old woman looked around to a small, shaded area of the garden, where a circular cluster of Silver Birch trees stood. "I'm no expert," she laughed, "but that looks like an ideal place for a small bluebell wood, don't you agree?"

Ella looked in the direction indicated, thinning her lips as she gave it a serious thought. "We had a little place like this near our house," she recalled. "I kept sayin' to mummy that it needed bluebells. Can I put a bench here, for when I want to think o' home?"

"That sounds like a magnificent idea, my dear. Now, how about those bluebells, before we show you around the villa?"

Ella nodded eagerly, then skipped off toward the trees. She slowed to a very deliberate stroll and began spinning. As she spun, a stream of magnificent white sparks began flying from the hems of her billowing peplos. The sparks flew slowly outward, gradually settling in place on the grass, before folding out of themselves into the most beautiful carpet of purple-blue. Each plant stretched out, popping new buds, until the green grass below became hidden. Ella looked about at her handiwork. "What do ye think, Selêne?" she asked.

The Moon smiled, loving the childish enthusiasm of her new protégé. "It's perfect, Mother. Now we just have to see about that bench." She held her hand out. "Let's head up to the villa and have ourselves some lunch. All this excitement has made me rather peckish."

They slowly and carefully made their way up the steps, Ella showing great patience as she assisted her mentor on the climb. Every so often, Ella would stop and gaze down at her new garden. Beyond the pond, and the trees that lined the bank, she could see other fenced, or walled, areas that would require exploring. One caught her eye; with white and pink blossoms, atop lots of tall trees, swaying in the breeze.

Selêne noticed the girl's interest. "That is the humanity garden, Mother." Ella turned, her eyes wide, seeking further detail. "The humanity garden is how we measure man's presence on Kiípos. For every child born, a new blossom appears, remaining there until such time as the Valkyrie take them on the first part of their final journey."

Ella looked again at the trees. "Does white mean boys, and pink girls?" She turned again, her curiosity rising.

Selêne smiled. "The colour of each blossom is not determined by whether the soul is a boy or girl. Why, sometimes a soul does not know if it's a boy or a girl until much later. Sometimes, what may appear to be a boy, may in reality be a girl; or vice versa. It takes some souls a lifetime of much pain and confusion, before they find their true self." Ella looked puzzled. "Do not think too much on this matter just yet, Mother. All things will be clear to you soon."

Selêne, too, looked down on the garden. "The trees are not so many now, after The Ripple. Not long ago, they were abundant, making that garden over ten times the size it is now." She sighed and, as she turned to resume the climb, said, "should these trees diminish much further, Mother, we may well lose all that is left. I fear that our work cannot start a second too soon."

At the top of the steps, a short path led to the front of the villa. A large arch framed the entrance, but there were no gates or doors to prevent access. Selêne held Ella's hand as they ambled through the arch into a large courtyard. "This was Mother Gaea's home, Mother, and now it is yours. It was open to everyone, at anytime, and she was never lonely. I hope you, too, shall be very happy here."

As they walked through the courtyard, surrounded by colourful walls of flowering climbing plants, the babbling of a running fountain and birdsong filling the air, Ella smiled at the old woman. "Selêne?" she prompted, "what happened to Mother Gaea? Where's she now?"

Selêne looked to the skies and sighed. "Ah, little one," she said quietly, "our Mother Gaea has rejoined the universe. Be it as a sprinkling of beautiful dust, or as a wisp of celestial cloud, we can only guess. But she is out there, somewhere, and that brings me comfort."

Ella carefully considered Selêne's answer. "Will she transcend to Sólaás?" the little girl asked.

Selêne's face glowed as her smile widened. "My, child," she said, caught by surprise yet again by the maturity of her new student, "you do learn quickly, don't you?" She cupped Ella's face in her wrinkly hand. "And there is much for you to learn."

"Mummy always says 'there's no such thing as a stupid question', if ye really want to learn."

"And your mummy is correct, Mother. You can ask anything, anytime, but, hopefully, our lessons will cover everything you wish to know, and more." She gestured for them to continue walking. "As regards Mother Gaea... as regards all of us Lunaá... We are but orphans of the universe, with no family but ourselves; created by Circe for a life of service to Kiípos. And, once that service is complete, to return our energies to the sweeping tides of the cosmos."

"But I had a family," said Ella. "Does that make me different?"

Selêne chuckled. "Oh, my sweet Mother Ella, you are certainly different to anyone in Lunaá. And that makes you a miracle. That's what makes you the miracle we all need."

A small step indicated the entrance to the villa building and, on entering, the bright space opening up before her was amazing. A clear glass ceiling, with the beautiful blue of the cloudless sky, and the sunlight, streaming through, made everything in the reception area shine. The walls and floors were a brilliant white; refulgent in Sólaás' glow. Large urns and vases, placed in strategic spots, allowed the colours of the various plants to jump out, vibrant against the sterility of the building.

Selêne picked up a little gong-mallet and tapped the small suspended bronze gong that sat on a shelf. A muted note rung out; not a crash, but a soft '*bong*', loud enough to carry, but not enough to seem harsh on the ear. Within a few seconds, a young girl appeared from around a hidden doorway. She wore a shimmering white stola, belted at the waist with a golden cord that matched the sandals that peeked out from beneath. Her long honey-coloured hair, tied near the end, hung forward over her bare left shoulder and, such was her poise, she seemed to glide across the tiled floor. She was of the same age as Ella, although slightly taller.

On seeing Selêne, her pace quickened, and her smile spread wide. "Welcome home, Aftí-Fengári," she said joyously, bowing respectfully. "We have missed you so much." Selêne embraced the girl warmly.

"It is nice to be home," she replied. "And I have brought someone with me." She smiled and turned, gesturing toward Ella. "Pandeia, I'd like to introduce Mother Ella. Mother Ella, this is Pandeia, the All-Bright. She is the illumination, the deliverer of moonlight."

"Welcome, Mitéra Fŷsi," said Pandeia, as she bowed once more.

"Pandeia shall attend your every need, Mother," Selêne added. "Anything you require, Pandeia shall be there for you."

Ella looked a little surprised. She smiled, firstly at Pandeia, then at Selêne. "I'm no' sure I need, or want, a servant," Ella said hesitantly.

Pandeia approached and took Ella's hands. "Oh, I am not your servant, Mitéra," she smiled, her gravelly voice and accent similar to Cassandra's. "I have the honour of being your Sŷntrofos... your..." She turned to Selêne, uncertain of the correct word.

"Your companion," smiled Selêne.

"Yes," enthused Pandeia, "your companion. I shall be your companion. Your friend, and companion." There was no doubting the enthusiasm in her voice, but Ella was still a little unsettled. Pandeia saw her reticence. "I am to make your life here pleasant, your tasks easier. It is my honour, my pleasure, to attend you, Mitéra. I, like many others, have volunteered myself for this duty."

Selêne joined the two young women and, placing a hand on either's shoulder, nodded and smiled. "Yes, Mother. Pandeia has volunteered her service to you, in order that *your* service be made easier. You have much to learn before we can set about our tasks, and Pandeia will lighten your burden." The little woman looked up to the taller of the three and, with a little chuckle, added, "she will also remind you to have fun, and laughter, amongst all the serious business."

"So, ye're no' just bein' *told* to help me?" confirmed Ella.

The girl shook her head excitedly. "Oh no, Mitéra. I offer my service willingly. And you would do me great honour in accepting." She held her gaze at Ella, awaiting acceptance and approval.

Selêne walked toward the doorway from where Pandeia had first appeared. "There will be much to exhaust you, in the weeks to come, Mother. However, we hope with Pandeia's help there will be much fun and silliness to remind us all that you are both still, for a short while at least, little girls; despite the tremendous responsibility thrust upon you. Now, shall we go find something nice to eat?"

X. INTO THE LIGHT

The tall figure stepped gracefully from the light and brushed their coat down, tidying themselves after the short, but turbulent, journey. Thin fingers combed through their long locks and straightened the wispy strands of their beard, shaking out the tiredness, before stepping forward towards the awaiting assembly. The light that had shone so brightly now faded, leaving behind the ornate white marble structure of the Sólaás Prime Diávasi.

Séntinell continued walking, with small, intentionally delicate steps, drawing forward the waiting ambassador. It was a small but important victory of recognition and stature; a vital diplomatic statement of equality in the face of the Supreme Boulé and, in particular, their leader, Archon Pollor Marik. The Archon smiled, increasing his own pace, and held his hands out to the visitor. "My friend, my friend, my friend," he enthused. "It is so good to see you again. It has been far too long since last you honoured us with your presence." He bowed as he clasped Séntinell's outstretched fingers. "How are you, Séntinell?"

The Luminára eyed their friend with some caution. Pollor Marik was an amiable sort, especially for an Archon, but this was a rather unexpectedly warm reception. "I am all the better for seeing you, Pollor. But I shall only be entirely at my ease once I have rested. I am not as young as I once was, you know." Séntinell glanced lazily about themselves — a subtle trick, often used in order to familiarise themselves of their surroundings, or threats, without arousing the suspicion of any bystanders.

"Solaás looks as splendid as it ever has," they added. The cursory inspection had established that there were no fewer than twenty guards behind the Archon — a significant, and unnecessary, number simply to welcome a friendly visiting envoy.

The gleaming marble spires of the White City shimmered brightly beneath the golden sky as the ranks of soldiers snapped themselves to attention, ready to escort the visiting dignitary. "We should dine together tonight, my friend," said Pollor. "My wife, as is her nature, is eager to hear tales of your latest adventures."

Séntinell hummed ruefully. "There are many who are eager to hear of these adventures," they replied, looking behind the Archon to the palace. "And I'm not sure they will enjoy the outcome too much." The two friends walked slowly toward the vast palace doorway. Séntinell felt uneasy — why so many guards? They turned, taking a quick glance over their shoulder at the following troops. "Are you expecting trouble, Master Archon?"

The politician laughed nervously. "Oh no," he said. "These..." He mirrored Séntinell's backward glance. "...

precautions... are merely to guarantee your safety, my friend."

"My safety?" laughed Séntinell. "From whom? What dangers could possibly confront me here? In the White City?"

Pollor laughed nervously once more. "I'm afraid your visit may be a short one, Séntinell. Lady Perse is not best pleased with the news of her daughters and, I'm afraid to say, is ready to lash out at anyone she believes connected with this tragedy. We are to be your shadow whilst you are in Sólaás, my friend."

Séntinell stroked their beard; this was not unexpected news. They had considered that Perse, reactive and permanently angry as she was, would look to exact her retribution on the first available victim. "And Lord Helios?" probed Séntinell. "What of the sun-god? Is he, too, looking to '*lash out*'?"

"Lord Helios took the news very badly." Pollor linked his arm into Séntinell's, and leaned closer so as to not be heard. "Helios' anger is directed mainly at Perse," he whispered. "He blames her for the enforced exile of his favourite daughter... and for keeping his grandson from him. Recent times have been... tense."

Once inside the palace doors, Pollor gestured for the guards to disperse. "This," he said, waving his hand in the soldiers' direction. "This is merely a show... a token gesture of Lady Perse's displeasure. She wants you to know that she does not welcome you here; that she considers you, in some way, responsible for events." Pollor raised his hands in the appeasement of Séntinell's intended rebuttal of his statement. "I know, I know, my friend," he comforted. "But grief, or anger, can blind anyone. Even Célestiaá."

"They wage wars for their imagined gods and religions. For land and territories. For the colour of their skins. They once waged war for the oil beneath Kiípos' lands and seas, now they wage war for its water. Tell me, Séntinell, is there nothing man won't fight over?"

The tall personage bowed. "I'm afraid that, when backed into a corner, self preservation becomes the overwhelming instinct of all living creatures, my lady. And, if the lack of food or medicines was not enough, mankind cannot last long without water. But, given the healthy supply of life essence man's wars have provided over the years, perhaps *thanks* for man's self-interest would be more appropriate... even if only grudgingly." Séntinell bowed once more.

The lady of Sólaás stretched on her chaise longue, her neck hairs bristling. "And it is from these leeches... these parasites, that the new rulers of Kiípos and Elŷsium have ascended? At the expense of my daughters? Explain this to me, Watcher... how are we to understand this turn of events? How are we to accept that the Célestiaá Rings are now in the possession of insects? If it were my decision, I would have Lord Helios crush the pathetic little rock here and now. Be done with the virus. Be done with the insatiable rash that is mankind."

"But it is *not* your decision!" boomed the stentorian voice, echoing through the halls that led off from the throne room. Séntinell turned to face the giant man of flames, now striding through the doorway toward the huge Volakas marble seat of power. The throne was an inelegant, crude construction; totally at odds with the highly crafted, polished seat, back and sides that comprised it. Four massive beautiful slabs of alabaster white, with slender ribbons of silver and pewter winding their way through, leaning—haphazardly—against one another; each holding the others in place. "Although I, too, would like to know why I shouldn't obliterate Kiípos."

Helios halted at the steps leading to his throne. When angry, he was of living fire, a true sun-god; the light in opposition to Haáde's darkness. As his ire receded, his flaming exterior diminished, revealing a strong, muscular blonde giant. The golden tunic, with the red fibulae adorning his right shoulder, bore the crest of Solaás. On his right hand, he wore the large, red jewel known as the Nuclei Ring; the source of his limitless power, and the tool from which everything in the universe was crafted.

Séntinell, as had Perse, bowed and knelt on one knee in front of the sun-god, who stood so tall that even The Lumináry had to look up to see his face. "Stand!" he thundered, as he took his seat. "I tire of this pompous deference."

Séntinell stood as ordered. "My lord," they began, "despite the recent tragedies that have befallen her, Kiípos remains the preeminent source of nutriment, not just for Sólaás, but for the entire universe."

"I know this, Watcher!" bellowed Helios, his fury bringing him to his feet, once more. "Am I not the creator of the universe? Am I not the maker of all that exists? Do not think to patronise me with your smarm, Lumináry. Remember your place, or you shall force me to provide a reminder."

The Lumináry bowed. "Forgive me, my lord. It is never my intent to offend. The point I was crudely making is that Kiípos is, at present, providing a bountiful source of life essence as never before. It would seem prudent to enjoy this period of plenty, as the human presence will not remain at recent levels for much longer."

Helios grunted and retook his seat. "I summoned you here to explain why I no longer have my daughters. And how and why my Célestiaá Rings came to be on the fingers of two humans."

"Aahh!" said Séntinell, nodding.

Perse had resettled herself onto her chaise. "Think carefully, Watcher," she cautioned. "What you say next may determine not only the survival of Kiípos, but whether we allow you to scurry back to Aether. I'm sure he is eager to learn of his brother's grief."

Séntinell stroked their thin beard, gathering their thoughts. "I'm afraid there is no palatable version of events that I can give. Certainly there is nothing I can say that will salve the wounds of loss that we are all experiencing."

"*Loss?*" screeched Perse. "You dare to tell us of your loss? What have you lost in comparison?"

Helios waved his hand, beckoning his wife to silence herself. "My apologies, once again, my lady. I did not mean to diminish *your* loss, only suggest that your daughters held a place in *all* our hearts."

"Do not use weasel words, Watcher," said Helios. "Tell it as it is. We know of Pasiphae's... ambitions. We are all too aware of her bitterness and anger toward her parents. Give us the facts of the matter; undressed, and free of garnished appeasements." Helios glared at Perse, his displeasure obvious and intense.

"I'm afraid, my lord, that the fault of this... tragedy... lies solely at the gates of Hades," explained Séntinell. "Lady Pasiphae has endangered the ongoing existence of man by her tinkering and tampering with the natural chemical and electrical constituent elements of the planet. It was initially her intention to destroy Kiípos in her path to the ultimate goal; the throne of Sólaás; the very seat you occupy at this second. It is only because of the selfless actions of our beloved Lady Circe, her son, Jacob, and her ward, Cassandra, that we are in any position to discuss this. I should also mention, not allowing their courageous contributions to be ignored, the assistance of Charon, servant of Haáde, and Brunhiíld and Marro; two simple humans, prepared to sacrifice themselves in order to save their fellow men. Theirs was a foolhardy jaunt, against all the odds; a last throw of the dice."

Séntinell wiped a tear from their cheek. "And it cost us *all*." They looked at Perse, a genuine sorrowful expression displaying their own true loss, their own true love. "And we shall grieve for *our* Circe until the ends of time." Séntinell's head lowered, bowing, aware that these utterings were bordering on insolence. Perse grunted, shifting uneasily on her couch.

"Are you saying that Haáde is plotting further treachery, Watcher?" Helios stood, his anger on the rise again. "Are we to at last wage war with Hades?" His face belied his anger; a hint of a smile hidden below the furrowed brows and red cheeks.

Séntinell raised a hand in appeasement. "I am satisfied, and thankful, my lord, that this is not the case. Lady Circe contended the universe needs both Sólaás and Hades; that neither can exist without the other. She convinced Lord Haáde of this inescapable truth, dampening his intentions, which were, I'm afraid to say, instigated and fuelled by Lady Pasiphae's resentment of... your majesties." They bowed, pausing for a reaction. Helios sat down.

"It was the actions of Lady Pasiphae that brought us to the brink. And it was her husband, and he alone, who extinguished the life of your eldest daughter. I should stress that Pasiphae was, by this time, beyond all reason; her hatred and entitlement blinding her to all sense. And it was to she whom you should allot responsibility for losing Circe. It was Lady Pasiphae's attack, her abuse of her Célestiaá Ring, that killed Lady Circe." The Lumináry bowed once more.

"And the rings? What of the rings?" asked Perse.

Séntinell smiled before sighing. "It was the wish of your daughter, Circe, that her ring be a gift to our Lady Cassandra. That she become mistress of Elŷsium and, in turn, Kiípos. That she, in partnership with your grandson, Lord Jacob, now the wearer of Lady Pasiphae's ring, restore Kiípos to the bounteous provider of life essence that she once was, whilst also reining in the excesses of man. Lady Cassandra is already proving to be a worthy monarch, a fitting torchbearer for Lady Circe's legacy."

"Lady Cassandra?" questioned Perse, incredulous. "And why is it not my grandson who wields both rings? He is Célestiaá, after all."

Helios roared. "Cease your endless whining, woman. You have no love for our grandson. You have denied his existence since the day of his birth. Do not pretend to have his interests at the forefront of your thoughts now. In fact, wife, I tire of your cynicism. *Leave.* Retire to your gynaeceum with your chattering maids; exercise your right to chirp and howl to your servants there. But, on the way, send Astris to me; I have need of her."

The mistress of Sólaás quickly raised herself from her lounging, huffily dragging her legs from the sofa, snorting in fury at the public slighting from her husband. She stormed passed Séntinell, who bowed, making sure to conceal the wry smile they couldn't help forming. As she disappeared from the throne room, Helios addressed Séntinell.

"She makes a good point, Séntinell. Why are both rings not on the hand of my grandson, and why is he subordinate to a mere human?"

"May I respectfully ask a question, my lord?"

Helios paused, surprised. No one asked questions of the sun-god; no one dared to presume the familiarity of seeking his views, or opinions, unless he volunteered those views. "I suppose..." he said, hesitantly.

"What do you know of humans, my lord? The male? The female?"

"I presume you are about to tell me, Watcher."

Séntinell nodded. "Indeed, my lord. Here.." Séntinell held their arms outstretched, turning, gesticulating at everything around them. "Here, you are lord and master over all. What you say is law, what you do is sacrosanct. You are unquestioned, and all do as you bid. That is how it should be." Séntinell could see the impatience growing in Helios' face. "But on Kiípos, on Earth, the female has male dominance *imposed* on her; through greater physical strength; and through emotional and psychological manipulation, amongst many other things. But the female is... *spirited*... shall we say? She has had enough of patriarchal suppression; of misogynistic repression; of being held back, and put down. It is, in my humble opinion, my lord, an overdue necessity that the female human now asserts *her* dominance over the male. Not, I add, for dominance's sake, but merely to achieve the simplest of outcomes; *equality*. This is not—and I stress I have no favourite—a merely whimsical battle of the sexes, a struggle for control; this has now become a matter of grave urgency if Kiípos is to have any chance of restoration; any chance of surviving in its present form."

Helios settled back into his seat, nodding for Séntinell to continue. "I have no doubts that Kiípos will survive, with or without the presence of humanity; but man is a curious, creative creature. And it would be such a shame if the universe were to lose such a marvel. Moreover, Lady Circe's decision to make man in the image of Célestiaá, to heighten man's intelligence, and make him caretaker of his world, was successful in increasing the flow of the life essence, was it not?"

The master of the universe sprawled across the width of his throne, considering the information given him. "What would you have me do, Watcher?"

"As much as I, amongst many I'm sure, would dearly love to look again upon the beauty of Lady Circe, there is no bringing her back. But she lives on, through her son, your grandson. And he is, if I may be so bold as to say, more than worthy of his position. But it was Lady Circe's wishes that Lady Cassandra take the role of leader, even above that of Lord Jacob. I feel she is the one who can bring about the realignment necessary in the gender hierarchy. In truth, she has already set several wheels in motion which may, given time, bring an end to the constant warring of the male. My advice to you, my lord, would be to leave Kiípos as is. If they succeed, then you reap the benefit. If they fail, then you are in no worse a position than you are now."

ﻋﻠﻋﻠﻋﻠﻋﻠ

Helios harrumphed, then looked toward the door. Entering was his youngest daughter, Astris. Helios smiled as he stood. "Ah, there you are, my dear," he said.

Séntinell turned to meet the new arrival and, when their eyes fell upon her, they gulped and, involuntarily, blurted out, "oh, my!" The Lumináry gave a stuttering bow and lowered to one knee, their gaze falling to the ground as a mild panic and bewilderment washed over them. "My lady!"

The girl looked at Séntinell in astonishment. "I... I...," she repeated, before looking to Helios and taking a knee. "Father," she said. "You sent for me?"

"Rise, my dear," said Helios. "I think I may have something that will interest you." He looked at the still kneeling Lumináry and gave a little laugh. "Well, well, Séntinell. You have finally seen something that takes your breath away, it seems. Please, stand."

Séntinell's head slowly rose, bewitched by the woman before them. "My lady," they repeated. "It is a pleasure to meet you." Séntinell was transfixed; before them stood the very image of Circe; slightly younger, perhaps, her brown hair a little shorter, and in a different style; her eyes a beautiful light blue, as opposed to hazel. But, despite these differences, she was the very double of her elder sister.

"This is Séntinell, Astris. The Lumináry; the Watcher; the Witness. They journey through the galaxies, the realms of time and space, from dimension to dimension, recording and reporting in service of my brother — your uncle Aether. But Séntinell is also the envoy, the plenipotentiary of Elŷsium." The girl smiled and held out her hand. In response, Séntinell knelt once more, bowing their head and kissing her hand. She giggled as the touch of their long fingers tickled her soft palm.

"Why do they kneel so much, father? Why do you kneel so much, Séntinell?" she asked, with an amusement enhancing her mellifluous voice. "I am not a queen." Helios stepped down and clapped the Lumináry on the back.

"Get up, get up," he said. "Enough of this nonsense. I have made my decision, Séntinell. Cassandra and Jacob shall keep their positions, and the rings... for now. You have served my brother, but now you shall serve me. More accurately, you shall serve Astris." The girl looked to her father in surprise, and not a little confusion.

"Serve *me*, father? How?"

"Do you think I am blind to your plight, daughter? How you go from day to day at court? Mouthing meaningless pleasantries to servile attendants, courtiers and sycophants; bored, uninterested, and unchallenged. You have longed for a purpose, a task, a reason to rise each day. Well, now, I am giving you this task. You are to go to Elŷsium, under the counsel of Séntinell. You are to learn all there is to learn about Elŷsium, about Kiípos, and especially about mankind. I want you to know your kin, your nephew; I want you to tell me about my grandson."

He removed a stunningly cut white diamond ring from his finger and held it out to his daughter. The Nuclei Ring glowed, and a red thread of light reached out, touching the white diamond, flowing into it, filling it as wine fills a glass until it, too, was a beautiful red. "This is not a Célestiaá Ring, Astris, but it will provide you with enough power and abilities to be of... *assistance*... to the stewards of Elŷsium."

Astris was beside herself. She lurched forward and embraced her father, pulling him tightly to her. "Thank you, Father. You will not regret this. I shall make you proud," she gushed, slipping the ring onto her finger. The jewellery immediately shrank itself to fit, and the diamond shone brightly, as if brought to life by its new owner.

The sun-god held her by the shoulders at arm's length and smiled. "I am already proud of you, Astris. But you need a challenge; you need to see something of the universe. Sólaás is your home, but the universe is out there —a marvel beyond comprehension—and it is time that you saw something of it." He turned to Séntinell. "I am trusting you with my last daughter, Séntinell. Show her what her sister created; teach her and guide her." He lowered his head and glared intently at The Lumináry. "Make sure they show her respect," he growled.

"You honour me, my lord," said the tall figure. "It will be a privilege." As Helios retook his seat, Séntinell bowed to Astris, who then wrapped her arms around them, squeezing them tightly, too. They smiled down at her. "Forgive me for saying, my lady, but you are *so* like your sister. Your very presence will brighten the gloom that has blighted Elŷsium since her passing."

"Thank you, Séntinell," she replied. "I know I am in excellent hands."

Séntinell bowed to Helios. "We will make Lady Astris most welcome at Elŷsium, my lord. She will make many wonderful friends, I am certain."

"She is not there to make merry," reprimanded Helios. Then, looking at the delight on his daughter's face, added, "well, not all the time. She is there to assess whether it serves Sólaás best for the humans to remain in control, or for alternative measures to be taken."

Séntinell bowed. "Of course, my lord. I shall keep that in mind." They then turned to leave, but hesitated.

"Is there something you wish to discuss, Watcher?"

Séntinell sighed. "There is one other matter, My Lord. But I am unsure how best to broach the subject. It may cause offence."

Helios sat up straight, leaning forward, his hand on his knee. "Speak up!"

"A long time agone, Apollo gifted Lady Cassandra the ability of premonition in rather... *tawdry*... circumstances. Well, at the time of her demise, Lady Circe passed certain... delicate... information to Lady Cassandra. Information, in the form of a vision; a vision that does not make much sense. Lady Cassandra's presentiment saw her at the Elysian Fields, an area of Elŷsium where the distribution of the life essence is determined. Before and behind her were two armies; massed ranks as far as the eye could see."

Helios frowned. "And you think one of these armies belonged to Hades? I thought you said they had convinced Haáde of peaceful coexistence?"

"But that is the strange thing, my lord," Séntinell said. "In the vision, Lord Haáde had aligned himself with what appeared to be the army of Elŷsium. An army that does not as yet exist."

"Ah, I see, Watcher," said Helios, nodding sarcastically. "And this is your roundabout way of asking if one of these armies could be mine; if Sólaás has designs on invading Elŷsium?" Séntinell squirmed and fidgeted uncomfortably. "Why?"

"I beg your pardon, my lord?"

"Why?" repeated Helios. "Why would I feel the need to invade my own terrain? Indeed, why would I invade when I could just wish Kiípos or Elŷsium away? I have always prepared my armies for an expected confrontation with Hades — not Kiípos, nor Elŷsium; but you tell me they are no longer required? I know nothing of the turpitudes of mankind, nor of the dreams of Kiípos' children, but I can say they do not involve Sólaás."

"Mmmm!" muttered Séntinell. The sun-god was correct. It made little sense that it would require the armies of Sólaás to overpower such a small sphere. Especially as Helios already had their souls in his possession, and under his dominion; if he wished, he could simply crush them with but a thought. No, there was nothing to be gained by invading Elŷsium.

"Now, leave me," ordered Helios. "I wish time alone. You should return to Elŷsium immediately, Watcher; my wife is not easily held at bay."

Séntinell bowed to Helios, then turned to Astris, extending an arm toward the exit. "My lady," they said. The young girl curtseyed and, with an excited chuckle, walked hurriedly, almost skipping alongside the large strides of The Lumináry. "Oh, Séntinell," she cooed. "I can't believe I'm leaving Sólaás. Will they truly welcome me at Elŷsium?" A worried look suddenly crossed her face. "I don't want them thinking I'm there as a spy."

"Oh, I'm certain you will receive a most generous welcome, my lady."

Helios smiled, delighted at making his daughter so happy; cheered by the excitement and enthusiasm in her now-fading voice, as both she and her new mentor disappeared from the throne room.

As they made their way toward the Diávasi, Pollor approached; alone, with not a soldier in sight. He bowed to Lady Astris, then, arms outstretched, gave a disappointed shrug of his shoulders. "It appears we shall not be dining together after all, my friend," he said, with a genuine sense of disappointment.

"I shall make it a priority to return as soon as circumstances permit," replied Séntinell. "But, for now, I must bid you goodbye." They smiled at Astris, then added, "we now embark on what we hope will be an exciting adventure for the young lady."

Pollor bowed once more and extended his arm toward the Diávasi. "My lady."

"Thank you, Archon Marik," said Astris, as she stepped toward the brilliant white light, closely followed by Séntinell. The light grew ever brighter, and the gate whispered an almost-inaudible 'sshh', as the pair disappeared into the radiance, until eventually swallowed by the portal. Pollor watched for a moment, then turned back toward the palace as the light dimmed.

He had only taken a few steps when the almost silent hissing of the Diávasi grew louder behind him as the gate reactivated. His shadow lengthened before him almost immediately as the light intensified and, as he turned back to face the gate, a massive flaming blade curved out from the illumination catching his abdomen; slicing effortlessly through him. He clutched his wound as his legs gave way and he fell to his knees.

"Who...?" he asked with a whimper.

He looked up to see an enormous silhouette fill the lit space; watching silently as the blade swung down once more, catching his neck, sending his now detached head tumbling across the shining tiles. The Archon's body slumped forward with a dull thud.

The giant stepped out from the light, sheathing his weapon; running his mighty hand through his long, golden locks as he looked impassively at the result of his swordplay. "No welcome committee?" he grumbled. "I should have expected nothing less."

XI. WOMEN WARRIORS

"I was onna-bugeisha; bushi class, defender of my household. I became onna-musha when I joined the great Tomoe Gozen at the Battle of Kurikaradani."

Chiyoko paced back and forth, spinning her naginata behind her back; the whirl and whoosh hypnotic as she nonchalantly passed it from hand to hand. "I was there when three hundred samurai of the Minamoto clan bested two thousand warriors of the Taira. I was one of only five to survive."

"I was there at the Battle of Awazu, where Lady Tomoe took the head of Musashi clan leader, Onda no Hachiro Morishige; despite his hiding among thirty of his horsemen."

"She taught me the bow. She taught me the katana. She taught me the naginata. I was taught by the best there ever was; Tomoe Gozen. My mistress, Lady Athena, has now charged me to teach you." She thrust forward, unexpectedly, swinging her naginata over her head, halting the tip of her weapon less than a millimetre from Melanie's nose. The terrified girl shrieked and, instinctively pulling her head back from the white shine of the twenty inch curved blade, fell backwards. Chiyoko smiled.

"Gooood!" she said enthusiastically. "You have some reactions, after all. You will both be here at sunrise, every morning, dressed in keikogi and ready to work."

"What will…"

"Ta ta ta ta…" reprimanded Chiyoko, wagging her finger, halting Katie's question. "I will teach you what you need to be taught. You will know what you need to know. To become masters of the katana would take years; we have three weeks to make you competent with *these* swords; hardly enough time to teach you anything. But, I will teach you basic kenjutsu, the art of the Japanese sword, and basic tantojutsu, the skill of the knife. You shall learn basic stealth and deception defence techniques of ninjutsu."

"Like a Ninja?" interrupted Melanie.

Chiyoko whacked the pole of her naginata on the side of Melanie's head. "Ow! Ye wee fucker! Will ye stop that?"

"No!" scolded Chiyoko. "*Not* like Ninja. Never use that term again. Understand?" Melanie grimaced as she nodded, rubbing the painful area. "I cannot make you onna-musha, but you will be Élementaá, and that will have to suffice."

Katie and Melanie had been sitting, as instructed, cross-legged, on small mats for over an hour. The numbness had become cramp; their legs stiff and sore. Chiyoko stamped the end of the naginata pole twice on the ground. She pointed the blade at two tree stumps, each about two feet tall, with a diameter of approximately half that, and about two feet apart from one another.

"You shall stand on one foot until you can stand on it no more. Then you shall stand on the other foot until you can stand on *that* no more. You shall repeat and repeat and repeat, but never with two feet on log at same time. Begin!" Chiyoko then sat cross-legged on her own mat, observing her students.

The two women hauled themselves to their feet, both groaning with the pain, but also at the thought of the impending exercise. They stood behind the logs, staring at each other, willing the other to make a move. "You first," said Katie, with a smile.

"Dinna start that bollocks again," smirked Melanie. "Get the fuck on yer log." She gestured with her head. "After 'three'," she added. "One, two... *three!*" They both hopped up onto the logs, struggling at first to keep their balance; eventually finding a steady stance. It didn't take long for the calf muscles, and ankles, to feel the strain, and each woman, only seconds apart, hopped quickly onto their other leg. Their initial laughter had quickly evaporated, as the physical effort of trying to balance undermined their mental determination.

They wavered, and they wobbled, then again hopped onto the other foot. The struggle intensified. Chiyoko watched. The pain was now excruciating, and sweat and constant groans were now emerging from both, as they teetered ever more shakily toward falling.

"Mel!" Katie whispered, purposefully, reaching her hands out. "Take my hands. We'll steady each other." Melanie gave a half smile as she jerked to her left, suddenly shifting her weight to compensate. She reached out, and the women clasped their hands together, immediately feeling more secure. The legs still quivered, and the calves still ached, but they held each other up. "Say when you want to change," Katie instructed.

"After three," Melanie prompted. "One, two, three!" They hopped up together, landing on the other foot, almost perfectly synchronised. Their hands grasped the other's forearms, making their posture even more secure. They smiled at each other, feeling far steadier, far more in control. This continued for several more minutes; each woman taking turn at indicating change.

"Enough!" barked Chiyoko, raising herself effortlessly to her feet. Katie and Melanie stared at her, arms clasped tightly, standing legs wobbling nervously. "Enough?" confirmed Katie.

Chiyoko nodded, a slight smile breaking her face, before returning to her usual stern visage as she pointed her weapon to the mats. "Enough," she repeated softly. The girls jumped down, grimacing as their exhausted muscles and limbs hit the hard ground. "What have we learned?" Chiyoko asked.

"That I should have gone tae the gym more often?" groaned Melanie.

"Ta ta ta ta..." reprimanded Chiyoko.

Melanie slowly raised her head toward the little Japanese woman, an accepting smile on her mouth, and she nodded. "We've learned that we're a team, and that we're much stronger when we work together."

"You are much stronger when you work together." Chiyoko nodded. "You do not yet realise what Élementaá will be; what Élementaá will be possible of. But it will all come from the two of you together. You are now irreversibly entwined; sisters; Onmyōdō... Élementaá."

She resumed spinning her naginata behind her. "Today we begin the task of making you a team. Getting you fit. Making you think. Finding the fearsome, fearless woman warriors you must become."

The sessions were gruelling. Chiyoko worked them hard; and hit them harder. She pushed their fitness to the limit as each exercise, each session, became tougher than the one before. 'Again! Again!', became the constant, echoing order barked out by the diminutive taskmaster.

Strength, stamina, and balance were the keywords drummed into them in the first two weeks; thin beams and logs being prominent features. They would spend hours on the balls of their feet, leaping from one beam to another, one log to another; sword in hand, performing complex arm exercises in tandem with each leap, squat, or roll. In the few breaks they were allowed, Chiyoko would educate the women on the ethics expected of them in honouring the traditions of kenjutsu.

The third week saw the introduction of a more principled style of swordsmanship; how to understand and employ the disciplines required to master traditional battlefield techniques. They were taught how to let their swords flow in smooth arcs; how to use their bodies as extensions of the sword, and the sword as extensions of themselves. There became an almost religious attention to every detail of handling the weapons; from the way they drew them from the scabbard, and held them, to the grace and balletic way they would wield them. They learned the respect with which they would cut down their enemies.

Then, just as the women felt in control of their bodies and weapons, Chiyoko ordered the wearing, once more, of vests, cargo pants, and boots. "This will be your uniform; these clothes should feel as invisible as keikogi." The familiar balance exercises felt like chores once more. They had to readjust their senses to compensate until, at last, the logs and beams again felt secure underfoot. Almost overnight, there appeared two skilled, athletic swordswomen; patient, disciplined, and ruthless.

Every few days, they would receive a brief visit from either Cassandra or Jacob; eagerly seeking progress updates. On the morning of the sixth day of the third week, Poseidon and Hephaestus joined the training party. Chiyoko sat the women down on their familiar resting mats. "You have, for now, reached a satisfactory level with sword. Today, you will learn the basics of psychokinetic influence."

"Psycho-what?" asked Melanie. Chiyoko drew her a displeased stare.

"Psychokinetic influence, or psychokinesis," repeated Poseidon, the warm tone of his voice immediately drawing the interest of his two new students. "Today you will learn how to use fire and water for your everyday needs; or as a weaponised extension of your swords and stones." The two women suddenly gained some much-needed enthusiasm as Poseidon sat across from them, cross-legged as were they. He placed a small white China bowl between them and, with a simple wave of his hand over the bowl, filled it instantly with cold water. Hephaestus quietly took a seat on the bench, watching as his colleague took centre-stage.

"Fuck's sake," laughed Melanie, "can ye do that wi' vodka?" Katie gave her a sharp dig in the ribs with her elbow, along with a stern, glowering look as she dropped her chin.

Poseidon laughed. "No, just water, I'm afraid."

The two women could see the water-master properly for the first time. He was not, Katie was sure, what most of the stories, movies or legends had depicted him as—violent and ill-tempered—a bearded middle-aged man with the build of an Olympian god. No, this Poseidon was much more... dreamy. He was tall, and slim; athletic, in a 'gym teacher' kind of way. Yes, that's what he reminded Katie of —a geeky school teacher—but handsome and clean shaven, with dense curly hair and piercing blue eyes. Katie sat forward, gazing at Poseidon, full of interest, as she cupped her chin in her hand, leaning her elbow on her knee.

"Do ye no' have a trident?" Melanie chuckled.

"Melanie!" chided Katie. "Don't be so daft."

Poseidon smiled as he looked at each of the women, his hand circling over the water, stirring the liquid just by his actions alone. "No," he said politely, "I have never had a trident."

"See, Melanie," confirmed Katie, "that was a daft question." She looked again at her tutor. "You were saying about Psychokinestics?" she queried.

Melanie burst out laughing. "That's no' what he called it, ye daft arse. It's psycho... psycho... well, it's something else."

Chiyoko had heard enough, and her patience finally snapped. "*Chinmoku! Chinmoku!*" she snapped. "*Silence!*" She stood behind the two giggling women, then whacked each in the ear with her staff. "You will show respect." Both women squealed, immediately raising their hands to their throbbing ears. They both glared up at the angry woman, but were met with every bit as severe a face staring back at them. "You will listen," she said, almost in a whisper, "and you will learn." She jerked her staff in Poseidon's direction.

Poseidon continued his circling action, and with no preamble, explained. "This is psychokinesis. The influence and control over inanimate substances or objects, simply by exercising your mind. Now you are Élementaá, you have the ability, through the swords and stones, to manipulate, to command the elements. You cannot create water, or fire, but you can use whatever is available to you, including drawing moisture from the ground, or the air if need be. Even the water content of your own bodies is yours to control."

"You can," interrupted Hephaestus, "in the same way you can draw water, *summon* fire, but only if you have a spark to draw it from." He relaxed back onto the bench, gesturing for Poseidon to continue. Unlike the water-master, Hephaestus was not so pleasing to the eye; bearded and scarred, he had a stocky build and a slight, but noticeable, limp. His manner was far more brusque; his consideration of others, or their opinion of him, not at the forefront of his mind. He was an impatient man, with the education of Élementaá seemingly beneath him.

"You can divert water," continued Poseidon, "drawing it to you, or sending it where you wish." The water smoothly rose from the bowl, stretching out into a thin rope-like cord. It circled around the three of them, gaining speed each time it passed. Melanie and Katie snapped their heads from left to right as they watched the water zoom by. "Not only can you displace any amount of moisture, you also have the ability to weaponise it."

The cord of water continued increasing its velocity, before shooting off toward the wall, hitting with such force it dislodged several small chips. "Wow!" exclaimed Katie. Melanie scratched her head.

Poseidon smiled at the women. "Now it's your turn. Now you truly become Élementaá."

Once training had finished, Katie and Melanie were met by Jessica, who led them down a corridor to a wing of the villa they hadn't been in before. "Cassandra has asked that we meet in the gynaeceum," she breezily informed them. "We can get a bit of privacy... away from the men," she laughed.

"What's the gyn.. the gynnie..?" asked Melanie.

"The gynaeceum," Jessica repeated, chuckling as she looked back over her shoulder to the bemused girl. "It's our retreat," she added. "Our space away from the men. As lovely as Elŷsium men are, they are still men, and it can be exhausting sometimes, dealing with their childish moods and behaviour. The gynaeceum is where we can just be women, talking about what we like, what we want to see happening." At the end of the corridor, she held her arm out, guiding them down to the right. "There's food, wine... *lots* of wine," she laughed, "and there are no men to spoil the party."

"A party?" Melanie's ears pricked up. "I could do wi' a party." She nudged Katie's arm, nodding enthusiastically. "Pity ye couldn't invite Poseidon, eh, Katie?"

"Oh fuck off," laughed Katie. "Don't talk pish."

Jessica laughed as she led them through a curtained doorway. The room was smaller than most of the others they'd been in at the villa. It was a cosy space, with plush sofas and cushions, and long drapes covered the glass doors that led to the veranda. The walls were a pleasant lime green, and thick rugs covered the coolness of the floor. As was always the case, there was a splendid assortment of snacks, meats, and cakes on display on a long table. Several ornate metal wine buckets sat below the table, multiple bottle necks poking their heads out from the packed ice that cooled them.

"Ah, ladies," welcomed Cassandra. "How was training today?"

"It was grand," said Katie. "I think we're gettin' the hang o' it all now."

"Well, apart from the water stuff," laughed Melanie. "Think I'd have more success tryin' to piss up a wall."

"Melanie!" scolded Katie, shaking her head. "What're ye like?"

"What?" replied Melanie. "Between Poseidon, and his water tricks, and Chiyoko and that fuckin' stick o' hers, my head's absolutely fucked."

Brunhiíld laughed loudly. "Do not fret so, Lady Katie. You are among friends here. We do not blush so easily, do we, Jessica?"

Jessica raised her eyes, chuckling as she poured some wine into glasses. "No, Brunhiíld," she agreed. "We do not blush so easily. I think you've made sure of that."

Brunhiíld laughed again, holding her glass high in a toasting gesture. "Aye, and here's to the overdue liberation of women's thoughts, words, deeds, and lives, as Katie and Melanie venture forth on their quest." She slugged the entire contents of her glass in one swallow, then wiped her mouth with the back of her hand.

"A quest?" Melanie seemed a little confused.

Brunhiíld belched loudly, then sat heavily onto one of the sofas. "Perhaps I should have said 'war'," she added.

"War?"

Cassandra gestured for Melanie and Katie to sit on the sofa next to her. "Brunhiíld, as usual, gets straight to the point. Let me explain. Élementaá are to be the new Muses," she began. "You will be the new inspirations, guides, and teachers of mankind. Élementaá will recalibrate man's morals, as well as his place in the... *pecking* order, I suppose." She sighed, then took a sip of her wine. "Unfortunately, there will be no shortcuts. Before we can reeducate, we will have to remove man's developed entitlement, and that will not be easy. And will most definitely take some time."

"And what, exactly, is that reeducation, Cassandra? What is it we're supposed to be teachin'?" Katie was voicing the curiosity of both herself and Melanie. What was their purpose? Why were Élementaá so crucial to the ongoing fortunes of mankind?

"Why, love, of course," smiled Cassandra. "The reminding of love, respect, and support of one another. The simplicity that man needs woman, and woman needs man. Men exert restrictions and limitations on women's choices simply to maintain control. Whole cultures are built on the premise that 'man knows best'. Until women are free to make their own choices about what they wear and do—even what they think and say—without fear of assault or disapproval, equality will not exist. There is no, or should not be, a dominant gender. All souls are equal; whatever their sex, whatever their gender. All souls have their part to play in the universe's survival. We are all, when it comes down to it, the continuing energy of Sólaás. Our physical forms are merely a temporary host for our true selves."

"And we're to preach *love*?," asked Melanie, hesitantly. "At the end of a sword?"

"Men must be *better*," stated Cassandra, "but they won't change unless we *force* that change."

"Jacob's concerned we might get a wee bit o' bloodlust," said Katie.

Cassandra's lips thinned, and she nodded her agreement. "I think that's because he knows how much of a cancer the Patriarchy is. He knows men will not give up their dominance lightly, and there *will* be much blood spilt. You may *well* find yourselves in a 'war', as Brunhiíld so delicately put it."

Katie finished the last of her wine, then stared at the glass, turning it in her fingers as she pondered the tasks ahead of them. "Jacob always had a wee bit o' the pessimist about him when he was a bairn. He wasn't there after the ripple," she said. "Even in a quiet wee place like Strath-sealgair, shit hit the fan. Makes me sick thinkin' about some o' the bastards that got their grubby mitts on the food, the water... Got their gangs to terrorise folk. Made lives a fuckin' misery for everybody..."

Cassandra swirled her wine in its glass. "No man, not even Jacob, can understand the everyday, the ever-present, gymnastics every woman puts herself through each and every time she ventures out into the world. No man, even in supporting his wife, his daughters, his sisters, will ever know the underlying fear—expectation, even—of attack, of assault, or ridicule. Of being talked down to; corrected, by the ignorant; objectified by those undeserving of their attentions. Every woman knows the tightrope they walk, but no man, even those who profess support, really know the extent to which woman have been driven."

"I canna believe how fuckin' low I sank," added Melanie. "Canna believe what I did... was prepared to do, just to get a meal... or to keep in those bastards' good books." She wiped a tear as she looked at Katie. "I canna believe the good people I turned my back on."

"Some men," said Katie, squeezing her friend's hand, "use sex as a torture, or a humiliation, or, as ye've experienced, simply to control. You were just played by the bastards, Mel. It wasn't your fault."

Melanie gulped the remaining wine from her glass. "Well, I'm up for this fight. If it means savin' more lassies from the shit I ended up in."

Brunhiíld poured more wine for the women. "I do not envy you, my friends. Men are stubborn shits at the best of times. In their minds, they are always right; even when they are so obviously wrong. Trying to take their control from them?" She shook her head and exhaled loudly.

"There *are* still many good men... caring men, on Kiípos," Cassandra reminded them. "But we cannot rely on men's support as we set about righting these wrongs. Many have set about forming new communities, but they are still the prey of the undeserving. Much of the misery on Kiípos was simply because they took the gift of love for granted; but it has not been forgotten entirely. This is exactly why finding these women, your Élementaá sisters, will be so important," she said. "They will be trained, armed, and given all the information they'll need to allow them to present an unarguable case to these communities. But, as with you two," she confirmed, looking seriously at Katie and Melanie, "the decisions of who lives, and who does not, will be theirs to make. Justice and retribution will be every bit as important as love, compassion, and mercy. But, the coming of Élementaá, these 'Angels of Justice', must reverberate around the world. All must know and fear the consequences of their actions. And that will take some time."

"Women-fearing men, eh?" mumbled Melanie. "That'll make a change."

"*God*-fearing men," corrected Cassandra.

"How did ye decide on who to recruit?" Katie asked.

"Séntinell has been invaluable in advising me," said Cassandra. "They know everything about everybody. They are The Lumináry, the Watcher, after all."

"Nosey bastard, if ye ask me," laughed Melanie. Her smile dropped, as a sobering thought crossed her mind. "Has that sneaky bastard seen us in the shower? Or..." She shivered. "Taking a shit? Have they been there when we were… ye know? Fuckin'?"

Brunhiíld patted her shoulder as she poured her more wine. "If so," she winked, "I hope you gave them a fucking magnificent show."

Melanie winced. "Oh fuck," she said, almost gagging. "I feel sick thinkin' about it." In an instant, the wine in her glass disappeared down her throat.

"At any rate, we have come to an agreement as to your first 'quest'," said Cassandra.

"Oh, aye?" Katie sat forward, on the edge of the sofa.

"Nothing too taxing. A little warmup for you to test your new skills."

"Aye?" asked Melanie, a little impatiently.

"Ladies, we are sending you home."

XII. UNDYING LOVE

Strath-sealgair, Scotland September 1986

"Ye sit out here a lot, don't ye?"

Cissy turned to find Ray leaning against the patio doors, wearing his familiar smile as he held out a mug of steaming tea. "Aye,' she replied as she reached out for the welcome hot drink. "There's somethin' calmin' about lookin' at the stars, don't ye think?" She sipped some tea, then held her arm out, beckoning Ray to come sit with her. It had become an evening ritual now; Cissy sitting out in the garden on Ray's parents' old rattan bench, in the semi-darkness, bathed only in the slightest of light that managed to filter through the curtains inside the patio doors.

The clear skies over this part of the Scottish Highlands escaped the light pollution of larger towns and cities, and the blueish black canvas of the Milky Way displayed itself with magnificent clarity. Cissy would, it appeared to Ray, repeatedly scrutinise the layout of the billions of twinkling constellations; not searching for anything in particular, just making sure that… well… everything was in its correct place. Cissy was blissfully happy on Kiípos; her life with Ray and Eric was undoubtedly bringing her great joy and satisfaction, but she was still a daughter of Sólaás. And she was still the Matriarch of Elŷsium.

Ray put her nightly ritual down to a simple enjoyment of the stars, a means of relaxing after a hard day at George Grant's cafe. He knew how hard she had been working; the long, grinding shifts throughout the height of the tourist season, which, thankfully, were now drawing to an end.

Ray looked up as he squeezed himself in beside her. "Aye," he agreed, "makes ye wonder about what's out there, doesn't it?" He held his own mug of tea in his left hand, wrapping his right arm around her shoulder as he kissed her cheek. "I mean, do ye think there's some other guy, sittin' in his garden on some other planet that we've no' heard o' before, havin' just as much luck as I'm havin'?"

Cissy leaned into him, resting her head on his chest. "Luck?" she asked. "Is that what it is?" She looked up at him, smiling as his eyes met hers. "Ye think yer just lucky?"

"How else can ye explain it?"

"Wellll…," she drawled, "I think you, Raymond Corrie, are only gettin' the happiness that ye deserve."

"Oh, come on," he remonstrated with an embarrassed laugh.

Cissy crossed her legs as she sat up and slurped her tea. She looked at him as she held the mug to her mouth with both hands. "Seriously," she affirmed. "I dinna think it's luck at all. I think the universe is givin' ye just what ye deserve. Yer a wonderful man, Ray. Ye work hard. Ye look after me, and yer a fantastic father to Eric. I don't think yer mum and dad could be any prouder o' ye. I couldn't be any prouder o' ye." She caressed his cheek, sighing as she looked into his eyes. "It's me that's the lucky one, Ray. I canna believe how everythin' I could ever want just showed up on my very first day in Strathsealgair. Landed in my lap." She leaned forward and kissed his lips, then returned to her previously comfortable position, her head leaning against his chest.

Ray snuggled into her and took a sip of his tea. "It is magnificent," he said, gazing up at the night sky. "But the two most beautiful stars are no' up there at all."

"No?"

"No." He gently turned her face toward him and leaned his forehead on hers. The young couple's eyes locked onto each other, and they exchanged smiles. "They're right there," he said, "in those beautiful hazel eyes."

"That you flirtin' wi' me again, Smiler?" There it was again, that overwhelming love that Ray could effortlessly invoke in Cissy. That feeling that, despite the multitude of galaxies, the endlessness of the growing universe, there was nowhere of significance compared to sitting on that rattan bench with the man she loved.

"Naw," he whispered. "I'm no' flirtin'. I'm just gettin' lost in those eyes, an' knowin' that there's nothin' out there…" He gestured to the sky with his head. "… that could ever outshine them."

Cissy snuggled into him once more.

"No one'll ever find anything as beautiful as those eyes… anywhere."

"Ye smooth bastard," she chuckled.

"Aye, that's me, right enough."

Charon stepped out from the villa doorway, having enjoyed the shade the canopied entrance afforded. The sun was at its highest as he shielded his eyes and watched the waggon roll up the track. He pulled at his tunic, still feeling a little awkward with this new attire, much preferring his old sailing leathers. He even felt more at home in his leather pteruges and breastplate than he did in tunics or togas, but he was an administrator now; considered an acceptable presence in Elŷsium, with responsibilities. How times change.

The villa was his home for now; Brunhiíld, his life; such massive and unexpected change from his days as an outcast. His plans to build a dream villa on the riverside at Elysia were well under way. But, for a little while, he was content to enjoy his new life, with the love of his life, at Strath-sealgair Villa.

He raised his arms in welcome as his friend and his son rumbled up the track. Ray was now keeping himself busy with his carpentry; today's visit was to deliver several items for the villa, and a special gift for Charon. "How ye doin', ye auld buggar?" Charon called. Ray laughed and held up two fingers, then pulled the reins, signalling the horse to stop.

"Less o' the 'auld'," he chided. "I think ye've got more than a few years on me." He tied the reins, then jumped down, striding enthusiastically toward the sailor. The men embraced tightly, enjoying the company that had been denied them for so long.

"Ye're lookin' well," said Charon. "Rimel is obviously good for ye." He looked up at the waggon, where Eric sat quietly. "Hullo, Eric!" he called. "Come down here and gi'e me a hug, boy."

"Aye, we're settlin' in up there," said Ray. "Couldn't have picked a better location. It's beautiful. And quiet." He glanced at Eric as he clambered down from his seat.

"How's Eric doin'?" Charon asked quietly.

"Well, he's still no' talkin' yet, but Grind's daughter, Jael, seems to cheer him up. She seems to be gettin' through to him... slowly."

Charon put his arm around Ray's shoulder, guiding him toward the villa. "She's a good lass, that one," he nodded. "Knows who she is."

Ray smiled. "She does that," he agreed. He stopped, suddenly, and turned back to the waggon. "I've got somethin' for ye," he smiled. "Somethin' to ease yer auld weary bones in that new villa yer buildin'." As Ray pulled the canopy up at the back of the waggon, Eric had caught up with Charon. The tall man hugged him warmly, ruffling his hair and kissing the top of his head. "Ye ok?" he asked, tilting his head down. Eric nodded and gave a slight, unsure smile. "Good!" bellowed Charon, "'cause we've got some fishin' to do on that massive lake back there. See if your dad remembers how to sail, eh?" Eric smiled briefly, once more.

"Here ye are," said Ray. He walked toward the villa carrying a rocking chair, similar to the one he had made for himself; but this one had a ship motif carved into the arm and head rests. "I appear to be a dab hand at makin' these things," he laughed. "I've had a ridiculous amount o' requests for them. They're calling me 'Rocking Chair Ray' in Rimel." He placed it in front of his friend, and gave the headrest a push back, letting the rocker do its thing. "Like it?"

"Ah ha ha," blurted Charon, inspecting the gift. "May I?" he gestured.

"Of course."

He sat down and rocked himself back and forth. "Oh, this is excellent," he laughed. "Brunhiíld'll have a job gettin' me out o' this, I can tell ye." He rocked a little more, before standing. "Best not wear it out on the first day, eh?"

Ray shook his head and sighed. "What kind o' carpenter do ye think I am, man?" He pulled the chair back as far as he could, revealing thin metal strips on the base of the rockers. "This thing'll last ye forever."

Charon shook his finger at his friend. "How could I have expected anythin' else?" he laughed, effortlessly picking the chair up, carrying it behind his back. "Was just sayin' to Eric, we should get out on a boat... see if we can't catch some nice fish for our dinner."

"Ye sure ye'd trust me on a boat again?"

"Well," mused Charon. "Ye trusted me in a rockin' chair. What could go wrong?" Charon looked seriously at his friend. "There's somethin' I better tell ye, Ray. Somethin' I should warn ye o'."

"Oh, aye?"

"Aye. We have a visitor; someone Séntinell brought back fae Sólaás. And she's... well, she's..."

"Cissy?"

Charon's eyes turned to the villa's entrance. Astris and Séntinell were making their way out, arms linked, enjoying some light conversation. The girl's eyes shone as she located the voice; eyes that Ray recognised from a lifetime ago. A huge smile crossed her lips.

"Raymond?"

✦✦✦✦✦

Ray's chin dropped. He felt as if he were eighteen again. The girl walked toward him, smiling, just as Cissy had the very time they'd met. "Cissy?" he repeated, his voice cracking as he spoke. Then, almost instantly, his heart sank as the hazel eyes he'd thought he'd seen revealed themselves as a beautiful sky blue.

The girl turned to Séntinell. "Am I *really* so much like her?" she asked.

Séntinell nodded, a warm smile emphasising their agreement. "Oh yes, my dear. You are so like her. I thought my own eyes deceived when I first saw you. And, if you need further confirmation, Raymond also sees the similitude, I feel."

Charon put his hand on Ray's shoulder. "Ray," he said, "this young lady is Astris. Daughter of Helios, younger sister of Circe, and an absolute joy." He looked up to the tall figure and smiled. "Séntinell, here, not so much," he laughed.

Séntinell waved a hand dismissively. "Oh, Master Charon, it is fortunate I know you're only teasing. It is so nice to meet you, Master Raymond." With a bow, they held out a hand. Ray shook it, instinctively, but could not take his eyes off Astris.

"Nice to meet ye," he mumbled. His heart was racing, and his head was a jumble. There, before him, right in front of his eyes, was the face that, so long ago, changed his life.

Astris approached and held her hand out. "You *are* Raymond, aren't you?" she asked. "Séntinell has described you perfectly." Ray shook her hand, his eyes flashing between Astris and Séntinell, unsure how the Lumináry could possibly have described him, the two never having met before. Astris giggled as Ray's hand went up and down. "Is this how people greet on Kiípos?" she chuckled.

"It is customary to kiss the hand, when greeting a Daughter of Sólaás," whispered Séntinell in Ray's ear.

Ray looked at Astris, still dumbfounded. "The hand?" He looked at his own hand, still reciprocating with Astris', as it moved up and down. "Oh, aye... the hand," he acknowledged. He bent forward, raising Astris' hand to his mouth, and gently brushed his lips on the soft back. "I'm...

I'm... Ray... Raymond!" he said. He smiled as he gradually composed himself.

"Ah! You're a smiler, Raymond. I can see why my sister was so taken with you." She giggled again, as she stared into his eyes.

"Smiler?" Ray's eyes teared up. "That's what Cissy used to call me," he said, realising he was still holding Astris' hand in his own.

"I never knew my sisters," said Astris. "You'll have to tell me all about Circe, Raymond. Everyone seems to have had a great love for her."

Ray abruptly released the girl's hand, his attention snapping back to the here and now. "It appears I didn't really know Ciss... *Circe*, either," he said. It was still difficult for him to equate the woman he had loved, with the woman so revered by all in this strange new place. Her sudden appearance, quickly followed by her demise in Hades, was so surreal that, even now, he wasn't sure if it had actually happened. He looked around, searching for Eric. "If you'll excuse me," he continued, "we have some furniture to deliver." He bowed his head and walked back toward the waggon, angry with himself for being so curt with the girl, but more so for thinking she could have been Cissy in the first place.

Séntinell placed their hands on Astris' shoulders. "Please be careful around Raymond and Eric, my dear. They have suffered so much and may not, I fear, have the same appreciation for your visit as the rest of us."

"Yes, Séntinell," Astris replied, her earlier glee diminished. "I sensed a great sadness... a great love; a love with nowhere to go. My sisters have somehow managed to rip this man in two. His heart and mind have both been broken." She stood in thought for several moments. "Perhaps I can..." Her words faded off, and her diamond ring glowed.

Séntinell placed a hand on hers, covering the ring. "As I say, my lady," they cautioned, "I would be very careful, if I were you."

Astris looked up at Séntinell's face, their concern evident. She watched as the man who had loved her sister helped his son remove several items of furniture from the rear of the waggon. "Yes. Yes, Séntinell. Raymond has endured enough from my family, I'm sure. I won't meddle." A sideways glance at the Lumináry, and a subtle smile, suggested otherwise.

༄ ༄ ༄ ༄

Ray couldn't take his eyes away from the mirror. He'd never worn a toga before—a tunic, yes, in the short time he and Eric had stayed here, but never a toga. It felt a little surprising, how well it suited him. He had never actually, even back on Kiípos, worn tailor-made clothing before, but Marro had done a splendid job. His tunics, the shirts and trousers he wore when at Rimel, and now the toga, too, all felt as if made just for him; not his usual off-the-rail bargain finds. It was sky blue, with a darker blue sash, and looked fantastic, even if Ray was still a little uncomfortable with the formality of it all.

A loud '*Bong!*' made him jump; the signal for everyone to head down to dinner. He looked about his suite. It *was* his suite, and *felt* like his suite, as Jacob had arranged for

175

both Ray's and Eric's quarters to be kept exclusively for them both. His natural tidiness was kicking in, making sure that all was in order before leaving. Satisfied, he took a last look in the mirror before heading out.

His and Eric's suites were at either end of a short hallway, and they both emerged from their quarters at the same time. Ray smiled as he saw Eric awkwardly shuffling out, pulling and tugging at the shoulders of his own white toga. "Ye look great, Son," Ray reassured him. He put his arm around the boy's shoulder and they made their way down a longer corridor toward the reception area.

A large square concourse opened before them, with the various diners emerging from several other corridors that led off to the different wings and accommodations of the sprawling villa. Sunlight shone through the large glass panels of the roof dome. The beams seemed to pick out Jacob and Cassandra as they stood by a small circular table, next to four attendants serving drinks from silver trays.

Ray felt a huge, but strange, surge of pride as he watched his youngest son assume the responsibility of leadership. It was still something he found difficulty in accepting; his baby boy now appearing older than himself. Before the rescue at Hades, the last time he'd set eyes on Jacob had been the morning of the car accident. Indeed, the son he'd known had been a far more reserved character, with the blackness, and growing immobility of his leg a constant worry. Now? Now he was the heir apparent; the natural successor to the throne of the universe. The son of a goddess; a goddess that he, Raymond Corrie, had loved.

There would always be, he knew, that constant disappointment at not seeing Jacob grow up. There would also always be the lingering fear and resentment of his and Eric's time imprisoned in the darkness of Hades. His own anxieties were, at times, overwhelming; he could not truly grasp how it felt for Eric, who had been Pasiphae's favourite plaything. It was little wonder the after effects were hammering at the boy every second of every day.

Tonight, however, raised several anxieties of a different kind. The Boulé had arranged a dinner in honour of Astris' visit, with as much pomp and ceremony as they could muster. There was to be a banquet, and speeches, as well as music and dancing. The council members took their places in a line by the doorway to the dining hall, with Archon Lusanne standing, noticeably, slightly apart from the rest; their various spouses maintaining a dignified distance to their side. As yet, there was no sign of Astris, and Ray was unsure as to what was expected of him and Eric.

Astris! Here was another source of anxiety for Ray. He hadn't intended on being rude, but his inner turmoil on seeing the girl had affected him far more than he was prepared to admit. Her similarity to Cissy was remarkable; an identical, yes, perfect, *double* of the older sister she had never met. All except her eyes; those weren't Cissy's eyes. Meeting her had broken his heart all over again, and he was determined that no-one should see his vulnerability, his sorrow, on full display. He had to stay strong for Eric, he reminded himself. He would remain civil... friendly, even... but would minimise his contact with the girl, lest his resolve crumble; and, he knew, it would not take much for his defences to fall.

The two Corrie men walked slowly toward Jacob, but it was Cassandra who noticed them first. She tapped Jacob's shoulder, whispering into his ear, then, with a huge smile, she made her way toward them. "Ray! Eric!" she cheerfully called. "You both look amazing." She embraced, first Ray, then Eric, paying particular attention to the young man's mood and demeanour. "You are sure you feel up to this tonight, Eric?" she asked, her genuine concern unmistakable. The boy smiled, then nodded.

"I'm sure he'd rather have been sittin' on his rocker," laughed Ray, "listenin' tae Jael's dulcet tones, instead o' chaperonin' his dad to a fancy do." Eric blushed, then nudged his dad's side with his elbow.

"Ah, Jael," replied Cassandra, looking over the men's shoulders to an approaching figure. "It's funny you should say that," she smiled, as her eyes met Eric's once more. She nodded in the direction behind him. Eric turned, unsure of what to expect.

Coming slowly, and unsurely, toward him was the most beautiful vision. Looking regal, almost queen-like, in a stunning silver stola, clasped with a large, glistening purple amethyst brooch, Jael shone as brightly as her jewellery. Her normally bobbed hair combed and scraped back, held in place by a matching tiara. Her figure-hugging dress, and bare left shoulder—crowned by her huge smile —made Eric gasp as he saw Jael, the woman, for the very first time.

"Hi, Handsome," she said, in her customary upbeat manner. "I hope I look as good as you do." She leaned forward, allowing Eric to kiss her cheek. He pulled back, holding her hand, as he gasped yet again. He still said nothing, but his smile was the perfect response as far as Jael was concerned.

"Ye look absolutely beautiful, Jael," said Ray, embracing her as he welcomed the girl into their company.

"Thanks, Mr Corrie," she blushed. "I'm not used to getting dressed up."

Ray smiled. "Well, ye have nothin' to worry about. Ye look stunnin'. And it's well beyond time ye called me '*Ray*', eh?" The young woman smiled as, once more, her shining eyes sought Eric's.

"Ray, it is," she said, her hand reaching out for Eric's.

Cassandra kissed Jael's cheek and sighed. "Such grace and beauty," she smiled. "Why has it taken so long for you to steal the show?"

Jael blushed once more, as her eyes sparkled. "Thank you so much, My Lady," she said shyly, reluctant to believe she could be anywhere near as beautiful as her hostess. "It feels so different to what I usually wear," she laughed, "but Lady Jessica assured me I look fine."

"*Fine?*" gasped Cassandra. "You look far more than fine, Jael. You are positively exquisite."

"Perhaps," breathed Jael, "but I don't look like that."

The group turned in the direction of Jael's stare. Entering through the main arch were Séntinell and Astris; the Lady of Solaás drawing the roof dome's sunlight directly to her, like the spotlights shining on the headline act on a stage. The mismatched couple ambled forward, the guests paying their respects, bowing and curtseying, and uttering the expected pleasantries. Astris duly returned the compliments with brief nods of her head, and simple hand gestures. As she came into full view, Ray's heart soared, and a wave of melancholy and longing washed over him. Her form-fitting white, silk stola glowed in the sunlight; her hair shone as it hung forward over her left shoulder, and her eyes sparkled like beautiful blue diamonds. But it was her smile... her *smile*... that grabbed Ray, pulling his heart back to the very first days of his time with Circe.

Cassandra linked arms with him. "The similarities are amazing, aren't they?" she whispered. "You know, Ray, I'm trying my best not to like her, so I don't feel like I'm betraying mother, but it's almost impossible." She patted Ray's hand. "It must feel like that for you, too?"

Ray sighed. "Cissy was everythin' to me. I never got over her, and the hurt was always there, every minute o' every day. I still have no idea what happened... down there... in Hades... but now I'm even more confused. I'm hurt, and I'm angry that I never knew who she really was." He watched Astris make her way toward Jacob. "And now I'm reminded o' her every time I turn around."

Cassandra patted his hand again. "Take comfort, Ray, in knowing you were everything to her, too. Mother talked endlessly of you and Eric. Console yourself knowing she missed you, and she, too, took comfort knowing you were there for the son she never got to know. Well, not until we brought him here." Cassandra's eyes followed Astris; she, too, unable to accept the likeness. "Mother would have given anything to get back to Kíípos to be with you, you know." Jacob caught her eye as he gestured for her to join him in receiving their guests. "I'd best go play hostess," she said, smiling sympathetically at Ray. "Please try to enjoy yourself tonight, Ray. You, more than anyone, could do with a little frivolity in your life."

Ray harrumphed. "I'll try," he said, with as much of a smile as he could raise. He continued watching Astris as she received the welcome from the Boulé members. He recognised the gestures and the movements, identical to the way Cissy would make them, right down to the smile.

As she moved from one councillor to another, she turned, looking straight at him; taking a second to let their eye contact say so much. She smiled, before being introduced to the next official. He felt his heart race, his pulse quicken, and the excitement of his first ever sight of Cissy.

'Oh no,' he thought. 'No' again.'

XIII. FATHER'S DAY

The Sun-God sat low in his throne, lounging back; his elbow resting on the side, his chin resting on his closed right hand. For the first time since the news of Pasiphae's and Circe's demise, he had cause to smile. It had been proving more difficult by the day to watch his last remaining daughter diminish through lack of purpose and direction. The visit—if it could be called that, as it was he who had demanded the attendance of Séntinell—could not have come at a more appropriate time. Astris had been distant for some time. Since the news of the loss of her sisters, Helios could only watch as her spirit, her energy, and her enthusiasm faded, like the final fluttering of a candle's flame caught in a breeze.

She hadn't known her sisters, but had always harboured the hope that, one day, she would travel to Elŷsium to meet Circe. Or, seeing as how she had no wish to visit Hades, Pasiphae would return home for a reconciliation with her parents. Neither of these scenarios was ever likely to happen and now any faint possibility had been crushed. Perse had not made the situation any better for her daughter—continually criticising and comparing her to her siblings, and showing her resentment at every turn.

Sending Astris to Elŷsium was not just a good idea; it was essential if there was to be any meaningful future for the girl. She had nothing to occupy her; she had no interest in any prospective suitors in Solaás, not that anyone came close to being suitable, anyway. Now she could experience something different. He had his own reasons, of course, for having Astris embedded in the higher echelons of Elŷsium's decision makers; his grandson was an unknown quantity—would he be a fitting heir to the throne of Solaás?

The question may have played on Helios' mind, but he was not about to find the answer. His musing was interrupted as the huge throne-room doors burst open with a crash so loud it echoed through the corridors of the entire palace. Helios jumped to his feet as the cause of the commotion made himself known.

A giant blonde stood in the doorway, his golden breastplate and vambraces gleaming as bright as his hair; the white leather pteruges of his skirt falling immaculately down his upper legs. His muscular physique, emphasised by two ornate golden armlets, made an impressive sight as he stretched to his full height. His raised chin and aggressive stance heightened his arrogance and contempt.

"Hello, Father," he said, sarcastically. "Have you missed me?"

"Aeetes!" roared Helios. "Are you mad? You know you should not be here."

Aeetes let out a short, haughty laugh. He glanced behind him to his left, sneering as a long line of Andromedan soldiers filed into the throne room, circling the walls around Helios' seat of power. "What is the meaning of this?" boomed the Sun-God. "Guards! Guards!" He studied the Andromedans curiously. They were man-like, to a certain point, but not the same as men. Their features were, it seemed, incomplete; where men's eyes, noses, cheeks, ears, and mouths had definition and shape, the Andromedans' were like unfinished physiognomies; lacking contour and detail, their clay-like complexion and blank countenance made each look the same as the next. They were identical in every way; their build, height, movement and mannerisms, all exact copies of the other.

Aeetes walked slowly toward his father. "I'm afraid there are no guards left to attend you, Father," he said, shaking his head as he looked at the floor. "Truth be told, they weren't very good guards at all, really. They did not put up much of a fight."

Helios stomped down from the throne, his fury rising, flames flickering on the surface of his skin. "What is the meaning of this, boy? What are these... these... *monstrosities*?"

"Tut, tut, Father. Please don't insult my... children." Aeetes continued ambling toward his father; his slow, deliberate gait bringing an air of menace to the unexpected intrusion. "Though, what do you know of children, Father? You could not wait to be rid of your own." He sidled up to his father and curled his lip. "The divine progenitor of all things, the king of the universe; the one true God!" Aeetes whispered mockingly. "I am surprised you recognise me,

Father. Seeing as I was but a babe when you discarded me to the outer reaches of nowhere."

Confusion was writ large across Helios' bearded face. "You know why we sent you to Andromeda, Aeetes. There cannot be two sun-gods in the same solar system; we would exhaust the finite resources in no time. That's why we gave you Andromeda; to rule; to do with as you wish. Aether was to guide you as you grew; show you how to create wondrous things. Andromeda was to be your very own playground."

"Oh, you gave me a playground, Father, but you never filled it with toys," Aeetes shrieked; the calmness and surety of before replaced by an outburst of anger and frustration. Flames flickered around his frame, his limbs stiffened as his height grew, and he was spitting in his childish tantrum. "You favoured your daughters over me; you gave them everything. You gave a slut—an undeserving slattern—a beautiful gift. And what did the cross-breeding whore do with it? She soiled herself in promiscuity. She sodomised herself with a human; tainted the bloodline of Célestiaá. She was not fit to be your daughter; not fit to be your favourite. *I* was your first-born. *I* should have been your favourite!"

Helios laughed loudly; a huge, roaring belly-laugh. "This is what peeves you, boy? That your sister received a tiny gift?" He roared with laughter again.

Aeetes shook with anger. "Do not mock me, Father. I warn you!"

"Oh, you warn me, do you, boy?" Helios looked his son up and down, his disappointment tempering his laughter. "You were always a querulous child. From birth, you were given to complaining; a peevish, grumbling little nuisance of a boy. There was always some grievance or other, even before you had your sisters to outshine you."

Aeetes' anger rose. His fists clenched ever tighter, his muscles flexed as his limbs shook. His flaming body stretched ever higher.

"Your temper was the real reason we sent you away. Even as a baby, your volatility was a danger to us all. Once you became a toddler, you were far too much to handle. That's why Aether suggested creating Andromeda for you. We had hoped you would calm yourself as you grew. Obviously not."

"You gave the whore Kiípos!"

"I gave Circe a *rock*," bellowed Helios. "She *created* Kiípos! She created Kiípos with her imagination, her ingenuity, and with her love. She made a world. She made life. She created *miracles* and made her father proud!"

Tears ran down Aeetes' face as his fury exploded into terrible, murderous action. His blazing right arm swung toward the head of his father, the flaming sword striking swiftly and true. He did not look. There was no need; he knew the outcome of his attack. He stepped forward, up the steps to the throne, smiling as his father's decapitated body fell quietly upon the gleaming tiles below.

Aeetes sat on the throne, closing his eyes and inhaling deeply through his nose, his massive body shrinking down to its normal size as the flames subsided. "Ah, so good to be home again. And now I am King!" He stared down at his father.

"Tell me, Father. Are you *now* proud of your little boy?"

Perse came running through the throne room doors, three of her maids scurrying behind. The news of Aeetes' return had reached her gynaeceum and, despite her reservations of him being in Solaás, the excitement of seeing her son had blinded her to the consequences.

As she entered, she collided with an Andromedan soldier; recoiling in disgust at the repugnant features of the man—if it *was* a man. It took several seconds to realise that he, and his companion, were dragging a body—a large, headless body—out through the doorway. As they passed, she did a double take, her delayed reaction making her doubt what she was seeing. The golden tunic, the red fibulae, even the build of the decapitated man were all too familiar, and her joy at the return of her son evaporated instantly.

She stopped in her tracks, holding her hand out toward her dead husband. "Helios?" she whimpered. "Helios, is that you?" Her eyes turned to the throne, where her son sat between two massive soldiers. Aeetes slouched lazily, almost lying on the seat, his legs apart; unconcerned his genitals were on full view. On the top step, between his spread-eagled limbs, Helios' severed head stared out. "Aeetes?" Perse called. "What have you done, Aeetes?"

Aeetes glanced in the direction of his mother's voice. "Ah, Mother!" he replied. "Come kneel before your new king." He remained slumped in his seat, gesturing his mother to approach. Perse traipsed toward her son, her footsteps heavy and unsteady. Tears streamed down her cheeks, but she wasn't sobbing; she wasn't anything. Shock gripped her, rendering her silent as she slowly made her way to the throne. She stopped at the base of the steps, staring at her son.

"Cover yourself, Aeetes," she snapped, averting her eyes. "Remember where you are! Remember who I am!"

"I said kneel!" Aeetes yelled, lurching forward on the throne, pointing to the floor. "Kneel before your king!" Perse, wiping her tears, remained standing, in defiance at what she was hearing. "*Kneel!*" screamed her son once more, his anger bringing him to his feet, the first flickering of flame licking his skin. He glared at his mother, his eyes bulging. "Chiliarch," he said, to the soldier to his right. "Have your men kill one of the maids." The Andromedan officer gestured to a soldier by the doorway, who then took a step forward and grabbed one of the screaming maids by her hair. In an instant, he had pulled her head back and run his sword across her throat. The two remaining maids screamed again, huddling together; their peer slumping forward as the soldier released his hold.

As the lifeless woman dropped to the floor in a pool of blood, Perse stared incredulously. She turned to her son in disgust. "What are you doing, Aeetes?" she pleaded. "These girls have done no wrong."

"I said, '*kneel*'!" he repeated. Perse reluctantly lowered herself to her knee. "That's better, Mother," he said as he retook his seat. "You wouldn't want to lose all your maids on our first day together, would you?" He tapped the Chiliarch's arm and pointed to the dead woman. "Get that thing out of my sight, Chiliarch. My throne room is no place for such unpleasant clutter."

"Aeet...," began Perse.

"Quiet, woman! You will speak only when your king allows." He held his hand up, silencing her, and watched as his soldiers dragged the dead maid through the doors, leaving a thin red trail as a reminder of his limited patience. "That's better," Aeetes murmured, sighing as he relaxed back in the throne. "Now, Mother, you may kiss my hand." His right arm thrust forward; straight, stiff—his fingers wriggling as they dangled before Perse.

"Why are you doing this?" she asked. "Your father...?"

"Kiss my hand, Mother."

"But, Aeetes... you've killed your father..."

"Kiss my fucking hand, woman!" he screeched. "Or shall we cull another servant?"

Perse swithered for a second, silently demurred, and leaned forward, hesitating for a second as Helios' Nuclei Ring thrust up in her face. Aeetes' fingers wriggled once more and Perse grudgingly brushed them with her lips. She rested back in her kneeling position. "May I stand now?" she asked sarcastically.

"Yes, yes, yes," he replied curtly. "Tell me, Mother, are you happy to see your son once more? The son you disowned so long ago?" He stared; his eyes drilling in to her as she stood.

Perse smoothed down her stola, then shook her head, allowing her long hair to fall back behind her shoulders, regaining her composure. "You were never disowned, Aeetes. You were allowed to grow, in a safe space for us all, but it meant that we had to separate you from your father. That's what happened; you know this."

"You sent me into exile!"

"You were not exiled," Perse snapped back, furious at her son's petulance. "We gave you your very own solar system; the largest space in existence; to do with as you pleased. And yet, here you sit, back in Solaás, and your first act is to commit patricide. How could you?"

"Actually, Mother, it was very easy—but it wasn't my first act. My first act was to remove the Imperial Guard. Father really should have protected himself better. But, alas, he could not learn from his errors, could he?"

"Why are you here, Aeetes?"

Aeetes held his hands out, gesturing to everything around them. "Why, I have returned to claim my inheritance, Mother. I have come to rule. I have come to bathe in the luxuriant tribute so enjoyed by my father; the tribute denied me when you sent me off to fend for myself. And, as it appears you have lost your beloved daughters, I would say now is the ideal time to do so."

"Your inheritance? You were told that your inheritance was here for you; safe, for when you would succeed Helios. You would then unite Andromeda with this solar system. You should know this, boy; Aether was to educate you on these matters. Until Helios' natural demise, you were to learn, and grow in Andromeda."

"'*Helios' natural demise*'. An interesting turn of phrase." Aeetes raised his leg, resting his foot on the throne, once more exposing his genitalia. He laughed at his mother's comments, and her disgust. "You expected me to wait another seven billion years before I could eat at your table? To remain alone in a distant kingdom; on a throne of no importance; with no wife to pleasure me, no heir to succeed me? And, all the while you intended allowing Circe's runt to supplant me as ruler?" He laughed once more, before dropping all expression on his face. "I have had enough of loneliness. I have had enough of a barren rock. I have had enough!" he screamed.

Perse's chin dropped, her mouth falling open in shock. "You are Célestiaá. You are a world-builder. Are you telling me that, in all the time you have been master of Andromeda..."

"King! King of Andromeda!" Aeetes corrected.

"... King... of Andromeda. In all the time you have been King of Andromeda, you never thought to create a life-form of your own? It never occurred to you that you could simply think yourself a wife; create her from the abundance of elements at your disposal? You never tried to create cities, or a people of your own?"

Aeetes looked about the room. "Do you not see the people I created, woman? Do you not see the *monstrosities* I have surrounding me?" The Chiliarch flinched at the slight. "Do these look like I succeeded? And do you think the females are any better? That I would lie with one of these... these... gargoyles? Had I the same patronage from father as Circe, or Pasiphae, then perhaps these malformations would have some aesthetic appeal—but I would *never* place my seed into one of them. I am not like my whore of a sister; content to lie with the creatures... the pets... she created. No, in my kingdom, Célestiaá blood will remain pure." He waved his hand dismissively. "But that is not important. I am here now for my rightful claim."

"Your rightful claim? You have murdered your father; what is rightful about that?"

"I will have my tribute. I will have Kiípos, and I will claim a queen. Tell me, Mother. Where is my sister? Aster?"

"Astris!" corrected Perse. "Your sister's name is Astris. And she will not be your queen."

"She will be queen if the king deigns it so." He took hold of his scrotum and held his testicles up, as if on display. "She shall perform her wifely duties; pleasuring me, producing an heir for me. She shall lie down in my bed; shall satisfy me; shall take my seed and be mother to my son."

"Don't be ridiculous, Aeetes," laughed Perse. "You cannot marry your sister."

Aeetes sat up straight once more. "You mock me again, Mother? You? You who whored out your daughter to our uncle; as soon as she was fuckable? You dare tell me what I can do?"

Perse feared his anger rising once more. "She is not here, Aeetes. She has left Sólaás."

"Left Sólaás? And where has she disappeared to, Mother? I shall have her return. Chiliarch, have a search party prepare for a trip to... Mother?"

"You will send no search party. She has gone to Elŷsium on an investigative trip for... for your father."

Aeetes smiled. "Elŷsium? Circe's fabled utopia? So, it exists after all," he mused. "A stepping stone to Kiípos. Now, that is very interesting, Mother. Am I to take it that my mongrel nephew is now King of Elŷsium?"

"There is no king of Elŷsium, but, yes, he has assumed stewardship since Circe's death."

"Then he shall have no problem bowing to his new king, then?" Aeetes sat back on the throne. "I shall have my army visit Elŷsium. My nephew will kneel before me, swear all life essence to me in tribute, and Aster shall become my queen." He fondled his scrotum once more. "In the meantime, Mother, *you* shall serve as my concubine; show me the love that I so sorely missed out on."

A sickening wave of nausea ran down Perse's shaking frame. "Your... *what*?" She blurted. "I shall do no such thing, Aeetes. I am your mother. How can you..."

"You are a woman; you have one purpose only. You will come to my bed, Mother, and perform your *womanly* duties. You shall spread your legs, and you will pleasure me; treat me like the king I am. If you refuse, or fail to please me, I shall have my soldiers work their way through your court; one by one, fucking, then removing the heads of your maids, your servants, and your courtiers. If you fail to please me, I shall pass you on to my Chiliarch, here; I am sure he would delight in the soft pleasures of a divine woman. Wouldn't you, Chiliarch?" The soldier stiffened at his post, uncomfortable at Aeetes' suggestion. Perse could feel herself stumble as she fainted, collapsing at the base of the throne steps.

Aeetes smirked. "Is that any way to welcome your first born, Mother?' He gestured to the Chiliarch. "Pick her up and take her to my suite. I am going to enjoy myself tonight."

XIV. ENTER ÉLEMENTAÁ

Katie and Melanie took their time saddling the horses, making sure their backpacks were complete, and that both were certain of what they had to do; and how they were going to go about it. The weeks of training had been tough but, Chiyoko assured them, they were both ready for their first outing as Élementaá; not, as they had been expecting, a recruiting mission, but a simple task, chosen by Cassandra, of freeing their former friends at the stables. If they were still there; if they were still alive.

They had learned some, but nowhere near all, of the swords and stones capabilities, but were still wary of what Cassandra had called the 'Diávasi', the 'inter-dimensional crossing'. The gate was a large, inscribed arch, built at the rear of the lakeside garden behind Strath-sealgair Villa, surrounded by cypresses, willow and ash trees. This was to be the first time they'd used the gate without Cassandra's assistance.

"The Diávasi is probably better known to you as a wormhole; a tunnel with two ends at separate, specific points in space," explained Cassandra. "They can be different locations; Elŷsium, Kiípos... even exact points on Kiípos. They may even, when required, bridge the gap to Sólaás and Hades. It is, I understand, possible to travel to different points in time, although we haven't quite figured how to do that yet."

She gave a little laugh, still feeling a little overwhelmed at the new resources and responsibilities given to her, but, seeing the questioning looks on the women's faces, their horror at her own uncertainty, she quickly regained her composure. "The tunnel is extremely short, barely noticeable, in fact. You enter and then, a few seconds later, you exit. Even when you travel from one point on Kiípos to another, you enter the gate, pass through here on Elŷsium, and continue through to your exit point. All in a few seconds. It's really amazing once you get used to it."

All they had to do was concentrate on the destination Diávasi—in this case Geata Dhè—then ride their horses through the light that the stones created in the arch. Simple, but still terrifying, particularly as they had no idea what they would find on exiting at Geata Dhè.

Jacob, Cassandra, and Ella—taking a break from her studies on Lunaá—had all come to see the women off. Cassandra took their hands, proud of how quickly they had reached this stage of their training. "You look strong. You look ready," she said. "I want to remind you both, there are no restrictions on what actions you take. No barriers to what you may do. You live by your own morals, your own decisions. If anyone... *anyone*... gets in your way, you have divine authority to remove the problem in whatever way you choose. You are your own law. You are Élementaá; Soldiers of Elŷsium."

Cassandra gave both women a long, tight hug before Jacob did likewise. "Ye'll remember that wee favour I asked?" he said to Katie. Katie nodded. "There're a couple o' wee things I need to do for myself anyway," she added. She turned to Ella and embraced the little girl. "Mummy won't be away too long. You keep workin' hard, and listen to Selêne, eh?"

The Earth Mother smiled and, sounding more mature and wise by the day, added, "I will, Mummy. You take care, and look after Melanie and Crumbles too. I love ye." It astounded Katie at how calm her daughter was; how accepting she had been with everything that had already been thrown at her. She held her hand out, offering a small canvas bag to Melanie. "A wee gift, so ye don't get hungry," she smiled.

Melanie took the bag and, loosening the draw-strings, peered, curiously, inside. "What's this?" she asked, poking her finger into what seemed dry soil.

The little girl giggled. "Ye'll see soon enough," she said, cryptically. "Ye just need a drop o' water." Ella gave Crumbles a final hug, then stepped back, taking Cassandra's hand.

"I'll take good care o' him, Ella," Melanie called, as she mounted Crumbles. "I promise." She guided the horse around toward the Diávasi, then looked over to Katie. "Well, here goes nothin', eh?"

"How far will the light go on?" asked Katie.

"Only about fifty paces," said Cassandra. "Then you'll see the other side. Take a breath before you exit, ready yourself for what you might find there. It will already be very different to what you left behind. Good luck, ladies."

The horses moved off, as if on just another walk. The light didn't frighten them as they slowly faded from view, like they were disappearing into fog. "We just have to wait now," said Jacob, squeezing Ella's hand.

Ella smiled. "Mummy needs to do this, Jacob. She never tells me what daddy did to her, but I know he was cruel." Jacob squeezed again. "Her and Melanie need to find themselves. Then they'll both be happier."

"How old are ye again, little lady?"

"I'm as old as I need to be," she replied with a cheeky smile.

✦✦✦✦

The horses strolled casually along the grass. The light, although not blinding, obscured the women's visibility of the surroundings. As they walked, they noticed the lengthening grass in the distance, and increasing numbers of fallen yellow birch leaves scattered everywhere. As they came to the edge of the light, the land opened before them; Geata Dhè.

They found themselves in the centre of the stones; wind and rain blowing fiercely into their faces, autumn leaves swirling about the overgrown, untended clearing. "Fuckin' brilliant," moaned Melanie. "It's pissin' down an' I've no' brought a coat." Katie felt the rain hitting her face and arms, felt the wind gust in her face and hair, but, strangely, there was no sense of feeling cold. The autumn chill, the wind, the rain, it was happening around them, not to them.

"Are ye cold, Melanie?"

The younger woman halted her horse. "No. Now ye mention it, I'm no'. My clothes feel wet, but I still feel warm. What the fuck?" She patted Crumbles on the neck. "Walk," she whispered. Bentley and Crumbles ambled forward, toward what was once the car park, and the light faded behind them. Jacob's abandoned blue car sat where he'd left it that fateful night. Nature continued reclaiming the area as grass, weeds and an assortment of other wild plants hid the now unused ground. The snacks kiosk looked much the worse for wear, as months of abandonment, neglect and the terrible weather had all taken its toll. As with the car, a wreath of golden leaves surrounded the base.

"What time do ye think it is?"

"I'm no' sure," said Katie. "It might be late afternoon, but the weather's shit enough to be any time o' day. Let's head down, see what the story is at the stables, eh?" They headed into the trees, onto what used to be a well-worn path for the horses; now, like everything else, unused and overgrown. The wind howled through the trees, with tremendous gusts throwing waves of dead leaves everywhere.

"That wasn't so hard, was it?" Melanie asked.

"Easier than I thought it was goin' to be," replied Katie. "The horses didn't even blink." She patted Bentley's neck, then smiled. "Beats showin' that awful fuckin' passport photo I had." They both laughed.

"I never had a passport," Melanie stated thoughtfully. "I've never been anywhere, really, except Glenaffric and Strath-sealgair. Me an' my pal did go to Glasgow once; sightseein' an' shopliftin'." She frowned at the thought of what used to make her happy, of what filled her old life. "And Elŷsium now, o' course. Fuck's sake... talk about extremes, eh?"

"I think we're gonna be seein' a fair bit o' the world if we're to get all o' these lassies for Élementaá."

"I'm still no' sure what this is all about, Katie. I know I nodded along wi' all o' the trainin', and the instructions, and everythin', but I'm still no' sure whit we're doin', no' really. Didna want to ask daft questions... come across as a stupid fucker. And the swords... the stones. Élementaá. What the fuck?"

"Well, we're building a team o' women to change the fuckin' world. To take it back from men. Ye get that bit, eh? And to do that, we need to find all o' these names I've been... well, *given*. This list o' names and places, all over the fuckin' world."

"Aye, I do get that bit," said Melanie. "But I don't have a clue what the fuck they were on about wi' the swords and the stones."

"Don't worry, I picked up some o' it." Katie assured her. "We'll get a chance to test these things while we're here, but, basically, they help us control the elements; to a certain extent. Watch this, I've been practicin'." Katie brought Bentley to a halt, then effortlessly unsheathed her sword from behind her. She held the sword out at arm's length. "If I concentrate, through the stones, to the sword I can..." She stared at the sword, for a few seconds. Nothing happened.

"Very impressive," said Melanie, clapping her hands. Katie frowned at her, then smiled.

"Shut the fuck up," she laughed. "Just keep watchin'." Katie refocused her concentration, staring once again at the sword. After a few seconds, she could feel a warmth flow through her, down from the stones; down her arm, out through the sword, the inscriptions glowing brightly. The surrounding rain fell toward the sword, onto the blade, as if being magnetically pulled to it.

"Ye fucker," exclaimed Melanie. "How the fuck are ye doin' that?"

"Keep watchin'," said Katie. Her face was showing signs of strain, as the physical effort drained the energy from her. She looked to a tree by the side of the path, then swung her arm toward it. The water shot toward the tree, in a concentrated stream, as if from a high-powered hose, breaking the surface bark. Katie held her arm steady for a few seconds before it dropped, exhaustion winning over. "Oh ye fucker, gi'e me a minute," Katie said, swaying a little in her saddle. "That's dizzy."

"Now, that was fuckin' impressive." Melanie gave a genuine round of applause this time. "How did ye do that? Can I do it?" The horses resumed their stroll as Katie regained her composure.

"I was practicin' in the bath; damn near drowned myself," she laughed. "Were you no' listenin' to anythin' they said? The gods that we met... Naátúr...? Well, Poseidon kept goin' on about drawin' the moisture, the very elemints o' water from the air, and the ground. He said it was 'at our disposal', our command, if we needed it. The same goes wi' the other stuff, apparently. Hephaestus said that if we have a spark, then we have fire and, if we have fire..!"

"Aye, ye listened to Poseidon right enough," Melanie laughed. "There was definitely a wee spark there, if I'm no' mistaken. Did he teach ye that in a 'private lesson'?"

Katie laughed. "Oh, fuck off," she replied. "I was just interested in what he was sayin'... the science, and..."

Melanie snorted. "The fuckin' science, my arse. Ye were flutterin' yer fuckin' eyelashes like a butterfly in fuckin' heat. An' I'm sure those tits o' yours grew an inch or two every time he looked at ye. And that walk..." Both women laughed uncontrollably as Melanie swayed her hips from side to side, almost falling off Crumbles.

Katie wiped the rainwater from her face. There was a pain in her side from laughing so furiously. "I had to listen carefully," she said. "They were ramblin' on at such a pace. I'm sure they thought we were far more intelligent than we really are." She looked at Melanie and laughed again. "Well, one o' us, anyway."

Melanie laughed again. "I was shit at science when I was at school... when I actually went to school. Was too busy fuckin' about wi' the lads, keepin' them on a string." She paused for a few seconds, thinking back on how she'd wasted her previous life. "Now, if I'd had a teacher like Poseidon..." The two women laughed again.

"He is a bit o' a hunk, isn't he?"

"He's no' what I thought Poseidon would be," said Melanie. "I thought he'd be a big, burly, beardy guy wi' curly hair... holdin' a trident and smellin' o' fish!"

"Aye," agreed Katie. "But he looks more like a... more like a..."

"A *teacher*!" they both chorused. They strolled on quietly, lost in their own thoughts.

"But he's no' Jacob, is he?" asked Melanie.

Katie looked ahead. "No. He's no' Jacob." She brought Bentley to a stop. "But we've got a job to do." She nodded ahead. Through the trees they could make out the outlines of the stable buildings, looking dark and sombre through the heavy grey rain.

"We'll tie these two up here," said Katie, already dismounting quickly. "We'd best keep a low profile 'til we figure out what we're up against." Melanie nodded as she, too, dismounted. She fumbled in her saddlebag for a biscuit, then scrunched it in her hand before allowing Crumbles his little treat.

❦❦❦❦

They carefully made their way down the last little slope toward the rear gate. Crouching low as they broke from the tree line, they ran toward the back wall of the stable; sidling along, listening and watching. At the end of the building, they paused, before Katie made a quick dart across the gate to the edge of the adjoining building.

She peered around the corner, into the yard. There was nothing. No one. Silence, save for the hissing of the constant downpour. The yard looked abandoned, with grass and weeds poking through the once-immaculate cobbles. The water trough sat idle, the fountain no longer working, with overflowing water spewing over the side. The heavy rain, and gloominess of the light added a melancholy to the space; a sorrow at the demise of what had once been a huge part of her life; what was, for a time, her entire life.

Feeling a little braver, Katie poked her head around the corner, looking down the entire length of the main block. At the far corner of the yard, a top half door swung loosely in the wind; an occasional creaking breaking through the hissing of the wind and rain. "Who the fuck dae we have here, then?"

The women turned, looking behind them in the voice's direction. A frowzy man stood at the edge of the tree line, his rifle raised, pointing directly in their direction, swaying between one and the other. Tall, unshaven, and looking as though he hadn't washed for some time, his long brown raincoat was torn at the left shoulder. He was calm and deliberate in his actions, stepping slowly forward.

Katie raised her hands above her head, gently pushing her chest out. "Well, hello there," she said, a welcoming smile on her face. "No need to be pointin' that thing at me, is there?" The man stared at her, keeping the gun trained directly at her.

"Who the fuck are..."

In a split second, Melanie cut off his words and flipped forward; her sword swiping sideways in a blur, slicing effortlessly through the midriff of the assailant. A dull thud, as the two halves of his body hit the ground, removed the threat as the girl knelt on one knee, her sword arm extended to her right; a perfect, elegant finish to the move, just as Chiyoko had taught.

Behind him, a young boy, of no more than sixteen, stood rigid with terror. His milky white face a sheet of fear. He dropped his rifle and raised his hands. A scrawny lad, he wore filthy jeans and, under a tattered green bomber jacket—that did little to keep the rain out—he wore a black T-shirt. "Please dinna kill me," he pleaded with a whimper.

"What's yer name?" asked Katie, moving quickly to kick the firearms from the reach of the second interloper.

"Grayser. Billy Gray. But everybody calls me 'Grayser'."

"This yer dad, Billy?"

"Naw. That's Sinbad. Harry Milne, was his name. He was a bit o' a cunt; kept goin' on aboot his time in the Merchant Navy, but he didna deserve…" The boy looked at Melanie. "Please dinna kill me." He was quivering, crying. Melanie wiped her blade on the dead man's leg, then re-sheathed it.

"Ye're safe… fer now," she said.

Katie looked down at Harry's severed parts. "Fuck's sake, Mel. He's no' gonna be much use to us now, is he?"

"Wasn't lettin' him fire off a shot at us." Melanie nodded toward the boy. "Anyway, the young lad'll gi'e us the info we need. Won't ye, Billy?" Billy stood shaking, staring down at Harry, sobbing and choking; mumbling unintelligibly to himself. "Billy!" snapped Melanie.

"Please dinna slice me in half," he pleaded.

"Where is everybody, Billy?" The boy continued staring at Harry. Melanie clicked her fingers in front of his eyes. "Billy!" she snapped again. "Where is everybody?" He flicked his eyes to Melanie, then Katie, then finally back to Harry.

"Dunno," he mumbled. "They left o'er a week ago, when they heard the army was gonna be here soon. Harry was sick, couldna go, so they told me tae stay wi' him. Had tae keep an eye oot for the soldiers, let them know how many, an' stuff." Katie wiped the rain from her face again.

"The women... the girls who were here... what happened to them?" she asked.

"Dunno," he mumbled again. The fear returned immediately as Katie had, without warning, drew her sword and placed it at his throat. The blade moved so quickly, it nicked Billy's Adam's Apple as he completed the word.

"I think ye do know, ye little shit," Katie said, calmly, and with such menace that Billy could feel the warm spread of his urine in his groin; the trickle of the stream down the inside of his right leg. "How could ye tell them about the soldiers if ye didna know where they went?"

"Please dinna kill me," he repeated.

"Please dinna fuck us about," said Katie. "We're no' in the mood to be fucked about. Okay?" Billy nodded slightly, wary of catching the blade's edge again. "Where are the girls?" she asked again.

"They took them, and the four horses..."

"Four?" exclaimed Katie. "There's only four horses? What the fuck happened to the rest o' them?"

"As they got sick, or lame, or whatever, they just shot them... butchered them for food. They dragged the remains aroun' the back o' the sheds there." He pointed behind the main stable block.

"And the girls?" asked Katie. "What about the girls?"

Billy's eyes involuntarily flicked toward the last unit. He started crying again. "I had nuthin' tae dae wi' it," he sobbed. Katie nodded for Melanie to go look inside the stable. "Once Giles was gone, Mull took o'er. He said that he didna gi'e a fuck aboot the lassies, that the guys could dae whatever they wanted tae keep them in line, keep them workin'. They left *her* as Harry's payment... tae keep him happy."

Melanie dragged the stable door open, peering inside. "Oh fuck," she squealed as she fell to her knees. "Katie!"

Katie nodded for Billy to go toward the open door. "I had nuthin' tae dae wi' it. Ye've got tae believe me."

Katie walked slowly toward the stable, sheathing her sword. As she approached, her eyes adjusted to the darkness inside. Through the dim light, near the rear of the space, she could see the naked body of a girl. Ropes had been tied around each of her wrists, then pulled tightly above her head, around the roof joists and stable posts, hoisting her arms so high her toes barely touched the floor. A further rope had been tied around her ankles and secured to a wooden tie post. Lengths of filthy, straw-like hair covered her face as it fell toward the floor. Her malnourished, skeletal frame was bruised and bloody; her feet were bloated lumps, with chunks missing where the rats had been enjoying themselves.

Melanie rose, then walked toward the girl, her tear-filled eyes drilling a hole into Billy's. Her sword came slowly from its sheath, before swinging through the ankle restraint. She put her arm around the body, taking its weight, before cutting the arm ties, catching the girl and laying her gently onto the dirt and straw on the floor. She knelt and leaned over, wiping the strands of dry hair away from the girl's face. "It's Claire," sobbed Melanie. "It's Claire."

There had been no love lost between the two girls but, seeing the beaten, broken result of her captors' abuse, brought an immense feeling of guilt to Melanie. Claire had always been a tough, uncompromising character, but always popular with everyone, always standing up for her friends. Except Melanie, of course. They were both far too strong willed to be friends, but now, seeing her like this, Melanie was realising just what she had missed out on in her earthly life. Being alone had always been shit, and, if only she could have seen it, Claire would have been an amazing, loyal friend.

She continued wiping Claire's face, removing the dirt with the bottom of her wet vest. She jumped as the girl's eyelids flickered and slowly opened. "She's still alive, Katie," Melanie exclaimed. "She's still alive." Katie crouched beside them, pulling her water bottle from her belt.

"Give her some water, Mel."

"She's tryin' to say somethin'." Melanie leant closer. "McGrory's... she's sayin' they've gone to McGrory's." She carefully placed the water bottle to Claire's mouth, tipping a few drops onto her parched, cracked lips. With a whip of her arm, her hunting knife flew, catching Billy in the throat, forcing him back as the tip sank into the door's timber frame. The boy dropped his rifle, his arms falling limp. Blood oozed from around the sunken blade as Billy gurgled and coughed, his eyes bulging, his breathing spluttering; his sneak attack, from behind their busy backs, halted.

"Fuck!" said Katie, walking over and kicking the rifle away once more. "Ye sneaky little bastard. Well, ye can just hang there for now. Hope that fuckin' hurts, ye little shit." She turned back to Melanie and Claire, kneeling beside her former employee.

"Is that you, Kathy?" she squeaked, her eyelids flickering as she tried to focus. "We all thought ye were deid."

Melanie gave her a few more drops of water. "Sshh," Melanie advised. "Don't try to talk."

The wounded girl's eyes flicked over. "Melanie?"

"Sshh, don't worry. I'm no' gonna hurt ye."

Claire smiled as much as she could manage. "No, I know ye winna." She coughed weakly, and blood spilled out of her mouth. "I've been waitin' fer the angels, an' I see ye now, Melanie. I see ye now."

Katie held her hand. "We'll get ye out o' here... someplace warm, get ye..."

Claire shook her head. "No," she whispered. "They raped me, and battered me. They've broken most o' my bones... I'm tired. I'm done." Tears began seeping from the corners of her eyes. "Finish me, Kathy. Please. The pain's too much." She tried to squeeze Katie's hand.

Katie's head sank, but she nodded her agreement, as she slowly reached behind her and removed her hunting knife. Cradling Claire's head in her arms, she bent over and whispered to the girl. "Close yer eyes, Claire, yer pain here's at an end. In a few seconds, ye'll be on yer way to Elŷsium. There, ye'll be amongst friends and family. Bless ye." She slowly drew her blade across the wounded girl's throat, and kissed her forehead as the last flickers of life faded away. Katie took Melanie's hand as both women shed a farewell tear for the dead woman.

"We have to bury her," sobbed Melanie. As they stood, Billy reminded them of his presence, gurgling and twitching away behind them. Melanie's hunting knife, thrown with such massive force, pinned him to the frame. He hung there, staring fearfully; his arms and legs giving an involuntary jerk every few seconds. The knife had pierced through the rear of his neck, sinking solidly into the wood. "He's just a fuckin' boy, for fuck's sake," said Melanie.

"Aye, he's just a boy, right enough," agreed Katie. "But he's a boy who's already learned that a woman is worth less than nothing. Thank you, Billy," Katie said, dryly. "We didn't really need a reminder, but..." She pulled the knife out with a twist, then watched the boy's body slump to the ground. "Now we *know* why we're here."

XV. THE THOLOS OF CIRCE

"You know what you possess, don't you, Cassandra?" Astris held Cassandra's hand, scrutinising the Célestiaá Ring, admiring the craftsmanship, the delicate detail, and the sheer beauty of the glistening gems. "I mean, you are aware of the monumental power you wear on your finger?" She looked up to see Cassandra's eyes also scanning the jewels.

"I know *of* its power," she confirmed. "But, as yet, neither I nor Jacob have been able to master its abilities." She sighed. "If Mother were here, we would not be struggling to provide for the influx of new souls. We would create the food, the accommodations, the weapons and whatever else we need. If Mother were here..." She sighed again, and turned, looking out from the veranda into the garden, toward the Tholos. "If Mother were here, the Boulé would not be thwarting me at every turn, and I would not be failing Mother's trust in me."

Cassandra turned again, facing Astris once more. The young Princess of Sólaás was smiling, her face bright with youthful exuberance. "But she is here," she said. "She has always been here. I'm sure of it now." Her wide eyes shone, her words suggestive of a clear oversight on Cassandra's part.

"I don't…" Cassandra was confused. Astris took her hand once more, and pulled her, insisting she follow. The girl stepped down from the veranda, eagerly making for the magnificent white structure.

"I sensed it as soon as I arrived here," she explained. "Circe's essence. It's here, all around us, everywhere, in everything, in everyone."

"That's a nice sentiment, Astris, but I don't…"

"Oh, it's not just a sentiment, Cassandra. It's the truth. I sense her… I can feel her… I can *hear* her." Her left hand gripped Cassandra's right hand so tightly, it hurt as she pulled. Astris pointed to the Tholos. "There! There is where we will find her!"

"At the Tholos?" Cassandra's head was in a spin. "But the Tholos is just a monument. A memorial. A place for us to remember her."

"Oh, it's much more than that, Cassandra. And we Célestiaá are not as easily dispensed with as you may think." She giggled. "The souls of Kiípos may have a finite existence, but not so the descendants of Sólaás. Our life energy will always return to the universe; will always exist in some form or other. Not… living… as such, but… well… as a presence." She stopped, almost as quickly as she had begun, looking, with great interest, at the carvings and inscriptions on the columns. "All we have to do," she muttered, as she made off once again, "is figure out how to bring her here."

Cassandra gasped. It had never occurred to her, or anyone else for that matter, that Circe would not simply die, as humans or animals die. Could it be possible? Could they, as Astris seemed to think, bring Circe back from wherever her essence had gone? If that were the case, then why had Circe shown her the vision? Why the battlefield, the young boy on the horse, the mysterious enemy? If she had known they could bring her back, why wouldn't Circe show how they should do that?

Astris was working her way from one column to the next; mumbling to herself as she ran her fingers over the engravings; her eyes darting up and down the columns, inspecting the etchings. No, not inspecting, *reading*. The ancient runes were not, as Cassandra thought, merely beautiful symbols—intricate decorations—they were columns of text; instructions. Astris let out a delighted squeal, quickly clapping her hands as she found what she was looking for.

She ran down the steps, back to Cassandra, her face beaming with delight at her success. "There is a way," she declared, "but, if I'm correct, we will need Séntinell's help."

"We can bring Mother back?" Cassandra felt giddy, as if drunk with excitement, overwhelmed by the mere thought of the possibility.

Sensing the hope she had built, Astris suddenly realised that, perhaps, a little caution may be required. "I don't think we can bring her back in physical form," she said, an attempt to lower the Princess of Troy's soaring, delirious expectations. "But, her consciousness, her being, her spark... we may reach that. We may be able to rescue her ethereal light... her spiritual existence." As much as she was trying to manage Cassandra's hopes, Astris could not contain her own excitement, nodding frantically as she considered the possibilities before them.

Cassandra fell to her knees, her heart thumping, her joy seeping out from her in a river of tears. "Oh, how I would so much love to set eyes on Mother once more. Even if only for a second."

Astris knelt before her, throwing her arms around Cassandra's neck, resting her forehead on Cassandra's. "Then let us at least try."

As their long, thin fingers traced their way down the column, feeling the indentations and carvings, Séntinell hummed and nodded; conducting, it seemed, a one-sided, internal conversation. Pausing occasionally, looking around to their companions with sometimes a frown, or a questioning gaze; before returning to their inner dialogue.

After some time, Séntinell turned, resting their left arm across their chest, their right forefinger tapping their lips. "Well?" asked Astris. "Am I right? Is it possible?" Séntinell sighed, then hummed once more. They looked back over their shoulder, as if to make sure the column was still there; still showing the same markings.

"I have to agree that the texts suggest so," confirmed the tall figure.

"Yes!" exclaimed Astris, making a little jump of celebration as she punched the air.

"But, and I must stress this," added The Lumináry, "I have never heard of such actions ever being discussed, or even mentioned, at any time, in any place, by either Célestiaá or man." Séntinell lowered their head, peering down their nose at Astris. "In fact," they continued, "I find it most interesting that Elŷsium's masons knew and understood pre-civilisation Hellenés."

They leaned forward lowering themselves to Astris' ear. "May I ask what you are up to, my lady?" they whispered.

"Up to?" she quietly replied. "I don't know..."

"Please!" whispered Séntinell, a gentle scolding in their tone. "I am The Lumináry. I have seen almost all there has ever been to see, my lady. I know a theatrical conjuration when I see one. I know when some*thing*, or some *texts*, should not *be there*."

Astris' cheeks reddened slightly. Her poker face disappeared, as she realised she could not deceive the towering figure, looming over her like a disapproving school teacher. She glanced, furtively, at Cassandra, who was straining to hear the murmured conversation, before sighing as she made eye contact once more with Séntinell. She turned to the Princess of Troy. "May we have a few moments, Cassandra? Please?" she asked, taking Séntinell's arm and leading them away from the Tholos.

"Would you agree, Séntinell, that my father sent me here to find a purpose?"

"Yes, my lady, I would agree with that. But..."

"And do you agree, that Cassandra and Jacob are barely keeping their heads above water? That they are drowning in the waves of life essence constantly arriving from Kiípos?"

Séntinell sighed. "What do you have in mind, my lady?" they breathed, accepting there would be no preventing her from interfering.

Astris smiled. "I have, very quickly, come to love Elŷsium, and those who live here. It pains me to see such a paradise struggle with the worthy tasks they administer. All I want to do is connect Cassandra with Circe's hypostasis. Give her a... a... boost. Help her utilise the Célestiaá Ring."

"Is that all you intend, my lady?"

"Well... it would be extremely pleasing to 'meet' my sister for the first time," she admitted. "Will you help, please, Séntinell?"

"This is most irregular, my lady, and there is no guarantee that this will work. Do you really wish to build Lady Cassandra's hopes up, for something that may be impossible?"

"I do not wish to cause any upset, so will let you counsel her on the possibility of failure, Séntinell. Though I do feel very confident of the outcome."

"Pray tell, my lady. Where did the texts originate? I have never seen them before."

Astris linked her arm with Séntinell's as they walked back toward the waiting Cassandra. "I spent much of my time in Sólaás in the vivliotíki; poring over Archon Marik's tomes. He is a very interesting, and educated man, Séntinell."

"I concur, my lady," agreed The Lumináry, unaware of the events unfolding in secrecy on Sólaás. "He is an amazing raconteur, and always has some very enjoyable tales to tell.”

“One of the most enjoyable of his works,” continued Astris, “was a hypothesis on the continuance of celestial emanation; the resultant ‘whereabouts’, after enforced dissemination, of higher entities, such as we Célestiaá. I simply... *borrowed...* one of his ideas, that’s all.”

The trio formed a small semicircle around the flame. “What do we do now?” asked Cassandra, staring into the beautiful swaying of the blue and orange.

“We will need both your rings to reach out,” instructed Séntinell, “through the flame and into the universe; seeking the very breath of Circe’s essence. It may be a fruitless search, I’m afraid, my ladies. But we can only try.”

“We shall succeed,” whispered Astris. “I know we will.” She reached her hand out to Séntinell, who then reached out for Cassandra’s.

“Once you connect with the flames, I shall guide us through the cosmos,” Séntinell prompted. “If we locate her, we can hopefully lead her back to the flame, back to a new home in the Tholos. *If* we locate her,” they repeated.

“Do we need to say anything?” asked Cassandra. “Recite any incantations?”

“No, no,” assured Astris. “Nothing of that sort, Cassandra. The texts have given Séntinell all they need. All we have to do is allow them access through our rings.”

The Lumináry took a deep breath, then gently squeezed the hands they were holding. Cassandra and Astris raised their other hands, those bearing the rings, and watched as both jewels glowed brightly. The stunning red of Astris', reaching out to the brilliant white of Cassandra's; strings of light twisting, entwining, creating a magnificent tendril of celestial power.

The flames danced and weaved in the hearthstone, stretching and shrinking, the end point searching for an invisible quarry. The two tentacles, fire and light, sensed one another; reached out to each other. The tips met, touching tentatively at first, testing each other, until flowing into a single continuous stream.

Séntinell inhaled deeply, their eyes rolling back in their head, until only the bright white of the globe-shaped part of the eye was visible in its socket. The Lumináry began muttering, unintelligibly; words far too quick and mumbled to have any meaning to the ordinary ear. After a few moments—moments that seemed a lifetime to Cassandra and Astris—the flaming light burst outward from the hearthstone, filling the inner circle of the Tholos.

Cassandra gazed about her in wonder. It seemed they were now, all three of them, standing at the centre of the universe. All around them, despite the darkness of space, millions of galaxies swirled and spun; some moving at spectacular speeds across the expanse of the heavens. Millions, billions of colours sparkled and glistened as distant planets, stars, and nebulas were born, lived, and died as they watched. Time was irrelevant as the universe spun and spun and spun.

A glance over her shoulder confirmed they were still in the Tholos, as, through the translucence of the immediate surrounding area, she could make out the lush green grass of the gardens. Her attention returned to the universe before them. They now appeared to be travelling, at speed, from one spot to another; rushing and darting; pausing only to search, just for a second, then onward to the next stopping point.

The hunt continued for some time. But then, without warning, they stopped. "Come forth, my lady," called Séntinell. "Come forth and find your way home."

Cassandra strained her eyes, peering into the depths of space until, at last, the faintest trace of a wisp of smoke meandered its way toward them. A thin lilac vapour, no longer than a finger; ethereal, translucent... *alive.* "Mother?" she called, a crack in her voice, a desperate longing for it to be so.

Séntinell squeezed their hands, once again, and the universe shrank back, away from them, returning them back to the Tholos as before. The writhing stream of light and fire disentangled, the red and white lights receding back to their original sources. The blue and orange flames danced once more, this time with a diamond-shaped lilac core; left then right, higher then lower; flickering and sparking. They danced and swayed, quickly then slowly until, finding the form it sought, the flame rose into the shape of a woman.

The burning figure looked down at her outstretched arms, studying her hands, then her legs, before gazing down upon the transfixed trio standing at her feet. She crouched, lowering to the level of her audience, holding out her hands. "Cassandra," she said, an echo, a reverberation to her voice; like a distant call from the depths of a large empty cavern. Cassandra reached out in response, her hands passing through the flame, unable to grasp the woman she so dearly needed to hold.

"Mother," she sobbed. Her hands continued their futile attempts to hold the flame but, despite this, she could *feel* her mother; a warm sensation—not those from the heat of the flame—coursed through her, filling her, making her feel whole once more.

For the first time since Hades, Cassandra felt her optimism rise.

The flaming woman reached out once more but, as Cassandra tried yet again to take hold, the form disappeared; rising as a single flame, as it had been before.

Cassandra turned to Séntinell, a quizzical, questioning expression on her face. "What's happened, Séntinell?" she asked. "Can you bring her back?" The flames continued their dance; the blue and orange, with its new lilac centre, writhing in the draught coursing through the columns of the Tholos.

Séntinell held their chin as they considered the situation. "It may be, my lady, that Lady Circe needs some time to... *adjust*... to her new bearing."

Cassandra stared at the flames. "She's still in there, then?" she mused. "How do we help her... *adjust*?" Astris passed her hand through the cool flames, testing the constituent elements, trying to find some evidence of her sister's presence.

"She's here," confirmed Astris. "At least, she has a hand-hold on the flame." The dancing coruscation sparkled and swelled, fighting with itself in deciding which way to move. Suddenly, the fire again took a woman's shape, briefly, for just a second, before reverting to its original form. "She will have to fight to inhabit the flame," Astris observed. "But she has an anchor, that is certain."

"Cassandra!" called the flame, a distant echo, low, almost inaudible.

Fear washed over Cassandra, the possibility of failure, of losing Circe once more, inducing panic. "Help her, Séntinell," she begged, her hands reaching out, redundant in their effect. "Please help her."

"I'm not sure..." Séntinell began, but was silenced as Astris thrust her ring into the flame.

"Éla se ména, Aderfí," she yelled. "Éla se ména! Come to me, Sister!"

The ring glowed brighter, sparking and crackling until, with a loud bang, the flame exploded outward, sending all three spectators flying. Séntinell sat up, almost instantly, peering into the cloud of smoke engulfing the hearthstone. "What have you done, my lady?" they gasped.

Astris lay stunned, a little shaken, shivering as the effects of the blast slowly diminished. She pushed herself up with her right hand, eager to see the flames. "I just... I just put a little of myself into it," she explained. Séntinell rushed over and helped her to her feet.

They turned, relieved to see Cassandra sitting up, no worse for wear. "That was extremely foolhardy, if you don't mind me saying, my lady." Astris looked up, rather sheepishly, the reprimand hitting the mark. "Are you alright?"

She looked at her hand, inspecting the ring, happy that there had been no damage inflicted on the jewel. "Yes," she confirmed. "I'm fine." A loud, hearty laugh came so unexpectedly it caught even herself off guard. "In fact," she continued, "I feel much better than fine. Circe is there. I'm now absolutely certain of that. And, while I agree it was somewhat foolhardy behaviour, Séntinell, I think I may have done the trick."

Cassandra stepped up to the hearthstone, waving the last of the smoke away. As it slowly cleared, the unmistakable form of before stood, more certain, more assured, in the centre of the hearthstone. A living flame, befitting of a Princess of Sólaás, her featureless face looking down upon them. She crouched, holding her hands out to Cassandra and Astris.

"My daughter, and my sister," she echoed. "How you both cheer my heart." The two women reached out, taking the softness of the flames in hand. There was a tangibility to her now—not solid, but neither was she ethereal—and they could hold her now, touch her.

"I... I can feel you, Mother," sobbed Cassandra.

"And I you," came the loving reply. "I am here for you, once more." The figure next looked to Astris. "My sister. How delighted I am to meet you, at last."

Astris, for once, was speechless. "I... I..." she repeated.

"I do not know how you brought this about," said Circe, "but I have much to thank you for, Astris." She squeezed the girl's hand. "You may not realise the enormity of your actions yet, sister. But we are one now. I am you, and you are me."

"My Lady," Séntinell cracked, an uncharacteristic outpouring of emotion as they kneeled in reverence before their beloved princess. "Elŷsium will rejoice at the news of your return."

Circe stood. "Please stand, dear Séntinell. I would ask that you keep this news to yourselves, for now at least," she asked. "I am not entirely at ease in this personification. It is, to say the least, exhausting to control, and I will need some time to become comfortable."

"Of course, My Lady," nodded Séntinell.

"May I tell Jacob?" begged Cassandra excitedly. "The news will thrill him as much as it delights us."

The flame nodded her agreement. "Jacob, yes, but no other for now. I'm afraid I must rest," she said. "Return before sundown, daughter, and we can talk again." And, with that, the form dissipated, returning, once more to its now lilac-centred blue and orange flame.

Astris and Cassandra threw themselves into a tight embrace, with Séntinell leaning over and hugging them both. "I can't believe it worked," said Cassandra. "Thank you, Astris. You do not know how much this means. Thank you."

Astris smiled warmly as she held Cassandra, omitting mention of the many strange, new sensations flooding through her since her intervention. *'I am you, and you are me'*. That's what Circe had said, without explanation of what that could mean. Astris had an inkling, however, as memories of Cassandra and Ray flashed through her mind; memories that she did not know of, prior to Circe's return.

She had no time to dwell on the matter, as Cassandra was already dragging both her and Séntinell toward the villa. Jacob had to be told as quickly as possible.

As the trio headed off with renewed enthusiasm, behind them the Tholos stood tall and grand. The blue and orange flame resumed its eternal dance, with the lilac diamond centre swaying in time. Then, for a few brief moments, the lilac core faded, replaced by a small sphere; a dark, ebony sphere. The small ball bounced erratically around the flame's centre, before fading out, replaced once more by the lilac diamond.

XVI. THE MITERÁ FŶSI

Ella and Pandeia scampered across the bridge, giggling excitedly, their bare feet thumping loudly on the ancient wood. Unsurprisingly, they were late once more, having spent all their time playing, rather than heading directly to the school. Pandeia reached the school entrance first, throwing her arms up in celebration of her victory. She cheered for a few seconds until a thought crossed her mind. "Did you let me win, Mitéra?" she asked.

Ella slowed to a halt, her breathing heavy, mostly through laughing rather than exertion. "Noooo," she replied unconvincingly. "Why would I do that?" Pandeia eyed her suspiciously. "And, please, Pandeia... call me Ella. *Please.*" Both girls leaned against one another, catching their breath, but still laughing in spasms.

"I don't think that would be proper, Mitéra." Pandeia gasped. "We can never disrespect the divinity of the Mitéra Fŷsi. Never."

Ella laughed once more. "Ye're funny, Pandeia. I never understand half o' what ye say. What does 'Mitéra Fŷsi' mean?"

"I'm sorry, Mitéra. Myself, and most of the inhabitants of Lunaá, still speak the original tongue, the first language; Hellenés. 'Mitéra Fŷsi' means 'Mother Nature', in your tongue."

"Can I learn Hellenés?"

"Of course, Mitéra. It will be one of your classes, and, I think, they will ask it of me to give you practice with the tongue."

"But first, you must attend *this* class!" The quiet voice was neither angry, nor authoritative. The girls turned to see Selêne standing just inside the classroom entrance, her usual smile lighting her face. The embarrassed, guilty looks on both girls' faces said far more than any apology could; but apologise, they did.

"I'm sorry, Aftí-Fengári," offered Pandeia, bowing.

"I'm sorry, too," said Ella. "We didn't mean to be late, Selêne. I promise we'll no' be late again."

Selêne nodded. "A few moments of joy and laughter are worth a few minutes of waiting, Mother. If Pandeia is helping bring that joy and laughter, then she is fulfilling one of her primary tasks, is she not?" Ella smiled as she stepped into the classroom. "And, yes, you shall learn some basic Hellenés, but not today," the old woman added.

Ella held her hand up. "May I ask just one question, Selêne?" The smile grew, and her eyes shone brighter, as Selêne gave her a nodded approval. "Pandeia refers to you as '*Aftí-Fengári*'..."

"Aaah," Selêne said. "She-Moon! Aftí-Fengári means She-Moon." Ella nodded her understanding. "I am pleased that your curiosity is not allowing anything to slip by you, Mother. That is why we shall begin today with the very basics of what you should know."

Ella raised her hand once more, and Selêne smiled. "Is it disrespectful for Pandeia to call me 'Ella'?" The old woman turned to Pandeia and gently placed her hand around, and on, the back of the girl's head.

"It is not," she said warmly. "Pandeia has shown the utmost respect at every turn, and it pleases, though does not surprise me, that you should wish her the same." The old woman kissed Pandeia's cheek. "If you are to be a true Sŷntrofos, Pandeia, we shall afford you the same regard as Mitéra Fŷsi. You may address Mother how you wish. Now, shall we begin?"

Ella, feeling more comfortable now Selêne had confirmed Pandeia's standing, paid more attention to the room she found herself in. Up to this point, her 'lessons' had been nothing more than little chats; of *Chaos!*; of the history of the world; of the decline of the equilibrium of Kiípos' health. Either in walks through the various gardens surrounding 'Tranquility', or in the courtyard garden at its centre.

Having expected to find a traditional classroom, she was a little surprised at just how empty the space actually was. There was no furniture, or colourful posters on the walls. Neither were there any activity tables, or games. There was nothing that was typical of any classroom she'd ever been in before. In fact, there was nothing at all, except three flat, rectangular cushions, laid out in a triangular shape, in the centre of the room. She followed Pandeia's lead, taking the cushion nearest to her.

The trio sat cross-legged, facing each other. "The first thing we shall explain, Mother," began Selêne, "is Lunaá. Kiípos' Moon. This is the only extraterrestrial body beyond Kiípos where humans have set foot. And, perhaps fortuitously, it and Kiípos shall remain the only celestial bodies mankind will have had the chance to pollute."

Selêne gestured to Pandeia, who raised her hands, palms upward. The room suddenly fell into darkness, until, in the centre space between them, the moon appeared, or at least, what seemed an exact holographic depiction. It glowed in the blackness, glistening, as if alive.

"Lunaá," continued Selêne, "is not only home to Naátúr—the caretakers of Kiípos—it also serves a much more important purpose; it is the anchor that holds Kiípos in her place in the universe. Lunaá moderates how fast, and how stable, Kiípos turns; creating gravity, regulating the seasons through which all life is born, lives, and ultimately transcends."

Ella raised her hand. "You have a question, Mother?"

"Why did the moon... Lunaá... look white to us, but, here, it's one of the most beautiful green places I've ever seen?"

"An excellent question," agreed Selêne. "The answer is sitting to your right." She held her hand out, gesturing to Pandeia. The girl smiled broadly and, as Ella watched, she glowed brightly; a brilliant, refulgent white light emanating from within her, stretching out until she became a hidden blur in the splendrous lustre. She held the light for several seconds, before returning to her normal self.

Ella looked up at the moon's image. She reached up, and with her right hand, gave the glowing sphere a little push. It began spinning, slowly, and the light radiated ever more brightly, illuminating the faces of all present. Ella was mesmerised. "It's beautiful," she murmured. Pandeia turned her palms into a more vertical position and the moon's image shrank, making room for a larger image of the earth. The beautiful blue world spun slowly, and Ella gasped once more.

"I introduced Pandeia as the All-Bright; the illumination, the deliverer of moonlight. It is she who brings the comfort of light to the darkest corners of Kiípos. It is she who, as you can see here, gives us insight into events and conditions on Kiípos. And, it is she who renders us unseen to the human eye. Unlike Elŷsium, Lunaá is situated, by necessity, in the same physical dimension as Kiípos."

Ella stood and inspected the largest globe she'd ever seen. "This is actually Kiípos? The real Kiípos?"

Selêne raised herself, gracefully standing without effort; she, too, now scrutinising the colourful ball. "This is Kiípos," she confirmed. "As it is, right at this moment."

"And where do we... Naátúr... fit in, Selêne?"

The Aftí-Fengári, with a long sigh of satisfaction, smiled and nodded. "You already speak of 'we', Mitéra Fŷsi. Thank you." Ella returned her smile.

"Over seventy percent of Kiípos' surface is water, and Lunaá controls the tides, creating a rhythm—a back and forth—that has guided all life on Kiípos for billions of years. Not just in the seas and oceans, but in all living things. The moisture in the air, the clouds. In the soils, and even in the physical chemistry of all living creatures. Over fifty percent of the human body, for instance, is simply water. Lunaá's rhythm of life influences the moods and behaviours of all things." Selêne watched as Ella continued studying the spinning spheres.

"It has been Naátúr's allotted task throughout the eons, to maintain the balance, the equilibrium, of Kiípos' varied climates and environments; to ensure the food chain is sustainable for all creatures. We work in team-ship and, through yourself, Mitéra Fŷsi, we provide the care and love that makes Kiípos the jewel in the crown of our universe."

Selêne looked forlornly at Kiípos. "These are troubled times, but, whatever happens, Kiípos *will* survive. I only hope we have enough time to repair the damage mankind's actions have done, before mankind disappears forever."

Ella continued inspecting the globe, occasionally spinning it; east to west, north to south, then back again. Selêne joined her as she hunted for her old home. "This is Kiípos as she is right at this moment, Mother," the Moon said. "Pandeia can locate any part of Kiípos you may wish to see. This is how, with Pandeia's assistance, you can observe every inch of land, every blade of grass."

Ella looked down to Pandeia, her wide eyes almost disbelieving what she was hearing. "Is that true, Pandeia? Ye can get really close in?"

The sitting girl laughed. "Of course it's true, Mitéra. Why would Aftí-Fengári lie?" She laughed again. "What would you like to see, Mitéra?"

"Can we see where my mummy is? She's gone back to Strath-sealgair. Can ye show me that?" Pandeia smiled and nodded enthusiastically. Then, with just a slight twist of her wrist, Ella felt like she was flying through space. Through the silent darkness of the outer atmosphere, the chill stung her cheeks as the first of the outer noctilucent clouds washed by her. Onwards she flew, into the Stratosphere, where a break in the clouds, as she tore through the ozone layer, warmed her face.

At last she entered Earth's upper air, and her ears almost burst as the sound of the rushing air and winds assaulted her hearing. Through the clouds, until, eventually, she could see the unmistakable outline of the large islands of Great Britain and Ireland. Still, she flew down, heading north toward Scotland. She could feel the wind on her face, in her ears; could feel the rain brushing her cheeks as she flew through more cloud.

Then west, toward the rugged mountain landscape of the Scottish Highlands. Down, down, down until she could see Loch Affric, then Glen Affric, Strath-sealgair and Geata Dhè. She came to a halt, high above the clearing, high above the stones. Rain was falling, and a strong wind carried thousands of fallen autumn leaves across the expanse, through the circle of rock giants, spewing out into the Glen's plummeting valley.

Ella looked around, watching for any sign of her mother, listening intently for any sound that wasn't the wind. She flew slowly eastwards, over the trees, past the stables, over the north edge of Strath-sealgair. Then, breaking the edge of the tree-line, two horses and riders making their way down the hill. "Mummy!" called Ella, unable to contain her excitement. The riders stopped.

"Did ye hear that, Mel?" asked Katie.

Mel twisted and turned in her saddle, scanning the surrounding area for the source. "Aye, I did. It wisna very loud, but I heard it, aye." Both women scoured the ground ahead, and the trees behind, but, satisfied they were alone, they continued their journey.

"Must have been the wind," shrugged Katie.

Ella stepped back and immediately found herself in the classroom again. She felt giddy with her excitement. "I saw them, Selêne. I saw Mummy and Melanie. They heard me when I called."

Selêne put her arm around Ella's shoulders and gave her a warm cuddle. "Yes, Mother, they heard you. That is because you are Mitéra Fŷsi. Your breath is the wind, and your laughter and tears are the very weather. Did you enjoy your first visit, Mother?"

Ella's smile could not have been wider. "My first visit? Ye mean I can visit again?"

"Oh, yes, Mother." She gestured at the floating globe. "This is the Diávasi Kiípou, the doorway into Kiípos for you, and any Naátúr you allow with you."

"A doorway?"

"Yes, Mother. This doorway, this crossing, allows you direct access to *any* of the Diávasi on Kiípos. You visited Geata Dhè and, had you descended further, you could have simply stepped through the gate into the stone-ring."

"I can walk through the gate?"

"Why, yes, Mother. The Diávasi Kiípou will take you to ground level. You then, simply, step through. As the Mitéra Fŷsi, you will have need to visit Kiípos frequently. There are many Diávasi at your disposal, in many of Kiípos' ancient sites; Geata Dhè, Machu Picchu, Uluru. We created the first such gate at Knossos, on what is now known on Kiípos as Crete. That is where Lady Circe, and Mother Gaea, made the first man, the first civilisation, and where *we* invested much of ourselves in Circe's grand plan."

Ella looked, awestruck, at the spinning globe; it's beautiful blue and green shimmering through the translucence of the intermittent stretches of cloud. "And I can go to any o' them?" Ella queried, still agog at the possibilities being presented to her. "Can I take Pandeia?" She looked at her friend, still generating, and holding, the terrestrial ball in place.

"Ah," said Selêne, "that may be a little tricky, Mother." She smiled at Pandeia, a gentle nod of the head instructing the girl to rest. Pandeia lowered her hands and the image slowly faded from view. "The All-Bright is the gatekeeper, allowing us the access we require, but also providing the means to return. She cannot visit Kiípos."

Ella placed her arm across her tummy, and her hand held her chin while she considered the situation. "Has the All-Bright *ever* visited Kiípos?" she asked.

"There has never been the need," replied Selêne, "Mother Gaea made her own gates. Pandeia is the first All-Bright to have this responsibility."

"So it's never been tried, then?"

"Well, no, I suppose." Selêne glanced at Pandeia. "Do you think you can maintain the gate whilst crossing through it, Pandeia? Could you reopen it from Kiípos' side?"

Pandeia sat still, staring at the floor while contemplating the difficulty of the task set before her. "It's possible," she said, uncertainly, "but I can't be sure until I try."

"Mmm," hummed Selêne. "Would you like to visit Kiípos, Pandeia?" The girl's chin dropped open, and her eyes shone as brightly as the moon had ever shone. She began nodding so enthusiastically Selêne felt she would do herself a mischief. "Very well," she confirmed. "But only for a quick visit. Enough to confirm it's possible, that's all. Yes?" The Moon looked to both girls, receiving the confirmation she required from two enthusiastically nodding heads.

Selêne placed a hand on both girls' shoulders. "You will step through and, if all feels well, you can close the gate, Pandeia. But only for a few moments. You must reopen it and return as quickly as you can. Do you understand?" The girls nodded again.

"Don't worry, Selêne," said Ella, her growing maturity in evidence once more. "We won't do anythin' silly."

Selêne smiled, then stepped back. "When you are ready, All-Bright," she said, gesturing to the space between them.

Pandeia and Ella clasped hands, giggling with nervous excitement, before Ella turned to Selêne. "Where should we go, Selêne?" she asked.

The Moon sighed. "Why don't you begin with something you are familiar with, Mother? Why not Geata Dhè?"

Ella giggled again. "Of course. Silly me," she chuckled, turning to Pandeia. "Geata Dhè, please, Pandeia."

"Geata Dhè, Mitéra," her friend confirmed, raising her free hand in preparation. "Ready?" she asked. Ella nodded and, almost immediately, both girls were flying toward the ancient stones. As they broke through the clouds, the weather had improved markedly; the sun was now shining, and the wind had dropped to nothing more than a light breath. They descended toward the centre of the stone circle which, unlike the surrounding area, was free of the faded yellow leaves shed by the thousands of silver birch on the mountainside.

Their descent slowed as it reached the ground. Ella turned to Pandeia, smiling brightly as she once again took her friend's hand, then took a step through the Diávasi Kiípou into the centre of Geata Dhè. They paused for a few seconds, ensuring all was well, before turning to Selêne. The old woman nodded her approval, waving the girls onwards into their adventure, but urged caution. "You may close the Diávasi, Pandeia... briefly... but please open it again immediately if anything feels... *off*."

ℓℓℓℓ

The All-Bright nodded her understanding and walked forward with Ella. Behind them, the bright light of the celestial portal slowly shrank until it closed, disappearing completely.

In their white peplos, barefooted, and without a supervising adult, the girls would have looked totally out of place to any passers-by; had the world not turned upside down. Pandeia stared at her feet, squeezing the wet grass with her toes, enjoying the sensation for the very first time. "It feels... strange," she said. "Not like the lawns of Lunaá."

Ella agreed. "It's *everythin'* about here that's different, Pandeia. The mountain air, the sunshine, the autumn chill. Elŷsium and Lunaá's *like* this, but it's no' the same. They're no' home... no' really." Her eyes flashed over to the viewing platform at the edge of the Glen. "Do ye want to see somethin'... *beautiful*?" Pandeia nodded eagerly. "Follow me," said Ella, as she ran off toward the leaf-covered decking.

They stood by the wooden security barrier, gazing down the long valley, its steep sides thick with thousand upon thousand of untouched Scots Pines. The autumn sunshine was breaking through the dark, low clouds; the rain, for now, ceasing its periodic cleansing of the mountainside.

Pandeia gasped at the sight. The dramatic, narrow steepness of the top valley, gradually widened further down into the Glen. With its evergreen carpet of pines, it shone like a stunning emerald under the heavenly rays of the sun. Ella smiled. "Mummy and me used to visit here all the time on our horses," she explained. "She always said it was her favourite place, growin' up wi' Jacob." She turned, leaning back on the wooden rail, staring at the stones. "She said they'd play here for hours and hours, only goin' home when it started to get dark. Back when she was a wee lassie."

Pandeia copied her friend's actions; turning, taking great interest in the rugged towers, and the eternal circle.

Ella sighed. "What's happenin' to me, Pandeia? I don't feel like a wee lassie anymore." It felt liberating just saying it, those words that had filled her head constantly since reaching Elŷsium. She could feel her personality veering back and forth; moments of sheer childish glee, mixed with sometimes overwhelming feelings of knowledge, of maturity and, most notably, responsibility.

Pandeia took her hand, reassuringly squeezing as she raised it to her mouth and kissed it. "To understand who you are becoming, Mitéra, you must first understand who I am to you. I am your Sŷntrofos. I am your friend, your companion, your confidante. But I am much more than this."

She turned, leaning her side against the barrier, looking once more at the stunning splendour of Glen Affric. "The universe is a mystery to most," she said, thoughtfully, weighing her words. "Time is a mystery to most, too. It is no coincidence that I appear to you the same age, the same height and, well, almost identical in nature and attitude, Mitéra. But I am far older than you can probably comprehend at this stage. I have been the All-Bright since the very beginning of time, but have only had *this* physical form since your arrival at Elŷsium."

Ella listened carefully, impressed with herself for not even considering an interruption. "I am your crutch. The assistance you shall need emotionally, mentally, physically... as you grow up far more quickly than you would have here on Kiípos."

"Is that what's happenin'?" asked Ella. "I'm growin' up?"

"You are the Mitéra Fŷsi, and yours is, perhaps, the greatest task ever set. It took Mitéra Gaea millions of years to know and balance Kiípos. To make her perfect. You do not have the luxury of mega-annum to learn all that Mitéra Gaea knew. We need you *now*. Not, unfortunately, as the amazing child you were on Kiípos, but as a fully grown Naátúr. And it is my honour, Mitéra, to guide you through this growing period."

Ella nodded, her understanding such that everything was already making sense. "I was a five-year-old when I came to Elŷsium, but I already feel much older. In my head, at least." She looked at Pandeia and smiled. "Do I look much older?"

Pandeia laughed. "You do, Mitéra. You are growing at an accelerated rate, as am I as your Sŷntrofos. Within the year, we shall both have the appearance of typical human teenagers. We shall be women grown. But your intellectuality shall continue to grow without restriction until you surpass even Mitéra Gaea's percipience and astuteness. You will truly become Mitéra Fŷsi."

Pandeia raised her hands, and the Diávasi opened once more. Ella smiled. "Best go have some fun while we still can then, eh?"

XVII. THE FIRST PICTURE

It was an arduous task, but only one of the many they knew would be required in their new ventures. The hole was easy enough to dig; the ground being so soft with all the rain. Claire had always enjoyed sitting, having her lunch, on the soft slope that looked down toward Strath-sealgair, and it seemed the right place to bury her tragically diminished remains.

Katie watched as her companion voluntarily dug out the last resting place of Claire's emaciated body, comforted only by the knowledge that her soul had moved on. Melanie had insisted—given her past tussles with the dead girl—she owed this one last little thing to her. With each day that had passed, Katie was ever more sure that her decision to bring Melanie was the right one; both for the girl, and, surprisingly, for herself, too.

By the time they had filled and firmed down the grave, the rain had eased to a light drizzle. The wind, too, had respected their work, dropping to a barely noticeable breeze. It had been difficult to gauge the time of day; the gloominess restricting the amount of daylight squeezing through the heavy clouds. Katie estimated, as much as the improved conditions allowed, that it was still only mid to late afternoon; enough time to complete Jacob's errand, and a little something she had to do for herself.

"Do ye think we should say a few words?"

Katie pondered the question for a few moments, then shook her head. "No, Mel. There's nothin' to be said. No words that can make this..." She looked at the grave, an intense anger rising inside her once again, then her head slumped to look at her feet. Her eyes blurred as her tears flooded through, and her hands came up to wipe them away.

Melanie threw her arms around Katie's shoulders and pulled her in, hugging her as tightly as she could. "Ye okay?" she whispered. Katie nodded, as the tears continued to fall like the rain that had only recently ceased. She gave a huge sniff, then hugged Melanie again.

"I'm so glad ye're here, Mel. Thank you."

"Thank *me*?" the younger woman replied, her own tears flowing now. "I'm only here 'cause you were forgivin' enough to gi'e me another chance. You saved me. I should be thankin' you, an' spendin' the rest o' eternity showin' ye how grateful I am."

Katie took the girl's face in her hands and kissed her forehead. "Ye're savin' me too, ye know. Ella's safe an' well. She's gonna be so well protected, an' so busy. An' I think we're gonna have more scenes like..." She looked again to the grave. "... this!" She sniffed, and she swallowed, and she regained her composure, wiping her eyes and nose with her arm. "I need to be tough... strong. I need to be responsible. You bein' here, it gives me that strength, it makes me responsible... for you, for me... an' for all the wee lassies like Claire. I wasn't really convinced that I was up to the job..." She took another deep breath as she looked for a last time at the burial plot. "... but now? Now I know I... *we*... have to be."

Melanie turned to look at the corpses of Sinbad and Billy, lying by the side of the stables where they had been unceremoniously dumped. "What will we do wi' these two?" she asked.

Katie sneered. "Leave them there for the wildlife. At least then they'll have been good for *somethin'*. Ye ready?"

Melanie smiled and nodded. "Where next, boss?"

"8 School Road," said Katie.

Bentley and Crumbles plodded along, as carefree as ever. As they turned onto School Road, the women were a little surprised at just how neglected it all looked. The long grass, the overgrown shrubs. The piles and piles of golden, brown, and orange leaves along the fences, walls and half-buried cars, still sitting where they had been as the ripple washed over them. The wind, although much gentler than it had been previously, was carrying autumn's litter along in waves; the whooshing, and the rustling, breaking what was an otherwise eerie silence.

The true state of the abandoned dwellings became clearer as they approached; doors and windows forced open when desperate raiders had searched for food, or water, as the crisis deepened. The hallways of open doors bulged, as did everywhere else, with the leaves that seemed to have no end. An ever-unfolding, uninterrupted, carpet of golden brown, highlighting a lack of human activity in this area; a lack of life.

Katie glanced over to the closed doorway of number 15; this would be their second port of call. The entrance to number 8, however, was wide open; the hallway an extension of the autumnal cloak. They pulled the horses up at the driveway and made their way up the path.

"I never asked," said Melanie. "But why are we here, exactly?"

"Retrievin' a family treasure," replied Katie. She gingerly stepped through the open door, each footstep met with the loud crunching of a hundred leaves. "Jacob said I'd find it upstairs."

"Do ye mind if I wait here? Feel kinda awkward..." Melanie gave a demonstrative shudder.

Katie smiled. "Aye, no bother. You stay here and give yer boyfriend, there, another biscuit." Melanie leant in to Crumbles and kissed his neck, as Katie made her way into the house.

The space felt very familiar. Her mum's house was of an identical design, even down to the small downstairs bedroom at the front. There was no reason to dawdle, as there was nothing reminiscent about the house anymore, and she made her way directly up the stairs to the main bedroom. Jacob had given detailed instructions. The brown envelope, marked 'Do Not Bend', would be in a compartment at the base of the wardrobe. There was no furniture other than the wardrobe, a chair, and the bed, where Jacob's disheveled sleeping bag still lay. By the wall with the window, the curtains still closed, was a rucksack, a dysfunctional tablet, and a scrunched up towel. 'He never was the tidiest, even as a kid,' she thought.

The wardrobe doors were open, with the discarded drawers lying to the front. The contents of the compartment all seemed undisturbed, being of no value to hungry, thirsty scavengers; not even the generous roll of euros. The envelope lay on top of some other personal documents, and Katie couldn't resist a look at Jacob's old passport. She smiled at the small round face staring out at her, trying for all the world to look as serious, and grown up, as he could. 'If only we could turn back time, eh? Start again...' she mused.

Katie picked up the envelope, sliding the contents out to ensure they were what she was actually looking for. The picture surprised her, saddened her. She recognised Ray, and a younger Eric, but had never seen Jacob's mother before. As the happiness jumped out from the photo, Katie was taken by how beautiful Cissy had been. The sight of them all together at such a joyous time, and knowing what lay ahead of them, brought a sigh to her breath.

Her mind wandered back to her childhood; the times with Jacob; losing him, then finding him again. Only for her hopes to be dashed once more. She closed her eyes, thinking back to their dalliance at the falls; how alive he had made her feel, turning her world upside down. Everything since, including seeing him with Cassandra, had all led back to the inevitable realisation, and disappointment, that they would never be together. She gave a rueful grin, and a hidden curse for the man she loved, before heading out the door, photographs safely in hand.

As she reached the bottom of the stairs, the sound of Melanie's voice drifted through the hallway from outside. Katie paused, and sat on one of the lower steps, just listening. The girl was chatting away to the horses, as if they were all best friends; seemingly with not a care in the world. Katie smiled. Not at the innocent chatter, but at the obvious transformation in her companion; from a bitter, calculating little whore, to a charming, friendly, funny young girl. 'She truly has been reborn,' thought Katie.

"You enjoyin' yersel?" she asked as she left the house.

"Me an' the lads have just been sharin' the biscuits," laughed Melanie. "That us?" she asked, nodding to the envelope. "Where next?"

Katie looked across to number 15 as she was securing the envelope in the pouch of her backpack. "Just want to have a look at my mum's old house. See if there're any clues to what happened to her. Ye comin'?"

Melanie glanced across. "Do ye want me to come? Will ye be alright?" Katie finished strapping the pouch, then nodded.

"Aye, might need somebody to lean on. Only if ye want to, though." The women patted the horses, then made their way over to the second house.

Katie tentatively tried the door handle, surprised that it pushed down easily; surprised that the door was unlocked. She pushed it open, and immediately pulled it shut again. "Oh fuck," she said, her gag reflex doubling her up as the stench of death puffed out the opening door. "Not what I was hopin' to find." She took a deep breath, then blew out again. "Think it might be my turn to dig a grave."

Melanie placed her hand on Katie's shoulder. "Do ye want me to have a look first?"

"Do ye mind?"

"Let me make her presentable for ye, eh?"

Katie nodded, taking a step back from the door. Melanie took a breath and entered the house, closing the door behind her. The smell was thick in the narrow hallway; a sickly, sweet invisible cloud that stunk like rotting fruit, mixed with cheap perfume. Once she'd overcome the urge to vomit, Melanie made her way down the hallway, gingerly pushing each door open.

The small bedroom to the left was tidy, but it looked some time since anyone had been in there. The living room on the right was a totally different matter. Adding to the smell of the so-far undiscovered cadaver, the pungent aroma of whisky filled the small room. Several empty bottles littered the floor by the settee, and around the coffee table. Still, there was no sign of a body.

Ignoring the kitchen, Melanie made her way up the stairs to the bedrooms. With each step forward, the stench thickened. She could almost taste it as she reached the top of the stairs, but continued on toward the main bedroom. Opening the door released even worse aromas, making her want to gag once more. The room was dark; the curtains closed. In the corner, lying on the bed, was what she had been looking for; the fully clothed body of a woman. It had long since begun its journey of decomposition, leaving just the almost-dried husk of leathery skin on a skeletal frame. The liquifying process had oozed toxic and gaseous excretions, ruining the fabrics of the clothing, the bedding, and the carpeting in the body's immediate area.

On the bedside table sat several empty pill bottles; different tranquillisers, painkillers, and other powerful drugs, consumed as the prelude to death. A quarter-full bottle of whisky sat on the table and, on the floor, lay a crumpled piece of paper. Melanie picked it up, unwrapping the heavily creased, almost cloth-like remains of a photograph. Through the thousands of little white veins, she could make out a man and a woman, drinks in hand. It was impossible to see the details of their faces as the picture was so crumpled.

She assumed it was Katie's mum in much happier times and tucked it into her trouser pocket. Being careful not to touch the corpse, Melanie leant over and pulled the thick top cover back and over, covering the top of the body. She repeated the process on her own side, making the scene ever so slightly more palatable.

Katie was sitting on the doorstep when Melanie returned. "Sorry, Katie," she said. "She's been dead a while now. In her bed, her own decision. The body's made a bit o' a mess, but I've opened the window and we can wrap her an' bury her, if ye'd want to." Melanie removed the crumpled photo and held it out. "This was lyin' by the bed." Katie wiped a tear, and bowed her head as she took the picture, unable to bring herself to look at it. "I'll take care o' it, if ye're no' up to it," Melanie added.

Katie wiped her eyes again, shaking her head. "No. No, I'm up to it, Mel. I'm just so fuckin' angry wi' m'self that, the last few times we saw each other, we always ended up arguin'. I can't remember the last time I told 'er I loved 'er." She stood, dusting the dirt down from the back of her trousers.

"At least ye know she's gone to Elŷsium, eh?"

"Aye. She's gone to Elŷsium." Katie nodded, pushing the door open again. "Let's do this quickly, while we've still got some daylight left. We've still got the hard bit to do."

XVIII. HARVEST FESTIVAL

The celebrations were already in full swing as Jael and Eric made their way down the path from the waggon park, mingling among the many other new arrivals. The music was loud, but not enough to drown out the barking of the stallholders, or the shrieking and laughter of the several small groups of teenagers, one of which was standing by a large table.

Although still morning, the sun's warmth was already leaving its mark, and Eric felt the need to pull his shirt away from his already-sticky armpits. His buttonless shirt and trousers seemed to hang on his still-emaciated frame.

He felt anxious at the prospect of meeting Jael's friends, and had considered not coming to the festival at all. The nightmares never stopped, and each new day was a challenge he was struggling to meet. Jael saw his distress and took his hand. He smiled at her, letting out a sigh, not so much of relief, but more an acknowledgement of not being alone. "You're with me, handsome," she whispered, leaning into him. "No one's going to upset you unless they want me to deal with." She winked, then squeezed his hand.

"Hey!" Jael shouted to the small group by the table. They all turned and waved, smiling as their eyes settled on Eric, their curiosity about to be satisfied at last. The stories of the broken, mute boy rescued from Hades were commonplace among the young, not just of Rimel, but throughout Elŷsium. It had become an almost daily topic and, as teenagers do, the stories had grown arms and legs in their constant embellishments and exaggerations. To most, it came as a relief to see a normal-looking, gawky and scrawny boy, no different to themselves.

There were three of them floating around a huge buffet of snacks; pies, sandwiches, chicken, fruit and other such delights. Several similar, large tables lined the 'street'. Tents, and marquees, erected behind each of the various stalls, and the hubbub of chatter, shouting, and music gave the area a carnival feel, and Jael's friends seemed very enthusiastic and boisterous. Eric looked about him, taking in the festivities.

Rimel was a small village with one street, and the main buildings of 'trade' lined either side. To his right, on the other side of the road, was the bakery; its doors wide open, and a large queue waited to sample the hot pies, pastries, and bread Biro, and Jael's mother, Clara, were eagerly distributing. Behind, and to the right of the baker's, down a slight incline, was the huge windmill; silent and idle, while the festival unfolded.

The Blacksmith's, also closed for the day, was a short distance from Biro's emporium, and looking up the street to his left, there was a clothing store, the butcher's, and a fruit and veg purveyor. Behind the table where they were standing, was a large storage barn and, down to the right, was the over-crowded saloon. An empty workshop and showroom, earmarked as an outlet for Ray's carpentry, was up the road to his left. Everywhere he looked, there were festival-goers mingling, or striding purposefully toward the saloon, or the baker's. At the very top end of the street, lots of tables and benches surrounded a makeshift stage and dancing area, in readiness for the end-of-day concert that crowned the Harvest Festival.

Jael squeezed his hand again. "Eric... these are my friends. The nicest weirdos you'll find anywhere in Rimel." She laughed, as the group approached them. "Actually, scrub that... anywhere in Elŷsium." Jael released her hold and leaned forward to hug the first of the group. "This is Monica, my best friend in all the world."

"Hello, Eric," Monica said, an effortlessly welcoming smile an attempt at bringing him immediately into the group. Monica looked relaxed in a simple lemon blouse and green linen trousers, with a floppy straw hat dangling down her back. "Jael told us all about you." She stepped forward and hugged him, awkwardly; Eric was not yet at ease enough to respond in kind. Monica leaned back and smiled. "We're all family here," she added, "we'll look after you."

As she stepped away from him, Eric's eyes were drawn to another young girl walking past the group, a few yards away. She was ambling toward the barn behind them, deliberately inviting Eric's gaze. She smiled widely, her eyes locked onto his, her hands combing her long black hair behind her.

"And this is Karl," said Jael, bringing Eric's attention back to the group. "He *works* at the blacksmith's," laughed Jael sarcastically.

"I do work," protested Karl. "Very hard, for your information. My dad wouldn't put up with me skiving... even if I could." He held his hand out. "Nice to meet you, Eric," he said. "Don't let these bossy women get the better of you. Especially this one..." He laughed at Jael and dodged as she made to give him a playful slap. He was a tall, thin lad, with a mop of curly brown hair that looked as if he'd deliberately pushed it upwards, and he reminded Eric of a boy he'd known at his school. He wore a white buttonless, v-neck long-sleeve shirt, with knee-length brown cotton shorts.

"And I'm Abigail." The voice came from behind Karl, and then a cute, round, smiley face appeared over his shoulder. She stepped out into full view, and it surprised Eric that she was the only girl wearing a peplos; cut daringly across the shoulder, and quite high above her knees. "But they all call me 'Abi'."

"Nooo," corrected Monica, "we call you Gabby Abi." The four friends all laughed together. Realising Eric was looking a little left out, Jael linked arms with him.

"You'll get used to them after a while, Eric," Jael reassured. "Now, who's for getting a drink?" The quartet nodded and agreed that a drink was just what they needed to get the day started. Jael turned once more to Eric. "We'll have to go into the saloon, just until the other stalls get set up properly, Eric. Do you want to come with us, or would you rather wait here?" Eric's face whitened. The thought of squeezing through the crowds to get to the bar, the deafening noise, and the claustrophobic feeling of having no escape route, all terrified him.

Jael put him at his ease. "You wait here, handsome," she smiled. "We won't be long."

"Is she your girlfriend?"

Eric turned, seeking the voice behind the question. Before him stood a slim young woman, much shorter, and possibly a couple of years older than himself; not as if that made any sense in Elŷsium. It was the girl from before, the one who had smiled as she walked past him. She wore dark brown trousers, and a loose, low-cut white cotton shirt, almost see-through in the sunshine, the darkness of her hair emphasised by the whiteness of her blouse. Her green eyes drew him in, and she smiled... naughtily, at him.

He nodded, feeling a little flustered as the girl eyed him up and down. "Lucky girl," she said. "Such a pity, though." She leaned forward, gently stroking his fringe across his forehead. "I'll bet she's told you she's gone to get drinks, right?" Eric felt his stress levels rising. Who was this girl, and why was she talking about Jael? He looked anxiously about him for his friend, but there was no sign of her.

"Hey, Cutie," she prompted. "Don't look so worried. I'll keep you company 'til she gets back. Though, knowing her, it could be some time." She laughed. Eric was unsure what to do. He didn't know this girl, but she was certainly acting familiarly. The girl leaned back against the wall, a teasing fluttering of her eyelids suggesting some not so innocent thoughts going through her head. Her eyes once again bored into Eric's. "I'm Eris," she said, "but I'll bet she's never mentioned me, has she?'

Eric gave a short, snappy shake of his head. "Thought so," said Eris, glancing away to her left. "She's always been a little jealous of me." She slowly returned her gaze to Eric and smiled. "Always terrified I'd steal whichever boy she was seeing. Whichever boy she was... fucking!" Her tone was anything but friendly, and Eric looked around for Jael. He made to walk away, but Eris took hold of his arm, halting his progress before it started. She rested her head against the wall, pulling her shoulders back. Eric's eyes lowered, staring toward her breasts as she pushed her chest forward; the low front of her blouse allowing a teasing view of the smooth curves sinking into her cleavage. He felt his heart beating faster, and Eris chuckled. "Do you like what you see?" she asked. "Has she let you touch her yet? Has she let you fuck her yet?"

Eric gasped, shocked at the directness of the girl's questions, and yet he couldn't draw himself away. She looked him in the eye and, despite resisting giving a reaction, he once again gave a brief shake of the head. Eris laughed again. "Really?" she probed, appearing surprised at his answer. "Well, you must be the only boy in Rimel that hasn't had the pleasure of slipping himself inside her. Would you like to fuck her?" Eris was teasing him again. "Would you like to fuck me?" she whispered, leaning forward into him. Eric could feel himself shaking, but was it fear, or was it excitement? He looked down at the girl's cleavage once more, her heavy breathing emphasising the two smooth, round mounds, rising and falling, hypnotising him. She suddenly lurched forward, pressing herself against him, pressing her cheek to his, her hand stroking his groin. "Would you like to slide your hard cock into my hot, wet cunt?" she whispered.

He was shaking even more violently now, panic overwhelming him; a hot sensation surging through his genitals. Eris laughed. The warmth spread further, lower; stress overwhelming him. Eris pulled herself away, looking down at his groin, laughing hysterically, drawing the attention of the surrounding festival-goers. The large, dark urine stain grew before his eyes and he gulped as the realisation of the crowd staring at him hit home. He looked from side to side, behind and before him; all around, men, women, children were pointing at him, laughing at him. Eris was shrieking as she, too, pointed to the offending wet patch, encouraging the crowd to mock him even more. Eric burst into tears as the girl stepped forward, and leaned into him once more.

"Pasiphae sends her love," whispered Eris.

Eric lurched back, staring at the grinning girl, her face now a wicked, contorted mask. The laughing, and the catcalls, all thundered in his head. He spun around and ran, trying to get as far from the ridicule as he could. Eris watched as he disappeared around the edge of the bakery building, heading down toward the windmill. Her laughing halted instantly, her work done.

"Eric?"

Eris looked over her shoulder. Walking through the crowd, carrying two tankards of punch, came Jael. "Eric!" she called again, looking frantically about her. Eris smirked as she walked past Jael, deliberately bumping her shoulder into the girl, spilling the punch from the jugs.

"I'm sorry," Jael said instinctively.

Eris sneered at her. "Oh, you will be!"

Festival goers streamed past on both sides, oblivious to her dismay. Jael twisted and turned, searching, scanning every face, every piece of clothing. Eric was nowhere to be seen. "Excuse me," she asked a passing woman, "have you seen Eric, the Corrie boy?" The woman just smiled and shook her head, continuing on her way.

Jael looked at the now-empty tankards, their contents lost as her arms fell redundantly to her sides, realising that Eric had gone. She was confused. Why had this other girl been so nasty? And what had she meant by *you will be*? She was sure she didn't know the girl; her dress had suggested she was from Elysia, so why was she here, and why be so nasty? Nastiness wasn't something she'd experienced at all since coming to Elŷsium so long ago. The girl was now leaning against the side of the saloon, staring at Jael; a sneering grin on her face. She nodded her head in the windmill's direction, smiling vindictively as she slowly raised her arm and pointed.

Jael's head snapped around in the direction indicated, peering through the throng of people. 'Why would she point at the windmill? Is that where Eric had gone?' The girl knew something, that was obvious. Jael placed the glasses on a barrel and strode purposefully toward Eris, grabbing her long hair and pulling fiercely down. "Where is he?" she roared. Eris screamed as her head jerked violently; retaliating, she punched upward, catching Jael fully on her chin. The unexpected blow caused her grip to break, and Eris pulled away, giving Jael a firm shove, pushing her over.

Jael landed with a thump on her backside. Eris stood over her, brushing her hair back with her hand, grinning inanely. "You looking for your boyfriend, dearie?" she shrieked. "The mute weirdo that grabbed my tits?" She looked around at the gathering crowd. "He *did*... he grabbed my tits." She glared again at Jael; a demented, wide-eyed stare. "Then, when I refused him, he *pissed* himself and ran off." She cackled hysterically, nodding frantically as she made eye contact with as many of the passersby as possible. Jael was still on the ground, realising the growing displeasure in the crowd; displeasure directed toward her.

Eris burst into tears as a nearby woman immediately embraced and comforted her. "First, the boy sexually assaulted me," she sobbed, "and then... and then... his girlfriend attacks me." The woman hugged Eris, then glared at Jael.

"You should be ashamed of yourself, girl!" More people came toward Jael, reprimanding her, abusing her. The mood was becoming very unpleasant and, for the very first time, Jael felt threatened and endangered. She quickly scrambled to her feet, dusting herself down; stepping slowly backwards away from the approaching mob. They were all shouting at her now. She glanced back at Eris, still being hugged by the woman, but she had turned her face to sneer at Jael; a wicked, cruel smile.

Jael ran off toward the windmill, crying as much in confusion as in any sort of pain. An overwhelming sense of dread washed over her; the feeling that life in Elŷsium had somehow, instantly, changed. It felt ridiculous, but this girl had somehow influenced the crowd. The further she ran from Eris, the lighter the mood in the crowds appeared. 'Well, of course it would,' she thought. 'They don't know what happened up there, do they?' She slowed to a walk as she reached the windmill.

The towering structure was a curious construction, the lower part of which was like a giant, circular dry stone dyke. The mix of black and grey stones looked almost speckled as the interweaving layers stretched from the ground to almost eight feet high; with a small wooden door at the front. Above the stones, the windmill was an entirely wooden conical affair, stretching another thirty feet. The huge red sails were still—the festival allowing everyone a day free from labour—hanging in a huge 'X', almost barring anyone entry to the door.

Jael looked about her, seeking any sign of Eric. She noticed the door, while not exactly open, was slightly ajar. It struck her as unusual, as she knew everyone who would normally work in the mill was up by the bakery, enjoying the celebrations; there was no one grinding the wheat today, so the mill should have been closed. She moved gingerly toward the door, hesitating as her hand reached out to push it open. Once again the ominous sense she'd felt earlier prickled through her skin, like pins and needles, but with a nauseous expectation making her want to vomit. She urged herself forward, pushing through the entrance and into the quiet, dimly lit workspace.

To her left was a high stack of flour sacks, recently ground and ready for loading onto the cart for delivery to the other village bakeries surrounding Rimel. Ahead was the mill, filling the centre of the space; a massive wooden contraption, with the grain chute and hopper sitting neatly atop the removable horse. The mill spindle dropped, from the driving mechanism high above, through the top of the vat encasing the stones, under which the enormous runner stone lay idle; as did its companion bed stone, hidden below the wooden floor.

The air was full with flour dust, a fine white cloud, raised up by the draft sliding in through the open door; and the poor light made it difficult to see. The floorboards beneath her feet creaked under her weight as she stepped slowly forward. "Eric?" she called tentatively. "Eric? Are you in here?" There was no answer, and she took another step. She paused, straining to see through the floating white speckles. Something wasn't right; she was still, but the surrounding wood continued to creak and groan. "Eric?"

Jael could feel the tears before she heard her own sobs. She knew she had to step forward, go around the mill, but her feet resisted, almost in fear of what they would lead her to. The groaning wood, the dimness, and the ever-intrusive flour cloud did nothing to ease those fears. As she rounded the mill, a shadow dimmed the light even further. Like a slow-swinging pendulum, the shadow moved from right to left, then left to right, the wood creaking in time with each swing. The urge to vomit returned without warning, and she violently expelled the contents of her stomach over the wooden vat.

Jael doubled over, collapsing against the vat, vomiting once again. She forced her tear-filled eyes upward to look at the shadow. "Eric?" she mumbled. Her eyelids flickered, then closed tightly—trying to stem the flow—before snapping open again as she knew what she had to do. Her hand pushed against the vat and she raised herself up, peering through the flour and the dust swirling about her. Against a flour sack lay a scythe, its handle within easy reach.

She jumped up onto the vat, and in a flash, the blade swung upwards. It smacked against the taut rope—shaking the pendulum bob, causing the shifting weight to blow a draft across the floury floor—but failed to cut it. Jael screamed in frustration, and swung her arm again, redoubling her efforts. Once more, the sharp edge failed to cut through.

Jael tossed the scythe aside, grabbing onto the boy, trying to raise his weight, ease the pressure on his neck. She was panicking now, screaming in sheer desperation. "Help! Help!" she screeched.

Behind her, Jael could hear the thump, thump, thump of someone padding their way through the windmill entrance, Biro's heavy footsteps resonating with the hammering beat of her heart. Above her head, the swoosh of the scythe effortlessly severed the rope, causing both herself, and Eric, to drop heavily to the floor.

Quickly gaining her composure, her fingers sank in behind the tightness of the cord around his neck, trying to ease the pressure on his throat. "Eric!" she screamed. "Eric!" The noose refused to budge, the pressure remaining. Jael looked to Biro, asking for the scythe once more, carefully slipping the point of the blade under the rope, curving it slowly around and up, shearing the fibres. "Eric!" she screamed again, her left hand behind his head, raising him to her; her right, cupping his cheek.

Her head lowered in an attempt to feel his breathing; nothing. She realised, through her panic, she should test his pulse; again, there was nothing. She tilted his head, placing her mouth on his, attempting to breathe him back to life. After a few desperate, futile attempts, Biro placed his hand on her shoulder. "I'm so sorry, Jael," the baker sobbed. "I'm so sorry."

The baker's daughter sat back, staring forlornly, through her own tear-drenched eyes, at the first man she'd ever loved; the first man to break her defences. She watched, sobbing, as the fine flour-dust settled, like the purest of snows, on the face of her love; settling as a sweet shroud, giving Eric an almost ghostly appearance as he lay motionless before her. Her heart broke as she leaned forward, placing her first ever loving kiss on the lips of her silent sweetheart.

XIX. A GIANT OF A MAN

The Road to Elah, The Levant 1063 BC

It had only been a few miles, but the eastward track to Shochoh seemed never-ending in the blistering heat. The waggons swayed back and forth, their soiled linen canopies clinging on by threads, the wheels almost fixed in the well-worn ruts of a thousand previous carts. The constant squeaking and creaking of the wooden sides and axles, as the vehicles rumbled along; the dust being thrown up all around them, and the thirst and hunger from their long journey were now taking their toll. "Take a drink, my dear," said the gigantic man. "We will soon be there."

"You said that two hours ago, my love," the woman replied. "And yet, here we are still, in the middle of nowhere." She looked from side to side. The now-familiar landscape showed little sign of change. Tufts of short, yellow grass, dried and baked in the sunshine, poked through the gaps in the rough stone terrain. Elah trees, and fig trees, broke the flatness and monotony of the trek, with any hills always seemingly distant. A snake slithered its way across the central mound of the track, hissing disapprovingly at the intrusion of the horses, waggons, and people. "I thank you for the offer, my love. But you are in more need of refreshment than I am. I shall leave the little water that remains. Just in case." She smiled at her husband, patting his hand.

Leaning over to her left, she peered back around the side of the waggon toward the following travellers. "Are you alright, back there?" she called. The elder of the two girls waved. The woman watched for several seconds, reassuring herself that all was well, before returning to the narrow, uncomfortable seating position that the width of her husband limited her to. She fidgeted in her discomfort. "May we stop awhile, Biro? I fear I have lost the sense of my legs." The man smiled through his thick beard, pulling back on the reins.

"Of course, my dear Naclara. Despite the displeasures of our journeying, I have to say I am in no hurry to reach our destination." The two horses slowed to a stop and Biro pulled back on the handbrake, straining to ensure a sufficient grip of the front wheel. He jumped down and hurried around, holding his hands up for his wife to steady herself. His bulging biceps, and forearms, had kept a tight grip of the reins, and now they easily lowered his much smaller wife from the carriage.

Naclara stepped down and immediately set about brushing the dust from her clothing. She wore a light blue summer simlāh; a rectangular outer garment of rough wool, crudely sewn together to leave the front unstitched, and two openings for the arms to go through. The wool was heavy enough to provide protection from the rain and cold, and even keep the warmth in at night, but was still light enough to wear in the mid-day heat. Below her simlāh, she wore a white linen sadin, with both garments coming down to her ankles. Covering her head, was a white keffiyeh; a large square piece of woollen cloth, folded diagonally in half into a triangle. The fold sat across her forehead, with the keffiyeh loosely draped around her back and shoulders, and held in place by a worn cord circlet. On her feet, she wore na'alayim; wooden sandals, with leather straps.

Biro wore a similar dark red sleeveless simlāh, with a white kethōneth, a loose-fitting under-tunic below. He, too, wore a simple white keffiyeh and plain na'alayim.

The two girls stepped down from the rear waggon and approached their parents. "Do you require water, Mumma?" the elder girl asked, holding out a clay bottle. Naclara put her hand to her head, steadying herself as dizziness came over her.

"Oh, yes, thank you, Jael. This heat will be the death of me." She took the bottle from her daughter, placing it against her forehead, attempting to cool herself, before taking a long, refreshing drink. She smiled appreciatively at the elder girl, immensely proud of how resourceful and independent she was. Jael was sixteen, headstrong, and sure of herself. She had already defied her parents' wishes by refusing to marry Izyan, the horse trader's son; he was twenty-three, far too old for her; in her eyes, anyway. And, at any rate, she had no desire to be married, to be a man's property; or to be confined to a life of cooking, cleaning, and producing babies. Not yet, at least; she would decide when she was ready, and who she would settle with. Her mother held a quiet, unspoken respect for her daughter for that. And now, here, in the middle of nowhere, Jael had once again defied her parents' wishes. "I do wish you had stayed home at Gath, Jael. My mumma and pappa would have taken care of you both."

"We couldn't stay, Mumma. Pappa needed all the grain, which needed both of the waggons. And we should stay together as a family in these times; we don't know what to expect when we reach the camp. The soldiers may make Pappa fight."

Biro laughed. "Fight?" he chuckled. "I have never been in a fight in my life. Despite my size, and I know everyone makes jokes, and calls me names about it, I think even your mumma could easily knock me over."

"Why am I here?" asked the younger girl. "I want to go home." There was no disguising her anger, and displeasure, at having to travel so far overland. Orpah was eleven, and seldom ever satisfied. "I want to go home to gramma and grappa. I don't like this heat. Why am I here?"

"You are here to keep me company, Orpah," explained Jael. "And we are both here to help mumma and pappa feed the soldiers. If they don't make pappa fight, of course. I will feed none of them if they do that."

"They will not make me fight, daughter," assured Biro. "I am a baker of bread and pastries, and I can do amazing things with bulgur and semolina. Our wagons carry grains and seeds. They carry neither weapons, nor warriors. The soldiers need my cooking skills, not my useless sword arm."

Jael grunted, unconvinced. "Well, if they do try to take you, Pappa, they will have to deal with me first." The huge man bent and hugged his daughter, kissing her forehead.

"And now I know I am truly safe," he smiled.

"I want to go home," repeated Orpah.

"I think it is too late to turn back," said Naclara, drawing the party's attention to the three approaching riders coming over the south-east ridge.

"The soldiers are here."

Effes Dammim, The Levant 1063 BC

The Philistine camp was situated just outside Shochoh, less than a mile from the valley. The Israelite forces had settled to the north of the valley; the sound of their camp easily heard in the quiet of night. The rumours were that the inactivity, the lack of confrontation, was because they were waiting for King Saul to arrive and oversee the battle. The Philistine soldiers were bored, and irritable. They had been camped at this place for over three weeks; watching and waiting; catching the occasional Israelite spies; but, mostly now, they spent all of their time gambling, squabbling and fighting amongst themselves.

They had given Biro and Naclara a large tent to the south of the camp. It functioned, not only as their dwelling for all four family members, but as the main camp kitchen. The soldiers had welcomed their arrival, and the novelty of fresh bread, and fresh foods; but, as time dragged by, with the rations and supplies diminishing, a tension had developed. It did not help this unease that the soldiers were now openly showing their interest in Jael and Orpah. Many had not seen a woman for months, and two pretty young girls were impossible to ignore.

A cistern, to collect rainwater, and provide fresh water, was situated one hundred yards behind their tent. Jael and Orpah would regularly take jugs and bottles to fill, but were now far more aware of the dangers presented by the soldiers. Each girl carried a knife, with one standing guard as the other filled the bottles and jugs; watching for prying eyes. They were now fearful every time they left the safety of their tent, even chaperoning each other when going to relieve themselves.

Biro requested an audience with Achish, King of Gath. He petitioned the monarch, asking that his daughters and wife be given protection, and a general and four soldiers arrived to escort the baker to Achish's tent. The general pulled the tent flap back, then held his hand out, staying Biro's entrance. "Remember, Breadman," he said, "stay bowed until his majesty addresses you." Biro nodded as he stepped forward.

He stepped through the flaps—his head bowed to the floor—and, despite his limited view, gasped at the splendour of the tent's interior. Woollen rugs and silk cushions were everywhere; golden goblets, vases, and urns littered the floor, and the smoke from an incense burner overtook the thick smell of spices. The tent was busy with chatter as the battle plans were being discussed. Biro made his way up the thin red carpet that led to the rear of the tent; toward the King of Gath. "My, he is a monster, isn't he?" proclaimed the king, as he caught his first sight of Biro. "A veritable giant! A real Goliath!"

Biro bowed once more before looking at the king, carefully avoiding full eye contact. "I'm sorry, your majesty, but my name is…"

"Silence, Breadman!" yelled the general. "Your name is what his majesty deems it to be."

"Ah, the Breadman," said Achish. "I must say, I prefer *'Goliath'*, don't you?"

"I do, your majesty." said the general. "Goliath it is."

Biro looked from the general to the king, a sudden realisation hitting him he was nothing more than a distraction or, even worse, an amusement to the assembled courtiers and military strategists. The king sat on a golden armchair. It wasn't grand enough to be a throne, but neither was it plain enough to belong to anyone but a king. He wore a beautiful emerald green silk simlāh, with a white silk kethōneth circled by golden cords. On his feet he wore intricately embroidered gold and green silk slippers. Despite his thick dark eyebrows and goatee beard, the soft complexion of his skin suggested a relatively young man.

"Why are you here, Goliath?" asked the king, now availing himself of some grapes.

"I am here to beg your protection for my family, your majesty."

"Protection? For your family? Is not the whole assemblage of the Philistine Army protection enough for you? You wish more than this?"

"It is from the soldiers that my daughters need protecting, my King. Their attentions are neither wanted, nor encouraged. My girls now fear leaving their mother's side."

Achish continued chewing his grapes. "Tell me, Goliath," he said. "Why are you wasted baking bread, when you should wield a sword in my ranks?" He threw another grape into his mouth.

"I... I'm a baker, your majesty. I'm not a soldier."

"Nonsense, Goliath! Look at you. You are amazing. You are magnificent. The very sight of you swinging a sword would strike fear into any man.

And any man is a soldier for his king, when the situation demands. Wouldn't you agree?"

"I swear I'm not a fighter, your majesty. I do not believe in conflict."

Achish sat up, bewildered. "I'm sorry," he laughed. "Did I hear you correctly? You do not believe in conflict? You think..." He laughed again, gasping in disbelief. "You think this war is wrong? Pointless? You think thousands of men have died in my name... for nothing?" The king laughed furiously, joined by his accompanying advisors, until the grape he was eating became stuck in his throat. He choked, thumping his fist against the chair arm.

"Help him! Help him!" the general screamed at a servant. The young man quickly poured a goblet of water and offered it to the king, who gulped it down, giving one last barking cough.

"I'm curious, Goliath," the king eventually said. "How would you settle this... dispute... between Philistine and Israelite, if not through war?"

The giant baker stood, mouth open, terrified at the course of events. "Answer the king," barked the general.

"I... I think that... I think that the deaths of thousands of young men are such a waste. Perhaps... perhaps..." Biro paused, uncertain of what to say next.

"Perhaps?" asked the king.

"Perhaps a designated champion from either side should settle the matter, your majesty. A warrior willing to fight in your name, therefore saving the lives of many." Biro could feel his panic rising. He looked back and forth, from king to general, then to the king again. "Perhaps King Saul would have his champion fight yours… ours."

The king sat, unresponsive, chomping on several grapes. He gestured to the servant to provide further water. Biro feared the worst. Achish looked to his general, thinking awhile, then nodded. "Send a rider to Saul," he said. "Put this unusual proposition to him. There is merit in not losing any more men." He continued nodding. "Yes, Goliath. Well done. You may go now."

"And my daughters, your majesty. Shall they have your protection?"

"Yes, yes," he waved impatiently. "If any man touches them, he shall lose his head. Now, begone. I wish to rest."

Biro smiled and turned to leave, happy with a most successful outcome.

"The king demands your presence!"

Biro looked up from his kneading and, through a cloud of flour, saw the general turn to leave the tent entrance. There was no preamble, no discussion. He dusted his hands and pursued the rushing military man past the campfires and idle soldiers. Without a word, the general raised the opening to the king's tent, nodding for Biro to enter. A thin smile crossed the face of his escort, causing a shudder to travel down Biro's spine; a terrible feeling overcame him.

"Biro, the Breadman, your majesty!" announced the general.

"Ah, Goliath," welcomed Achish. "I have good news. Saul is open to your suggestion and will put forward a champion. At first light tomorrow, we shall put an end to this war, one way or the other. What do you think of that, Goliath?"

Biro wasn't sure how to respond. It didn't matter, as he wasn't given the chance. "You, Goliath! You shall be my champion!"

"Me? Me, your majesty? But I am not a fighter, sire. I have never held a sword in my life. I cannot win this challenge for you. Please… please choose someone else." His heartbeat was racing, sweat pouring from him. He looked to the general, who simply stood with the same smile fixed on his face.

"Yes. Yes, you, Goliath. You will stand as my champion, else your entire family shall face the consequences. Or, are you a coward?"

Biro felt nauseous, felt tears filling his eyes. "I'm not a coward, your majesty. But, how am I to defeat a trained champion? How can I hope to match an experienced soldier? I'm no coward, but I have no wish to lose you this battle." The general couldn't help letting out a laugh.

"Do not be so naive, Goliath," laughed Achish. "If you lose, then we are none the weaker. As you yourself have said, you are not a soldier, and we shall simply launch our attack. Just as Saul shall do, should you win." He thrust his hands forward, as if pointing out the obvious. "Have him fitted for armour," he said to the general, "and give him a sword." The king sat back, relaxing in his golden chair. He waved his fingers, gesturing for Biro to leave.

"This way… *Goliath*," said the general, taking Biro's right arm; the same sickly smile still glued on his face.

⁂

There had been no sleep. Nor had there been a chance to see his wife, or his daughters. Instead, they held him, alone and afraid, in an empty tent on the opposite side of the camp from his loved ones. He couldn't eat; he couldn't drink.

Biro sat on a stool, staring at his clothes, lying folded in a neat pile on the straw mattress he hadn't used. He now wore a short green panelled kilt, with a wide hem, and tassels falling down the side. Above his waist, a ribbed corselet, with thin upward-curving leather strips, covered a linen shirt. By the entrance to the tent sat, on top of a small circular shield, what the general called a "feather" headdress; a leather cap with an ornamental headband from which a row of slightly curving reeds, not feathers, stood upright, forming a style of diadem. The worn, cracked short sword they had given him provided little reassurance. Biro despaired, questioning how effective his armour would ultimately prove.

The first hints of sunrise peeked through the tent opening. A horn, sounding the call to muster, and the sounds of frantic activity outside, shook him to the core. A feeling of hopelessness washed over him, and he leaned forward with his head in his hands. "You should have something to eat," said a voice from outside the tent. Biro raised his head. He was cold, with a strange sense of displacement; he knew he was here, but he felt like he was actually somewhere else. At least he wished he was somewhere else. The horn sounded once more, and Biro threw up.

As the minutes passed, the soldiers' preparation intensified and, before long, Biro was being marched up a long track toward the Valley of Elah. There were squads of soldiers everywhere; marching on the track, over the gorse, in fact, anywhere that was flat enough to march on; all heading toward the valley. The unbroken, open space suddenly led uphill into a forest of Elah trees. The further he walked, the louder the din from the growing ranks on either side of the valley. Chants, and songs, and insults were reverberating all around, and Biro felt his fear growing. "I have to piss," he pleaded.

"Be quick about it," retorted his escort.

His hands shook as he tried to concentrate. The sensation of needing to relieve himself had been so strong, but nothing would come. Nothing. After a minute or so, the escort banged his sword on his shield, unceremoniously ending the unsuccessful toilet break.

As he made his way out from the trees, a cool breeze whistled down the length of the open space that now stretched for several miles in either direction. A slight, downhill gradient led to a dried out creek at the bottom of the valley, but every inch of ground on this side seemed occupied by Philistine soldiers. Biro looked across the valley, horrified at the scene before him. Thousand upon thousand, chanting and banging their swords on their shields; a tumultuous thunder, beneath cloudless skies. Horns blasting out tunelessly, drums beating relentlessly. It hadn't occurred to him how many Israelites would be on the other side, but he was certain, there were far more than anyone would have expected. The rumours had been wrong; they hadn't delayed waiting for Saul; they had simply delayed to maximise their numbers, and they heavily outnumbered the Philistines.

The escort led him to the front of the column, where the general waited. Biro had not, to this point, paid much attention to the man; but, here, faced with death, he wanted to see the individual who was effectively serving him his death sentence. The short, bald man, who was a little overweight, especially around the middle, stood like a child in front of the large, muscular baker making his way down the incline. The general, despite his colourful corselet, and clutching his flamboyant feather headdress, was not an impressive specimen; he had only seemed so in Biro's moments of confusion and panic.

"Over there," he said, pointing, "by the white horses. That's your opponent. Just keep walking and, when you meet him, kill him." He looked at the escort and laughed. "What could be simpler? Eh, Goliath?"

Biro continued his walk without breaking stride. As he reached the frontline of the soldiers, a tremendous cheer went up. "Goliath! Goliath! Goliath!" they chanted, banging sword on shield. The Israelite horde, on seeing Biro, responded with their own chants, their own shield banging. On the horses, where the general had indicated, the riders were pointing at him, and giving orders to the man standing between them. All three men were laughing. Biro flexed his fingers, re-gripping the handle of his shield, and making sure the arm strap was tight enough. He did likewise with his right hand, strengthening his hold on his sword. Behind him, the Philistines chanted. "Goliath! Goliath! Goliath!"

He could now clearly see the man he was to face. It wasn't a man; it was a boy. A small boy—no taller than his youngest daughter—with a pale complexion and dark shoulder-length curly hair. He wore a white knee-length tunic; no armour, or shield. His weapon was a wooden staff, although he appeared to be holding something small in his right hand. Biro felt extremely uncomfortable; even more so now that he realised he was going to kill, or be killed by, a child no older than Jael.

Biro continued walking, and his opponent started out toward him. The Israelites roared. The

Philistines roared back. The boy looked at his staff, then discarded it to his side, stooping to scoop up a small stone, which he inspected, then rejected. He did this four times, rejecting the stone he had picked up, tossing it aside. The fifth stone he collected appeared to satisfy his requirements, and he turned to face his army, holding the stone high so they could see it. The Israelites roared again.

There was now only twenty yards between them. Within seconds, the boy had dropped a sling from his hand, loaded the stone, and twirled the weapon around his head. Before he knew what was happening, Biro buckled as the small rock smashed into his forehead, between his eyes and just above his nose.

His vision immediately blurred. He felt sick and fell to his knees. The Israelites roared. Biro dropped his sword, falling forward onto his right hand. He could hear the cheering, and the banging on the shields as he vomited. Blood ran down from the gaping hole in his forehead, blinding him further. He was shaking violently, and could feel the warmth of his urine, now, at the time of his helplessness, running down his thigh. The roars of the Israelites continued, but he could hear the padding of someone running toward him, getting closer.

The footsteps halted, and the boy gathered up Biro's sword. "We shall feed the bodies of your Philistines this day to the birds of the air and to the wild beasts of the earth," he said. "Make peace with your heathen gods, Goliath. For now, you go to join them." The blind, concussed giant looked up in the voice's direction.

"My name is Bi…."

The sword swung, cleanly, completely separating Biro's head from his body, his feather cap flying off. The dead baker slumped to the ground. His head bounced, then rolled awkwardly, halting at the feet of his decapitator. The boy grabbed the head by the beard, raising it in victory, presenting it to the Israelite horde. As they roared once more, they ran, as one, toward the shocked Philistines.

The Philistine front ranks ran forward, joining the battle. There was a mighty thunder-like thud as the two bodies of men clashed, shield to shield, sword to sword. Shouting and screaming filled the valley; a horrendous song of death, accompanied by the rhythm-less clanging of metal on metal. Within seconds, faced with overwhelming Israelite numbers, many of the Philistine ranks broke away, fleeing west toward Shaaraim. The Israelites swarmed forward, relentlessly pursuing the enemy, ultimately as far as Gath and Ekron.

They scythed and slashed through the feeble resistance presented by the disassembled Philistine army; trampling over the fallen, and pursuing the terrified and wounded. Up the incline and through the trees, the swarm continued. The Israelites cut the Philistines down in their thousands, their hundreds and, ultimately, one by one, until they left none alive.

The wave of death continued onward through the trees, down the slope and into the remnants of the Philistine camp, where Naclara, Jael, and Orpah waited for their husband and father.

None were spared.

Biro lay where he fell. There was a strange calm; a silence; a peacefulness suggesting there had never even been a battle; that it was all just a dream. He could hear birdsong, could feel the gentle breeze caress his face, but he still couldn't see; all was dark.

Two birds now warbled their cheery, hopeful song. The breeze still made its way across the valley, and the warmth of the early morning sun was now touching his skin. He felt as if he had just woken after a deep sleep. A tiny dot of light appeared in the darkness, gradually growing until a bright, white light filled his eyes. He could hear voices; two women were chatting as they approached from the distance.

The white light slowly turned to blue, and Biro realised he was looking upward to the cloudless sky. It was a beautiful morning. He sighed; relaxed and content. The beauty of the blue canvas was broken, as the two women towered over him, one either side. To his left, a tall woman, wearing a long gold stola, with long brown hair that fell from her face as she gazed down at him; her wonderful smile making his already warm contentment even more complete. To the right, a similarly dressed woman, this one in green, with lighter coloured hair, but just as warm a smile. They seemed, to his eyes, to stretch away from him into the beautiful blue haze of the morning sky.

"Good morning, ladies," he said. "Isn't this a lovely morning?"

"It is, indeed," said the lady on the left, holding her hand down to him. "May we help you to your feet, Biro?"

Biro smiled. "You know my name? Well, that's a turn. I had almost forgotten it myself. They kept calling me…"

"Oh, we know what they named you, Biro," interrupted the other woman. "But we know who you are, sweet and gentle giant. You are the reason we are here."

The first woman clasped his outstretched hand and pulled. Biro heaved himself up into a sitting position. "I am?" he asked. "Did my wife send you?" He looked about him, struggling to turn to see behind. A puzzled look fell on his face. "Where is everyone?" he said, as the memory of recent events formed in his mind. "There was a boy," he recalled. "A small boy… with a sling. Where is everyone?" he repeated. "My wife… my family?" Biro struggled to his feet. He looked about him again, his gaze falling upon the headless body lying close by, and the thousands of fallen soldiers that littered the ground all the way to the trees. "What….?"

"Please be calm, Biro. The worst is over, and the best is yet to come."

"Who are you?" he asked, anxiously scanning the valley. "And where is my family? My wife? My daughters?" He turned in the direction of the camp. "Naclara!" he shouted. "Naclara!" Biro ran toward the trees, but his big, heavy frame soon slowed; he continued, walking as quickly as he could. He was out of breath and his limbs were aching, but still he pressed forward. "Naclara! Jael! Orpah!" he cried.

The women followed. "Shouldn't we stop him, Mother?"

"I think it best he sees the reality, Cassie," said Circe. "There is nothing left for him here; he belongs in Elŷsium now."

"And what of his family? Do they not deserve a place in Elŷsium?"

"His family?" Circe asked.

"Yes, Mother, his family. The wonderful man we have come for, was shaped by his family. He is his family, and they are he. Are they not worthy of our hospitality?"

Circe watched the despairing man lumber toward the trees. "He would be lost without his family just as much in Elŷsium, as he would be here," added Cassandra. Circe nodded as she considered her suggestion.

"You know, I think you're right, Cassie. We shall take them all."

XX. SHADOW OF THE SUN

Aeetes stood, preening himself, naked in front of the mirror. He ran his fingers through his golden locks, gazing at his side profiles, and sighed. "It feels so good to be back home again," he said. He turned, side-on to the mirror, and posed as he flexed his muscles, admiring his athletic physique.

He picked up a robe, draped it over his shoulders, and walked toward the bathroom. "The people are delighted to have a powerful leader once more," he opined. "They had tired of the disinterest with which my father treated them. Now they know what I expect of them. Now they know the consequences of displeasing their king."

He stepped down into the blistering hot water and sat on the shelf seat at the side, raising his arms back onto the floor edge above him as he leaned back. "It *is* good to be back home," he repeated, "but I thought there would be more for me to do." He looked back over his shoulder toward the bedroom, listening for a response, grimacing when none came.

"Did you hear me?" he shouted. "I thought there would be more to entertain me." He turned again, but still there was silence.

Her tears fell, seeping into the softness of the pillow; her humiliation seeping into her heart. Lying naked on her side in the bed, the silk top-sheet discarded around her ankles, Perse coiled herself into a foetal position, pulling her knees tightly into her chest. There were no sobs, no choking cries; she was still the Queen of the Universe, after all. No. There were just the silent tears.

Yes, she was still Queen of the Universe, but now she was also a reluctant concubine for her son. She was now the always-available whore with which he would pleasure himself. At least, she felt like a whore; a whore who lay down, spreading her legs, regularly and often. Not for money, no—nothing as tasteless as that. No, her wages were the lives of her courtiers, her maids, her subjects; not that she'd accepted it at first. Aeetes had held true in his threats, his promises that, were she not to lie down for him, many would pay with their lives.

At first it was a single maid, or a footman. Then, when she continued to resist, his anger led to the destruction of entire villages. Despite his deranged savagery, Perse had tried holding on to her pride, her dignity. She wished he would spare her the humiliation of conceding in front of her subjects; that he would be done with the performance, and just force her; violently, if that's what it took to show publicly what a monster he was. At least that would spare her honour. But he was too vain for that. He may be angry, but he was also patient enough, cruel enough, to slaughter as many innocents as it took. He waited until his mother knelt before him, begging him to call off his murder squads.

She would never forget that sickening look on his face, as she declared before the assembled aristocracy of Sólaás her obsequiousness to accommodate his sexual demands. The sneering grin, his enjoyment of her degradation, and the ultimate insult, as he demanded she take him, there and then, performing an oral act which had no intent other than humiliation. In full view of the court, her fall from Queen, to little more than a demimondaine, a doxy, a slut. She was now the pet of the new king, and he would, from then on, take every opportunity to empty his seed into her. He was no longer her son; he was her tormentor. He was her abuser, and her hatred for him was more intense than that which she ever felt for Haáde.

Yes, there was little for him to do; for he lacked imagination, creativity, or even the wit to realise what power he now wielded. He was little more than a petulant bully; an arrogant, conceited despot with a sense of entitlement as great as the Universe he now ruled over. Not for him the ambition of world-building. Not for him the possibility of rescuing Kiípos from its current malaise. He wanted everything, but he wanted it served up to him; on a plate; in his bed; at his feet.

And, now, all that there was for Perse was involuntary servitude and disgrace. She wiped her tears, disgusted with herself that she did not have the courage to take either her own, nor her son's life. Now she would just lie and take it. Now she was defeated.

"Are you still lying there, feeling sorry for yourself?" Aeetes sneered as he returned from his bath. "Get up, woman. Clean yourself, and make yourself presentable." Perse did not respond, instead continuing to squeeze herself ever more tightly. "Get out of that fucking bed, you pathetic bitch," he screamed, ripping the top sheet away from her legs. His fragile patience had already run thin.

"You can make all of this stop, Mother. You know you can."

"I will not let you defile your sister," Perse mumbled.

"Defile?" Aeetes laughed, mockingly. "I shall not defile her. I shall make her my Queen. She will bear my children, and she will be happy doing so, keeping the blood of Célestiaá pure." He stood by the side of the bed, his genitals directly in Perse's eye-line. "But first you must tell me how I can enter Elŷsium. There seems to be no gateway from Sólaás, no Diávasi that lets me through. And, of course, I cannot set foot on Kiípos lest it burn to a crisp. So, how do I get to Elŷsium, Mother?"

Perse smiled, taking pleasure in knowing that her daughter was safe, for now, in the otherworldly environs of Elŷsium. It was a curiosity that she couldn't quite grasp; how could Célestiaá have so much power, and yet not easily move between the dimensions they themselves had created? Séntinell had explained Circe's difficulties in returning to Kiípos after Pasiphae's Reavers had attacked her at the human hospital. They described how, separated from her Célestiaá Ring, she had despaired of ever seeing her beloved Raymond, Eric, and Jacob again.

She knew, too, how Pasiphae had wormed her way onto Kiípos; manipulating Jacob's presence, using Circe's own ring to build a bridge through the waterfalls, through a freak of the weather she had somehow conjured. It was this trickery that had allowed her access through Circe's

Diávasi. For the moment, these crafts seemed beyond the limited intelligence of Aeetes; a deficiency Perse had never thought helpful until now.

"Elŷsium is out of your reach," muttered Perse. "Astris is out of your reach. Choose another queen and enjoy your stolen kingdom."

"Spare me your simpering, your false mourning for my father. You had long since grown tired... bored, even, of his company. And I'm certain, despite your protestations, you are enjoying the attention a younger stallion is giving you." He leaned down, placing an arm either side, his face right in hers. "Do you, Mother? Do you enjoy my attention?" he asked sarcastically.

Perse lay still, nausea creeping over her. She stopped herself from answering; stopped herself from angering him further. A quiet, distant *'ting'*, indicating a request for an audience, drew Aeetes' attention. He slowly raised himself away from the terrified woman, his eyes never breaking contact with hers.

"Enter!" he barked. There was no attempt by Perse to cover herself; her modesty long abandoned, replaced by a resignation, an acceptance of her newly diminished status. It did not concern her if anyone—servants, soldiers, traitorous sycophants—saw her nakedness. If it thrilled them, then fine. If it embarrassed Aeetes, even better; but she doubted her son could ever have the self-awareness of feeling such discomfort.

A servant entered the bedroom, bowing, avoiding eye contact with his king. He passed a message, then backed off again, bowing continuously until he left the room.

"Well, well," muttered Aeetes. "It would appear that madness has taken hold of the palace. Apparently, there is a flaming brazier in the throne room that is calling my name." He sat on the bed, laughing hysterically. "And, would you believe it, Mother? The voice is claiming to be my sister."

Aeetes entered the throne room, his usual entourage trailing behind. Awaiting him was Archon Alin Dóul, formerly Pollor Marik's deputy, now promoted as his successor. Alin had none of the sophistication Pollor was renowned for; none of the impressive demeanour, or stature. He was a weedy little man, looking even less impressive in his ill-fitting dark green tunic. His greasy grey locks, and crooked nose, and the constant perspiration dotting his forehead, betrayed his permanent fear of failing, or displeasing.

He was, mostly, an inconsequential toady; a man who would say whatever would ingratiate him, whatever would curry favour. In short, he was the ideal sycophantic courtier.

Alin bowed low as Aeetes swept into the new heart of his kingdom. "Welcome, Gracious Majesty," he said, as if speaking directly to the floor, such was the depth of his bowing. Aeetes afforded him his usual arrogant side-eyed sneer, befitting the contempt with which he viewed anyone who was not Célestiaá born.

"What of this?" Aeetes probed, waving the cryptic message. "What nonsense is this?"

Alin held his arms outstretched, directing Aeetes' gaze toward a brazier. There was nothing of note about the grilled coals, not that the new king could determine. So, why the urgent request for his presence?

"I warn you, Dóul... this had better not be a waste of my time." He sat on the throne, staring at the burning slack, straining to see what he should look for.

"Oh, I would not dream of wasting His Gracious Majesty's precious time, My King," oozed Alin. He stood by the brazier, he too staring into the depths of the embers. Realising that nothing was happening, Alin grasped a poker and stoked the coke briquettes, throwing up a flurry of sparks and smoke. He stepped back, anticipating some magical response. Still, there was nothing. He looked desperately into the flames. Then, when Aeetes made to stand, he fell to his knees in search of mercy. Sweat seeped from every pore of his shaking body; fear of Aeetes' already-infamous wrath and justice making him tremble.

"What is this?" roared the king, drawing his sword. "You would interrupt..."

"*Brother?*" came the echoing call from the flames.

Alin snapped his eyes directly to the brazier. "There! There, My King," he gushed. "The flames call for you."

Aeetes stepped, hesitantly, down the steps from the throne, his sword half-drawn; his eyes fixed firmly into the bright red fuels. A black smoke emanated from the ashes, though not behaving as one would expect smoke to. It rose, slowly swirling back into itself, almost as if standing; almost as if trying to take solid form.

"Hello?" Aeetes asked quietly, uncertainly. He looked back at his courtiers, making sure none were mocking him.

He removed his sword completely from its sheath, the hairs on the back of his neck bristling, the first flickering of flame tickling his arms. Was this fear he was feeling? He wasn't sure, he'd never felt fear before. But this was unexplained strangeness, perhaps even sorcery. In his long exile in Andromeda, he'd heard tales of the magics of Kiípos' wizards and witches; of warlocks and, even more unsettling, the necromancers who dabbled in dealings with the dead. Of course, he knew about the life essence; and how the souls of each spirit transcended to Sólaás or Hades. But these necromancers, these mysterious creatures who defied the laws and natures of Sólaás, were to be avoided at all costs.

Over many millennia, he had sent spies across the skies in search of news and intelligence of the dealings in his father's many kingdoms. Kiípos had become a particularly interesting topic for Aeetes and his advisors. Though none had ever actually set foot on Circe's garden world—always quickly retreating through fear of discovery by Aether—his spies had discerned much about the behaviours of the inhabitants of this blue and green wonderland. Indeed, humanity, or the *fleas*, as Aeetes knew them, had exceeded even Célestiaá in their technological and scientific advances.

Their religious and spiritual beliefs and ceremonies, as reported by his information gatherers, fascinated him. But it was the necromancers who terrified him. If his spies were to be believed, not only could they communicate with the dead spirits of those departed to Sólaás and Hades, these shamans could control and manipulate these souls once in their new destination. And it was this possibility that was always at the forefront of Aeetes' concerns; betrayal from within. So, yes, he was familiar with fear.

Invading Sólaás, even defeating Helios, had been the simplest of tasks. But, what if the necromancers of Kiípos could undermine the new king? Take advantage of his unfamiliarity with his new realms? He dare not mention his insecurities to his advisors, and certainly not to his subjects, for they would be certain to call these agents of death to their aid. He was not a fool—he was fully aware of how despised he was in his new home. This would change over time of course. Not with love, or mercy; no, once he had established his rule with brutal force, his subjects would learn to fear him. And fear is more powerful than either love or hate. Fear keeps the fearful in a state of indecision, a state of inaction, of subjugation. Fear encourages the weak to betray the courageous, the rebellious. But only if he could keep the necromancers at bay.

"Hello?" he called again to the flames. "Who are you?"

The smoke swirled, and the coals cracked and sparked. The smoke-column grew taller and taller, taking the form of a giant shadow-woman.

"Why, brother," the echoing voice chimed. "Do you not know me?"

Around him, Aeetes' courtiers drew back, fearful of the deathly sound of this terrifying voice. Aeetes, too, felt his courage failing, and he took a step back. "No, I do not know thee, shadow. Are you a necromancer, dark stranger? What do you want with us?"

Aeetes caught the shadow unawares; this was not what was expected. The King of Andromeda, the Usurper of Sólaás, cowering in fear of... what? Myths of human lore?

Stories of magic, of the raising of the human dead? Why was he so afraid? The dead do rise, their essence journeying to first Elŷsium, then Sólaás or Hades. It was surprising, then, that the new King of the Universe should be in thrall to pathetic, infantile ghost stories.

The shadow-woman had come to Sólaás in search of an ally; someone to facilitate her return to the celestial realms; to bring about an end to her enforced exile. She had expected a strong, powerful king—a man with whom she would negotiate, trade benefits—not this superstitious fop. This was no king, this was an arrogant, entitled dictator; a man ignorant of his power, merely glorying in his privileged position. Here was a man-child; used to getting his own way, not accustomed to anyone contesting his wishes.

And now, much to her delight, a great opportunity appeared; now, she could take the initiative, and wield the power of this fool to her advantage. She could never have hoped to confront Helios; his dim-witted son, however, was a different story. He had made her succession so much simpler. The dirty work, the hard part was done; Helios was no more, and Sólaás was there for the taking.

The smoke swirled violently, whooshing as it rose and fell, sparks jumping furiously from the embers. The shadow laughed loudly, echoing through the throne room, its darkness spreading through the space, slamming the throne room doors shut, swallowing all light 'cept that from the brazier. The courtiers screamed and fled back toward the walls, leaving Aeetes alone to face the visitor.

The shadow-figure grew ever larger, its laughing ever louder. "Yes!" it bellowed. "Yes, Aeetes, I am indeed a necromancer. I am the Queen of the Necromancers, the ruler of the dead. I was Pasiphae, your sister; first-born daughter of the murdered king Helios; Queen of Hades, and wife of Háade. Now I come to claim reparation for the unconscionable wrongs inflicted on me. Now you shall know me as *Persephone*!" The smoke swirled, faster and faster, growing, the whirlwind becoming ever more agitated and aggressive.

"Now!" boomed the Necromancer. "Now, I demand your service, your armies, and your kingdom. Free me from these dark, empty peripheries, or watch as I turn your filched dominion, your conquered, unwilling allegiants to ashes."

Aeetes shielded his eyes as the fire sparked explosively once again, the light stabbing the eye as the surrounding darkness seemed to fold in on them all. The courtiers squealed and huddled tighter against the walls. "Watch," shrieked Persephone, "as I swallow Sólaás with the embers of my desires!" Her reverberating words filled the hall, bouncing from the walls, piercing the ears of all assembled. The brazier rumbled, and sparked, and, without warning, there came a flow of lava from within its heart. Bubbling out, hissing as it met the tiled floors, groaning as it stretched out toward the cowering King.

"Tell me," begged Aeetes, "what do you want from me?"

Persephone sensed her victory; her spectacular performance successful in cowing her simple-minded half-wit of a brother.

"The Nuclei Ring," she declared, pointing down at his hand. Aeetes stared at the magnificent jewel, trembling on his coward's hand. He quickly removed it, pulling it off, holding it high in offering to his tormentor.

"Here, take it," begged the king. "Spare me... take these peasants... but spare me, and I shall be your man."

"Throw it into the flames," ordered Persephone.

Without thought, Aeetes did as instructed, then scurried backwards on all-fours toward the wall beside the courtiers. The fearful, tearful shrieks and cries as the throng parted, fleeing the bringer of their ruin, drowned out even the loudest of Persephone's laughs. The brazier roared, and the shadows smothered, and covered, and terrified the kneeling crowd.

They watched as the shadow-woman stretched tall, before stepping down from the crown of the coals; towering above them, the shadow glowing brighter, brighter, ever brighter. Until, at last, the light slowly abated, leaving the throne room in total darkness.

After a short time, the shadows relented; easing back, like the going out of the tide, until they retreated once more into the depths of the brazier. Persephone looked down upon her new subjects, as they stared in terror at her. The giant shadow-woman was now a solid, living being; her bearing and stance that of a strong, young woman; her features those of a wrinkled, haggard old shrew. Her leathery, puckered face, with heavy bags beneath her eyes, brought nought but fear to all who gazed upon her. Her long, grey straw-like hair fell to her waist; lifeless, and without shine, looking as dead as she did. For that's what she resembled—the dead come back to life. The blackness of her stola was as deep as the night, and the aura that emanated from her was as terrifying as death's final consuming kiss.

"Hear me and tremble," she began, her skeletal arms, with loose skin hanging off the bones, pointing; her words almost hissing, as if spoken by a snake. "I, who was once Pasiphae, Princess of Sólaás, Daughter of Helios The Slaver, Queen of Hades, and wife of Haáde The Wife-Murderer, avow here and now, that I shall not rest until I have my revenge. I shall deliver retribution upon those who have wronged me. All hail Persephone, the new Queen of the Universe."

Aeetes crawled forward, still down on his hands and knees. He knelt up, clasping his hands, beseeching his new queen. "My dearest sister," he grovelled. "I..."

Persephone looked down at him, repulsed by his kowtowing; ceasing him in mid-speech as she held her hand up in reproach. Aeetes gazed upon the Nuclei Ring on her bony finger, glowing a much darker red than before; a living shadow at its centre, angrily crashing from side to side in apparently futile attempts to escape. In that moment, the deposed usurper realised the confidence trick which had just been played on him; swallowing hard, understanding how easily he had conceded all his power to his cunning sister. Persephone was no necromancer, no manipulator of the dead. She was Célestiaá—as was he—but now she was the most powerful of them all; and he had just gifted her the universe.

Persephone crouched in front of her brother. She lifted his chin with her skinny, wrinkled finger; a cold, deathly hand, then cupped his face. She smiled a hideous, taunting smirk. "What a disappointment you are, Brother," she hissed. "I find it difficult to believe you could actually best our father. Tell me," she continued, "where is our mother?"

Aeetes gasped, and his head snapped back toward the throne room doors, involuntarily providing Persephone with confirmation of Perse's survival. She looked up at the grovelling, snivelling congregation, each trying harder than the next to gain a place of safety behind his or her neighbour. "You!" she barked at Archon Alin Dóul, her voice feeling as though it had fingers gripping his throat. "Bring the Queen Mother Perse to me." Dóul struggled to his feet, shuffling his way backwards toward the door, his customary grovelling bow in evidence once more for this new liege.

Persephone turned her attention back to her kneeling brother. She gestured for him to stand, scrutinising him, inspecting him as he did so. "I must say, Aeetes," she said, "you are a remarkable physical specimen." Aeetes' ingrained narcissism brought a smile to his face. He watched as Persephone made her way up to the throne, taking her place as the new queen. She stared at him, her eyes stabbing into his, a sneer running across her thin, crinkled lips. "But beauty does not a powerful ruler make. Tell me, brother, how did you expect to succeed our father, when..."

"Well, I..." Persephone thrust her hand up, silencing him.

"Do not think to interrupt me, Aeetes," she asserted. "I have had my fill of insult and betrayal. I shall brook no disrespect from an imbecile." Aeetes, in his umbrage, made to approach Persephone, but did not get far. She stood, striking out with her hand, sending him flying backwards; rendering him prone, bleeding from his mouth and nose. "You shall approach only when I allow it," she spat. "You will speak only when I allow it. In fact, brother, you will eat, sleep, piss or shit, only when I allow it."

She looked to the edges of the room. The sobbing and crying were now jarring on her. Once, they had been a source of pleasure; the rewarding results of her tortures in the cells of Hades. For now, however, they were beyond being annoying. "Leave us," she screamed. The courtiers did not need any further convincing, scrambling over one another to be the first to leave. Her focus rested on Aeetes once again.

"You are not a king, Aeetes," she said, so matter-of-factly it stung. "You will not rule Sólaás. You will not rule the universe. Instead, you shall lead my armies in an assault on Elŷsium, Kiípos, and, most importantly, Hades."

The deposed tyrant bowed his head in shame. In mere moments, he had fallen from the lofty position of king, to the subordinate service of being a mere soldier. He cursed himself for his foolishness; he cursed Persephone for her deception.

"I shall, of course, reward you for your service, brother. Once I have the throne of Hades, and the head of Haáde as my trophy, you will take care of Sólaás in my stead, thus maintaining the balance of darkness and light. I shall rule from the Shadowlands, with all future tribute delivered directly to me."

Aeetes was unsure whether he should feel angered or relieved, but continued to stare at the floor. "An assault on Elŷsium is impossible, sister," he mumbled. "There is no gateway, no entry to Circe's paradise." He wiped the blood from his face. "I have tried," he said, as if that were the last word on the matter.

Persephone laughed a little; a laugh derisive in its tone. "As I said, you are no king." She sat quietly for a few moments, considering her brother, weighing him up further. "If I give you the means to enter Elŷsium," she mused, "will you guarantee the retrieval of the Célestiaá Rings from the humans?"

Aeetes looked up; Persephone had stoked his interest. "You have a key?" he asked. "A way through the dimensional barriers?"

"I do," confirmed Persephone. "And you shall have the means to take the armies of Sólaás and Andromeda into Elŷsium. My armies. You shall retrieve my Célestiaá Ring, besides that which belonged to Circe."

Aeetes considered the possibility. "And what of our nephew? He is Célestiaá after all?"

"Half-Célestiaá," she reminded him. "Half-Célestiaá. And what you do to him... what you do to any you encounter is up to you."

"If I do this," he asked, "I can have Astris as my queen?"

Persephone lowered her shaking head, once more disappointed, but not surprised, at Aeetes' short-sighted self-interest. "I have no interest in anything but the rings. You can keep whatever... *spoils*... you win in Elŷsium. Just bring me those rings. I shall have need of all the power I can muster if I am to face Haáde."

She smiled, her wrinkled face contorting into the most hideous of masks. "And face him, I most certainly will."

XXI. MCGRORY'S FARM

The large pall of smoke, emanating from behind the milking parlour, billowed in the strengthening wind. They could hear the echoing sound of male voices—although unintelligible from this distance—arguing, and joking, as the men went about whatever it was they were doing. A solo guard sat on the roof of the cowshed; paying more attention to his mates below, than his duties above. Smoke was also discharging itself from the farmhouse chimney; a sure sign that someone had taken up residence.

Katie and Melanie lay on the ridge, scoping the farmyard and buildings, trying to calculate the numbers and locations of their quarry. The nearest edges of the farm were about a hundred yards over the field, but they had an unobscured line of vision directly into the main farmyard. The large milking shed was to their left, with smaller barns and sheds dotted down either side of the farmyard, and the two-storey farmhouse to the right.

"They seem to have a fire back there," said Katie. "We can use that when we go down."

"A fire? What have ye got in mind?" asked Melanie.

"Ye really weren't payin' attention, were ye?" Katie smiled and shook her head.

"Well, they kept goin' on about the elements, an' then rumbled on about 'psychokinetic influence'... an' Poseidon kept smilin'."

Katie sighed. "We can use the fire like we can use the water. Just have to figure out how." She continued watching the men. Two people appeared from the farmhouse; a man, and a woman wearing nothing but pants. He was pulling her along by her hair; her body stooped over, her feet tripping and skipping in the mud, her arms flailing as she tried to keep up. "An' we better figure it out quick!"

The man's pace quickened, causing the woman to stumble, eventually tripping onto the ground, spinning as she fell. They could hear her scream as she hit the floor. A second scream, even louder than the first, split the air as her tormentor gave her hair a violent tug, and he continued dragging her along the dirt. He halted his walk, kicking out at the woman as she lay prone, his boot flying into the poor girl's unprotected face. "Get the fuck up," he shouted, before kicking her a second time. She struggled to her knees, then her feet, as he dragged her without waiting.

"Do ye recognise her?" asked Melanie.

"No. But I think we should get down there. I've seen enough. We'll just have to take our chances as far as the numbers are concerned."

The four men looked toward their approaching colleague and the poor bedraggled girl he had in tow. They laughed as he cursed at her, jerking her, pulling her; her legs swaying wildly from side to side as she struggled to keep her faltering balance. The group had assembled around a metal dustbin, which they had filled with broken wood; now aflame and providing some much-needed warmth and light in the growing gloom. They had long since abandoned their task in the barn in favour of warming their hands, and whinging at the current state of their lot.

"Who put that fucker Hog in charge, anyway?" complained one.

"Ye gonna tell him he's no'?" suggested another.

"I just might. I'm gettin' right pissed aff wi' sleepin' in a fuckin' barn, while he lords it up in the hoose, shaggin' these bitches like they're his ane personal fuckin' harem. Who the fuck dis he think he is?"

"Go on, then, Gaz. Go an' tell him ye're no' happy. If he disna kill ye on the spot, then he'll slice yer gut an' tell us tae finish ye aff. An', tae be honest, between the stink o' they fuckin' horses, the cow shit, your fuckin' moanin', an' the fact that my balls are freezin' aff, I might just dae it m'self, anyway. Shut the fuck up, fer fuck's sake."

"Looks like he's throwin' us a bone," added the man on the roof, nodding toward the approaching pair. The girl's body was covered in mud, her pants now invisible, and her face hidden behind a bloody mask. Her tormentor gave her hair another powerful tug, pulling her in front of him;

eventually dragging her so forcefully that she fell to the ground once more. In his hand, he clutched a fistful of greasy, unwashed blonde hair that had come detached. A look of disgust crossed his face as he eyed it, shaking it loose from his grip; relinquishing his responsibility, or interest, in the pathetic woman now whimpering hopelessly as she lay face-down in the dirt.

"Hog's had his fill wi' this ane," the man said. "Says ye can dae what ye like wi' her, then..." He shrugged his shoulders.

"Then what?" asked Gaz.

"Then ye dae what ye like wi' her, if there's anythin' o' 'er left." He stared at Gaz, shrugging his shoulders once again, impatient with the other man's ignorance. There was a great whoosh, and a shower of sparks flew out from the bin; catching everyone by surprise as the roof guard tumbled down silently into the improvised brazier, tipping it over.

"What the fuck?" shouted Gaz, staring at his dead associate; a massive hunting knife protruding from his forehead. The thumping of boots on the cobbles of the farmyard caused the men to look around. Running toward them, swords unsheathed, a gap opening between them, were Katie and Melanie.

"Use the fire, Mel!" Katie shouted.

"The fire?" Melanie stared at the fallen bin, with the hot ashes and burning sticks littering the surrounding ground; the fallen guard's clothes alight. 'Oh, the fire,' she thought, as she understood Katie's suggestion. She lunged forward, bending down on one knee, pointing her sword directly at the flames. Taking a deep breath, she calmed herself and concentrated through the sword—the inscriptions now glowing brightly—feeling the warmth at her neck as the stones, too, glowed. In less than a second, the bin exploded with a loud but dull '*boom*', sending a huge shrapnel-filled fireball outwards, engulfing the surrounding group.

The men screamed as the searing heat, and brightening inferno, swallowed them in its ever-growing circumference, setting their garments afire, turning them to human torches. They flailed, and they squealed, running aimlessly and blindly in panic as the bin's metal shards lodged themselves deeply into their limbs. Gaz rolled and writhed on the ground, trying, in futility, to douse his painful overcoat. Melanie's eyes widened at the results of her work. "Fuck's sake," she mumbled to herself. "Didna expect that!"

The prone girl looked through her bleary, bloody eyes, confused at the events both in front and behind her. The man who had dragged her through the mud had frozen where he stood. He stared at Katie as she closed the gap between them in a millisecond, barely blinking as she jumped and somersaulted, sword swinging, cutting horizontally through his neck, separating body and head. The girl gasped as the man fell to the floor without a sound, or even a spot of blood. She couldn't take her eyes from Katie, who had landed on both feet, crouched, looking directly ahead with both arms extended low behind her.

Melanie had by this time reached Gaz, ending his torment as her sword pierced his heart. She reached down by the bin, through the flames still flicking the downed guard, and retrieved her hunting knife. She felt no pain; the opposite, in fact. There was a coolness in the fire around her skin, and it mesmerised her for a second. She turned her hand in the blue light, awestruck at what was happening. A shout, from the direction of the farmhouse, broke her reverie and she looked up to see another girl being ushered out; a human shield protecting the man behind her. It was Gail, a girl she'd worked with at the stables. She was terrified, her hands fumbling down by her sides, as if trying to grasp something that wasn't there; her feet shuffling along in an unsuccessful resistance of the force behind her.

The man had his left arm around Gail's neck, pulling her tightly to him, revealing as little of himself as he could; making himself as small a target as he could. His extended right arm was forward, pointing a handgun at Katie. "Stop where ye are, ye bastards!" he shouted. He continued shuffling forward, training the weapon at Katie. "Drop the fuckin' sword, ye bitch!"

Katie cautiously walked toward him, her sword pointing out to the side and downward. "Let her go," she said firmly, her voice echoing across the farmyard. The man did not reply, instead letting off a shot, the crack of the gun causing Gail to squeal. Melanie gasped as she watched. Katie turned quickly to the side, dodging the bullet, feeling the whoosh of air as it passed her cheek. She stared at the man. "Let her go," she repeated as she resumed her slow steps in his direction. He fired again. Once more, Katie instinctively turned to her side. This time she winced as the projectile grazed her cheek, breaking the skin and drawing blood, but still she continued her advance.

"For fuck's sake!" he screamed, as his frustration got the better of him. "Will ye just fuckin' die?" He pushed

Gail to the side and, with both hands holding the gun, fired off several rounds toward Katie. He immediately staggered backwards on his heels as the force of Melanie's hunting knife thudded into his head; slumping to the floor on his backside, the back of his head thumping back against the farmhouse wall. Gail immediately grabbed the dropped gun, emptying the remaining rounds into Hog's chest.

Melanie ran over to her partner. "Are ye a'right, Katie? Did he get ye?"

Katie sheathed her sword and dusted herself down. "I'm fine, Mel," she replied. "He only grazed me." She watched as Gail was now beating the pistol grip into Hog's head as he lay with the knife handle pointing to the sky. She then turned to the sobbing girl lying in the mud. "You see to Gail, Mel, and I'll take care o' the young lass here." Melanie nodded her agreement and made over to where her former co-worker was still assaulting the dead man.

As she walked toward the mostly naked girl, Katie wiped the blood from her cheek. The wound stung, but it wasn't serious. "Hello," she whispered to the girl. "You're safe now. What's your name?" The filthy wretch looked through her straggly hair; her face a mess of mud, tears, and blood. Katie crouched down and offered her hand. "You're safe now," she repeated. The girl's terrified eyes were darting from one place to another. Her breath was rapid and laden with panic. She tried to scramble away from Katie, her limbs thrashing through the muddied water from the recent rains.

"Dinna touch me!" she squealed, her entire body now trembling with terror.

Katie pulled her hand back. "Sshh!" she mouthed. "It's ok. We're here to help." The girl halted her retreat. Katie smiled and held her hand out once more. "We're here to help," she repeated. "Are there any more o' this lot that we haven't seen yet?" The girl stared, wide-eyed and shivering, but didn't answer. Katie tried again. "Are there any more men on the farm?"

"This isna a farm anymore," the girl cried. "It's a slaughterhouse. It's a fuckin' abattoir."

"What's your name?" Katie asked again. "I'm Katie. That mad ginger fucker there's Melanie." Katie smiled as she watched Melanie comfort Gail. She turned again to the terrified girl, still shivering violently as she sat in the mud. "We're here to make ye safe, darlin'. We're here to help."

"Kayla," the girl mumbled through her trembling lips. "My name's Kayla."

An enormous cloud of steam rose as Katie poured the hot water from the kettle. "Tell me if it gets too hot for ye," she instructed. She knelt by the side of the bath, soaping up a soft face cloth, as Kayla sat with her knees hunched up to her chin, her arms clasped tightly around them. Her trembling, whether through fear or the cold, had continued, and she hadn't spoken a word since giving Katie her name.

As the soft cloth wiped away the dirt and the blood from Kayla's face, it was only then that Katie realised how young the girl was. "So, Kayla, eh?" she asked casually, not wishing to startle the girl by being too direct. She needed answers but knew tact was crucial. "How old are ye,

Kayla?" The girl didn't answer, but it was becoming more apparent as the grime disappeared that she couldn't be more than fourteen or fifteen years old.

Katie continued gently washing the girl, desperately trying to keep her anger from boiling over. It was obvious from the multiple cuts and bruises that Kayla had been seriously and repeatedly abused. There was a bite mark on her left breast; finger marks bruised into her arms from where her abuser, or abusers, had held her as they defiled her youthful body. Her scalp was bloody red from the violent removal of large chunks of her hair; the incident in the courtyard had not been the first time they had dragged her around.

"Do ye live here, Kayla?" Katie attempted another line of questioning. "D'ye know Alex McGrory?"

"He was my granda'." The words came out in the softest mumble, barely audible, even in the quiet of the bathroom. Her eyes fell upon Katie's as she stopped washing the girl.

"Was?" asked Katie. "He's no'... he's no'...?"

"Dead? Aye, he's dead. They bastards killed him!" She pulled herself tighter into herself, then returned to staring into the water.

Katie resumed her task, reeling at the tragic, if not surprising, news. "I'm so sorry to hear that," she said. "Alex was a lovely guy..."

"He was weak," Kayla mumbled. "He let them in."

"What happened?" pressed Katie.

"He's buried, sort o', in the field back there." She raised her tear-filled eyes. "Along wi' another two o' the lassies that they brought."

Katie placed her hand on Kayla's arm, squeezing gently as a show of sympathy. "It must have been awful for ye," she said softly, "but you're safe now."

Kayla turned and stared at her, tears streaming down her face. "Safe? *Safe?* There's nae safety any mare. Ye'd have been as well lettin' them kill me, tae. There's nothin' here. There's naewhere tae go. There's nothin'. Naebody's *safe.*"

The girl was in shock, and Katie saw little point in pressing her further. She continued washing her in silence, until Kayla finally relaxed enough to stretch her legs out, sitting more normally, less fearfully in the bath.

"Well, if anybody else comes, they'll need to get past me and Mel first. We'll be downstairs if ye need anythin'. Okay?" Kayla nodded as she sat in the warmth of the suds-filled water, still shivering, and still not fully trusting the two strange women.

Katie descended the stairs back to the farmhouse living room. In the far corner, Gail lay on a couch, sleeping under a blanket. Melanie sat on an armchair, hunched over, staring at the fire as it blazed furiously, large blocks of wood spitting and cracking. "You okay, Mel? You feelin' the cold?"

"What the fuck are we, Katie? I mean, we baith died, didn't we? Are we ghosts? Or what? What the fuck are we?"

"I'm... I'm sorry, I'm no' sure what ye mean?"

"Those things we did out there. I wasn't expectin' that. What the fuck are we?"

Katie sat on the second armchair, gathering her thoughts as she looked into the flames. "Well... well, we're

Élementaá," she said, matter-of-factly. Melanie looked up and gave a muted, dry laugh.

"And what are Élementaá, exactly? A few weeks ago, we were women. Now? Now, we're Élementaá. Now we're killin' people. Now we're doin' fuck knows what. I'm a fuckin' wizard wi' fire, you wi' water... Shit! Ye even dodged bullets. Dinna say ye didna; I fuckin' saw ye. An' since when am I a bloody Hawkeye-impersonator wi' a huntin' knife? An' by fuck we've baith become fuckin' handy wi' these swords, haven't we?" She wiped away a tear with the heel of her hand. "Ye know what, Katie? Up 'til today, I thought this was all just a great big laugh; somethin' that was goin' on around me; a fuckin' dream, or somethin' I was imaginin' through some drunken headfuck. I thought it was my heid tryin' to make some sort o' sense, some sort o' meanin' for Allan stranglin' me." She prodded the fire with a poker. "But we're just goin' fuckin' mad aren't we?"

Katie moved over, crouching alongside her friend's chair. She put her arm around Melanie's shoulder and kissed the top of her head. "You're right, ye know, Mel. This is totally fucked up. Totally mental." She stared into the red-hot coals, collecting her thoughts and memories; considering everything that had occurred since Allan had left her, too, defiled and dead. She lowered herself, kneeling, then sat on her heels.

"When Cassandra first appeared in front o' me, I felt like you did now — confused, upset and, most o' all, I think, really fuckin' angry. Allan had..." Katie paused, deciding not to go down that particular rabbit hole. "Anyway, Cassandra spoke to me an' I thought I'd gone crazy. This beautiful woman, this Trojan Goddess, was just standin' there, smilin' at me... holdin' a fuckin' sword for fuck's sake. An' behind her, my wee lassie... lookin' absolutely stunnin' in her wee silk dress. I thought my head had exploded. Then, I took Ella's apple. Ate it. An', from then, even though nothin' made any sense, I just went wi' it all. I accepted it."

She put her hand on Melanie's cheek and turned her face, looking into her eyes. "This is all real, Mel. All o' it. We're no' just killin' people, we're rescuin' them as well. Just think what would have happened to these lassies if we had left them wi' these bastards any longer."

"An' what'll happen to them now? We just gonna leave them here, for some other fuckers to take advantage o' them?"

"For now, at any rate, they'll have to manage as best they can. They'll have to be strong for themselves. I only wish we'd got here earlier. We might have saved Claire. We might have saved Alex and the other lassies. Poor fuckers. But, we're here now. We've been given abilities, weapons, an' a mission."

Melanie laughed ironically. "A mission fae God?"

Katie laughed softly, too. "Aye. It seems that way, doesn't it? A mission fae God. But God's no' what we thought, eh?"

"It is fucked up though, Katie! Think about it. The son o' a carpenter, the son o' a genuine goddess, reborn in some heavenly paradise. An' we're to go around preachin' love, respect, an' equality while, at the same time, havin' to kill anybody that disna agree wi' us? Does that no' ring a bell wi' ye? Swap Élementaá fer Disciples, an what do ye get?" Melanie looked questioningly at Katie, genuine concern and bewilderment framing her tone. "An' why us?

Ok, you at least knew Jacob, were close to him. But me? I was just a wee slapper, a troublemaker that fucked up my own life, as well as loads o' others. Why did ye choose me? Why was I the first name ye thought o'? To go searchin' an' killin' our way around the world, spoutin' 'love' an' 'tolerance' an' all that shit. Why? It couldna just be that ye felt sorry for me. There must've been somethin' else, somethin' more. So, why?"

Katie didn't have any answers. She took Melanie's hand. "I did feel sorry for ye, Mel. I did think ye deserved a second chance. I hear what ye're sayin'—it does seem... well, coincidental, all that stuff. But, if ye think there's somethin'... *biblical*... goin' on, well, I can't see it. True, I knew Jacob, but he's wi' Cassandra now. An' I think I was picked simply because I'm Ella's mum, nothin' more than that. Why was my wee Ella chosen? Ye'll need to ask Cassandra, she's the boss in all o' this."

Melanie smiled—a little, but not completely, reassured that she was not totally crazy. "So ye dinna think it's to do wi' the Bible, then?"

"No, no' the Bible, but Cassandra did say somethin' about 'The Muses'."

Melanie screwed her face up. "Muses? What the fuck are Muses?"

"I think, originally, they were the inspiration for artists, musicians, and, well, any auld clever sod. Cassandra said she wanted Élementaá to be the new Muses, the new inspiration for the world that's left."

"Were they in the Bible?"

Katie slowly grinned. "For fuck's sake. On second thoughts, maybe you're right," she said, cheekily. "Your name is 'Eve' after all. Mibbee you've got some bigger part to play in rebuildin' the world, just as Ella has."

Melanie pushed Katie over. "Oh, fuck off," she laughed.

"Eve!" repeated Katie, laughing hysterically.

Melanie fell to the floor, trying to pin her cackling friend's shoulders back. "Fuck off," she laughed again.

"Evie. Evie-pooh," continued Katie. "Evie the Élementaá — saviour o' the world." Both women rolled onto their backs in front of the fire, choking with hilarity.

"Oh... fuck off, ye demented cunt," coughed Melanie.

"Aye," Katie agreed. "We're demented a'right." She looked over at Gail, sleeping soundly on the couch. "We'll stay wi' these two the night, an' head back to Elŷsium in the mornin'. For now, freein' them'll have to be enough. Once we round up the rest o' Élementaá, we'll get a better idea o' how many nuts we're gonna have to crack."

"Muses, eh?" sighed Melanie, nodding. "Sounds like we're puttin' a band back t'gether."

XXII. THE DIMENSIONAL BRIDGE

Lunaá sat high, her silver light shining like a glistening coin, looking on silently as billions of stars twinkled in the blue blackness that filled the clear sky above them. She looked down upon the garden, keeping the secrets of the Eternal Flame's new inhabitant to herself.

The air felt cool, with no hint of a breeze, and the silent still of the night was in tune with Lunaá's hushed presence. The slight crunch, as their footsteps pressed into the lush grass carpet, barely broke the silence as Cassandra, Jacob, Séntinell, and Astris, paced slowly around the Tholos. Eventually, Cassandra voiced her concerns, to no one in particular. "Mother said 'before sundown'. It is now well after sundown. Where is she?" She looked from face to face, but there was no answer.

Astris made her way up the steps to the flame. She held her hands on either side of the hearthstone, bowed her head, and closed her eyes. A red glow drifted from her ring finger, probing the flame, seeking her sister's presence. "Are you there, Circe?" she muttered to herself. She cocked her head to the left, listening intently for any response. After what seemed an age, a spurt of flame, followed by an exaggerated swaying from side to side, signified Circe's arrival.

The flame stood tall, the womanly shape taking control once more. "Circe?" asked Astris. The flame bowed her head, looking directly at the young Célestiaá.

"It is," came the echoing reply. "I am so pleased to see you again, sister."

"Where were you, Mother? We were worried," Cassandra called, stepping up to greet the presence.

The flame turned and crouched. "I have news," said Circe. "Where is Jacob? Is he here?"

Jacob stepped forward from the darkness, his face a picture of wonderment. "I'm here, Mum," he said. "I didn't dare believe it... Yet, here ye are." He looked, incredulous, to Cassandra, then to Astris. "How is this possible?"

"Many are the mysteries of the universe, Jacob," Circe said softly, "and there is still so much for both you and Cassandra to learn. But, we have very little time."

"Please don't go again, Mother," begged Cassandra.

"No, my dear, it's not my leaving that should concern you." She stood, then looked about her, as if in search of something, or someone. "When you found me, Astris, you also made your presence known to Pasiphae, who, much like myself, was in flux out here in the Nowhere." She looked about her again. "I sensed her energy, but could not see her. I have searched but have not seen, nor sensed, her presence since. I know she gleaned much information from our previous contact, and I fear she may attempt to enter the physical dimension once more."

Jacob placed his arm around Cassandra's shoulder. "The physical dimension?" he asked. "Is that possible? Can we bring you back into this dimension, here, now?"

The flames fluttered, their brightness rising and fading, as she crouched to see him better. She held her hand outstretched, reaching for his. Jacob was a little unsure, but Cassandra smiled, nodding her encouragement. As he took her hand in his, her warmth flowed through him, a wave of motherly love which required no words. "I would dearly love to return to you all, Jacob," she sighed. "But that would be foolhardy in the extreme. It amazes me that Astris even created this bridge." She looked about her new form. "Thank you for this, sister. But, attempting to come through, to breach the Ether, would leave me in a highly unstable form, physically and mentally. This... here, what you see before you, is as close as we can ever be. And that is far more than we could have had, if not for Astris and Séntinell."

Cassandra held her hand out. "So, you're confined to the Tholos, Mother?"

"I'm afraid so, my dear. Or, at least, I'm confined to the flame. But that is a blessing we did not have before, is it not?"

"Yes, Mother."

"You mentioned Pasiphae?" Jacob reminded her.

"Yes, Jacob. I fear Pasiphae will, in her usual selfish ignorance, look for an escape into the physical dimension. Perhaps here, perhaps Hades. She may even attempt to enter Sólaás."

"And that's a problem?"

"It *is* a problem, Jacob. We Célestiaá are the personification of nuclear power; living atoms; reflections of the Big Bang, as you'd have known it on Kiípos. We are the Children of *Chaos!* At the centre of every atom is a nucleus. If that nucleus was to break apart, it would release vast amounts of energy, which can initiate massive explosions. That is how man developed nuclear weapons. The atoms of Célestiaá are, however, billions of times more powerful, more volatile, than anything ever discovered on Kiípos. If I were to attempt reentry into the physical dimension, my atoms would, as would Pasiphae's, almost certainly enter a state of immediate degradation."

She stood and, yet again, scanned to her left, then right, still searching for her twin. "Her mental state, her anger, were already beyond reason when last we saw her in Hades. It does not need much thought to determine how dangerous she would be if she were to resume physical form. Madness and explosive volatility are a much greater threat to the universe now than anything that may happen to Kiípos."

Astris frowned. "Are you in any danger, Circe? You appear to be wary of your surroundings."

"I am in no immediate peril, sister," she replied, "but I am wary, and uncertain, of Pasiphae's whereabouts and intentions." Circe turned her attention to Cassandra. "I suspect recent events may have some connection to the vision you saw, Cassandra."

Astris thought carefully, holding her hand up, scrutinising the glowing red jewel on her finger. "If you cannot enter the physical dimension, can we bring the *flame* into our mediacy?"

The living flame stood still, considering the question put to her. "I'm curious, sister. What have you in mind?"

"It seems to me, you are achieving a symbiotic compatibility with the flame. Would it be possible for us to create a synchronistic coexistence, whereby your essence remains outside the physical dimension, but your consciousness attains a permanent presence here in Elŷsium?"

"But I have a presence, here, in the flame."

"And that presence is limited to the confines of the Tholos. What if we could transmute the flame? Transfer your consciousness, through a tiny sliver of flame, into the jewels on our rings?"

Circe's flaming hand rested on her chin as she considered the unusual hypothesis. Cassandra held Jacob's hand, a million questions running through her head, but no words coming to her mouth. Everything was happening so quickly. She was still coming to terms with the idea of Circe being back in their lives, albeit in an intangible form, and now Astris was trying to find a means of bringing her even closer. And was Circe correct? Had recent events begun the inevitable countdown to the envisaged battle at Elysian Fields?

Circe gave a little laugh, a disbelieving shake of her head. "I may not have met you till now, little sister, but I wish I had known you for much, much longer. You have an extraordinary mind; a perception bordering on genius. How do you propose to do this?"

Astris turned to Séntinell, who had, till now, stayed patiently, and silently, to the rear. The Lumináry stepped from the darkness, nodding their approval. "I sense you have need of my... talents," they said, smiling at Astris. "I must agree with Lady Circe, my lady. You are an amazing thinker. A superior intellect of the highest magnitude. But I must caution..."

Astris held her hand up, staying Séntinell's next words. "Yes, I know the risk, Séntinell. If we succeed, Circe's essence will create an invisible tendril, like a thread through a canvas, permanently breaching the dimensions."

"And what would that mean?" asked Cassandra.

"It means," said Jacob, "that the very escape route that mum warned about would be there for Pasiphae, if she were to find it. Am I right?" He looked, firstly at Séntinell, then to Astris.

"If she hasn't found it already," said Circe.

Astris took Jacob and Cassandra by the hand. "My father sent me here to find my purpose in the grand plan. I am now seeing what that purpose is, for the first time. I am sure of it." She turned to Séntinell, once more. "By my calculations, Séntinell, if we seal the gap tightly enough, there should be enough of a hole for Circe to stretch through, but no way for Pasiphae to breach the gap. Do you agree?"

The Lumináry paced up and down considering Astris' assessment. "I agree that, without her Célestiaá Ring, Pasiphae is much weaker than she was." They hummed, and haahed. "And, it would be nigh impossible for her to carve a way through. Provided, of course, we ensure the strictest of seals were put in place. That nothing short of a Célestiaá Ring would be needed. Yes, yes, it could work."

"How do we do this?" Jacob held Cassandra's hand, squeezing a little tighter than he meant to. The significance of what Astris and Séntinell were proposing had his heart racing. Cassandra, too, was swept up in the excitement, her emotions bubbling over at the prospect of having Circe in their lives once more. Even if only in ethereal form.

Astris stood by the hearthstone, beckoning them all to join her. Séntinell pulled their sleeves up to the elbows. "Well," they said, "we simply create a spacial gateway, as we did before. This time, however, we shall extend the terminus from the hearth and into all three of your rings." They gazed up at Circe's flaming silhouette. "You are in agreement with this procedure, my lady?"

She smiled at Astris. "My little sister believes this will work. I trust my little sister," she confirmed.

"Very well," said Séntinell, waving their three companions closer to the hearthstone. "All three rings must be inside the flame when I open the gateway. Lady Circe can then inhabit them all in equal measure." They turned their attention back to Circe. "I would urge you bring as much of yourself through as possible, my lady. The less residual energy left in the Nowhere, the better. Makes it more difficult for Lady Pasiphae to detect."

Circe nodded as she crouched in preparation. Séntinell held their hands out, placing them slowly into the flames, indicating the others do likewise. As all four stood—arms outstretched—Séntinell took a deep breath, and their eyes rolled back in their head, once more, with only the bright white of the globe-shaped part of the eye visible in its socket. In the depth of the hearthstone, the rings glowed brightly and the strings of light stretched out from each, entwining as they reached up through the height of the flames.

The lilac core intensified, pulsing brighter, then dimmer, before shrinking down to the size of a tiny ball. Circe's fiery form gradually softened, back to the original shape of the dancing flame, and the lilac ball exploded into a trillion particles. Slowly, they found their way into the entwined strings of light, feeding down the line; making their new home in the gemstones of the rings. The flames died down, and the strings drew back to the hearts of the rings.

Séntinell withdrew their hands, and their eyes returned to normal. Each of the ringed trio then removed their hands, eager to take in the wondrous glistening reflection now emanating from their bejewelled fingers. In each of the Célestiaá Rings, the red-rimmed lilac sliver seemed to jump from one white diamond to the other; an erratic, random to-ing and fro-ing, bringing the rings to life. The beautiful red jewel on Astris' ring now had a vibrant lilac dot, constantly circling its circumference; throbbing, like a heartbeat had just been activated.

Each of the wearers could now feel Circe's presence coursing through them. Astris, in particular, was more aware of the warmth her older sister had instilled. *'But we are one now. I am you, and you are me'*. She now realised what Circe had meant. Her sister was not only present in the jewel on her finger, she was now a part of her, physically and mentally. Her sister and her symbiont. Her blue eyes, now imbued with tiny flecks of hazel. The memories of Circe and Pasiphae growing up together—twins in eternal conflict—filled her mind. Of meeting Raymond Corrie, and the beautiful joy and love that was felt in such a brief instant of time. The pride, the care, and the concern for her much loved Kiípos, now bringing a realisation of Astris' true purpose, her true worth, and her true destiny.

"Astris?" Cassandra's muted voice broke through the distant contemplation she had occupied. "Are you alright, Astris?"

The Princess of Sólaás smiled, although, slightly shaken by her new condition, it took her a few seconds to regain her immediate bearings.

"Yes... yes, I'm fine, thank you Cassandra," she said, although that was not entirely true. As she looked at her companion, memories of Cassandra's past relationship with Circe sprung into her mind. She wanted to reach out and touch the daughter she'd adopted all those thousands of years before; wanted to console and reassure her that Circe was back from the Nowhere. Not in her original form, no, but hosted in the shape of her sister, both now sharing the same atoms. Both now sharing the body of perhaps the most powerful Célestiaá yet. Two daughters, and the amplified abilities of Helios' gifted ring.

Séntinell stepped over to Astris, taking her hands, concerned at the stunned, almost concussed look on her face. They sensed something. They weren't sure what it was, but there was definitely a more powerful aura around Astris now. "Are you sure, my lady?" they asked. "You look a trifle unsteady."

Astris calmed herself. "Yes... yes, dear Séntinell," she confirmed. "I was just a little unprepared for the surge of energy the ring absorbed, that is all." She smiled at The Lumináry, who seemed satisfied by her answer. As she turned toward the villa, Séntinell watched the young princess closely, suspecting more to her reaction than she was prepared to admit. Their suspicions were further heightened when Astris looked back over her shoulder, and, for the briefest of instants, her eyes flashed as bright as the sun.

XXIII. THIS DYING WORLD

"They speak no words of comfort, no words of hope," explained Selêne. "They know nothing of love, nor sympathy, and they provide no means of escape or recovery. They are the wrath, the anger, the ire. They are the *Consequences*: the natural justice mankind has wrought upon himself. They are long overdue, but now they are here. And there is no escape."

Ella sat quietly. She was already familiar with the Moon's sometimes flamboyant, and often over-dramatic, descriptions of events, places, or even just the meal on her plate. It was also a common occurrence for Selêne to tell little jokes, or funny stories, or heart-tugging anecdotes of her times with Mother Gaea. What was never in doubt, was the great love and empathy that radiated from the little old woman.

"Today," she continued, "we must take stock of our priorities on Kiípos, Mother." Pandeia held the world in the centre of the room as she had before. "Mankind is still our best hope of curating this earth. But the floods, and the forest fires... the rains that fall, and the heat that dries, are not our only concerns." Selêne nodded to Pandeia, who, with a simple gesture, spun the earth, changing its appearance from blue and green, to grey, with areas of red highlighting the extent of the poisoned sectors; areas where life was gradually disappearing.

Selêne placed her hand on the globe. "Man's fascination for nuclear power has left us with a difficult problem. Where there were once power stations, there are now open sores. Gaping boils of festering poison." She slowly spun the ball, emphasising the scale of the spread of radiation pollution.

"When Pasiphae's ripple destroyed all means of electricity, it also rendered useless Kiípos' nuclear reactors' cooling and power-regulating systems, as well as any emergency safety systems. These effects were compounded by others, and chain reactions in the multiple cores spun out of control. Tremendous explosions triggered large fireballs, and the ensuing fires in the reactor cores have released large amounts of radioactive material into Kiípos' atmosphere. This radiation has since been carried great distances by air currents. As you can see, Mother, there are many areas infected by this nuclear cancer. Many species suffering now, many more at continuing risk."

"Vast areas of Kiípos are now contaminated; the forests, the rivers, the cities. The initial loss of mass food production has now been exacerbated by the ruination of vegetation and plant life. This, in turn, has caused a decimation of wildlife. All life on Kiípos is being forced, compressed, into much smaller land areas, while the radiation continues to close in on them." Selêne shook her head. "More living creatures competing for less food, in ever smaller habitation. The *Consequences*!"

Ella joined Selêne as she inspected the damage. "We have to treat the sores, don't we?" asked Ella.

"We do," agreed Selêne. "That is our most pressing task. We must treat the sores, then, somehow, remove the residual radiation clouds; stop the sickness from spreading; tend the ailing regions."

"How do we do that?" asked Ella.

Selêne sighed, slowly turning to look upon her student. "I was hoping *you* may have some suggestions, Mother," she chuckled.

Ella walked slowly around the spinning globe. She loved Selêne's sometimes dark sense of humour, but her thoughts were bent entirely on the glowing redness; the inflammation, scattered across what were once the wealthy, technologically advanced regions of Earth. As she passed Pandeia, they exchanged eye-contact and subtle smiles.

"We have to isolate the sources o' the poison, suck it out, and plug the wounds," Ella said, finally.

"Very good," complimented Selêne.

Ella stopped walking, placed one arm across her chest, and covered her mouth with her hand as she thought deeply about the 'how' of what they must do.

"Have you ever heard of '*transmutation*', Mother?" Ella and Selêne came together once more. Ella closed her eyes and smiled as her mind plucked the information from nowhere.

"Transmutation," Ella recited, "is the conversion o' one chemical element into another."

"Wonderful," said Selêne, applauding enthusiastically.

Ella smiled again, incredulous. "How do I know this, Selêne? I had never heard o' that, no' until you said it. So, how can I know this?"

"You are the Mitéra Fŷsi, my child. The knowledge of millennia is yours to know. It is still, I know, strange, these new feelings and experiences, but, while you may not realise it, you are, even now, learning at an incredible rate." Selêne smiled and gestured for Ella to sit. They both lowered themselves to their respective cushions, sitting in their customary cross-legged positions. The globe disappeared as Pandeia lowered her hands. "Would you like to explain 'transmutation' to our Mother, Pandeia?" The Moon and the All-Bright exchanged smiles and nods of their heads.

"In these conditions," Pandeia said, "a transmutation means transforming active atomic nuclei, either through a *chemical* reaction or another *nuclear* reaction." She smiled, adding matter-of-factly, "we need to *attack* the sores."

"Good," continued Selêne. "Long ago, man's alchemists experimented, in their ignorance, with transmutation; attempting to turn base metals, such as copper or lead, into gold or silver. They had, at this time, no real understanding of the atom, or the nature of matter. Truly, they did not know with what they were playing, but their experimentation did bear fruit in unexpected ways, leading them to many other discoveries. The many chemical reactions they uncovered, for instance. But chemical reaction alone cannot affect the nuclear changes required to create the scale of transmutation we need in our present dilemma."

Ella leaned forward, her hands clasping her ankles as she pondered the problem. "So," she said, slowly, "what we need… is somethin' wi' enough power to… what? Blow the nuclear out? Like a candle on a birthday cake?" There were a few moments of contemplative thought by the small group.

"Are we talking about *photo*-transmutation, then, Mitéra?" asked Pandeia.

"Photo-transmutation?" asked Ella. "What's that?"

"What does your mind tell you, Mother?" prompted Selêne.

Ella closed her eyes, her eyelids blinking rapidly whilst shut, as she accessed her subconscious bank of knowledge once more. Her eyes snapped open and a huge smile covered her face.

"I see you have a solution, Mother," observed Selêne.

"I think so, Selêne," she said, hesitantly. "If I understand it correctly. We have to bombard the 'sores' wi' an alternative radiation; enough to stimulate the atomic nucleus until it becomes a subatomic particle. If we do that, it should immediately decay enough to render it safe." She looked, questioningly, to both Selêne and Pandeia. "Have I got that right?"

"Well done, Mother," smiled Selêne. "We bombard it with an alternative. Gamma radiation is required, lots of it, directly targeted at each of the many sources. We cannot do that from here, and we shall also have need of a vacuum to, as you so eloquently put it, 'suck the poison out'."

"Hmm," muttered Ella. She sat looking at the floor as she considered the difficulties. She had nothing. Yes, she had somehow figured out what should be done, but did not know how they were to accomplish it. She looked to Pandeia, for support as much as anything else, but, she too, just smiled and shrugged her shoulders.

"I'm sorry, Mitéra," she said. "This is beyond my limited abilities and knowledge."

"Hmm," muttered Ella again.

A deep sigh caught her ear, and she turned to look at the Moon.

"I'm sorry," Selêne lamented. "But we now find ourselves in the most unfortunate of positions. We need an inordinate amount of gamma in order to quell the nuclear threat. For our task to succeed, the most efficient way to produce this gamma is by using the most powerful of lightning strikes." She sighed once again. "For nature and science to work hand in hand on Kiípos, each member of Naátúr has their own specific responsibilities. To produce this gamma, we shall need the assistance of someone who has, well, kept themselves distant from us Naátúr since Mother Gaea's passing."

Ella and Pandeia were mystified. "Who is it we need, Aftí-Fengári?" mumbled Pandeia.

Selêne took a deep breath. "Make ready, ladies. We have a journey to make. And it may not be a pleasant one."

⁂

The trio made their way along the dry tracks, chatting, laughing, and joking; filling the otherwise monotonous hours with stories of fun. Occasionally, Selêne and Pandeia broke into songs that Ella presumed were ancient Naátúr folk songs. Gone was the earlier despondency as Selêne regaled them with stories of the gods, and the demigods and, the more she opened herself to Ella, the more the young girl grew to love her.

The waggon, pulled by two beautiful greys, rolled along. A gentle sway, seemingly in time to the birdsong, and the sound of running water, provided a calming backdrop to the fresh air and sunshine. It was incredibly pleasant, and the journey, despite being long and, mostly, uneventful, was really quite enjoyable. The forests, and the fields, the streams, and the rivers, all passed them by. The lush greenery of the land was still a mystery to Ella. For all her short earthly life, the moon had been a great, bright white ball in the sky. Now it was as lush and beautiful as anything she'd ever experienced back home in Strath-sealgair. Cypress, Olive, fir and pine; small, tall, wide and narrow; the trees and shrubs were all shapes and sizes.

There were sheep and deer on the higher slopes; horses—dozens of them—running free through the valleys. Goats clung to craggy cliff faces, as the landscape rose and fell. It stretched out into the distance and closed in on them in narrow ravines; but all the time the track remained remarkably smooth and level.

"It may surprise you, Mother," said Selêne, her familiar manner so light and casual, it felt to Ella that she'd known the little woman forever. She sat up front with Selêne, who had a very loose hold of the reins, while Pandeia knelt on a thick cushion on the waggon bed, leaning forward into the gap between them. It appeared to Ella that Selêne wasn't actually controlling the horses; they seemed to know exactly where they were going and were in no real hurry to get there.

"It may surprise you, Mother," Selêne continued, "just how many of Lunaá's inhabitants enjoy farming, or even just tending the simplest of gardens. There is such a natural affinity with growing things, it seems strange to think of the sometimes violent and destructive traits many have been burdened with."

Ella scanned the distant hills. Much of the land was covered in forest, but there were large open spaces of identifiable fields. Ella could make out the various cottages and villas to whom those fields belonged; occasionally, they would pass quite close to some homes, and the tenants would shout and wave. It was surreal to think that every one of the 'country folk' they encountered was actually Naátúr and had their own particular place in the grand plan.

After every couple of hours, they would find a place to stop for rest; usually by a stream, or a small spring, allowing the horses to drink and their own legs to stretch. They rested, this time, at the top of a valley; horseshoed, on their side, by thousands of emerald fir trees, and there was a small lake at the bottom. The path they were to follow was visible as it exited the tree line. Running alongside the length of the lake, it then meandered its way upwards toward a gigantic mountain in the distance.

Ella shielded her eyes from the sunlight as she stared across the expanse. "Is that where we're headin', Selêne?"

Pandeia stood next to Ella, also shielding her eyes. "Is that really where he lives, Aftí-Fengári?" she asked, with no little amount of awe.

Selêne joined the pair and sighed. "Yes, my dears," she said. "Atop that mountain is our first great task. Convincing him to help us."

The waggon finally reached the top of the steepest part of their climb, the last hour being the most troublesome of the journey. The horses made little fuss, plodding along, taking their time as they clipped and clopped over the loose stones, and fallen branches that now littered the pathway. Unlike the meticulously manicured countryside behind them, this was now a far less impressive landscape, looking almost... neglected.

Pandeia was the first to comment on the debris. "Are you sure he will see us, Aftí-Fengári? This does not look very... welcoming."

The wind was much stronger at this height; the gusts snatching and grabbing at the trees and shrubbery; skittering the branches across their path. Dark clouds gathered overhead, and the rumble of thunder assisted the winds in making the final stages of their journey far less enjoyable.

"Ye still haven't told me who we're goin' to see, Selêne," prompted Ella.

Selêne pulled the horses up and stared directly ahead. The path was now perfectly straight. To their right, the trees climbing up the steep incline swayed and groaned and, to their left, the edge of the path became nothing more than a steep cliff face. About five hundred yards in front of them, two large wooden gates loomed. Behind the closed entrance, carved into the mountainside, was a massive subterranean cave-castle; its external tall round columns and turrets imposing in their severity. She turned to face Ella and, placing her hand on the girl's shoulder, she gave a rather forced smile.

"We are seeking an audience with the Lightning God, Mother. We are hopefully going to save the saddest being in Lunaá from his self-imposed exile." She shook the reins, encouraging the horses to move on.

"We are about to meet Lord Zeus."

XXIV. THE STORM COMETH

"Jael?"

A puff of white blew up, a cough, and a shudder, as the young man jerked and shook himself back to life. Jael raised her tear-drenched eyes, her breath held, as she stared, disbelieving, at the white face and the frantically blinking blue eyes. "Eric?" she asked. "Eric?" She brushed his hair back, wiping the flour from his face. "Eric?" she repeated once more.

He locked his eyes onto hers; wide, desperate, searching for reassurance. "Jael!" he said again. Her arms pulled him tightly as she clasped him to her, sobbing, kissing his cheeks, his lips, his forehead.

"Careful, girl," advised Biro, "you may just kill him again if you pull him any tighter." He leaned down, sliding his arms under the boy, scooping him upwards, effortlessly. "Let's get him somewhere more comfortable." The giant man turned and made toward the mill door, Jael shuffling alongside, her hand clasping Eric's for all its worth.

Eric lay cradled in the safety of Biro's arms as the baker pounded his way up the path toward his home. "The girl," sobbed Jael. "The girl. I'm sure she had something to do with this, Pappa. I'm sure of it."

"Girl? What girl, daughter?"

"There was a girl, my age, maybe older. She was outside the saloon. A nasty, spiteful girl, and I think she had something to do with this. It was she who told me where to look for Eric." She wiped away the never ending tears with her sleeve.

"Who was she?" Biro enquired, glancing at his distressed daughter, his angry tone and facial expression something Jael had never known before.

"I don't know, Pappa. She was alone, and I have never seen her around here. She dressed like the merchants do in Elysia, so why was she here?"

The gathered revellers stopped their celebrations, the throng parting, curiously straining their necks for a better view of the unfolding drama. "What's happened, Grind?" called one. "Has the boy had too much ale?" yelled another, as he and his group joined each other in laughing at the hilarity of his question.

"Hush you now!" boomed Biro, his anger bubbling beneath the surface. "Someone fetch Master Raymond," he barked. "Quickly!" He looked down to Jael. "We'll get Eric comfortable. Then we shall find this girl, if she's still here." He gave a reassuring smile, then continued his pounding homeward.

His great foot crashed against the door, sending it flying inwards. "Clara?" he called. "Are you here, Clara?" His foot lowered, catching the swinging door, softening its progress as it made its way forcibly back toward him. He turned, entering his home sideways, gently ensuring Eric's head did not hit the doorframe, and strode over to a long couch beneath the open window. With a gentleness belying his massive bulk, Biro lay Eric on the couch.

Almost immediately Jael had knelt by his side, squeezing his right hand in her left, stroking his cheek with her right. "You're safe now, Eric," she whispered and kissed his forehead. His eyes never left her, and she let out an involuntary laugh as tears rained onto her arm, barely noticing the constant drip, drip, dripping. "You said my name," she gushed. "You said my name, and it was the sweetest sound I've ever heard." She wiped her eyes and leant forward and kissed his lips. "I thought I'd lost you, sweet boy."

Eric held her gaze, a look of confusion flashing through his eyes. He smiled. "Jael," he whispered, "you saved me?" Jael looked around to her father, who smiled his approval.

"*We* saved you," she nodded. "*We* saved you, Pappa and I. And I'm never letting you out of my sight ever again." A cough behind her, a reminder from her father they had a task to undertake, brought the realisation that her promise would be delayed somewhat. "But first I have something to do."

"Clara here will take care of you, Eric," said Biro, leaning across his daughter's shoulder. "Won't you my dear?"

A mess of curly hair appeared around Jael's other shoulder, and the ruddy red cheeks were separated by a comforting smile. "Of course I will," she said. "It will be my utmost pleasure." She turned to the kitchen. "Orpah!" she called. "Orpah, bring some water, as quick as you can." She hugged her daughter. "Don't worry about Eric, Jael. We'll look after him. You go with your father, find this girl."

Jael nodded, then bent down, giving Eric a farewell kiss. "I'll be back as soon as I can," she whispered. Eric nodded, making Jael smile even more, making her heart skip even more. As she stood, however, her resolve to find Eris hardened. "Let's go, Pappa," she said.

⸙⸙⸙⸙

The crowds had grown as the Harvest Festival wore on. The drink was flowing; the bands were blaring out their well-practiced staples, and all around there was a tumultuous, cheerful chatter of men, women, and children lapping up the sunshine, the food, and the company.

Biro and Jael wandered methodically through the throng, carefully checking each premises as they passed, carefully scanning each face as they came into view. Jael had provided Biro with a brief description of the girl - from what she could remember, at any rate. Every now and again, Biro would ask, 'is that her?', and each time Jael would shake her head as she scrutinised the next face to appear.

As they approached the saloon, a distinctive, perfect-sounding voice could be heard, piercing its way through

333

the surrounding noise. "She's over there," pointed Jael. She had not seen Eris, but the clarity of the vowels, the entitlement, the supremacy of her words as they cut the air, left Jael in no doubt. Here was the mischief maker they were looking for.

Jael's pace quickened as she barged her way through. Then, there before her, leaning against the saloon as she had before was Eris—teasing, flirting, and pulling the strings of several young men—encouraging two in particular to fight over her. "Don't listen to her," Jael warned, "her voice is poison."

The men turned toward Jael, curious as to who was interrupting their attempted courting. Eris smiled as Jael approached. "Make her go away, boys. This promiscuous slattern wants you all to herself." She laughed as her suitors all made to halt Jael's progress. "Be as rough as you want, gentlemen. I believe she likes it rough."

Jael continued undaunted and, as she reached the first of Eris' puppets, she dodged his outstretched hand, pushing him to the side. The others moved forward, each determined to be the deserving victor of Eris' promised affections. From behind her, Jael heard a massive roar and, suddenly, her father was ahead of her, swinging his fists, grabbing and throwing the men aside. Her assailants were no match for Biro's raw power—unleashed in fury at his daughter's predicament—a whirlwind of bruising knuckles and sledgehammer blows.

"You will not lay a finger on my daughter," he bellowed. "Stay down... *now*! Or else... I shall put you down permanently."

The would-be attackers all held their place, terrified of the fired up man-mountain. Biro strode toward Eris, his eyes locked onto hers. "You will not approach me, you ignorant ogre," Eris ordered, bringing her psychological manipulation to bear. "You will stay where you are."

Biro continued his march, his feet pounding the ground in his anger. "You will stay where you are," Eris repeated, a little more uncertainly this time. As the enormous man drew nearer, Eris felt a queasiness she'd never known before. "Stop! I order you!" Biro drew closer. Eris felt herself sidling along the wall of the saloon; felt fear for the first time. Why was this gigantic oaf immune to her control? "I order you again, brute," she tried one more time. "I am the Goddess of Strife and Discord. The Mistress of Mischief. Stop there, you cannot hurt me."

"But *I* can!" Eris turned to find Jael next to her, her fist swinging toward her face. The blow landed fully on Eris' nose, the loud crack as it broke almost drowning out her pathetic squeals. She fell on her backside, tumbling back against the wall, the pain of her bloody nose, and the confusion of what was happening, making her feel, for the first time, totally out of control of the situation.

Before she could get her bearings again, a giant hand grabbed her by the front of her blouse, lifting her effortlessly into the air. Biro pounded his way down toward the windmill. "Get out of my way!" he roared, the crowd parting before him. He recognised a boy standing by the side of the path. "You! Tom Skillers! Go find your father. Have him ride immediately to Strath-sealgair Villa. Tell him to bring Lord Jacob to the mill. Go on, boy! At once!" The boy ran off and Biro continued his relentless advance, Jael trying her best to keep up.

As he fell below the shadow of the great sails, his right boot stretched out, almost taking the mill door off its hinges; the resultant bang as it crashed open, further terrifying the flailing girl in his vice-like grip. He stomped to the far end of the mill. Then, after casually discarding Eris into a pile of empty flour bags, he flicked a wooden lever which raised the tarpaulin canopies covering the side of the mill. Light flooded in and Eris raised her hand to shield her eyes. The sudden bright light, and the silhouette of the giant, standing in the dust cloud created by the disturbed flour, further unsettled Eris.

She dragged the back of her hand across her bleeding, broken nose, disbelieving of the ease with which these illiterate, ill-mannered bumpkins had bested her. She looked up again at Biro, standing, feet apart, with his hands on his hips. "You will pay for this, you overgrown troll," she snapped, the words hissing out with as much venom as she could muster.

Biro tapped his finger against his temple. "I can feel you… in here," he said, "but you're wasting your time, girl."

"You fool," she retorted. "No mere male can resist the temptations I offer. You are but too stupid to realise this just yet." She smiled, a sneering, contemptuous acceptance of Biro's resistance, but a smile laced with the expectation of her eventual success. "But you will."

Biro laughed. "You have never met someone like me before, have you, girl?"

"And what is that, Ogre?"

"A man you cannot tempt with anything. A man who has everything he could wish for."

"There is no such thing," scoffed Eris. "All men want more. All men want what they cannot have. It is in your nature. And you, you grotesque monstrosity, are no different."

As Jael joined him, standing by his side, wrapping her arm around her father's arm, Biro looked down at her and smiled. "I am a simple man, yes. But I have family, and friends... gained through love and respect, not fear and manipulation. You are not of Elŷsium, girl. This is obvious. You will tell us where you are from, and why you are here."

He crouched close to Eris' face. "Or you will find that a 'simple man' does not necessarily mean a 'patient man'."

❧❧❧❧

"How's Eric? Is he okay?" Ray peered through the floating white flour dust; the permanent thin cloud created as the draft from the door, and the now-open tarpaulins, flowed through the mill. The girl sat where Biro had thrown her—on the pile of empty, flour covered sacks—her fury undiminished. As they stood just inside the closed doorway, he couldn't quite make out her features; couldn't yet tell if he recognised her.

"He'll be fine, Raymond. I have sent Jael home to be with him."

"And he spoke? He actually spoke?"

"Aye," nodded Biro enthusiastically. "He spoke. He said her name, and I don't think my daughter will ever forget that moment, her devastation so quickly turning to joy."

Ray smiled as he took in the news. He wasn't surprised at the development; Jael had been the constant, the

337

lighthouse, that Eric had so desperately needed in order to find his way back from the internal darkness that had so completely engulfed him. "I don't think anyone else could've managed what Jael has, Biro," he said, placing his hand on the huge man's arm. "I thought we'd lost Eric to the misery and despair that Pasiphae had poisoned him wi'."

"You do know he tried to... he..."

"Aye, I know," nodded Ray. "But Jael saved him. She never gave up on him. And I love the lassie for that. Now ye say he's talkin', and he and Jael... Well, I don't know about you, Biro, but I couldn't think o' a better, perfectly matched couple. So, right now? Right now, I couldn't be happier for my boy." He stared down to the far end of the mill. "Right! Suppose we better have a wee word wi' this little madam, eh?"

"She said something that caught me by surprise," Biro said quietly as they strolled through the mill. "She called herself the 'Goddess of Strife', making particular mention of 'mischief'. I have to say, I did feel a cold shake go through me when she uttered these words. It was then I knew of her malcontent; of her cancerous influence on those around her. I have sent word for Lord Jacob to come as quickly as he can. I think this goes a little further than mere mischief."

"Hmm, startin' to sound all too familiar, and no' in a good way," Ray mused as they approached the sitting woman.

"Ah, Raymond! We meet again," smirked Eris, taking a surprisingly calm and friendly posture.

"Do I know ye?" he asked, feeling as if he knew the face, but could not place from where. "Who are ye?"

Eris' lip curled up in a mocking, condescending sneer. "Oh, you know me, Master Corrie," she smiled cryptically. "You may not recognise me, however, as each time we met, you were, of course, slightly distracted by Pasiphae's... *attentions*. Her sexual peccadilloes required feeding, after all."

A panic ran through Ray. Pasiphae? She was an agent of Pasiphae's? Why was she here? How did she get here? Both he and Biro now realised the enormity of the situation before them.

"I am Eris," she said, casually. "And I am here as a herald; a harbinger; a deliverer of your doom. My Lord, Haáde, shall soon bring about the end of this pathetic paradise, taking you as his subjects as he strikes down, once and forever, the blight that is Helios." She smiled again, so matter-of-factly, it chilled them to their bones. "Prepare for your Armageddon, you witless curs."

Biro folded his arms. "Not the most charming of women, is she?"

Ray was far more interested in her claims. "Haáde backed down from his war wi' Helios," he stated. "I was there. He killed Pasiphae and let us all leave. Why would he wage war now?"

Before Eris could answer, the sky darkened in an instant, as if the tarpaulins had once more shut out the light of the day. The sunlight that had been streaming through the canopies suddenly disappeared. A crack of lightning, followed instantly by a loud rumble of thunder, precipitated an intense downpour of fast-falling rain. The deluge fell directly on Eris who, far from being discomforted, stood with her arms raised, reaching for the sky. She looked directly upwards, allowing the rain to wash across her face, and she laughed hysterically as she repeatedly cried, *"It begins! It begins!"*

Biro pulled the lever, dropping the tarpaulins once more. The rain was kept outside, but Eris remained standing on the sacks. "It begins!" she cried again, running her fingers through her drenched hair. Her eyes snapped back onto Ray, and her hands made their way down her chest, pulling her soaked blouse tightly against her skin. The wet cotton clung to her like a second skin, revealing the fullness of her breasts, and the pink protrusions of her small, yet firm, nipples. Eris' green eyes drilled into Ray, and she ran her tongue slowly, seductively, along her lips.

"My Lord is coming," she purred. "Join me, Raymond. Let us pleasure ourselves in celebration, and anticipation, of his arrival. Kill this monstrous halfwit, then sate yourself in my gift. Save yourself. Join us as we create our new universe, our new..." Biro's fist brought her hysterical monologue to an abrupt end, and Eris slumped unconscious to the floor.

"Didn't take ye for someone who hit women, Biro," mused Ray.

The giant man looked down at the crumpled woman and shrugged his shoulders. "I don't," he confirmed. "But I have no qualms about dealing with poisonous snakes." He winked and smiled at Ray. "Anyway," he added, "didn't want you to get tempted."

Ray sighed. "No chance o' that. She isn't my type."

XXV. A NEW DILEMMA

The light dimmed behind them as Bentley and Crumbles sauntered through the Diávasi. They weren't expecting a welcoming party, but it delighted Katie and Melanie to see Cassandra and Jacob waiting on the lawn.

"Welcome back," called Cassandra, breaking into a light jog toward them. "How was it?"

The women climbed down from the saddles and both were met with a warm embrace. "I'll take the horses back to the stable, if ye want to update Cassandra, Katie," offered Melanie, laughing as she petted Crumbles' neck. "Think the lad here needs a wee treat after his exertions."

Cassandra held Katie by her shoulders, genuinely concerned as to how the first sortie as Élementaá had gone. "It was emotional," nodded Katie. "Hang on, Mel," she called, reaching into her saddlebag. A familiar looking brown envelope appeared in her hand. "For you," she smiled, passing the envelope to Jacob. He carefully opened it and removed the pictures.

"It's more for my dad," he said quietly. "I'm hoping it'll be a pleasant surprise for him and Eric." Cassandra peered over his shoulder, seeing the Corrie family as a group for the first time.

"That's beautiful," she said. "What a beautiful family." She gave Jacob a hug. "I'm sure Raymond will be delighted, both with the picture and, of course, our other news."

"Other news?" Katie was intrigued.

"I'll catch ye in a wee while," said Melanie, making to move off with the horses. Katie nodded in acknowledgment.

"Other news?" she repeated.

"Aye," said Jacob, "we've had some developments while ye were away."

"Oooh, developments?" cooed Katie. "Tell me more."

The trio ambled back toward the villa, Jacob and Cassandra regaling the tale of how they had found Circe's essence in the flames; and how her essence had now been housed in the gems of the three rings. Their excitement was infectious, and Katie was caught up in their delight at having such momentous news.

Their joy was brought to an abrupt end as Jessica came running from the villa, with Marro following closely behind. "Jacob!" she called. "Jacob!" She reached the group, out of breath, trying desperately to catch her words. "Jacob," she panted. "You have to get to Rimel, immediately. It's Eric. There's been some sort of accident." She doubled over, her hand on Jacob's shoulder. "Give me a sec," she wheezed, "not used to this much exertion."

"An accident?" Jacob pressed.

Jessica nodded, trying desperately to get her breath back. "An accident, yes. He's alright, I think, but Grind says you have to get there... there's someone he thinks you should see. Sounds serious."

"I'll get changed and head off. Can ye arrange a waggon, Jess?"

"I'm coming with you, Jacob," said Cassandra.

"I've already asked for the waggon to be readied," added Marro. "It will be at the front of the villa for you."

Cassandra turned to Katie. "I'm so sorry, Katie, I wanted to learn of your trip but..." She gestured toward Jacob.

"That's okay, Cassandra. Chiyoko told us to report to her as soon as we got back. I'm sure she'll have our next task all ready for us." She laughed, adding, "Don't want to get on her bad side, do I?"

Cassandra clasped her hands. "No, I don't suppose you do," she laughed. "We'll talk properly next time we meet." She looked to the skies, surprised at how quickly the clouds had gathered. "We'd best get going. It looks like there's a storm coming." The women embraced, then Cassandra and Jacob said their goodbyes before disappearing into the villa, accompanied by Jessica. Marro walked with Katie and they made their way inside.

"How was your trip?" he asked.

"Enough to focus our minds on what we have to do, and how hard it's gonna be. I think Mel will need a wee bit o' time to get her head around it all, but I'm convinced we're up to it."

"I don't think anyone's in any doubt of that," Marro said. "Chiyoko will give you more details of your next trip, after you've rested. But it seems you ladies will be off on a trip to Central Africa."

"Africa? Fuck's sake," laughed Katie. "Is it too late to start collecting Air Miles?"

The further they travelled, the worse the storm became, but, at least, they were now just a few minutes from Rimel. The dark, heavy clouds were not their usual blueish grey, they were a deep, angry purple. And, with each lightning strike, a spectacular redness swelled within, like a giant beating heart.

"I don't think I've ever seen rain so heavy." Jessica leaned against the window, watching thousands of beads of water being chased down the pane of glass by thousands more. Every few seconds a heavy gust would rattle the glass, the raindrops hitting with such force it sounded like thousands of little stones being thrown against the carriage.

The carriage wheels were now sinking ever deeper into the saturated and now flooding track. The horses, as powerful as they were, were feeling the strain of hauling the bulky coach, with every step pulling their hooves further down into the mud, sucking them into an ever tightening grip.

"I can't believe how dark it's become," commented Jacob. "It's surely still just afternoon, isn't it?"

"It is," confirmed Cassandra. "This is, without doubt, the worst storm I have ever experienced in my time in

Elŷsium." She looked at Jacob with increasing concern. "I really have a bad feeling regarding all of this, Jacob. I wish we could contact mother. I thought the rings would allow us to see her whenever we wished."

"I did, too," he responded, with obvious disappointment. "I can feel her presence, in the ring, but she seems to be spendin' more time wi' Astris. It's almost like she's bondin' wi' her." He leaned closer to the window, looking upwards at the swirling thunder clouds, cursing the weather. "If this has somethin' to do wi' yer vision, Cassie, I only wish we'd had more time to understand the rings."

"If this is the beginning of the war," Cassandra said, "then we are fortunate there's a battle scheduled at the Fields in two days. If we use those combatants, at least we will have a small army at hand, even if this is not what they've trained for."

The horses trudged their way through a group of trees before the track opened up into the Main Street through Rimel. The festival had long since been abandoned, with the revellers scurrying off to the dry safety of their homes. The rain persisted in its deluge, the torrential shower now sitting two inches above the track, each drop hitting with such force they seemed intent on bouncing as high as they could.

The street was lined with discarded ale glasses, tankards and trays; foodstuff, thrown away as the crowd hurriedly dispersed, and several tables blown over under the heavy gusts still hammering the windows of the carriage. The driver followed his instructions, heading through the small village and down the slope toward the windmill. The slope resembled a river, as the torrent flowed directly toward the massive structure below. The mill sails, although still locked in place, were struggling to break free, assailed as they were by the gales howling across the skies.

The waggon curved round in front of the mill entrance, coming to a halt in a significantly deep puddle. Biro quickly pulled the mill door open, placing a sturdy, upturned box by the carriage steps for the passengers to alight safely. He held his hand out aiding, first Cassandra, then Jessica, with Jacob bringing up the rear; each stepping carefully over the sandbags Biro had lined the doorway with. There was little point in any greetings, as it was impossible to hear above the howling of the wind, and the almost constant crack and rumble of the thunder and lightning.

The giant baker was shouting inaudible instructions to the driver, gesturing for him to get himself and the horses up to the livery stable; instructions the driver had no hesitation in following.

Biro slammed the door shut behind him, quickly placing a securing spar across the holding brackets, keeping the wind out. He turned to greet his visitors who, despite how briefly they had been in the rain, were all soaked to the skin, shivering from the freezing bite of the wind's blast.

"Welcome to you all. I have lit a brazier to provide some warmth for you," he said, guiding them further into the dark building. Dark, despite lanterns being lit and hung from some of the lower rafters, giving some rather subdued lighting. The rain continued falling, its *rat-a-tat-tat* against the high wooden structure of the mill amplified in the relative quiet below.

"How's Eric?" asked Jacob.

"He's doing fine," Biro replied, thoughtfully. "He gave us quite a scare, but he's being looked after at my home for now. Master Raymond has gone up, and Jael and Clara will take good care of him."

"Thanks, Biro," said Jacob. "I couldn't have asked for better carers. So, who's this person ye want us to meet?"

Biro nodded toward the back of the mill. "I have her tied up back there. She's quietened down somewhat, but you may get more sense out of her than we did."

"Who is she?" asked Cassandra.

"Says her name is 'Eris', but it's *what* she claims to be that's worrying me." He held his arm out, encouraging them to follow.

"'Eris'? It can't be the Eris who... Are you sure she said 'Eris'?

"Oh, I'm sure, right enough, my lady."

They made their way around the huge milling machine, curious as to what they'd find. Sitting on a pile of sacks, her hands bound to a wooden pillar, looking bored, Eris looked up as the new arrivals came into view.

"Ahhh," she purred. "The Halfbreed and the Trojan. My, I am in distinguished company, aren't I?"

"You hold your tongue now, girl," chastised Biro. "Show some respect."

Eris' eyes narrowed, and she glared at Biro. "When he comes, you impotent Minotaur, you will learn exactly what respect means."

"When who comes?" probed Jacob.

Eris slowly turned her head, a wicked smile forming on her lips as she looked deep into Jacob's eyes. "Oh,

Jacob, you know of whom I speak," she gushed. "Did he not show you his mercy when last you met?"

"Merc... Haáde? What's Haáde got to do wi' this?"

"The storm!" she yelled. "The Storm! It is the precursor of your doom, you insignificant bacteria. When Lord Haáde comes, he will flush the virus of humanity out of existence, and claim the twin entities of Kiípos and Elŷsium for his own." She sprang to her feet, stumbling, as the restrictions of her bindings pulled her hands back. "Here, in this antiquated backwater," she laughed, maniacally, "shall land the first blow in the fall of Helios' universe. Here, shall mark the first day in the new cosmos, and, from this plane, the darkness will spread and shall swallow you all."

Jacob held Eric's head in his hands, their foreheads resting on one another. He looked his brother in the eye, then pulled him tightly to him. "Fuck's sake, big brother," he laughed, as tears slipped down his cheeks, "how many times am I supposed to lose ye?"

"I'm sorry," Eric whispered.

"Don't ye dare be sorry, ye daft buggar. Ye're here, ye're alive and, fuck me, it's good to hear yer voice again." He pulled himself away, wiping his cheeks with his hands. "But we've got to get ye away from here."

Jacob stood in front of everyone, drawing their attention. On the couch, next to Eric, holding his hand, sat Jael. Ray, Jessica, and Cassandra sat at the dining table.

Clara held Orpah in front of her as they stood by the doorway.

"The situation is this," Jacob explained. "We believe this girl, who has seemingly been able to influence others, mainly men, but not exclusively, is an agent of Hades. We've left Biro to guard her, as she doesn't seem able to influence him."

"Only Mumma can make Pappa do anything," laughed Orpah.

Jacob smiled at the girl. "She's somehow managed to breach Elŷsium's dimensional borders, and is apparently just amusin' hersel' while she waits for Haáde to attack us. That's what she claims, anyway. Accordin' to her, this storm is him preparin' the way for a massive incursion by Hades' armies."

The group sat quietly, digesting the news. "We've sent word," Jacob continued, "to Charon and Brunhiíld, who've been makin' arrangements for a battle at the Fields, two days from now. They're briefin' the combatants on a new task... the defence o' Elŷsium. They will, hopefully, buy us a wee bit o' time to try to get Astris and Circe's help."

A murmur rippled around the room as the urgency struck home. "What do you need us to do, My Lord?" Clara stepped further into the room, Orpah following behind.

Jacob smiled at the baker's wife, her resolve clear on her face. Here was a woman who had no intention of running away. "Well, first," he turned to Eric. "Jessica'll take ye on the coach, back to Strath-sealgair Villa. Ye have to get back and warn Astris. We'll need her and Circe to try to fight Haáde off. Séntinell should be sent to Sólaás to warn Helios, and to ask for *his* help."

"How do ye know the battle'll start here, at the Fields," Ray asked.

"We're makin' the assumption that Haáde'll want to get the Célestiaá Rings as soon as he can." Jacob exchanged glances with Cassandra. "He'll know where to find us."

"Well, I'm goin' nowhere," affirmed Ray. "I've had enough o' that bastard and his wife. Gi'e me a sword."

"I'll fight, if you give me a sword," declared Jael.

Jacob smiled at the girl. "I know ye will, Jael. But I'd like for you to travel wi' Eric and Jessica. Look after this wee buggar for me, eh?" He turned to Clara. "The word has to get around all the surroundin' villages, and riders should be sent out to all parts o' Elŷsium. The more we can get to come fight the better. Me and Cassandra will try to figure out how to use these bloody rings properly. We know this Eris doesn't like bein' around the rings. Seems to limit her influence, so we'll keep her close to us."

He looked each and everyone of them in the eye. "This might just all be a false alarm, but I don't think so. War is comin', I fear."

XXVI. HAPPY

"What is in the rucksack? What have you got there?"

Katie looked up, pausing in repacking her bag. The short black man stood about twenty feet from her, his legs slightly apart, pointing the rifle directly at her. He had emerged, silently, but highly agitated, from the bush, slightly up the incline where it was at its thickest. He carefully made his way down to the clearing, taking small sideways steps, keeping the rifle trained on his target. Scanning the area to his left and right, Katie watched and listened for further intruders, until satisfied he was alone.

She smiled at him as she stood, then looked down at the embers of the campfire. A thin but constant wisp of white smoke wafted upwards. "Mmm. Élementaá, my arse," she muttered, as she kicked some more dirt over the offending area, finally snuffing out the remains of their fire. "Well, who do we have here?" she said. He was surprised by how tall she was, her statuesque figure stretching up as she stood. He quickly wiped away a bead of sweat as it dripped from his forehead to his cheek, before gripping the rifle with both hands again.

His eyes never left her as she stood facing him, her black cargo pants tightly hugging the curves of her hips, tucked neatly under elastic at the top of her black leather army boots; her grey vest clinging to her torso, highlighting every curve, presenting her perfectly packaged chest for eager viewers. The smooth surface of her upper chest displaying her necklace, the five rare stones glinting, reflecting different colours in the sunlight.

She stretched her long arms out, raising them in a circular motion, making every inch of movement count; slowly pushing her breasts out as she reached up and pulled her long brown hair back behind her head, tying it together with a rubber band. "Come closer," she said. "Don't be shy."

"Didn't you hear me, woman?" His deep voice booming out the words, almost staccato-like. "What is in the bag?" He was becoming increasingly impatient, with more large beads of sweat running down his face and arms. He took a step forward. "Answer me!" he shouted.

Katie smiled again. "Oh, you don't want to know what's in my bag. You want to know why there are two bags, and two horses, but only one woman. That's what ye should be askin' yerself."

The man froze, surprised at the audacity of his would-be captive. "I should... *what*?"

She returned to packing the equipment away. "Ye're no' very bright, are ye?" she queried. He gave a slight, sardonic laugh as he stepped closer, gripping the rifle ever tighter. He was about thirty years old, his hair close cropped, with the facial stubble of several days unshaven.

Muscular and slim, he wore army-issue combat trousers and boots, but his green vest had several holes, and a large tear up the left seam.

"I am not... *what*?" he asked incredulously. "I am bright enough to know that it is I who has the rifle... and you who are at the other end of it." She looked at him, the smile still beaming out, unsettling him. "Stop that! Tell me what you have in the bag. Do you have food... water... ammunition?" Katie continued with her work, arranging the now-clean cooking implements and dishes in an orderly manner in her pack.

"We don't use guns," she said, thoughtfully, looking up at him again, "*because* you always need ammunition. No, we use something *much* better." The man took another step forward, his anger increasing, pulling the rifle into his chin, threatening to fire. As he prepared to squeeze the trigger, his eye caught the glint of metal to his right. His right arm felt the searing heat slice through, and his left arm buckled under the weight of the heavy rifle, his fingers prising themselves open. He screamed as he watched the lower half of his right forearm drop to the ground, short bursts of blood spurting out of the remaining stump. His knees gave way as he shrieked in panic.

"Sorry I took so long," said Melanie. "But why is it so fuckin' hard to have a shit in the bushes in this fuckin' place?" She kicked the rifle—still with the lower right arm gripping the trigger—away from the writhing assailant, then kicked him over onto his side. "That ye tryin' to blind another silly fucker wi' those weapons o' yours?" she laughed. Katie laughed back at her. "Well, if ye've got them, flaunt them," she said, pushing her breasts together and up, making them even more prominent. Melanie laughed again. "Lucky bastard," she muttered, enviously, shaking her head. She stood over the pathetic, terrified pile squirming on the ground.

"We're lookin' for Raissa," she said in a loud, monosyllabic tone. "Ra-is-sa! Do ye know where she is?" The man continued to roll and writhe, crying now. "Gi'e me fuckin' strength," she cursed.

"Fuck's sake, Mel," Katie reprimanded. "Do ye really need to dismember every fuckin' man we meet?" The young girl held her hands to her side in a questioning manner, mouthing, 'What?' She bent down and, grabbing the injured man's vest, pulled the long, steel blade through her hand, cleaning the few drops of blood that had clung to her sword, before sliding it over her shoulder and into the sheath on her back.

"He was goin' to shoot ye, Katie. I know Cassandra says nothin' can kill us, but I'm no' wantin' to test that out unless we really have to." She rolled the man onto his back. He was no longer screaming, just breathing rapidly, giving a little pathetic wheeze each time he exhaled.

Katie squatted down by his side. "We're lookin' for a girl called Raissa," she said calmly. "We were supposed to find her in a village about here, but there's no sign o' it. Tell us what ye know and, if it's o' any use, we'll mend yer arm... well, sort o'... and then send ye on yer way." The man stared at her, his eyes wide with fear, his good arm clutching the stump, trying to stem the flow of blood.

"You have cut my arm off," he stated, superfluously, his voice now a high-pitched squeak.

"Aye. Bravo, smart lad," said Melanie. "Now, start talkin', or I'm gonna consider takin' your cock, as well."

"You are devils," he complained. "You have cut my arm off."

"Oh, for fuck's sake," said Katie. "You pointed a fuckin' gun at me."

"It is not loaded," he bleated. "I found it back there, where the village used to be." He was crying, once more. "I only wanted some food. That's all. Just some food. I have not eaten for three days. I just wanted some food."

A loud 'ssshhhh' caught his attention as Melanie unsheathed her sword once more. She grabbed his injured arm and smeared the curved blade over the open wound. He shrieked again as a searing heat burned deep into the limb, cauterising the skin, the blood, the nerve endings... glazing over, making a perfect seal. She then opened her water bottle and poured a generous stream of cooling liquid over the stump.

"There ye go. All better now," she said sarcastically.

"You truly are devils. You are a red-haired devil," he wailed, even more fearful of Melanie now. She shrugged as she stood. "I've been called a lot fuckin' worse," she opined. He stared at her, making sure that she was backing away from him. This woman, too, wore black cargo pants and army boots, with a brilliant white v-neck t-shirt. She had an identical necklace, with five very strange, different coloured stones. Both women looked perfectly cool, the heat of the day having no apparent effect on them.

"Calm down, for fuck's sake," said Katie, getting a little impatient now. "What's yer name?"

"Happy," he replied, snapping his attention back to Katie. "My name is Happy."

Melanie burst out laughing. "Fuck off," she screamed. "*Happy*? Fuckin' *Happy*? Oh, my giddy fuckin' aunt! Ye've done nothin' but whinge since ye got caught tryin' to shoot her, ye fucker." Katie laughed, then made a hand gesture suggesting her companion, too, should calm down.

"Were you from the village, Happy?" she asked. The man looked at Katie, her face now a much-needed source of friendliness and reassurance. He nodded. "What happened? Where's the village?" He looked from one woman to the other, unsure whether to trust them. "Do ye know Raissa?" Katie pressed. He nodded again. "Where is she?"

"They took her. They took them all,"

"Who? Who took them?"

"The Ba Rushimusi... the game poachers. They now call themselves Ingagi Nshya... New Gorillas." He sat up, still clutching his injured arm, satisfied that the crazy women would not cut him into pieces. "They are raiding the villages on the mountainside, stealing the food, the water... anything they can get. They take the women and girls, and kill the men and boys."

Katie went into her pack and pulled out a water bottle. She removed the lid and offered it to Happy, the man gratefully swallowing as much as he could with each gulp. "They burned the village down and threw the bodies of the men into the well. The women, taken, led farther up the mountain. I survived only because I was returning from a trip to Musanze. They have a camp by the Bisoke Crater Lake, near the border with DRC, and it is common for them to raid both sides of the border now. If there *is* a border now."

"By the crater lake?" groaned Melanie. "The Diávasi? For fuck's sake, that's where we started from. We've been wanderin' around in circles fer days. Would have been as well campin' there, then waitin' for them to come to us, Katie."

"We didn't see any smoke as we made our way here," said Katie.

"It was two weeks ago when they came," said Happy. "We have had a lot of heavy rain, which has doused the fires. I would take you there... but there is nothing but death."

Katie looked around the mountainside, hoping to see some sign of human activity, some clues of where to go. "Don't the Rwanda Defence Force patrol this area?" she asked.

"Hah! The RDF!" He spat to his side. "The RDF have scurried back to their holes in Kigali. They do not care for the people. They have never cared for the people. Since the ripple, they are the same as the Ingagi Nshya, looking after themselves and the bastard government, keeping the food and good water from the people. The Ingagi Nshya are the power here now."

Melanie gave Katie a knowing smile. "Well, I'm up for a fight," she said.

"How many Ingagi Nshya are there, Happy?" Katie probed. She pulled an oat bar from her bag, unfolded the napkin wrapper, and passed it to the starving man.

"This group? Fifty... sixty? But there are many, many such groups. Too many. I have been scavenging the hills for food since the attack. I am alone and dare not approach any village, as they will kill me on sight. They will not chance me being Ingagi Nshya."

"And how many women and girls?"

Happy looked shocked. "About... forty. You cannot be seriously thinking of trying to free these women?"

"We're here for Raissa," figured Melanie. "If that means killin' sixty scum bastards... and freein' forty women, then bring it on. I'm ready to kick some arse."

"You are crazy," Happy squealed. "The guards will kill you as soon as they see you and, at any rate, Raissa will be dead by now. Probably."

Katie was securing her pack onto Bentley's saddle. She strapped her sheath around her shoulders, fixing her sword firmly in an angle across her back, much like Melanie's. "Why do ye say that?" she asked.

"Because Raissa is a devil like you," he said. "She shows no respect, and she does not know fear."

"Sounds like the girl we're after, right enough," Melanie nodded.

"We would be better getting to safety. I doubt Raissa will still be alive. They will rape her, then they will kill her," advised Happy. "They will do this with many of the women, as they will not want to feed them." Katie turned and offered her hand to Happy, gesturing for him to stand.

"Then we better get a move on, hadn't we?" she said.

"No, no, no," Happy protested. "I am going nowhere, and certainly not toward Ingagi Nshya."

"Look, Happy," Katie sighed. "This is quite simple. Either ye show us where they are, or Mel will take your head off. Your choice." He turned to look at Melanie, who stood with a big smile on her face, unsheathing her sword yet again.

"Ok, ok," he said. "I will take you close, but I will not fight. I cannot fight, now that you have taken my hand."

"Stop fuckin' gripin'," said Melanie. "Ye're still alive, for fuck's sake. Ye've lost yer hand... ye canna wank wi' it anymore... but, are ye in any pain? Are ye?" Happy looked at his wounds. There was no pain, or discomfort, just a strange feeling that something was missing. Katie offered her hand, once more, pulling the conscripted guide to his feet.

"We have about two hours o' light left, then we'll stop for the night. Behave, and ye can have some o' Mel's delicious veggie stew."

"Sarcastic bitch," retorted Melanie with a laugh and a shake of her head. She mounted Crumbles, gently patting him on his neck. "Hello again, handsome," she whispered, the horse giving a welcoming nod of his head. Katie mounted Bentley and pulled Happy up behind her.

"How far to their camp?" she asked.

"If we stick to the trails, at least half a day, probably more because of the rains. But, I don't think this is a good idea."

"Oh, for fuck's sake, Happy," interrupted Melanie. "Cheer the fuck up!"

The lower slopes were thick with bamboo forest, the trails often narrowing, forming difficult gaps for the horses to squeeze through. Although the climate was pleasantly warm, the nights were cooler because of the altitude, and the temperature was already beginning to drop. This did not present a problem for the women; they were now apparently unaffected by external temperatures, feeling neither overly hot nor cold.

Recent rainfall had made much of the ground thick with mud, hampering their progress. Where it wasn't mud, it formed slippy inclines, testing the horses' ability to stay on their feet, and the riders' ability to stay in their saddles.

At regular intervals, they found abandoned gorilla nests, the most recent circular beds looking fresh and numerous, suggesting a healthily populated group nearby. "Do ye think we'll see any?" asked Melanie, barely containing her excitement.

"The gorillas keep on the move during daylight, but they usually only travel about a mile or so each day, so maybe. These nests look fresh," said Happy. "This family must be about twenty strong." He raised himself, pushing up on his thighs, straining to see through the bamboo.

"Will they come back here?"

"It is unlikely. They build new nests each night, then move on the next morning. They sometimes do not go very far from the old nests, but, since the ripple, they are being hunted yet again, so will try to keep moving." He turned back and forth, left then right, then slumped back down onto the rear of the saddle, disappointed.

"The bamboo is their principal food, but they are now the food for the Ingagi Nshya, and their numbers are falling once again."

"How do ye know so much?" asked Katie.

"I was a Ranger at the Nature Reserve... before. The gorilla population, and the golden monkeys further north, was slowly increasing, but... *now*? The poor creatures are in even more danger than before. We, too, should be careful of Ingagi Nshya patrols."

They continued their sluggish ascent, picking their way carefully through the various thick patches, making slow progress mostly. In the more level areas, the trails were drier, and they increased their pace on the firmer ground. "Is it bamboo all the way to the top?" asked Melanie.

"When it gets to the higher slopes, we will come to a band of Hagenia and Hypericum forest. I suggest we wait till we get to these thicker areas before we stop for the night. The dense floors will give us cover, and protection from the Ingagi Nshya patrols. It will also be easier to hear them. After that, as you near the summit, the mountain opens out to much shorter shrubs... Senecio and Lobelia bushes. It will be much easier for *them* to see *you*."

As they climbed, they saw no more signs of gorillas, and the bamboo began thinning out, gradually being replaced by taller, thicker plants. The trees were much greener, with long straggly leaves dangling down from the moss-covered branches. Bryophyte cushions padded out from the tree limbs, and ericaceous shrubs filled many of the gaps between the trees. Happy directed them off the main trail, through a narrow gap in the shrubs, and into an area that had a small but well protected flat area. The light was fading, and the women set about their now-practiced routine.

Katie helped Happy down from the horse before untying her pack. She removed the canvas roll from the back of the saddle, placing it next to her pack beside a massive Hagenia, then removed the other packs from Crumbles. Showing an amazing dexterity, she quickly cleared a large area of brush, and gouged out a bowl shape in the ground in readiness for a campfire. As she kicked and threw suitable logs and branches into the bowl, Melanie was unsaddling the horses. She looked at Happy. "Are ye goin' to make yerself useful, Happy?"

"What can I do? You have cut my arm off... and it is incredibly itchy."

"Ye can get some firewood while Katie gets the bivvies up, for fuck's sake."

Katie laughed. "I wouldn't piss her off, if I were you, Happy. Her hair might be red, but her touch-paper is definitely blue... light it an' she'll go off like a fuckin' rocket!"

The man walked off, mumbling to himself in Kinyarwanda, shuffling the forest debris in search of suitable logs. Melanie continued to tend the horses, laying out two bowls of water and two small blocks of compressed hay. She sneaked a broken biscuit to Crumbles, whispering, 'Don't tell Bentley, eh?'

Katie already had a decent fire going and was now unpacking the bivouacs.

Happy looked on in wonder. Where had Melanie found the water and hay? How had Katie got a blaze going in just a few seconds? These women terrified him, and the more he saw, the more he suspected sorcery... witchcraft! He looked at his stump, replaying the injury in his mind. The girl had swung her sword, certainly, but now that he thought about it, he had felt no pain, just the intense heat as the sword passed through his arm. Then, of course, she had used her sword to seal the wound, stop the bleeding. He was an intelligent man—he reminded himself—but if not witchcraft, then what? He continued his ineffectual and distracted rummaging, as the women were finishing the shelters.

"How the hell do we take care o' sixty o' these bastards, Katie?" whispered Melanie.

"I'm workin' on it," she replied. "This might take a wee bit o' theatrics, I think. We'll need to scare the shit out o' these cowardly fuckers. Spook the shitebags. It's mibbee time we found out what the swords, and the stones, can really do."

"Cassandra advised we stay inconspicuous. That we don't attract attention," Melanie reminded her.

"Come on, Mel," she said, with a mischievous smile. "Ye've been on your best behaviour for long enough. Bet your dyin' to let rip on these cunts?" She gave a nonchalant shrug. "A wee bit o' *magic* might make it easier to convince Raissa into the bargain, eh?" The corners of the young girl's mouth rose slowly into an agreeing smile. They secured the final bivouac, then high-fived each other.

"Now, let's have some o' yer delicious veggie stew."

"Cheeky cunt," said Melanie.

Happy watched as the women quickly, and with amazing efficiency, threw a meal together. Melanie concentrated on the stew and seemed to produce, from what seemed a saddlebag of soil, a variety of carrots, sweet potato, onion and parsnip; which she deftly peeled and chopped with a rather serious looking hunting knife.

Katie had, somehow, snared a decent sized rabbit, skilfully skinning and roasting it over an improvised spit. She then stripped the meat, chopped it and added it to the boiling vegetables. The abundance of food, besides the boiling pot of coffee, was very welcome to Happy's empty stomach; but he couldn't help wonder at where, and how, the women were so readily finding their resources. There was no fresh water in the immediate vicinity and, while it was possible to find wild vegetables in the area, Melanie seemed to have an amazing store ready at hand. It came as no surprise when she produced a small container, from which she added a thickener, and then a gravy to the stew.

They enjoyed the meal and the coffee before washing the cooking equipment, mess trays, and cutlery. Happy sat nursing his amputated arm, watching, listening as the women chatted, inanely at times.

The fire crackled and spat; a burst of sparks exploded upwards, illuminating the clearing for several seconds. "Ye don't look very happy, Happy," Katie observed. "Did ye no' enjoy Mel's stew?" Although impressed with the speed with which they had built it, he could not understand why they had built such a large fire. It was far more than they had need of; just to boil water and stew.

"The fire is a mistake. The Ingagi Nshya will see it from miles away."

"Good! It'll save us time if they come to us."

"You want them to come to you? You English are crazy!" He stood, looking frantically about him for an escape route, or a hiding place.

"English?" Melanie repeated. "Who the fuck are ye callin' English, ye little shit?"

"Who are you? Why are you here? And what do you want with Raissa?" His voice was, once again, growing higher in pitch; his panic rising yet again. A branch cracked under an approaching foot, somewhere in the trees.

"I'd get down if I were you, Happy," said Melanie, slowly standing as she emptied her coffee mug to the side. "There's about to be some... *fireworks*!" Happy immediately dropped to the ground and scrambled into a furrow below one of the taller trees. He crawled as far under the bushes as he could, whimpering in fear of the approaching guerrillas.

Melanie drew her sword and swung it in a circular motion around her head. The flames rose in a column, growing hotter and brighter. Brilliant white, a temperature of over 1300°C, the light and heat shining out, illuminating much further into the jungle. Katie, too, was circling her sword, drawing the many days of rainwater, the very moisture, from the ground; swirling it around them, faster, and faster, into a fine mist. The mist circled, whooshing, growing louder, as if Katie had drawn the wind itself. She looked about her, watching for the advance of the Ingagi Nshya. Waiting, biding her time, her sword moving smoothly, effortlessly around her head. Melanie's sword continued its arc around her head. She, too, scrutinising the trees in search of the enemy.

"Come on, ye bastards, show yerselves," she called. They duly obliged, cautiously picking their way past the surrounding trees; quietly making their way through the darkness toward the light of the fire, their eyes wide in fear of the vision before them. "How many on your side, Katie?"

"I see eight. You?"

"More. Twelve, possibly. Ready?"

"Ready. 3... 2... 1... *Now!*"

In unison, their necklaces glowed brightly, the inscriptions on the swords glowing, as the two women spun, pointing their weapons at the fire. The mist flew into the flames, immediately becoming thick steam, hissing as it rose skywards. Katie again circled her sword, drawing the steam down and outwards, filling the clearing, confusing the attackers, obscuring their vision. They were shouting now, breaking their disciplined approach, rushing forward into the clearing, into the steam. As they reached the fire, a realisation fell upon them. The women were no longer waiting. They were now on the move, behind them, beside them, slicing and hacking. One after another fell, the glint of silver flashing through the grey white of the steam.

In panic, the Ingagi Nshya fired their guns; indiscriminate and frenzied, cutting down their own comrades as fear gripped them. The steam thickened, the hissing grew louder; the swords swung faster, deadlier. In less than thirty seconds, it was all over. The gunfire ceased, the swords stopped swinging... the steam dissipated, floating gently toward the skies; leaving just the bright glow of the fire, receding as it cast its light upon the circle of carnage. In a small corner of the clearing, the two horses stood, chewing; unconcerned, and uninterested.

The women systematically worked their way around each of the Ingagi Nshya, plunging their sword deep, ensuring none survived. They counted twenty-one.

"Superb," smiled Melanie. "That leaves less than forty for tomorrow."

"You can come out now, Happy," called Katie. "Happy?" She looked over to the furrow. Happy was rigid with fear, his eyes wide, his mouth quivering, unbelieving of what he had just witnessed. Katie walked over and held her hand out. "You're safe, Happy. They're all dead." Still, the man just stared at her, until, with a jolt, he rose onto his knees.

"Safe?" he asked, with a fearful, ironic laugh. "Safe? How can I be safe in the company of witches?"

"We're no' witches," laughed Melanie as she walked over to the cowering man, then crouched in front of him and smiled. As he considered returning her smile, she jerked her head forward. "*Boo!*" she exclaimed. Happy recoiled backwards, losing his balance and toppling over. Katie leant forward and, again, offered her hand to him. She pulled him to his feet with his good hand.

"We're no' witches, Happy," she confirmed.

Melanie leaned close. "Or maybe we are," she whispered. The man just stared at her. "Whoooooooh!" she said, wiggling her fingers in his face. "And we're *Scottish...* no' fuckin' English, ye prick!"

"Then you Scottish are crazy!" He dusted himself down as best he could.

"Yep!" agreed Katie. "And we crazy Scots are fuckin' knackered. It's late, so we'd better get some sleep. You can have that bivvie there, Happy." She pointed to the lean-to nearest the horses.

"What? You cannot be serious. You are going to sleep among the dead?"

Melanie looked about her. "They're no' goin' anywhere," she said matter-of-factly.

"God will punish you for this," Happy declared. "He will serve justice upon you."

Katie sniggered. "Oh, Happy," she said. "It was God who sent us here. And *she* will be most happy wi' our work."

XXVII. THE LIGHTNING GOD

The tall, wide wooden gates were less than cooperative. It was impossible to tell the last time they had been opened but, at this particular moment, they were refusing to budge even an inch.

Pandeia and Ella pushed and pushed, but lacked the strength to trouble the barricade. The clouds were growing thicker, the rumbles of thunder louder and longer and, just as the light was fading, the winds rose, and the trio felt the first drops of rain hit their faces.

"We must take shelter for now," advised Selêne, looking around for anything that may act as cover. The trees to their right swayed and groaned in the building storm; the ferocity of the branches, as they whipped back and forth, deterring any thought of comfort there. The only possible protection was for them to hide underneath the coverless waggon. "Quickly, ladies," advised Selêne, "under here."

Ella eyed the waggon, not yet sure there was nothing to be done. She looked up at the top of the gates, and back to the waggon. The rain was growing heavier by the second, and the thunder boomed. "Bring the waggon in front o' the gate, Pandeia," Ella shouted. "I can climb over."

The All-Bright nodded in understanding. Holding the reins, she circled the horses, bringing them alongside the gates. Ella ran over to Selêne, who was trying to cover her head with the blanket she'd stowed in the waggon. She helped the Aftí-Fengári below the cart. "I'll try to open it from inside," she mouthed as the thunder clapped yet again.

Ella climbed onto the waggon and stretched as high as she could. She couldn't quite reach the top and, for the first time ever, cursed in her frustration. Pandeia leapt up and gestured the offer of a help-up. Ella nodded and raised her right foot into Pandeia's clenched hands. With a loud grunt, she powerfully lifted Ella's foot, as Ella, too, pushed up, grasping for the top of the gate.

Her hands curved over, and her feet scrambled frantically up the soaking wetness of the unrelenting barrier. She pulled herself up with such force that she flew over the top of the gate, disappearing instantly from Pandeia's vision. The rain soaked the All-Bright's face, and she blinked repeatedly as she bowed her head, wiping her eyes. "Mitéra!" she called. "Mitéra! Are you alright?"

The storm raged on. The thunder roared, and the rain hissed as it pelted the waggon bed around Pandeia's feet. In only a few minutes, the light had all but faded into darkness, and Pandeia now feared for Ella's safety. She jumped down, reaching under the waggon, pulling herself next to Selêne. "The Mitéra Fŷsi has disappeared, Aftí-Fengári."

Selêne smiled. "Our mother is very resourceful, Pandeia," she said, struggling to be heard over the thunder. "I don't think we should be unduly worried just yet." Behind them, the loud creaking of moving wood filled the gaps in the thunderclaps, as the gate swung slowly open.

The two Naátúr shuffled around to find Ella gamely pulling the huge wooden door. Her feet splashed and slipped beneath her, and she was covered from head to foot in dark brown mud.

"Hurry!" she gasped. "I canna hold this much longer."

Selêne and Pandeia scurried from under the waggon and through the small gap Ella's efforts had created. As they passed through, Ella's feet gave way, slipping in the growing muddied waters. The gate crashed shut and Ella splashed to the ground, her backside thumping into the mud.

Pandeia reached down. "Are you alright, Mitéra?" she asked anxiously. Through the poor light, and the rain, and the brown mud that now covered her, Ella's eyes shone out. The whiteness of her teeth as she flashed a massive smile came as a relief to her two companions.

"Well," she said, sitting in her puddle, shaking the mud and wet from her hands, "we're in, at least. What now?"

Pandeia leant forward with both hands and pulled Ella to her feet. The rain continued its ceaseless assault, and the thunder rumbled. They found themselves in a large courtyard, with nought but mud, and puddles, and dead branches. In truth, it looked as though they'd stumbled into a long-abandoned ruin of a castle.

All three were now sodden and in need of some hot refreshment and food. Before them, the columns at the entrance to Zeus' home rose like the bars of a giant prison cell; ominous and off-putting. Behind the columns, the doorway into the castle was the deepest darkness; a blackness so disconcerting it caused Pandeia to step back.

"Are you sure we should be here, Aftí-Fengári?" she asked fearfully.

Ella took her hand, squeezing it gently, her support and reassurance most welcome. "It's alright, Pandeia," Ella affirmed. "There's nothin' to hurt us here." She looked to Selêne, her heart breaking for the sadness she felt in this dark place. "There's so much hurt here, Selêne. So much sadness and grief."

Selêne clasped Ella's other hand. "My, you really are so insightful, Mother." Her lips thinned, and she nodded slowly. "Alas, you are all too correct. Before we can mend Kiípos, I fear we shall have to repair the most broken of hearts."

They stepped between the centre columns and up several steps into the castle entrance. They were thankful for the shelter from the downpour, but a cold draft was escaping from within the darkness of the cave. Pandeia took the lead. She held her hand out in front of her, and immediately illuminated the high archway in which they stood.

A long corridor led into the cave before fanning out into a wide arboretum. As with the outside, the space was dark and in deep neglect; the various shrubs and trees, and an area where an extensive range of orchids once grew, all lay in disrepair. Most were dead, beyond saving.

Pandeia increased her luminosity, revealing, on either circular side wall, two staircases rising to the next floor. The group carefully stepped through the clutter and gingerly made their way up the steps, behind much of the failing greenery, turning into another short corridor.

As they exited the passageway, the light flared out to fill a massive reception area, or, perhaps, what had once been a ballroom. The beautifully tiled floor, and the ornately decorated walls—a kaleidoscopic swirl of brilliant, lustrous colours—looking just as depressed as the building which housed them. Here, too, was an abundance of neglected, dying plant life.

"Douse that light," came the gruffest of shouts. "It offends mine eyes."

Pandeia looked to Selêne, who gestured for her to lower the brightness slightly. "Is this the welcome you offer your visitors now, my lord?" Selêne asked, in the general direction of the unseen objector. She stepped ahead of the young girls. "Come out... come out and greet us, old friend."

A loud banging noise, a door being slammed shut, echoed from the far right corner. A shuffling of feet, dragging their way across the filthy floor, was accompanied by a huge, dark, lumbering blur. As the light fell upon him, Zeus held his left hand up to shield his eyes. In his right, he held a large horn which, judging by the slopping spillage as he lurched toward them, was full of ale. His once-white tunic was now a stained, ragged sack. It had obviously been some time since he had bathed, such was the ingraining of the dirt on his skin, and the greasy, matted state of his hair and thick beard. The foulest of stenches preceded his approach.

"Must we have these cheap conjurations?" he growled. "These disrespectful lanterns, mocking my tragedy, demeaning my mourning?"

"And must we," retorted Selêne, "endure the mewling whimpering of false and exaggerated bereavement, my lord?" She stepped purposefully toward Zeus. "It was, as far as I am aware, Mother Gaea who perished. And yet, here in these halls, it is you who carry the stench of the dead. You who seem intent to mock thyself."

"How dare you," bellowed Zeus. "How dare you invade my home—uninvited, unsympathetic—insulting both myself, and the memory of the Mitéra Fŷsi." He threw the horn of ale in their direction; his lack of coordination such, that the missile came nowhere near. "Begone, foul harpy," he spluttered, "for I wish to be alone."

"*You?*" declared Ella, ambling toward the drunkard. "*You* are Zeus? You're the reason we've slogged all the way up here?" She stood, her head shaking, her hands firmly on her hips.

Zeus froze in his tracks, completely flummoxed. He stared down at Ella, squinting his eyes, disbelieving of what he was seeing. "Wha.." he stammered. "What... who..." He looked to Selêne. "What is this impudence, Selêne? That a filthy guttersnipe should address one such as I?"

"Filthy is it?" snapped Ella, her dander up. "I'll have ye know I got filthy helpin' my friends... no' feelin' sorry for myself in some dark hole. No' drinkin' myself into oblivion. And '*one such as you*'? Don't make me laugh. Look at ye, you're a disgrace."

Selêne stepped forward and placed a calming hand on Ella's shoulder. "Tell me anything just said that is untrue, Zeus, and we shall depart immediately," she challenged.

"Bah!" roared the Lightning God. "Begone, I say. Begone!" He gestured awkwardly, swinging his arm for them to leave.

Selêne approached the flailing drunk. "We shall leave only when you answer our plea."

"Your plea?" Zeus laughed. "So, you *are* here to beg my help? I should have known it was not for my welfare."

Selêne sighed. "But it is, albeit indirectly, *all* of our welfare that shall benefit if you agree to our request, Zeus."

"And you think to win my favour by inflicting this...," he gestured wildly at Ella, "this... mud-splattered rodent on me." He stared, too, at Pandeia, squinting his eyes once more. "And where in Helios' name did you find the sprite? Do as I say, dim that infernal light, girl!"

"Rodent?" Ella stomped toward Zeus.

Her directness caught him by surprise, and he flinched and took a step back. "Stay back, rodent," he ordered, though not with as much confidence as he tried to muster. He shook his head, his sorrow and anger competing as he tried to compose himself. "I'm sorry, Selêne," he breathed, "but you have wasted your time." He turned, seeking to return to the refuge of his quarters.

"Wait," called Ella. "Are ye so willin' to languish in yer own decrepitude; to meekly fade away? Buried here, under yer mountain?"

Selêne looked to her protege, completely stunned by the change in tone, demeanour and, most noticeably, maturity. No longer was she a little girl; now she was truly the embodiment of all life on Kiípos. Her grace, composure, and confidence were now shining from her. She seemed to grow up in this instant.

Zeus stared at her with renewed interest. "Who are you, girl?" he asked, a fear now in his voice. "Who are you?"

Ella held her hands out in friendship. "I, Lord Zeus," she said, with a heart-warming smile, "am the Mitéra Fŷsi. And we've come to ask for yer aid."

Zeus laughed, unconvinced. "The Mitéra Fŷsi is dead, little one. And my heart died with her. She was the beat of my heart, the blood through my veins, but now my heart beats no more. So, please, just leave me to myself... and I shall leave you to..." Before he could finish, Ella began slowly spinning, her arms outstretched, drawing more light from Pandeia; brilliantly, warmly, filling the ballroom. Ella's tunic flared at the hems, from which red, and orange, and yellow sparks began flying out; floating out, and up; restoring the colour, the vivacity, the life back into the vapid, crestfallen hall.

The plants stretched, and strained, and pulled themselves up, to reach once more for the light. Their leaves sprung forth, life and growth restored. The Lightning God, Pandeia, and Selêne all looked on in wonder; their smiles befitting of the joyful scene unfolding around them.

Zeus' eyes fell back to the filthy little girl but, in her place, stood a beautiful, youthful vision. Gone were the mud, and the dirt. Her tunic, too, was now a brilliant white, her hair lustrous and shining with health and life. But most of all, she had grown, transformed. No longer a small girl, now she was the Mitéra Fŷsi. Now she was a young woman.

"I *am* the Mitéra Fŷsi," repeated Ella, her tone now soft, friendly... loving. In her outstretched hand, she offered an apple. "And, Lord Zeus, we really need your help."

They waited on the large, spacious veranda. As with the courtyard entrance, leaves and broken twigs littered the floor; swirling loosely in the intermittent breeze that darted in and out. The storm continued, unabated, the thunder and the rain just as intense as before, but making little impact on their surroundings.

Zeus had led them through the decaying, neglected corridors of his castle, mumbling and complaining of how *all* had left him; *all* had deserted him in his time of grief. In truth, his attendants had all been chased and cajoled, insulted and bullied into departing their positions. The sorrow of the Lightning God had come perilously close to driving him, if not mad, then to the extremes of intransigence and unreasonableness. His decline into alcohol, self pity and self loathing, had been swift, as news of Mother Gaea's death reached his halls.

He loved Mother Gaea. There was no doubt of that, but she was devoted to her care and responsibilities for Kiípos. Her love for him was far less obvious, far less certain. It was not that she *didn't* love him—she loved everyone—but her commitment to him was not as full, not as complete as his was to her. She loved him... *seasonally*! *Occasionally*! Her visits were always on her terms; staying only when *she* wanted. It seemed to Selêne that Zeus had, in his grief-stricken mental state, elevated Mother Gaea's affection for him to levels far beyond the reality.

She watched Ella and Pandeia as they sat across the table, laughing and joking as they always seemed to do. But they were far different now. Ella's blossoming had not been an isolated event; Pandeia, too, had grown beyond the childhood personage she had inhabited. Both were now beyond adolescence—in appearance, manner, and behaviour—and before her sat two extremely intelligent, articulate, and vivacious young women.

To look at, Ella was now at the older end of her teenage years; tall, graceful, and, with a little sprinkling of freckles across her nose and cheeks, an unaffected younger version of her mother. Her facial gestures, her laugh, and even the way she would flick her hair, were all direct mimicking, whether or not intentional, of how Katie behaved.

Pandeia, not surprisingly, was a wonder to behold. Of course she was; she was the All-Bright, the illumination, the deliverer of moonlight. She had been carefully selected as the ideal Sŷntrofos for the new Earth Mother; and how perfect that selection now seemed to be. Her honey hair, and her golden eyes, sparkled as she smiled. The looks, and the body language between the two confirmed Selêne's suspicions - they loved each other. They had a bond, a shared life experience of lives not yet lived, of memories not yet made. They were meant for each other. And in that realisation, Selêne's hopes for Kiípos, for humanity, and for the future of the universe soared.

The table was empty except for a fruit bowl that had long since been tended, and an empty water jug; redundant, as the Lightning God had other, more inebriating preferences. The apples and pears had rotted, over ripe. At least they *had*, until Ella placed her hand on the table, bringing life, colour, and flavour back to the decayed and pulped treats. Here was another reason for Selêne to rejoice; Mother Ella was intuitively embracing her new skills, effortlessly employing the miracles with which she was so abundantly imbued. Selêne smiled as she caught the subtle little hand-squeeze between her two protégés.

Ella turned and smiled. "Ye look awfully pleased wi' yourself, Selêne," she said warmly.

"I have every reason to be pleased, Mother." The Aftí-Fengári reached over, taking both girls by the hand. "We are far more blessed than we could ever have imagined. And I truly believe you shall bring our salvation." She smiled at Ella, then looked to Pandeia. "*Both* of you," she confirmed.

"Can I ask a question?" Ella's face suggested uncertainty, puzzlement.

"Of course, Mother," replied Selêne. "It is your prerogative to ask what you like, and my responsibility to answer as fully as I can."

Ella sat still for a few moments, considering her words. She and Pandeia exchanged eye contact, and Ella smiled and sighed. "I don't for a second want to sound ungrateful," she said, as reassuringly as she could, "but why is all o' this happenin' to me? Why am I *older* me?"

"Ah," said Selêne, "to the crux of the matter as usual." She squeezed the girls' hands, then stood, making her way around to their side of the table. She cupped Ella's chin in her hand, raising it gently to look into her eyes. "Sometimes, Mother, the universe requires certain... entities... to grow at an accelerated rate in order to achieve its designated, or desired, function, or potential. In your case, the universe needs an adult Mitéra Fŷsi to tend Kiípos' wounds." She appraised Ella's response, seeking her continuing understanding. "On realising that Lord Zeus was neither interested in, nor taking seriously, your pleas, you actively triggered your own physiological development. You are the Mitéra Fŷsi, the cultivator of all living things; the hand that tills the soil; the Universal Granger. You, quite simply, make things grow."

Ella nodded and smiled. "And I brought this on Pandeia, as well?" She looked to her Sŷntrofos, holding her hand as she gazed into her eyes. Pandeia seemed to glow with pleasure as Selêne, too, squeezed her hand.

"Of course, Mother," she said warmly. "Regardless of whether we intended such consequences, it would appear you have chosen your life partner, and she will mirror your own development." Selêne looked into Pandeia's eyes. "She will compliment you—in every action, every desire, every need—for she is the light and the love within you, for now and always." She repeated her customary hand squeeze and smiled. "And, in doing so, Pandeia will become the Aftí-Fengári when my time comes to depart."

Pandeia jumped to her feet. "Aftí-Fengári," she exclaimed, "you cannot mean this. I can never replace you." Her eyes welled as her emotions, her love for the little woman spilled out.

Selêne sighed as she embraced the girl. "Oh, please do not fret, my dear. I have quite some time before I leave you all. But, you must realise, Pandeia, as partner to the Mitéra Fŷsi, you are her equal now." She looked to Ella and chuckled. "Unless Mother thinks otherwise, of course."

Ella approached Pandeia, wrapped her arms around the girl's neck and pulled her closer, tightly embracing her. She leaned back, allowing their eyes to settle into each other, then leaned forward, placing the softest of kisses on Pandeia's lips. "Oh, I think Pandeia's more than my equal, Selêne," she said softly, a warm smile now underlining her teary eyes. "She's everything. I love her. And I hope she feels the same."

The All-Bright, too, was now teary-eyed; her heart pounding at the acknowledgment of, not just acceptance, but much more than that. Yes, she had loved Ella from the first, but did not dare to presume equality, or anything other than service and friendship. "Yes," she whispered. "Yes." A warm flush filled Selêne as she watched the first demonstration of their love; the first physical declaration to one another, as they kissed as lovers in admission of their devotion.

"Love is surely the greatest, and most beautiful mystery of the universe," smiled Selêne.

A crashing bang, as a door slammed shut, drew the trio's attention back inside the castle. "Down to business," said

Ella, wryly, as she turned to face the approaching Lightning God.

Zeus had changed his clothing and, while not exactly bathing, had at least *attempted* to clean himself up. His still soaking hair had been dragged back away from his face, his beard dripping wet. A fresh tunic, albeit a little tatty, further improved his appearance. He made his way toward the veranda, a rather sheepish look betraying his shame for his previous behaviour. "My apologies, Selêne... Mitéra Fŷsi," he offered, his head bowed. "You did not find me at my best."

"Mmmm," hummed Selêne. "And are you at your best now, my lord?" Her disapproving tone left no doubt as to her displeasure. His eyes looked up from his still lowered head, and he grunted an acknowledgment of sorts.

"I am truly sorry," he confirmed. "You were seeking my assistance?"

Ella stepped forward, holding her hands out, taking Zeus' in her own. "I really am sorry for your loss, Lord Zeus," she said, her genuine sympathy coming through in every word. "But it was a loss for everyone else, too. And now we have to make sure Mother Gaea didn't die for nothin'."

Zeus gripped Ella's hands tightly. "Thank you," he replied. "For too long I have hidden here, in solitude, mourning my loss, never considering that others, too, may grieve in their own devastation." He gestured for them to sit. "My hospitality is, I'm afraid, far lacking in what it once was. Would you like some..." He looked about him for some suitable offering but, except for the rejuvenated fruit on the table, there was nought.

"It's ok," Ella reassured him. "We can eat and drink later. First, we have to ask ye somethin'." Zeus sat, leaning forward, his hands on his knees, nodding in anticipation. "Kiípos is in a perilous state," Ella said. "The actions o' Pasiphae, the ripple, and the subsequent repercussions, have left vast areas uninhabitable because o' nuclear contamination. People, and wildlife, are ill, or are dyin'; plant growth has suffered, crops have failed, and food is becomin' almost impossible to find for all life in these parts o' the world. Rain, when it does fall, is also contaminated, and further impairs the growin' process."

Ella selected a pear from the bowl and bit deep. She paced slowly around the table. "We all agree," she said, looking to Selêne and Pandeia, "that what's required, before I can even begin to restore anythin', is a purge o' all the contamination." She paused, holding the pear in front of her, looking at Zeus through steely, determined eyes. "That's where you come in, my lord."

XXVIII. A CALL TO ARMS

"How much time do ye think we have?"

"Your guess is as good as mine," replied Charon. "A week? A day? An hour? We're guessin', right enough, but we have to assume they're comin' soon." It brought Jacob a strange comfort, hearing his dad's friend talking in an accent that was so familiar to them both. He felt as if in the presence of the most trusted of family friends; that he wasn't alone in this most critical of times.

They watched the ranks of 'soldiers' filing onto the field, each taking up their own small space in line; the tiny spot where they would pitch the tiniest of tent; the tiniest spot that would become their last home, for however long they had to wait.

Thousands of transient souls, made ready for their final journey to Sólaás, or Hades. Thousands of transient souls, of men, of women, who had come to make peace with their gods. Now they were the last defence of the living world; the unwitting defenders of Elýsium, and of

Kiípos; the last line Haáde would have to cross before his assault on Sólaás.

"D'ye think they're ready enough?" asked Jacob.

"They'll just have to be. We have what we have." The sailor looked at Jacob. "How confident are ye o' this 'vision' o' Cassandra's?"

Jacob grimaced. "Don't tell her, but I was only fifty-fifty, up 'til the point where Eris pretty much confirmed it. There are a few details that haven't quite matched up, but this doesn't look like a normal storm. Didn't really think it would be Haáde, though, if I'm bein' honest."

"Hmm," grumbled Charon.

The rain continued to hammer into the ground; the thunder continued to rumble, and the angry clouds swirled in their purple wrath. The two men stood, somewhat sheltered by the canopy of trees surrounding them. From their vantage point at the edge of the de facto battlefront, they could see the various sections of troops. Once, they had expected to be pitted against one another; now, they were lining up as allies.

"What if ye're wrong? What if this isn't where Haáde'll hit first?"

Jacob turned, walking back inside the tree line, taking shelter under the bivouac Charon had erected for them. A small fire warmed an ancient coffee pot, and Jacob sat on the small logs they'd chosen as stools. As he poured, he stared out toward the vast open space stretching out into the horizon. "In her vision, Cassandra is adamant it's the Elysian Fields. And I... well, I've just had this... feeling... that this is where we're supposed to be. He'll want the Célestiaá Rings, even though he seemed happy for us to leave Hades wi' them. Somethin's changed since then. I *can* feel it." He handed a small mug of black coffee to his friend. "But I'm still findin' it hard to believe Haáde's behind this."

"I have to agree wi' ye," Charon said, taking his seat on the spare log stool. "When he spoke to me, just before we left, I didn't get the sense that he was bein' dishonest. Haáde is a lot o' things, but he's no' a liar. He doesn't have to be." He sipped his coffee. "And yet, this Eris, as mad as she is, seems absolutely convinced that Haáde's comin'."

"Pity the weather's so shit, eh?"

"Well, what do ye expect?" added Charon, partly stifling a laugh. "Ye're Scottish. Ye've got rain in yer DNA."

"Aye," sighed Jacob. "Did ye ever see Eris, ye know, on your trips to Hades?"

"No. I'd heard o' Eris, o' course, but never met her. Actually... always thought Eris was a bloke." He laughed, ironically, standing as he shook the last drops out of his coffee mug. "Keep gettin' reminders that I've gone through eons knowin' fuck all about anythin'." He kicked Jacob's boot, pointing to the far side of the field.

A large group of horse riders were circling the corner next to the distant tree line. Jacob peered through the rain. "Is that...?"

"Brunhiíld? Aye, that's her. The Valkyrie'll be our cavalry, when the time comes."

"How many do we have?"

"Well, Brunhiíld has re-called all that were down on Kiípos, so there'll be a tidy amount. And, what of Cassandra?"

Jacob turned to look toward Rimel and sighed. "Cassie's got the short straw right now—playing babysitter to our friend Eris."

❦❦❦❦

"We've met before, you and I." Eris was, once more, sat on the flour sacks, calmed down enough to appear rational, if not helpful.

"Have we?" responded Cassandra, feigning interest. "I'm sure I'd remember one such as you."

"Oh yes," continued Eris. "You were but a child, of course. Well, when I say we've 'met', I actually mean I was once in the same room as you."

"Really?"

"A wedding. A wedding I was not invited to..." Cassandra looked up as Eris' anger came to the surface once more. "My sisters were invited, but not I. Oh no, not the mischievous minor goddess of discord."

"Your sisters?" Cassandra suddenly found herself curious.

"You are a fool, Trojan," Eris laughed. "You think you know all there is to know. You think your pathetic visions and foresight give you some sort of higher intellect and understanding. But you know nothing."

Cassandra adjusted her seating position, paying full attention to the girl. "Tell me, then, oh magnificent goddess," she said, "tell me what it is I don't know."

Eris smiled, her lips thinning, her eyes narrowing. "Ha," she spat. "Your malediction, gifted you by Apollo.

The war that destroyed your homeland. You think these were just random acts? The results of fate? How stupid you are."

The mention of Apollo and reference to Troy hit Cassandra like a sledgehammer. She cautioned herself, however, reminding herself that this was, after all, the goddess of mischief, the sower of discord. "Do you have something to say, or nay? Either tell me, or be quiet."

"You think Circe was some perfect woman, don't you?" Eris asked. "Well, she was no better than Pasiphae; two manipulating dreamers, idealists of the worst kind. Creators of their children, neglecters of their 'pets'." Eris stared hard, her hatred on full display. "Yes, pets. That's all we were to the daughters of Helios."

"Who?" demanded Cassandra. "Who do you speak of?"

"Why Naátúr and Caátastroph, of course. We are cousins, brothers and sisters, united as the discarded progeny of Célestiaá."

Cassandra scoffed at the idea. "You may have been Pasiphae's pet, but I certainly wasn't Circe's. I was treated as a daughter. You make no sense, girl."

"Then listen, and all shall become clear. The wedding I speak of... your family attended, as guests of King Peleus, and his new wife Thetis, a sea nymph of great fame. All were invited, human and god alike. All except Caátastroph, of course. There was to be no acceptance for us, the children of Pasiphae."

Eris laughed as she recounted the fawning, sycophantic worshipping of Naátúr. "You think you know all about the goddesses you graciously invite to Elýsium. You pander to their whims, and yet you know nothing of their vanity, their narcissism. Hera, Athena, Aphrodite. Those beautiful effigies of womanhood?" Eris spat at Cassandra's feet.

She pulled at her bonds, raging at the situation she found herself in. "But I showed them," she chuckled. "How dare they ignore me. I snuck in. Of course I did. The wedding. I snuck in, and, oh my, how much mischief I wrought. And all it took was an apple to show these vainglorious, preening dolls up for what they really were."

Eris sneered at Cassandra. "How easily your kingdom fell."

"My kingdom? What do you mean?"

"I threw them an apple. The fools. I threw them an apple. *'To the fairest'*, it said. They couldn't help themselves. Hera, Athena and Aphrodite. They all fought for the apple, the fools. Embarrassing themselves and Naátúr. Then Zeus, in his usual drunken state, brought your brother into things."

"My brother? What nonsense do you speak?"

"Paris! He was your brother, was he not? He was chosen, on Zeus' splendid advice, to decide who should win the apple. And here is where man's greatest failing came to bear. Corruption! All offered Paris incredible bribes; land, victory, fame. But it was Aphrodite who played the winning hand. Her offer of the most beautiful woman in the world—Helen—was too much for Paris to refuse. And so Paris gave Aphrodite the apple, enraging Hera and Athena. It was they who ultimately engineered the kidnapping of Helen, and the subsequent war that destroyed what was Troy." Eris fell to her side in fits of laughter. "And here you are, playing hostess to the very women who brought about your demise."

Her laughter abruptly halted. "A strange turn of events, don't you think?"

Cassandra was devastated, her head swirling. "This cannot be true," she cried. "You lie!"

Eris settled back and sighed. "Believe me or no, Princess of Troy. I do not care. It is all water under the bridge, and shall soon be lost in the darkness of my lord. You will be but just another forgotten spec of what was once Helios' failed universe, as will all."

Eris inspected her bindings for no other reason than something to do. "I'm sorry," she said, quietly.

Cassandra's jaw dropped. This was the last thing she was expecting to hear from this highly strung woman, whose moods seemed to swing from one extreme to the other. "And for what, exactly, are you so sorry?"

Eris glanced over, quickly returning her eyes to her ties. "I am sorry that we shall not see the results of your Élementaá. I commend you on your resolve... your ambition, even. It would be quite the thing to see a world where women were, at the very least, the equal of men. But we do not yet live in that world, do we?"

Cassandra nodded thoughtfully. "Men will not hand us equality," she said. "It is up to the strongest of us, the bravest of us, to lift our sisters out of the mental and physical shackles that have been imposed on us for too long."

Eris met Cassandra's eye contact and, for the briefest of moments, an understanding was held between the two women. Then, with the simplest of smiles, that moment was gone.

"You cannot survive what is coming. My lord shall unleash the might of Hades, and all shall fall before him." Eris sat up straight, resuming her belligerent, disagreeable self.

"And what do you get out of it?" asked Cassandra.

"I am his consort. I shall deliver an heir, and I shall be his right hand."

"That does not sound like 'at the very least, the equal of men'. That sounds like a woman selling herself for position and power."

Eris sighed. "But '*at the very least*' I shall *have* position and power, while you shall have nought but dust and darkness."

"Then we must find some way of bargaining with Lord Haáde, mustn't we?"

"'*Bargain*'? And with what do you think you can treat with the Lord of Darkness?"

Cassandra held Eris' glare. "Not what. *Who*?"

XXIX. GUERILLAS & THE MIST

Katie woke to the sound of intermittent raindrops hitting the canopy. It quickly became a heavy downpour, a constant drumming on the top of the canvas. She looked out into the clearing. Melanie was standing outside her bivouac, near the fire pit; naked, washing herself in the natural shower. Uninhibited, relaxed; aware that Happy was watching her desirously. She had no interest in him; she had no interest in any man now, but would let nothing prevent her from cleansing herself of days of dust and dirt. *'If he can't control his dick, that's his problem, and he'd pay a price if he got adventurous'.* Still, it would do them no harm to keep him on-side for the rest of the journey. She was in no doubt that he hadn't seen a naked woman for some time, especially a young, fit woman. A young, fit woman caressing herself with soap; massaging her breasts, touching her intimate areas... why not give him just a *little* thrill?

Happy realised that Katie was watching him, and quickly pulled the flap of his bivouac down; embarrassed and ashamed of his voyeuristic lapse. It had been such a long time since he had been with a woman, but that was no excuse for spying on the girl, he reprimanded himself. He lay back, closing his eyes tightly, trying to ignore his erection. He could not make out what was being said, but the two women were now talking. He peeked through a tiny gap in the canvas. Katie, too, was now availing herself of the teeming rain; her pale, naked figure stretching and twisting against the dark green background of the sodden trees. Through the rain, the two nude women looked like goddesses... no, not goddesses... Mountain Nymphs. He watched in wonder, in excitement, aroused... his good hand now stroking himself. He looked from woman to woman, his excitement growing... until his eyes picked out a body. The Ingagi Nshya. Amid this surreal, erotic spectacle, there still lay the hacked and dismembered corpses of the previous night's attackers. He pulled the flap back again and lay on his back, eyes shut, crying.

"Man, this feels good," said Melanie.

"Aye, I was startin' to feel a crust o' dirt settlin' on my arms," laughed Katie.

"Can't say I miss makeup, or spendin' hours tryin' to look good so men would notice me. Men can go fuck themselves."

"If they could do that in the first place, then mibbee they wouldn't have been such nasty shits to women." Melanie hesitated, her arms dropping to her sides. There was steam coming from Katie.

"A hot shower? How the fuck are you gettin' a hot shower?"

Katie smiled, her arms wrapped around herself, her hands exaggerating her washing strokes, making a show of it. "The stones," she replied. "Thought about it, last night. If we can use the heat from the fire, then why couldn't we use the heat from our own bodies? That's why we don't feel the cold; our body heat! Just think it. It's nowhere near as hot as I'd like, but fuck's sake, it feels brilliant. So much better than a cold shower."

Melanie closed her eyes and focussed her thoughts. Within seconds, the water warmed and the washing experience became even more enjoyable. "Whoooo Hoooo!" she wailed at the top of her voice, the sound filling the clearing.

Happy was now convinced he was in the company of Banshee Witches.

After a short time, the rain ceased, almost as quickly as it had started. Happy poked his head through the flap, relieved that the women had now dressed and were preparing a breakfast. The sun's heat was already evaporating much of the rain water, and thin clouds of mist were floating off from the large leaves of the surrounding vegetation. The fire was already ablaze, a coffee pot boiling away.

"Mornin', Happy," called Melanie. "There's coffee in the pot, and a bowl o' hot water for ye to wash wi'. I'm doin' some toast." She held up a long fork with a piece of bread at the end. The man didn't respond, just huffily splashed his face and arms, then looked around for a towel.

"There is nothing to dry myself with," he said.

"Oh, sorry," replied Katie. "We don't normally use towels now," she added, cryptically, before pulling a dry rag from her pack and throwing it over to him. "There's coffee in the pot, an' Mel is doin' some toast."

"I am not hungry," he muttered. Katie's eyes met Melanie's, her impatience growing with the sulking man. Melanie nodded at him, urging Katie to say something. She wandered over, sipping her coffee.

"You ok, Happy?" The man just grunted. Katie crouched in front of him.

"Listen," she said. "Ye came at me wi' a gun and, as far as we knew, ye were prepared to shoot me. Had you no' done this, then ye would still have yer hand. The world has gone to shit, Happy. Billions o' people are dead, or on their way to bein' dead. We," she looked around to Melanie, "are goin' to make sure that many o' the *right* people, many o' the right *men*, end up dead. You are still alive, even after ambushing me. Think yourself lucky that ye only lost your hand."

She stood, looking directly at him for a few seconds, then turned, throwing the remnants of her coffee to the side. "You've got five minutes, while we saddle the horses. Then we move. We're here for Raissa, no' you. If your no' comin', then you'll no' be *goin'* either." As she strode off, Happy watched her, with an icy dread coursing through him. This beautiful woman was a demon, not a nymph, and he now knew that any goodwill was gone.

The women ate their toast as they went about packing up the camp, in much the same way as they had the previous day. Their efficiency was something to behold but, despite that, the events he'd experienced since entering that clearing made him wish they'd just killed him, and been done with it. It was clear from Katie's threat that, if he was not willing to show them the way, then he, too, would end up as company for the fallen Ingagi Nshya. The truly terrifying thing was her lack of emotion; he knew she would take his head off without a further thought.

True to her word, they had packed, mounted and were ready to go five minutes later. Katie held her hand out, pulling Happy up, on to the rear of the saddle, and they were, once more, on their way.

❦❦❦❦

"Why are you here? Why have you come to Rwanda?"

Happy was, once again, trying to assert himself. "We told ye," said Melanie. "We're here for Raissa."

"What do you want with Raissa?"

"Raissa will soon become the most important woman in Rwanda. The most important woman in Africa. We're here to... teach her... to advise her." Katie was trying to be a little more diplomatic than she had been earlier.

"You are wasting your time. Raissa listens to no one."

"She'll listen to us. Rwanda was a pro-woman country before the ripple, and is still majority female. But, no matter how successful women were in public, that success didn't even extend into their own homes. They were still at the beck and call o' their men. That's about to change, and Rwanda is the perfect place to make that change." Happy burst out laughing.

"You are feminists. You are just two crazy feminists... come to fill our women's heads with your American nonsense. They will never listen, they know it is just selfish talk. They know their men know bett....."

396

Before he could finish, Katie nudged him off the back of the horse and he fell into a crumpled heap in the bushes by the side of the trail. By the time he'd recovered his senses, she was standing over him, sword drawn.

"After all you've seen in the last twenty-four hours, you're still comin' out wi' the same old shite that every man, everywhere, believes. That women are the weaker sex. That women can't do anythin' without a fuckin' man." He crawled out onto the trail. "Do ye want to see just how weak we fuckin' are, Happy? Do ye?" Happy looked up at her, in fear of her sword swinging down on him.

"I am sorry," he pleaded. "I am sorry." Katie smiled at him.

"Don't worry. I'm no' goin' to kill ye. I want ye to see what we do to the rest o' these Ingagi Nshya fuckers. How much further?"

He pointed up the hill.

"The trees end up there, about one hundred metres. Then it is low-level vegetation, all the way to the crater lake. They will see you before you can get near them." Katie's eyes followed his pointing finger. She thought for a second.

"Why have they camped up here? At the top o' a volcanic mountain. It doesn't make sense."

"They will not stay here very long. They usually occupy the old safari hotels, coming out just to raid the villages."

"Mmm. Hotels? Sounds familiar," mumbled Katie. "Right then. Sooner we get started..." She gave a quick whistle and Melanie jumped down from Crumbles. "We'll tie them here, Mel. It gets more open just up there." Melanie looked up the hill.

"How we gonna play this?"

"Well, last night's theatrics worked. We need some mist," Katie smiled. "You stay here wi' the horses, Happy," she ordered, this time without a smile.

The women made their way to the edge of the forest and scanned the ground ahead of them. They were much closer to the crater lake than they'd expected. There was a long, level stretch of ground, covered with what seemed to be long grass and waist high bushes. Disappointingly, there was no sign of a camp. That would have been far too simple. But, in the distance, they saw an Ingagi Nshya patrol; two men on horseback, six on foot.

"Shall we follow them?" asked Melanie.

"It'd be rude not to," agreed Katie.

Katie drew her sword and began circling it above her head. Once again, their necklaces glowed, and she drew the moisture from the ground and from the trees behind her. Melanie, as she had back at the shower, channelled the heat from her body, through her sword and into the swirling moisture. The warmer air surged through the water, and as it met the cooler surface of the ground, almost immediately, a wide bank of mist swirled about them, surrounding them, concealing them. As they stepped out from the forest, the mist spread out across the ground, moving with them, ahead of them.

They walked at a brisk pace, hoping to catch up with the patrol as soon as they could. The mist now covered an extensive stretch of the open ground, concealing them as they closed the gap. Pockets of mist on the top of the mountain were not unusual for this time of the morning, so the patrol continued on its way unconcerned. Eventually, they took a turn downhill, back toward the tree line, much further along the mountainside. Katie was the first to spot the tents making up the temporary encampment; there were seven in total; one large tent, with six smaller ones surrounding it. The poachers had also built a makeshift pen, in which they had herded the women and children; they were all sitting down, hunched, despondent and fearful. They looked a bedraggled mess but, far from being about forty strong, there could be no more than twenty in the confines, none of them uttering a sound.

The women came to a halt near the top of the ridge, looking directly down at the campsite. There were two armed guards by the pen, with another three sitting around a fire a few yards away. There were little groups, dotted sporadically, in various spots in the camp and, from their vantage point, they counted twenty-three. As the patrol entered the camp, several men emerged from the largest tent. There was a lot of unintelligible shouting, and one man gesticulated aggressively down the mountain, roughly toward where they had camped the previous evening. Their attackers were, it seemed, from this group, and their absence was causing concern. The patrol immediately turned around and set off in the massacre's direction.

"Well, that gets rid o' eight o' the fuckers," said Melanie. "How do ye reckon we deal wi' the rest?" Katie was watching intently, inspecting the camp in search of any weaknesses they could exploit.

"It'll be easier if we can keep the women and kids in that pen, out o' the killin' zone. But we'll have to take care o' they guards first, and hope that the prisoners don't panic and bolt." She fingered her necklace, turning the stones on the chain. "Élementaá. Earth, water, fire, air, and space." Melanie turned to look at Katie, recognising the calculating tone to her voice.

"Ok, let's have it," she smiled. "What the fuck is cookin' up in that heid o' yours?"

"Earth, water, fire, air, and... *space*," repeated Katie. "Élementaá! We can, apparently, control and manipulate *all* o' these elements. That's what they said, didn't they? Back at Elŷsium?"

"Aye, that's what they said. But I wouldn't place too much faith in what I remember," laughed Melanie. "Have ye got a plan?"

"I think so. But we have to head back a bit. I want to try somethin' out, without riskin' the poor sods down there." She looked back over her shoulder. "Let's head up toward the crater. Get a bit o' breathin' space. If this idea works, then we'll be able to take all o' these bastards out, easy as fuck."

"Ya beauty," said Melanie, but then, after a thought, "and what if it doesn't work?"

"Aye, well. We'll cross that bridge when we come to it."

ﻣﻤﻤﻤ

The plan was ambitious but, despite the lack of any guarantee of success, seemed like the most painless way of freeing the prisoners. Well, painless for all but the Ingagi Nshya.

Katie returned to their initial spying position and waited. Melanie had the more arduous task of circling around the encampment, approaching from below, through the trees. Once in position, she withdrew her sword and held the necklace stones in her hand, breathing slowly, lowering her heartbeat. She then closed her eyes and made a mental push through the stones, a gentle nudge that Katie felt at the receiving end. They still didn't understand the stones but, with every passing moment, they were learning more of their capabilities, feeling more confident in pushing their limits.

Katie sat, cross-legged on the grassy ridge, holding her sword in both hands at arms' length at the height of her chin. She took a deep breath, cocking her head to both sides, relaxing her neck muscles. The practice session had worked, but it had also been very stressful, straining her muscles to the limit. And that was just on a small target. This was going to be much tougher, and she didn't know how long she could hold it in place. She looked directly at the camp, concentrating on forming an imagined circle around the tented area; an imagined dome over the imagined circle; creating an empty, invisible 'snow-globe' over the camp. The pen was safely outside of her target area. It wouldn't be affected... she hoped.

'Here goes nothin,' she thought.

The stones glowed, and she felt warmth flowing through her arms, down to the sword, which glowed brightly. She stared at the camp, then began slowly breathing in, inhaling as much as she could take. As she did so, down in the camp, the air was being quickly sucked out of the 'snow-globe', creating a vacuum, making breathing impossible for the unsuspecting Ingagi Nshya. They clutched their throats, gagging for breath, panicking in their ignorance of what was happening to them. The campfires fluttered, straining to stay alight, before snuffing out with a whimper; the rising smoke held inside the snow-globe circling around and down, filling the kill-zone.

As Katie had begun her attack, the stones on Melanie's necklace, and the inscriptions on her sword, glowed brightly, too, signalling for her to carry out her part of the plan. She circled her sword around her head, concentrating on the campfire by the pen. The guards were standing now, stretching and straining to see what the commotion was, confused as to the activity and panic in the camp. Melanie pointed her sword at the fire, gripping the hilt tightly, then snapped her arm toward the guards, aiming the flames at each of the poachers. A streak of death, with extraordinary rapidity, force and power; an unnatural blowtorch of immense temperature that consumed in seconds. The burning men ran aimlessly... shrieking and writhing... before falling to the ground, their very skin melting from their bones. The prisoners were all on their feet, crying and screaming, scurrying as far back in the pen as they could.

Katie had inhaled as much as she could take. She let out a massive exhalation of breath, then immediately resumed inhaling once more. The men in the camp were falling rapidly, bewildered and terrified... and breathless. As she once more reached capacity, dizziness took hold, exhaustion overwhelmed her, and she slumped to her side, unconscious; her sword lying to her front, the stones dulled once more.

Melanie was now in and about the camp, finishing those who were still clinging to life, her sword deadly swift... deadly accurate... *deadly*. She worked her way, methodically, around each of the poachers, confirming their death, before doing the same inside each of the tents. Satisfied that none were alive, she turned her attention to the terrified women and children in the pen. Sheathing her sword, she gestured for them to calm down. "You're safe. You're all safe now," she repeated over and over. Turning to look up the hill toward her partner, the severity of the other woman's condition suddenly became apparent; there was no movement at all from her. "Wait here!" she said, firmly, to the now-free prisoners.

"Katie! Katie!" she screamed as she ran up the hill, her leg muscles aching with the strain, her lungs bursting. She fell to the side of the unconscious woman, lifting her upper body into her arms, pushing the hair from her face. Her hand reached behind her and pulled her water bottle from her kidney pouch. Gripping the lid between her teeth, she twisted the bottle until open, and splashed some onto Katie's face, giving little slaps, trying to wake the woman. "Katie! Katie!" Her eyes opened, slowly, and it took a second for her to get her bearings, to focus.

"Well, that was new," she mumbled. She looked up at Melanie and smiled. "But, don't let me do that again... at least, no' until the next time, eh?" Melanie hugged her tightly.

"I thought... I thought..."

"The women?" Katie looked down the hill, Melanie's gaze following her.

"They're scared shitless," she said. "Best we get down there, explain yet again that we're no' witches." Katie struggled to her feet, leaning on Melanie's shoulder for balance. She paused to get her breath, then leant down to pick up her sword, stumbling forward as the dizziness returned with a vengeance. Melanie caught her in time, then gathered the weapon up for her.

"I think we'll just take a wee stroll down, eh?"

"Aye, better no' chance anythin'. No' at your age," Melanie laughed, still concerned at the condition of her friend.

Back at the camp, the prisoners were still at the rear of the pen, huddled together, crying and terrified after seeing the terrible mass extermination. "If you sort this lot out, I'll go get Happy and the horses," Melanie said. Katie nodded, still a little uneasy on her feet. Melanie hesitated, but Katie gestured her to go. She walked over to the paddock, looking about the pathetic survivors... starving, dehydrated, injured... many near to death. There were twelve adults and nine children, ranging in age from about three to fourteen. They cowered as she approached, squeezing together in the pen's corner.

"We're lookin' for Raissa," she said. They gave a communal howl, then huddled even closer together. "Please, don't worry... we're here to help. Is Raissa here?"

"I am Raissa." A voice came from the back of the group. The women to the front turned and parted as a young girl, no more than fourteen years old, limped gingerly through the gap. "I am Raissa," she repeated. "What do you want with me?"

Katie smiled. "This will take some time to explain," she said. "When did ye last eat?"

"We have been at this place for two days, and had nothing. Before this, perhaps three days, was the last time. They do not feed us, and many have died. The children, here," she turned and pointed to the little people, the little bags of bones, "they are almost gone, too." Katie looked around to the tents. The campfires had all been extinguished as she withdrew the oxygen, but the pots of stew, and the spits were still hot.

"There's plenty o' food there, if ye can see past the bodies," she suggested.

"We are used to death," said Raissa, coldly. "Eating among these monsters will feel like victory." She gestured to the others to go feed themselves. "What do you want with me?" she asked again.

"Oh, nothin' much," shrugged Katie. "We just need ye to protect the women o' Africa."

ﻋﻠﻴﻜﻢ ﻋﻠﻴﻜﻢ ﻋﻠﻴﻜﻢ ﻋﻠﻴﻜﻢ

They sat around the now-reignited campfires, eating and drinking, laughing and chatting; almost as if they had forgotten the trials and traumas of the previous weeks. Some children, the desperately ill ones, required feeding by hand, treated like newborn babies as their limbs were too weak to feed themselves. Even so, this did little to dampen the mood of liberation now flowing through the group.

Katie sat by a fire with Raissa, watching the women take care of the children, before thinking of themselves. It was impossible to tell which children belonged to which woman, or even if they belonged to anyone. The sense of community and shared responsibility was very clear. Raissa looked about the camp at the scattered bodies, then at Katie with a mix of suspicion and curiosity. "What did you do here? You and the red-haired girl? What did you do?"

Katie sipped her coffee. "It's difficult to explain," she replied. "It's much easier to show ye, but we can't do that here."

"Is it magic?" asked Raissa, a slight tone of wonderment in her voice.

"No, it's no' magic." The voice came from behind Katie. She turned to find Melanie and Happy leading the horses to the tent behind them. "It's... well, science... an' nature... an, well... *stuff*." Katie stood and gave the young girl a tight hug. Raissa noticed Happy and hurriedly limped over to the man, punching him hard in the face.

"Why is Happy with you? He sold us to the Ingagi Nshya... traded us for his own worthless life. Why have you brought him here?"

"No, no, no... she is mistaken," he said, holding his hands up in front of his face, cravenly skulking back toward the tent. "Hello again, Raissa. I saved you. They would have killed you all," he added in an unctuous, ingratiating manner.

'Ssshhh'. Melanie's sword was instantly out and at the man's throat.

"Is this true, ye little shit?" She kicked him from behind, and his legs buckled, bringing him to his knees. He was panicking now.

"They promised they would take care of you," he bleated.

Raissa punched him again.

"You snivelling bastard. Your wife was among the first they killed. Your... your child... your child was among the first they killed. And yet, here you are, still trying to worm your way out of trouble." She punched him a third time.

Melanie's sword fell slowly away from the man's neck. She looked at Katie, her eyes welling up, suddenly reminded of the enormity of her own past actions; her own betrayal of Katie, and the girls at the stables. How selfish she herself had been when aligning herself with Giles and Allan. They may not have openly killed in the same numbers as the Ingagi Nshya had done, but, she felt, there was still blood on her own hands, if even indirectly. "Katie?" she pleaded, tears already leaking down her cheeks. Katie embraced the weeping girl.

"Ssshhh," she whispered. "Don't even think to compare yourself wi' this piece o' shit. You didn't betray your family, or anybody ye had any loyalty, or responsibility to. And, anyway," she wiped the tears away, lifting Melanie's face up below the chin, "you are more than making atonement for your actions. You are Élementaá. *We* are Élementaá. We are *sisters*." They hugged again. Melanie nodded, regaining her composure and belief once more. She wiped her nose with her arm and gave a wee laugh.

"I must look a sight, eh?"

"Aye," agreed Katie. "Sort your puss out. You're makin' me look good." She gave a wink and turned back to Happy. He was looking up at her with wide eyes; a sickly, cowardly smile on his face, and sweat and desperation oozing out of every pore. Katie turned to Raissa.

"What do ye want to do wi' him?" Raissa looked shocked.

"It is not for me to decide, surely. It is the responsibility of the elder women." She looked back at the others, many of whom had approached, cussing and hissing; their loathing of Happy there for all to see. The women, too, looked to Raissa.

"We are here, only because of you... because of what you gave up, just to keep us alive," said one woman. "You should decide what happens to this louse."

"What did ye give up, Raissa?" asked Katie. Another woman stepped forward.

"She gave up her innocence. She gave up her body. She gave up her soul." The woman wiped a tear from her eye. "She gave up herself. For us!" Katie turned to Happy, nodding in understanding of Raissa's sacrifice.

"I am no one," said Raissa. "I do not have this power." Melanie walked over to her and hugged her. Then, holding her by the shoulders, she looked into her eyes.

"Have ye heard o' Joan o' Arc?" The young girl nodded.

"Well, you are Raissa o' Rwanda. You are the woman who will protect and lead the women, no' just o' Rwanda, but throughout Africa. You *are* this power!"

"Here's the deal, Raissa," said Katie. "We'd like ye to come wi' us. We'll take ye somewhere to be trained and equipped for yer task. There is a price to pay but, in return, ye'll be given certain... *gifts*. I can't explain everythin' right now..." She looked around the growing group, aware that her explanation might provoke fear and superstition if they didn't understand. "But, I promise, it'll be to the benefit o' all o' ye." Melanie still held Raissa's shoulders.

"What would ye give for these women and children?" she asked forthrightly.

"I would give anything."

"Anythin'?"

"Yes, anything."

"Would ye give yer life?"

Raissa hesitated. She sensed that this was not a hypothetical question and looked around the camp; the children were now, for the first time in weeks, laughing and, whilst none of them had the energy to play, looking unafraid.

"Yes."

Melanie turned to Katie and stepped away from Raissa.

"What shall we do wi' him?" Katie asked.

Raissa glanced at Happy and, as she turned to walk away, said, "kill him."

Melanie's sword swung before Raissa finished talking, a *swish* and a *shikht* as it sliced through Happy's neck. Raissa walked over, facing Katie. "Do ye have any family ye want to say goodbye to?" asked Katie.

Raissa glanced over her shoulder, taking a last look at Happy.

"Not anymore," she said.

XXX. A Daughter's Decision

"There's the villa, not far now," declared Jessica, trying hard to impart as much reassurance as she could. But, inside, terror and relief were battling each other. "We're almost there."

"I'm no' goin' back," sobbed Eric. "I'm no' goin' back to Hades. I'll... I'll..." Jael gripped his hand, as the boy's dismay increased with each flash of lightning, or clap of thunder.

The carriage rocked from side to side, as the driver urged the horses onward; he himself fearing the might of the storm now playing out around them. The horses drove forward, ignoring their own uneasiness, their own anxieties, as they sought the sanctuary of the stable they knew lay ahead.

"We'll be alright, Eric," assured Jael. "We'll soon be under proper cover."

The carriage raced through the gates to the villa compound, mud and water spraying up from behind each wheel, a shower of brown rain left in their own wake. The horses banked sharply around the front entrance, pulling up in a massive splash of water. The side door immediately flew open, and the passengers disembarked, each jumping down, ignoring the facility of the steps. Jael and Eric helped Jessica over the sandbags that now offered the villa some limited protection from the growing flood besieging her. Without hesitation, the driver snapped his reins, urging the terrified animals into one short, last journey, seeking the comfort and safety of the villa stables.

The villa foyer provided an instant shelter, a harbour from the natural bombardment, and the new arrivals felt, for the first time since leaving Rimel, some sense of safety. "Follow me," said Jessica, as she hurried up the wide hallway and into the reception area. "Marro!" she called. "Marro!"

Within seconds, a familiar face, accompanied by two maids, appeared from an archway to the left. The couple fell into each other, tightly embracing; a loving kiss banishing the pain of being parted.

"Are you alright?" asked Marro. "The storm..."

"I'm fine," Jessica smiled, nodding in confirmation. She looked to the maids. "Please take Eric and Jael to Eric's suite, and have some food prepared." The young maids bowed and gestured for the young couple to follow.

Jael nodded, linking arms, leaning her head onto Eric's shoulder. "I'm going nowhere without you, Handsome," she whispered. "So, let's go get cleaned up." The young man immediately relaxed, following Jael as she headed off in the direction indicated by the maids.

Jessica watched them leave the reception, then turned her attention to Marro. "Where's Astris?" she asked.

"I would imagine she'll be in her suite. Why? What's wrong?"

Jessica clasped his hand and marched off toward the visitor's suites. "Oh, Marro," she exclaimed, "it's so much worse than just an accident."

"Forgive me, Jessica," he replied, a little puzzled. "But Eric looks just fine. I thought…"

"There's far more to it than we thought, Marro. It looks as if Haáde is preparing to invade."

"Haáde?"

"The storm. The storm is a precursor…" She dashed around a corner, dragging Marro behind. "There was a girl," Jessica continued, "an evil little madam, she was. She was responsible for Eric's… *accident*. And I think she's here to cause as much disruption as she can. Before…" Her face said all that Marro needed to know. She stopped abruptly, her eyes full of realisation. "Is Séntinell still here?"

"I assume so," nodded Marro. "They haven't left Astris' side since arriving here."

Her hands clasped Marro's, and she took a deep breath. "We should send Séntinell to warn Helios. He has the armies that Elŷsium doesn't, and will surely come to our aid."

"You go to Astris," offered Marro, "and I'll go find Séntinell. It sounds as if time is of the essence." Jessica gave him a last kiss before rushing off once more.

"Every second could be crucial," she called, looking back over her shoulder.

"Astris!" called Jessica as she ran down the corridor leading to the large, sumptuous suite. "Astris, are you here?"

"I'm on the veranda." A muted voice confirmed the presence of the young woman. Jessica made her way through the lounge area, and out through the doorway.

Astris was leaning on the balustrade, watching the storm as it continued to vent its anger. The purple clouds rolled across the skies; darker than ever, gaining pace as the day wore on. She wore a navy silk stola with, unusually, a woollen shoulder wrap. "It's a little chilly, don't you think?" she opined.

"Astris!" panted Jessica. "I'm so pleased I've found you."

"Why, Jessica," Astris giggled, "have you been running?"

"Yes," wheezed Jessica. "We have an emergency."

"An emergency? What sort of emergency?" The Princess of Sólaás gestured to a cushioned seat, taking an identical one just opposite.

Jessica looked upwards to the clouds, the rumble and crack of thunder and lightning sitting regularly above the loud, constant hissing of the rain. "This storm... it's not a normal storm. It's something more," she gasped.

Astris gazed outward. "We, at times, have similar storms on Sólaás," she said. "Well, similar, but for the rain. They are usually far more appealing to look at."

"No, you don't understand. This storm is covering the arrival of Haáde and his armies. Elŷsium is about to be invaded."

"Surely not," mused Astris. "Why would Haáde risk war with my father? I assumed, from what I was told of Jacob's and Cassandra's trip to Hades, that there was peace, however uneasy, between Hades and Sólaás. You must be mistaken."

Having finally caught her breath, Jessica told of Eris, and her mischief-making; her manipulation of Rimel's citizens and, in particular, her behaviour leading to Eric trying to take his own life.

"I was to ask if you, and Lady Circe if you can contact her, could lend your..." She gazed at the glowing red ring on Astris' finger. "Your power and abilities... to aid in whatever defences we can muster. Marro is asking the same of Séntinell, hoping they can enlist assistance from Lord Helios."

Astris considered Jessica's request, then stood once more, approaching the balustrade as she took in the thunderous weather raging before them. "Circe? I could attempt to contact her, but she comes and goes. Her presence here is fleeting sometimes, not yet guaranteed. I feel she may need some time before becoming a reliable ally in terms of affecting matters."

Jessica sighed, disappointed. "I understand," she said. "I think Jacob was counting on the additional power source of your ring. He and Cassandra are still struggling to master theirs." She stood, making to leave. "Can you, at least, try to contact Lady Circe? Any help would be appreciated."

Astris turned, smiling as she bowed. "Of course, Jessica," she confirmed. "I shall do so immediately."

Jessica felt a little more at ease, sure that Astris would be successful in recruiting Circe's help. "Thank you," she nodded. "Now, if you'll excuse me, I must get cleaned up, out of these filthy clothes."

Astris walked with her, escorting her from the suite, watching as she made her way up the corridor.

Astris returned to the heart of her suite, pausing as she considered the turn of events. "Did you hear all of that?" she asked.

"I did," came the response.

She walked over to the wall mirror. Looking back at her, the unmistakable hazel eyes the only differentiating feature, the spirit and essence of her sister. "I'm not comfortable lying to my new friends, sister. They are looking to me... looking to *us*... for help."

"I know this will be difficult," replied Circe. "It is difficult for me, too, Astris, but it has to be this way."

"Are you sure of what you say, or are you still riddled with uncertainty?"

"I am now certain, little sister. Our father is dead. Murdered by either Aeetes, or Pasiphae. It is the forces of Andromeda and Sólaás that now stand on our doorstep. Séntinell has confirmed it as so."

Astris sighed, holding back her tears. "Father? Dead? How can this be? Are our brother and sister so deranged, they would destroy the universe for misguided revenge? And Séntinell? Marro is searching for them right at this minute. What will they say when they are found?"

"They will not be found, Astris. I have despatched The Lumináry on a further, more pressing commission. One that must not fail."

"Which is...?"

"Séntinell is currently en route to Hades, tasked with enlisting the armies of the Dark Lands, in support of the meagre resistance we can provide here in Elŷsium."

"Will Haáde's armies be enough, do you think?"

"No," replied Circe. "They cannot possibly arrive here soon enough to be of any immediate aid. They shall join the fray at a later time, but they will not alter the course of events. There will be no force strong enough to resist the combined might of Sólaás and Andromeda. Elŷsium *will* fall."

"Then why...?" cried Astris, her emotions bubbling over. She had loved her father, had grudgingly loved her mother. But, now, realising the extent to which her other siblings had gone in their hatred of her parents, she felt, once again, as she had always felt - alone.

"It will be your task to evacuate everyone at Strath-sealgair Villa..."

"Where to, Circe?" she sobbed. "Where on earth can we possibly escape to?" Astris was now deeply upset. She knew this was a betrayal, an abandoning of her new family. How could Circe be so clinical, so detached from the fate she was leaving her loved ones to?

"That is exactly where you should head, dear sister. To Kiípos. To Earth. To the land of the very beginning, out of our siblings' reach. You speak Hellenés and will adapt to the climate more easily there."

"And what of Raymond? Are you so ready to leave him here?"

Circe sighed. "I cannot lie, Astris. When you brought me back, it had occurred to me I could, through you, have a life once again with Raymond. That you, too, could experience the joy I had of loving that man. Had he returned to Strath-sealgair Villa with Eric, that may well have been possible, despite what is about to unfold. But Raymond has chosen to fight alongside our son, and we can only wish him well."

Astris sat on a couch, raising a hand mirror before her. "And you will not intervene, Circe? Not even to save Raymond? Not even to save Jacob, or Cassandra?"

"We.... neither of us... can get involved, except for rescuing as many as we can from here, at the villa. The die has been cast, Astris. There is no going back, and only one inevitable outcome. We must now prepare for what comes after."

Astris lowered her mirror and wiped a tear from her eye. This was not what her father had envisaged for her. This was not the exciting adventure that she had welcomed with all of her boundless enthusiasm. She raised the mirror once more. "Does Cassandra suspect what is in store?"

Circe's lips thinned at the thought. "I doubt it. I don't believe Jacob has any inkling either."

Astris felt her tears flowing more quickly. "I'm sorry, Circe. I can't understand why we can't help Jacob. Why are we turning our backs on him? Why must he do this alone?"

"He won't be alone, Astris," Circe reassured her. "But only Jacob can do what has to be done. It is by virtue of being a Human Célestiaá that Jacob has this responsibility. Otherwise, all mankind would fall. At least this way there is a chance to salvage something from the ashes."

"And the vision you gave to Cassandra, is that, too, to be discarded, sister? Along with all that you built, all that you created?"

"No, Astris. The vision will come to pass, but not, perhaps, as Cassandra has seen it. Hers was a more metaphorical interpretation, but the principal actors will all be there. The time *will* come when my grandson confronts the enemy, but Cassandra did not see everything. Cassandra did not see the end."

"My heart breaks for her, Circe," cried Astris. "My heart breaks for us all."

"Dry your tears, dear sister, for we have our parts to play, and the time is nigh that we play them. We must have courage, and we must have faith that others, too, will hold strong in their roles. If not, then all is lost."

XXXI. THE RISING OF THE SUN

The rain seemed to intensify—if that were even possible—as the defenders of Elŷsium took their positions; forming ranks across the breadth of the field. There was no particular method used to decide which combatant stood where, or which sections would be responsible for... well, anything. This was not, after all, a military unit. This was merely several thousand souls who just happened to die on Kiípos, then find themselves in Elŷsium at the worst possible time; theirs was the unfortunate duty to defend all life on Earth. Theirs was the responsibility to defend all life in the universe.

A more ill-prepared army would be difficult to imagine; the young, the old; the brave, the timid; all with but a symbolic sword to protect their armour-less bodies, their blouses and tunics already soaked to the skin.

A scattering of Rimelian men and women had roused themselves and joined the cause. These, too, however, were merely here to make up the numbers. Innocents, naïve in the belief that they could, at best, delay the hordes of Hades until Helios would come to their rescue. Farmers, butchers, traders - a hodgepodge of terrified, poorly armed and untrained decent folk, with not a single piece of armour among them.

The only section that could remotely be compared to a proper fighting force was the Valkyrie; several thousand mounted she-warriors, each intent on honouring their legacy as the bringers of heroic souls. They sat astride their mounts, eager to join the battle, eager to sacrifice their own life essence if necessary. No price was too much if it meant saving the living.

The storm had reached its zenith; a crescendo of thunderclaps so loud, they seemed in concert with the lightning flashes, and the horizontal rain. The enemy was not yet in sight, but their entrance music had already brought fear to the fore. The lines of defenders were nervous; skittish; many ready to forfeit their glorious deaths, in exchange for the eternal servitude of Hades. Many were ready to flee. Courage, when most needed, now seemed in short supply.

Jacob and his 'generals'—Charon, Brunhiíld and Biro—remained sheltered under a makeshift belvedere, surveying the scene before them. Ray leaned against a table, a short-sword in his hand. Cassandra stood to the side, a firm grip on Eris' arm. All had managed to grab some of Charon's tatty old leather armour and, of course, Jacob and Cassandra had kept the armour they'd worn to Hades. It was supposed to have been a reminder of their courage; a sobering memento of how close oblivion had come. Yet here they were, staring at their doom once more.

"What's the plan?" asked Ray.

Charon looked over his shoulder, a muffled laugh at his friend's dark humour. "Who the fuck needs a plan, eh?" he joked.

"Well," said Jacob, "if we did need a plan, it looks like we've run out of time to make it." He pointed out across the expanse. The dark clouds they'd become accustomed to, rolling menacingly low across the skies, now began a downward path; making their way to the ground, far across the length of the fields. As they touched the soil, the purple blue cover spread across the width of the Elysian Fields; forming a pulsing angry wall, a gate through which the ruin of mankind, and all things good, would come.

"Thank you," muttered Charon, as he kissed Brunhiíld for possibly the last time.

"For what, my love?" she whispered. "It is I who should thank you."

"You were my dream," he breathed, "and in bringing my dream to life, you brought *me* to life. I shall love you forever, be it in our brief life here, together, or in the glorious death that now awaits us."

Brunhiíld looked out across the field and smiled. "Do not be hasty in your despair, my lord boatman. Death is but the doorway to our next life. And I shall find you in that next life." She kissed him, passionately, fully, then found her strength as she looked in his eyes. "You have my promise. The word of the Valkyrie."

The wall of cloud throbbed, like a heart beating with internal life, swirling as activity increased on the other side. Then, deep in the centre, appeared a massive black shadow; a silhouette of immense stature; a figure ten... *twenty* times that of a normal man. Waiting.

"My Lord!" screamed Eris, yanking her arm free from Cassandra, pushing the Princess of Troy to the ground as she made her escape. She ran. Faster, faster, increasing the margin of escape from her captors—reducing the distance to her safety—rainwater and mud splashing up around her. Undeterred and never slowing, rain washing down her face, Eris bolted toward the shadow.

Cassandra hauled herself to her feet, immediately chasing after her escaped prisoner. "Cassandra! Wait! Don't..." shouted Jacob, caught unawares by the sudden turn of events. Cassandra was deaf to his pleas; the thunder, the rain, the lightning, drowning out all but the sound of her own heavy breathing as she continued the pursuit of her quarry.

The two women ran and ran, one intent on escape, the other intent on capture. The distance was further than Eris had calculated, but still she ran, Cassandra in never-wavering pursuit. The clouds loomed large, the silhouette larger still, the great shadow towering overhead. Then, as Eris drew near, the shadow stepped forward, emerging slowly from the cloud.

"My Lord!" Eris screamed in ecstasy. Her pace slowed, and Cassandra could see the gap between them closing. Eris' tear stained, and rain soaked face peered up in exaltation as her lord appeared. She watched, excited, exhilarated, as her run fell to a light jog, and then a few faltering steps. Her exhilaration turned to horror as the shadow emerged as light; bright sunlight. Her lord was not hers; indeed, it was the very opposite of hers. Looming out of the shadow, as her footfall became heavy, her momentum causing her to trip, and to splash, was the Sun-God himself. Not Helios, no, but Aeetes.

The rain disappeared as she entered the now sunlit area before the approaching giant. She stumbled further as Cassandra crashed into her, sending her forward, falling onto one knee. Eris quickly grabbed her pursuer by the arm, pulling herself to her feet, sending Cassandra sprawling into the mud. She did not hesitate and ran back in the direction whence she came.

Aeetes glanced downward at the insects before his great might. The now warm and bright sunlight, bursting from the opening which he himself had created, shone down on the scrambling woman flailing in the pool of mud. The light picked out the gleaming jewel on her finger, focussing Aeetes' attention on the Célestiaá Ring. His eyes widened, and he bent down, wrapping his great left hand around Cassandra, picking her up as if just a doll. The terrified woman screamed, her terror piercing the ears of the Sun-God. He immediately squeezed his hand, crushing the bones of his helpless captive, her body falling limp, with consciousness drifting slowly out of her.

Jacob felt as if his heart was about to explode. He looked to the ring, attempting to draw any sort of reaction, but the ring did not respond. "Who is that, for fuck's sake?" he yelled. "Where the fuck are Astris and my mum?" He looked about him. The terror on the faces of his army told all he needed to know; Aeetes already had the upper hand; psychologically, physically, and actually.

Aeetes dropped his left arm to his side, Cassandra flopping around like a neglected rag doll, her arms and legs swinging loosely. Raising his right arm high, he called, simply, "Forward!" His massive arm swung down and to the fore. Behind him, the portal through which he had stepped swept open, as if a giant gust of wind was blowing the clouds away. On either side, vast columns of Andromedan soldiers marched through; regimented, heavily armed, heavily armoured. They funnelled outwards, taking up positions on both flanks, with more soldiers marching up the centre; a never-ending stream of identical warriors, striding purposefully to war.

Following them came the range weapons. Massive trebuchets, and scorpions. Ranks of archers, thousands of mounted cavalry. Aeetes' forces seemed endless, and they filled the landscape ahead of the terrified Elysians.

The sunlight spread forth from the portal, the rain diminishing and the clouds breaking. The storm that had blighted Elŷsium for so long evaporated in mere minutes; leaving beautiful blue skies, and a gigantic army at the other end of the waterlogged and muddied field. Aeetes looked toward the enemy, hoping for a glimpse of his sister, then glanced down at the Chiliarch standing to his right. The Chiliarch raised his arm, awaiting the command from his master.

"You may begin," Aeetes said.

The Chiliarch dropped his arm and within seconds, the trebuchets and scorpions let loose their missiles of destruction. The huge metal bolts, and the enormous rocks hurtled in high trajectories, falling indiscriminately into the massed ranks of Elŷsium's army. The archers ran several hundred metres ahead, then quickly formed in lines, before they too began their assault, firing high into the air, arcing their arrows in accord with the larger weapons. Beneath the arch of death, Eris continued her renewed attempt at escape, now just a hundred yards from the Elysian lines.

Behind her, Aeetes waved his right arm. A burst of heat from the Sun-God rippled out across the battlefield, instantly drying and solidifying the ground ahead. The cavalry set out on the flanks, careful not to stray into the paths of the flying death being meted out by the unemotional, uncaring servants of the Sun. And, as if practiced to perfection, the foot soldiers set out on their march toward undoubted victory.

"We have to do somethin'," yelled Jacob. "We're sittin' ducks like this."

"Aye," agreed Charon. "Biro," he shouted, "take the centre section. Brunhiíld, the right. I'll lead the left." He gave a loud whistle and waved his arm. The Valkyrie set out to meet their mounted counterparts, sorely outnumbered, but not lacking in intent.

"I'm with you," assured Ray, stepping up behind his old friend.

The three sections all moved forward as one, seeking to engage the incoming Andromedans. Eris had now reached the 'safety' of the Elysian army. "The ring!" she screamed at Jacob. "You must use the ring." Jacob stared down at his finger, willing the ring to do something... anything. There was no response. He closed his eyes, silently calling for his mother to appear.. to help them in this time of dire need. Again... there was no response.

For better or worse, they were on their own.

XXXII. REFUGEES

The rain had, thankfully, stopped, and sunshine was once again bathing the grounds of Strath-sealgair Villa. Birdsong, and that freshness, that smell in the air, that can only be found after a massive storm, suggested the worst had passed. The white of the villa shone out, like a beacon of hope in this now besieged paradise. A call to the fearful, the desperate; the weak and the old. Here was the place to provide comfort in this time of need.

Astris knew better, however.

The lines of evacuees, pair after pair after pair led by Jessica and Marro, trudged their way through the Diávasi; most uncertain of their destination; all uncertain of their future. The maids, the waiters and waitresses, the cleaners. Stable hands and Blacksmiths. Cooks and bakers. Farmers and villagers from the areas surrounding the villa, all making their escape from the invading hordes. Each carried the minimum in a pack on their back; a change of clothes, a rolled up mat to sleep on, and a tarpaulin sheet to be used as a bivouac cover. And what could only be called a packed lunch, of bread, ham, cheese, fruit and water. All making their escape into an already troubled world - Kiípos.

"Is there nothing we can do?" sobbed Jael. "We're just going to leave them all behind?"

Astris, too, was crying. "I'm afraid so, Jael," she said. "The enemy is overwhelming. The best we can do is to save as many as we can from here... before we, too, are overrun."

Eric looked at her finger, the beautiful red jewel gleaming, with the lilac edge glistening in the sunlight. "But ye have a ring, Astris," he said quietly. "Can ye no' use that to... well, *do* somethin'? Anythin'?"

Astris placed her hand on Eric's shoulder, her eyes falling to the ground. "I'm sorry, Eric. There is nothing I can do. We have to leave here... for now, at least. It's not ideal, I know, but we can find some sanctuary on Kiípos. And we can pray to the universe for a solution."

Jael was outraged. "Pray?" she gasped. "Pray? To whom should we pray, Astris? The Gods? The Goddesses? We have a goddess right here, standing in front of us, unwilling to use her powers. And what of Circe? She saved Jacob and Cassandra before. She freed Eric from Hades. Where is Circe, now, when we need her even more?"

"I..." Astris shook her head. There were no words to answer Jael's question; no explanation that could placate the heartbroken young couple.

Jael looked down, nodding her head in her certainty. "I thought so," she said. Jael turned slowly to Eric, taking his hand as she led him away. "Let's get our packs, Eric," she muttered. "There's nothing left here for us."

Astris watched as they both joined the line. She sobbed into her hand, feeling, for the first time in her existence, the urge to be sick. The nausea that comes from being helpless in the face of tragedy. She had left Sólaás, hoping to leave her loneliness behind; hoping to be welcomed into a new family, finding new friendships; to make a meaningful life for herself. And now, here in the apparent tranquillity that sat around the villa, she was alone. Truly alone. Her father was dead. Her brother was now the instigator of a crime most heinous; her sister's return soured in her willingness to abandon all that she'd loved, all that she'd created.

And for what? Circe had never explained the reasons behind their fleeing Elŷsium, or their reluctance... no, not reluctance... *refusal*... to help. So, now, here she was, alone —Circe had not appeared since their talk through the mirrors—and without friends; embarking on a journey into the unknown. Oh, if only Séntinell were here to advise her, to comfort her, and tell her everything was going to be alright.

Astris watched the last of the lines—the two hundred or so refugees fleeing Elŷsium alongside her—disappear through the light of the Diávasi. She then made her own way through, pausing as she exited the light at the other side. One last look back before raising her ring finger and closing her eyes. The ring glowed, sending out an invisible pulse. Then she turned, leaving the fading Diávasi behind.

In the garden at Strath-sealgair Villa, the once beautiful white arch now cracked and crumbled, slowly falling to the ground. A pile of white marble lay below a swirling cloud of white dust. The Diávasi, the celestial gate, was no more; ensuring none could follow, but, also, that none could return.

XXXIII. DEATH OF A DREAM

The battle was over before it had begun. Aeetes' forces swarmed around the flanks of the isolated Elysians, cutting down those on the fringes and squeezing the main body back in on itself. The thunder of the cavalry charges on either side seemed to make the screams and shouts of the foot soldiers sound even louder. The Valkyrie engaged on the right flank, but were struggling to hold the Andromedans back.

The trebuchets and scorpions discharged their loads at a frightening frequency, with each projectile exacting devastating damage to the ill-prepared Elysian forces. They fired, and fired again, stopping only when the Andromedan foot soldiers reached their targets.

Jacob continued to swing his sword into the never-ending tide of Andromedans, whilst the Elysian troops tried valiantly to force the onslaught back. He once more attempted a surge of power through the Célestiaá Ring, but, as before, there was no response. To his right, Charon, besieged by the first wave, was falling back in retreat, but there was no sign of Ray.

Biro had redirected his section back to support the right flank, and was pulling Brunhiíld free of the grabbing arms of her assailants. The attack was unrelenting, and the pitiful barrier breached; the defending Elysians crumbling under the weight of Aeetes' troops.

Aeetes strode toward Jacob, then stood like a tower; a giant — tall, strong, and imposing. In his left hand, hanging limply, still clutched like an unloved rag doll, was Cassandra. She was alive, barely, despite the giant hand crushing her, breaking her ribs, squeezing the breath from her. Aeetes raised his arm, holding her above his head, her limbs flopping uselessly about her; displaying the broken women as if a trophy. She dangled, her arms loose and her chin on her chest. "Here," he thundered, "is your 'Mistress' of Elŷsium. Give me Astris, my sister, and you can have *this*; or watch as she crumbles and breaks like the straw she is. It is your choice, nephew."

Jacob stepped slowly toward Aeetes. "She's gone," he yelled. "Astris has fled. She's safe."

"Hmm!" hummed Aeetes. He turned his head upwards, contemptuously inspecting the now-worthless woman. "Then I have no further need for this. You can have her."

Cassandra slowly raised her head, looking directly at Jacob. Her hair covered most of her face, but he could see the tears streaming from her pain-filled eyes, the blood oozing from her mouth. She smiled, silently, painfully mouthing 'I love you'. Then, as Aeetes' grip tightened further, the sickening crunching of her shattering bones gave way to her final ear-piercing scream.

"No!" shrieked Jacob, as he dropped his sword and fell, defeated, to his knees.

Aeetes glared at the sobbing wretch kneeling before him and laughed. He glanced once more at the dying woman in his hand, then threw the broken body at Jacob. Cassandra hit the ground directly in front of the weeping man, contorted and crumpled, throwing up a cloud of dust as she skidded into his knees. Jacob gathered her up into his arms, his anger now overpowering his grief. As he looked into the once-beautiful brown eyes, now dull and vacant, he wiped her hair away from her face, touching her cheek as he placed his forehead to hers.

"I love you," she whispered, clinging to the last moments of life.

"And I love you," Jacob sobbed. "But, the vision. Our son?"

Cassandra mustered the slightest hint of a smile. "He was never mine," she mumbled. "He was never mine. I understand that now. I am not the Divine Creator. You must find..." Her words trailed off, and her wheezing breaths ceased.

Jacob's heart pounded, his tears and saliva merged in long strands hanging from the edges of his mouth. He gently took Cassandra's hand in his, clasping their fingers together one last time. And, as he squeezed, the Célestiaá Rings glowed; dimly and weakly at first, but then they shone bright; their heat surged through him and gave him a renewed strength.

Aeetes glared down at Jacob. In his arrogance, the Sun-God had failed to remember he had one of the Célestiaá Rings there, in the palm of his hand. He cursed his foolishness, drawing his sword as his anger reached its limit, flames bursting into life across his torso and arms. "The Rings!" he bellowed. "By order of Queen Persephone, give me the Rings!"

Dragging himself to his feet, clasping Cassandra tightly to him, Jacob looked about him in search of his allies and friends. Biro and Brunhiíld were close-by, but there was now no sign of Charon. "Biro!" he called. "Biro! Over here!" The man-mountain was limping whilst dragging the barely conscious Valkyrie back from the battle. "We have to go! Now!" yelled Jacob. The rings glowed brightly as a large, circular portal opened behind him, the dazzling light painful to the eye. The baker and the she-warrior dragged themselves toward the opening.

"Take me with you." A voice, behind him and to his left, made him turn. Eris, her right foot raised into the chest of a dead Andromedan, pushing him from her sword, looked directly at Jacob. "Take me with you, and you shall have the armies of Hades at your side."

Jacob sneered, turning toward the portal. Eris grabbed him by the arm. "Take me with you," she repeated, "and we shall avenge your Princess of Troy. If you want Haáde's attention, then you will need me. You cannot do this without me." Jacob hesitated, and Eris sped past him to the portal.

"Charon!" cried Brunhiíld. "Find him... please!" Biro plucked her up and stumbled through the gateway as Jacob scanned the surrounding mayhem. Charon was nowhere to be seen. A loud roar to his right made Jacob aware of Aeetes, and a group of Andromedans, making their way toward him. The giant sun-god raised his mighty arm, swinging his flaming sword at Jacob's head.

"Shit!" Jacob mumbled, before grabbing his own sword and stumbling toward the light; ducking as Aeetes' great weapon swung overhead, quickly willing the gate firmly closed behind him as he collapsed to the ground. As the last tiny gap of the gate disappeared, the tip of Aeetes' sword sheered off, remaining inside the escape area, dropping by the head of the prone Jacob and Cassandra. The master of Elŷsium closed his eyes, as at last, all fell silent.

EPILOGUE

The darkness hung around him like a silent, disapproving accuser. All was still, the emptiness almost shouting at him, forcing him to consider the events just done; but only for a few wistful seconds. A rush of wind swept through the trees and over the clearing, chilling his cheeks, bringing him to his senses. He could feel his heart beating furiously, thumping against his chest. He could hear his breathing — rapid in's and outs of short desperate sucks and blows.

He lay there in the darkness; in the quiet; gradually feeling at peace with the chill, and the smell of pine and birch. He smiled at the familiar smells of his childhood; the welcome brush of fresh air on his cheeks that he'd loved since his very first breath. It seemed so easy just to stay here, lying on the grass, soaking up the mountain air, with not a care in the world. So easy. But he did have cares. And, most importantly, he had people who were depending on him; people who were now at the mercy of the Andromedan invasion.

Jacob opened his eyes, praying he was simply waking from a terrible nightmare, only to find the nightmare was real. Before him was Cassandra's lifeless face; cold and humourless, loveless, dead. In the darkness of night, she looked strangely serene, relaxed, and at ease in her death. The beauty of her face quickly blurred as the tears of realisation burst through his eyes and his anger soared. The shouts and sobs of his companions suddenly filled his ears.

"Where's Charon?" cried Brunhiíld. "Where's Charon?"

Jacob felt himself being effortlessly lifted, carried a few yards, then placed down beside the distraught, kneeling woman. Biro then returned to collect the fallen Mistress of Elŷsium, the Princess of Troy. He laid her gently, tenderly, down by Jacob's side. Jacob sat up and dragged his sleeve across his eyes, clearing his vision. He scanned the scene surrounding him, bittersweet at the tragedy of his unplanned homecoming, his return to Geata Dhè.

Biro knelt in front of him. "What do we do now, Master Jacob?"

In the centre of the stones, next to his own dropped sword, the broken piece of Aeetes' sword glowed brightly; the red heat hissing as it met the cool air of the Scottish Highlands. Jacob eyed the red-hot shard. "I don't know, Biro," he mumbled. His eyes then fell upon the Célestiaá Ring, that was still aglow on Cassandra's dead hand. "But I think we need to keep the rings and that sword-tip safe until we figure out what to do." He gently lifted his lover's hand, removing the ring that was no longer of any use to her. The ring's light faded as it left the woman's finger.

Biro ambled over to where the sword-tip lay and, ripping a strip of cloth from the bottom of his shirt, wrapped it into a bundle before slipping it into his trouser pocket.

Jacob forced himself to his feet. "Brunhiíld?" he asked. "Are ye hurt?"

"Where's Charon? Did you not see where he was?"

"I'm sorry, I couldn't see him. Are ye hurt?"

"I have a few cuts; nothing that won't heal. My heart, however, is back there, in Elŷsium. We have to go back."

"We can't go back," Eris said. "We wouldn't stand a chance. Aeetes has won; he has Elŷsium."

Jacob picked up his sword and looked around the clearing. How strange it looked to him now, this place that he'd known since childhood; this place that was the scene of his earthly death. The stones, of course, were just as they'd always been for millions of years - tall, rugged, imposing. The grass area inside the circle showed the remaining scars of Pasiphae's attack; scorching still blackened the ground, despite the fresh green grass that was now fighting through. In the shadows, he could just make out the silhouette of the car he'd brought to the stones, still parked, but just as dead as it was after the ripple.

Brunhiíld had crawled over, and now knelt beside her fallen friend. She took Cassandra's hand in hers and raised it to her lips, kissing it softly. "Farewell, Lady Doll," she whispered. "My brave, beautiful sister. Thank you for everything." The Valkyrie raised herself and she, too, surveyed the strange land around her. "What is this place, Jacob? Where have you brought us?"

"This is Geata Dhè, Brunhiíld. Down there..." He pointed down the slope, into the darkness. "Down there, is Strath-sealgair. I've brought us home."

"We should bury Cassandra," she said. "I would prefer a pyre, a more honourable send off, but a burial will have to suffice."

Jacob bowed his head. "I'll do it," he said. "I have..."

"No, Jacob," interrupted Brunhiíld, placing her hand on his shoulder. "I am a Valkyrie. I am the last guardian of the pure in soul; and there was none more pure than our beautiful Cassandra. This shall be my final act, my final honour, as Valkyrie, for, once this task is done, my eyes will look for naught else but vengeance. I shall seek retribution. I shall see Aeetes on his knees, and I shall have his head as he begs for mercy."

"Aye, well," said Jacob, "we have to figure out how we go about doin' that." He looked over to Eris. "How do we get to Haáde?"

Eris smiled. She had a smugness about her now, a sense of power, knowing Jacob needed her. "In good time," she said. "You had better be nice to me, hadn't you?" She shrieked as she felt her hair being pulled back, and the coolness of a blade at her throat.

"Do not test us, girl," hissed Brunhiíld. "I have taken many lives tonight. Do not think I would hesitate in taking yours. Speak..."

A sudden surge of light to their rear, startled them into turning toward the stones. "Everyone, swords at the ready," boomed Brunhiíld, "they've followed us through."

Biro took his place to Brunhiíld's left, Jacob to her right; all three bracing themselves for the imminent attack.

Eris, too, made herself ready. The stones crackled, the electrical fingers splaying from column to column. The light continued to intensify, compelling all four to shield their eyes. Peering through their fingers, they could now make out two tall, thin, faint silhouettes coming through the light.

"Be ready," advised Brunhiíld. She dropped her hand from her eyes. "Show yourself," she shouted, "and be ready to die!"

The shadows drew closer, growing larger with each passing second, until the nodding heads of two horses poked their snouts through the edge of the brightness.

"Well, that's no' much o' a fuckin' welcome," retorted Melanie.

συνεχίζετα

COMING NEXT

CÉLESTIAÁ:

ETERNAL RETURN

THANK YOU

Thank you very much for purchasing this title.

I hope you enjoyed it!

If you have a spare moment to return to where you purchased
the book and leave a review it would be much appreciated!

Reviews help new readers find my work and decide if the book
is for them, along with providing helpful feedback for my writing.

I hope you continue the journey with me.

ABOUT THE AUTHOR

Mick Carty is an author born in Dundee, Scotland. Having dabbled in *careers* as a
motor mechanic (apprentice), soldier, salesman, truck and coach driver, he now
spends his time, when not daydreaming or making things up, as a driving instructor.
Resilience, optimism, imagination and courage. Hope, dreams and excitement. He
hopes you will find all of these things somewhere in his musings.

mickcartyauthor@gmail.com